CONTEMPORARY AMERICAN FICTION

DROWNING

Lee Grove teaches creative writing, contemporary American fiction, and American detective fiction at the University of Massachusetts in Boston. His first novel, *Last Dance*, published in 1984, was described by Robert Parker as "piercingly observed and elegantly said, a wonderful first novel." *Drowning* is his second novel.

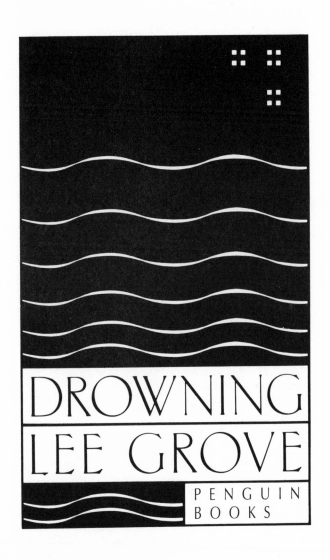

DROWNING
LEE GROVE

PENGUIN
BOOKS

PENGUIN BOOKS
Published by the Penguin Group
Viking Penguin, a division of Penguin Books USA Inc., 375 Hudson Street,
New York, New York 10014, U.S.A.
Penguin Books Ltd, 27 Wrights Lane, London W8 5TZ, England
Penguin Books Australia Ltd, Ringwood, Victoria, Australia
Penguin Books Canada Ltd, 10 Alcorn Avenue, Suite 300, Toronto, Ontario,
Canada M4V 3B2
Penguin Books (N.Z.) Ltd, 182–190 Wairau Road, Auckland 10, New Zealand

Penguin Books Ltd, Registered Offices: Harmondsworth, Middlesex, England

First published in the United States of America by Viking Penguin,
a division of Penguin Books USA Inc., 1991
Published in Penguin Books 1992

10 9 8 7 6 5 4 3 2 1

PUBLISHER'S NOTE
This is a work of fiction. Names, characters, places, and incidents either are the
product of the author's imagination or are used fictitiously, and any resemblance
to actual persons, living or dead, events, or locales is entirely coincidental.

Grateful acknowledgment is made for permission to reprint an excerpt from
"Faith Healing," from *Collected Poems*, by Philip Larkin. Copyright © 1988,
1989, by the Estate of Philip Larkin. Reprinted by permission of Farrar, Straus
and Giroux, Inc. In Great Britain, this poem appears in *The Whitsun Weddings*,
by Philip Larkin. Reprinted by permission of Faber and Faber Limited.

THE LIBRARY OF CONGRESS HAS CATALOGUED THE HARDCOVER AS FOLLOWS
Grove, Lee.
Drowning / Lee Grove.
p. cm.
ISBN 0-670-83458-0 (hc.)
ISBN 0 14 01.7325 0 (pbk.)
I. Title.
PS3557.R736D76 1991
813´.54—dc20 90–50549

Printed in the United States of America
Set in Garamond no. 3
Designed by Francesca Belanger

for Terry

with special thanks to my family,
Kathryn Court, Caroline White,
Theodora Rosenbaum, Lois Wallace,
and Alice Cutler

In everyone there sleeps
A sense of life lived according to love.
To some it means the difference they could make
By loving others, but across most it sweeps
As all they might have done had they been loved.
That nothing cures. . . .

I'd like to bash Venus' ribs in.

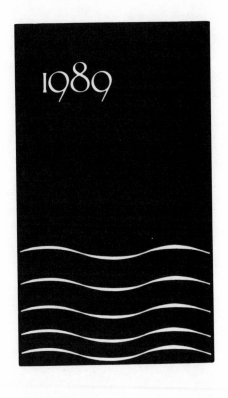

From my window I can see Denis as he mows the lawn. His back is to me. He never looks up. He is totally absorbed in his work. Blades of grass stick to his bare legs, his sweaty shoulders, like mayflies; but he does not pluck them off. He has turned out to be a much finer gardener than Lydia, ridding the earth of whatever scourged her roses. They only started to bloom the year after she died, the year he took control of the lawn. He mows slowly, and with care. Cautiously, as if he still had reason to be cautious. I'd worry more, I suppose, were he operating a power mower, since he is always barefoot.

Dana, as usual, complains about the old hand mower, asks me why I haven't junked it yet. I could answer her by simply pointing to other *objets* around this house that are even more out-of-date, like the furniture downstairs, or the car in the garage. Both cars. "The squeal of it, Father," she says. "How can you stand it? It's worse than chalk scraping on a blackboard. And he spends hours out there on the lawn." I tell her she should be glad the lawn runs out eventually, becomes sea wall, beach. I do not tell her that my gardener is afflicted with spiritual progeria; that, like his parent, he prefers communing with antiques, or with things destined to swiftly become antiques. His back is strong. He does not hunch over. From up here he could almost pass for a teenager, or a young man momentarily down on his luck, making up for it by putting in a hard day's labor at something he loves. Time has stopped for him. He does not yet resemble what he in fact is—a middle-aged man, two years shy of fifty, adrift and immobile at the same time.

Some cry of angst, unheard and unanswerable, not the whine of the lawn mower, is what disturbs Dana. I'll hear her pacing the hallways well after midnight and think, *Light sleeping, maybe that too is passed down through the genes.* I am often awake when she stops outside my door, considers knocking, refrains, and then continues her restless walk, her stalking. I know that between the grinding of Denis's mower and the grip of her own insomnia she will find little comfort here, and so will leave, with her daughter, after three days at the most. And that, I am not sorry to say, doesn't displease me. She has begun to drink heavily again, surprising no one. To have been nursed by a mother full of bile leads one almost by instinct to harsher bottles.

As for outer, not inner, noise, I should inform Dana that the sound of the mower is but a peep compared with the racket made by her daughter's radio. Jessie showed me the radio her first day here, a square white box, more like a fat plastic Chiclet than a radio. I was initially fooled into thinking its compact design some updated version of Art Deco. Then I noticed the glossy red plastic lips protruding from the front of the box, like painted worms, lips that open and shut whenever Jessie turns up the volume. Its weird-looking plastic teeth clack in time to whatever dreadful music happens to be playing. Jessie says the trade name for her radio is the Blabbermouth. Her aunt Roo sent it to her for a birthday present. I assume Roo's husband includes it among the smorgasbord of specialty items he sells on the road. That he can make a living at this dumbfounds me. Though I recall that, ten years ago, he peddled equally outlandish things, apparently with great success, and they now command exorbitant prices on the flea-market circuit, as "camp" antiques. I have never met my daughter Roo's husband, never seen him. But I have some sense of him from these gewgaws of his, which I would rather not see. Up until just recently, gorgeous pastel buildings from the thirties in Miami were left to scab and go to ruin. Egyptian movie palaces, so abundant once and so splendid, have been ransacked like mummies. I shall not grieve when I depart this earth if the only durable, playful, enchanting work of art our craftsmen can produce is a plastic radio with wormy lips.

What is cacophony to me may, of course, be sweet music to another. And vice versa. Dana does not know that the sound of Denis's mower comforts me with its stabby thrusts, its dull whine, its staccato pauses. For what Dana cannot hear—how could she? she spends at most only a week or so of the year here—is the rhythm beneath the screech, Denis's rhythm. The mower with all its crotchets may fight him. But he mows so steadily, until he takes his predictable afternoon break, that the noise is like that of a sea gull whose petulance has become more or less routine. And against the sound of the ocean, that petulance is no more grating than the buzz of a housefly.

I watch my son, I realize, in probably much the same way my father watched me, back in '33. Neither of my parents had known then about my respite in the hospital, or what had landed me there. All they knew was that they had a shattered near-thirty-year-old child on their hands, someone who'd dropped his magnificent career and left Chicago and could no more design a repoussé leather chair than build a birdhouse. My parents let me drift and heal at my own pace, pretending I was on some internal safari. But they spied on me nonetheless—desultorily, inefficiently. I spied on them too, since that was a crazy time for all of us. One of my father's best friends, I remember, a banker, had called him at home, the morning of March 3, while we were still having breakfast, and told him to come to the bank immediately and to bring a gladstone, if not a steamer trunk. The bank was going to close down for good the next day; so was every bank in the country. The banker was warning only a chosen few. My father never told me what was in those suitcases he brought back with him later that morning and which I helped carry up to my parents' bedroom. He assumed I was still in some other world, climbing a candelabra tree in Kenya, canoeing on Lake Nyasa, pursuing a flight of Kavirondo cranes, still "totally out to lunch," as Jessie might say. As a result, my mother, at dinner, could quite unguardedly ask my father questions about her jewelry, her silver. "Shouldn't everything be safe?" she said. "What if we need rubies to buy bread?"

That night, after Felice had finished the dishes and gone home, I remember hearing noises in one of the rooms upstairs, hammering noises. The sounds conveniently muffled my own footfalls as I tracked down the source. The door to my parents' bedroom had slipped open a notch, and neither had heard or noticed. My father was scooping out plaster from a hole in the wall behind the bedstead. My mother was shifting a pearl necklace from one hand to the other, as though trying to assess its weight. The bedspread gleamed. Double eagles covered the length of it, along with an assortment of silver spoons. On the floor lay the open suitcases, one filled with money, the other with what I guessed rightly were gold certificates. They looked like crazy prospectors, my parents: spooning for gold. Then I saw my father start to wall up the hole with wads of certificates.

The noises went on all night, from room to room. I prayed the house would not burn down. I was a fanatic about burnt matches the next week, and double-checked the kitchen every night to see if Felice by accident had left one lying near something flammable. I also prayed my parents had drawn up an exact map of their diggings. They had. Three weeks later, they returned all the gold to the bank. My mother's panic had been exaggerated; similarly, my father's. As I floated through the house that year, I couldn't help noting the irony: I was far more walled up than that money had been—and I couldn't be returned.

I love this house, have loved it as dearly as my parents did. It is one of the grand Mizner homes in Palm Beach: delightfully asymmetrical, stuccoed without and barrel-tiled above, liberally flamboyant, a charming hodgepodge of Venetian and Moorish ornamentation. Trefoil arched windows poke through the inner walls like rococo portholes. The cypress beams in the living-room ceiling give the house a boatish feel too, as though the builders had had their hearts set first on a galleon, then changed their minds and opted for a palazzo. Yet the prow of the boat remains. The French windows open onto a spacious lawn, and the lawn races down to the sea wall. My rooms are endless. Likewise, my grief.

My father was lucky, I suppose, in those few good choices he'd made. He'd moved to Florida in 1925, the year The Breakers burned to the ground. That he was a fine architect and designer, that he'd cut his teeth at some point earlier in his career with one of the architects rebuilding The Breakers, made him a shoo-in for the cerebral-work crew. He was a Houdini with stone and wood and wire: he could make them change properties; and he passed that all on to me. But what he designed and helped build at that hotel was the landscape. His zest for working on commercial buildings had shriveled when we lived in Chicago. By the mid-twenties, ornamental facades had given way to sterile, concrete sheaths. Gropius and Mies van der Rohe, he used to tell me, were senseless killers, the Leopold and Loeb of architecture. Maybe his hands were simply tired of stone, and what he longed to sculpt now was earth, like his grandson. I outstayed him in Chicago, only because adventurous ornamentation flourished still in the interior-design trade. My departure had nothing to do with failing desire.

After he had planted the last palm tree, my father seldom went back to The Breakers. I remember he told me that the hotel had been named The Breakers because of the sound of the waves breaking against the shore, the sound you could hear every night from your hotel room, the sound I hear as well, from my own windows. But irony is more often cruel than amusing, he said. What was breaking then, in the late twenties and early thirties, were careers, fortunes, lives. The broke, he said, could never stay in The Breakers.

The crash, so miserable for so many, proved his good fortune, however. He'd bought not only this house but others too, once their bankrupt owners had bailed out. Less thrifty investors got badly burned in Florida real estate. But not my father. He got burned in another way.

Were he alive today I would tell him: unsparing irony can also be sparing. The waves still break—monotonously, beautifully. And my broken child, my son, continues to mow the lawn, never once looking at the water, perhaps not even hearing it.

If this house could somehow float away, neither Denis nor I would be missed by this town, which we have for the most part ignored for decades. It is a silly town, Palm Beach. But you can be assured that if this house really were to set sail, a television cameraman would turn up here in a flash. Four years ago some Balkan freighter crashed into some woman's private sea wall, sat there like a Noguchi sculpture; and she and the scow made headlines for a year. A new career had been launched for marine debris, as "found art." The aerobics woman downstairs told me the town is agog over the foolishness of a hoodwinked millionairess, who purchased sight unseen an estate in East Hampton which had twenty-four bedrooms, only to learn later that what she'd acquired was a bordello and that all the bedrooms were the size of broom closets. The town is kept alive by this—tales of ancient lesbians killing themselves out of unrequited love by diving headfirst into empty swimming pools, of young trollopy sorts making requited love to musical instruments or household pets.

Jessie, Dana tells me, is itchy and moody mostly because there is no television here. But that has been the one rule I've laid down for my boarders: radios and phonographs, yes; television, no. And I have done that not to be crotchety. In this house a person can summon up all the images he or she needs from the stones, the vaulted hallways, the damask roses outside, the churning waves. One should see visions here, not television. That's all that keeps one going, besides Motrin.

My world is quieter than Denis's. But it has its sounds too. The peeling of hinges; the snipping of crystal mounts; the flutter of mounted stamps when I turn the album pages, almost like butterflies moving their wings for the first time though still restrained by the chrysalides. I suppose I water flowers too—flowers, animals, islands, volcanoes. This two-shilling sixpence violet-blue and black pictorial of the snoek, the snake mackerel, from Tristan da Cunha, for example. When I squirt it with benzene, a watermark emerges on the back of the stamp like invisible writing—a multiple Saint Edward's crown with the initials *CA*. Some watermarks are more festive, less stuffy. On a few of my earliest stamps from Jamaica, the Queen Victoria issues, pineapples pop up behind her head once the stamps are wet. And turtles pursue each other in circles on the backs of stamps from Tonga, perhaps to make up for the even slower, far more lifeless images on the face of the stamps. There are watermarks on my son as well. But I cannot read them. Except for one.

Dana knocks twice and then walks in. I can tell she is peeved. She expects me to lay down my stamp tongs at once and listen. When she was living in Boston she was miserable. When she returned to New York, she became even more disagreeable. The city is aging her, feeding her anger. She is only fifty-four, but she looks much older. Perhaps physical menopause is starting to take its toll. She has been in spiritual menopause now for over a decade.

I do not wish to aggravate her. I can still be polite to my own child. I ask her how many are expected for this family affair tomorrow.

"Jessie and myself. Denis, of course. And I assume your boarders. Maybe others. Who knows?"

"I won't hold my breath."

"She could still bend."

"If she could bend, she would have attended her mother's funeral."

"She calls people more now. She's into channeling."

"Whatever that is. If it has anything to do with television, I'm afraid I'm not interested. As for calling, I hear her sometimes—in my head. But that's not the same."

"Must we invite the racing windbag?"

"Yes. For men who've lost what he's lost, nothing else matters but killing the silence."

She leaves as abruptly as she entered. She isn't happy with any of the boarders I've taken in these past ten years, ever since Lydia's death. But why let such an enormous house go to waste? Emptiness has a tendency to reverberate when too many rooms are left unfilled with human breath. Besides, my boarders keep me company in their own peculiar way, though we seldom run into one another. I charge them no rent; I simply give them space in which to hibernate or disintegrate comfortably. The communal refrigerator is the only sticky wicket. Everyone keeps his or her own food on separate racks. But sometimes a treat that Denis will have made for just the two of us will vanish, and I never know where to point the finger of suspicion. The polo player generally blends his dinner and dessert, turning them both into successive tumblers of scotch. The boy with the trains is anorexic. The latissimus lady is the most likely culprit, except she binges on the sort of food only Puritans could abide—celery stalks, Triscuits, zucchini bread. I still mourn the loss of Felice, who left the week after Lydia collapsed from her stroke in the garden. The meals in this house suffered an irreversible decline. Even though she handled spice containers like maracas and overdosed everything with salt, no cook whom I tried afterwards could compare. So we do it all ourselves. Now, when I totter down to the kitchen at odd hours late at night, I will often find nothing in the refrigerator but radishes, yogurt and goat cheese, and Cuban TV dinners featuring globs of black beans and *fufu de plátanos*. For an old man stalking some Proustian madeleine to resuscitate a long-dead sweet tooth and perfectly willing now to raid someone else's rack, none of this suffices. I have no idea who amongst my boarders wolfs down the *fufu*.

But were there no boarders, Dana would still be unhappy. This tiny burst of good fortune she is experiencing—the Upper

East Side gallery show, this public interest in her work—really offers her no joy. She only grits her teeth all the more and looks glum. I cannot, for the life of me, understand why anyone would bother with her photographs. They are as minute as my postage stamps, if not tinier. The enormous mats she has designed for them reduce the images even further. In order to get a close look at these "candids," I'm forced to use my philatelic magnifying glass. But I see nothing in her work that in the least resembles what I see in my stamps—no exotic flowers or butterflies, no zebus or barra canoes, no proud mahogany bodies. She says her images are "retro-neo-Arbus," as though that word alone conferred some three-starred, invincible status. "You know nothing about current art trends, Dad," she tells me. "You live in the world of Atget." But she is wrong. I lived in the world of Walker Evans and Man Ray and Brassaï. Not that that finally matters.

Tomorrow I shall be eighty-five. But the day, to me, is just another day. I cannot say I look forward much to whatever fête Dana is planning. Denis has always been able to put his capable hands to good use in the kitchen as well as the garden. The cakes he makes for me can almost stand up to Felice's. Though when he frosts them, he does so more generously, with chocolate or sometimes peanut butter frosting. He must know how taste buds flag as one grows older. But Dana, apparently, has forbidden him the use of the kitchen tomorrow. Her perfect cake no doubt conforms to the stringent requirements of her less-than-Platonic ideal photograph: it must germinate in some designer bakery, it must sell for at least a three-digit figure, and it will probably be no bigger than a petit four. Surely Dana knows what everyone in this family knows. This party, like all parties here, died on the drawing board over twenty years ago, even before the day one daughter departed from the party table forever.

I've never been good with birthdays. I always forget them— my own, as well as my children's. Death days are what I remember. And they are never cold days. When they stick in the head, they leave a burning sensation rather than numbness or chill. Living in a hot climate alters one's conventional notions of finality. Death seems palmier here, less flinty.

I have not seen snow now in more than fifty years. Midwestern winters were reason enough, I suppose, for my parents to have packed up their bags and migrated down here. My father often said that Florida was as close as we would ever come to living in paradise, in spite of the occasional coral snake and the more menacing alligators. My mother put about as much faith in paradise as she did in banks, both commercial and terrestrial. Sometimes she worried that a tidal wave might crash upon the shore and carry her out to sea while she was at her lawn table in the middle of a game of solitaire. That never happened, though later I wondered if my father had ever wished it would. Were he or my mother given the choice, death by water might have been kinder. Neither deserved to go as quickly as they did, or in such a way. When I think of them, I see them strategically positioned against greenery, always—my mother lazily drinking glass after glass of iced tea under a palm tree, my father artfully maneuvering urns of flowers on the lawn as though he were playing some sort of gardening chess game. One is forever lounging, but restless; the other is forever upright and restlessly moving. I cannot envision the two of them scrunched together, trapped in something that might as well have been a cufflink box. Emerald green is what I see, not tango orange, fireball red. Denis, when he's mowing the lawn and tending the flowers, reminds me often of my father. I realize now that my mother's fear was well-founded. A tidal wave did indeed sweep one of us away. If not more than one.

The ocean is a gorgeous blue today. Sky blue, ultramarine. But when it turns grey, when a white scum floats on its surface like dirty milk, I remember Lake Michigan and Chicago, and the drear, interminable winters, and the snow that, it seemed, nothing could melt.

I met her during a snowstorm—on a terribly chilly night

when the snowflakes stung like hornets. I had gone for a toboggan run one Friday night, or perhaps it was a Saturday. One tends to regard as highly farfetched, I know, the notion of tobogganing in Chicago. One does not wish to have joggled, or contradicted, that myopic vision of a flat Midwest with bumps no larger than anthills. The toboggan slide at Palos Park might not have been steep according to Aspen standards, but it was a leg-aching climb for anyone over sixteen. I had made my own toboggan. Its scrolling curves pleased me immensely. It was both furniture and vehicle, a sort of Récamier couch-boat. When I reached the top of the hill, my toboggan in tow, three young women and a young man were preparing for their descent. Two of the women were tucked together like spoons, their long coats bundled over them like blankets. The third woman was waiting for the young man, who was anchoring the toboggan, to move back just a little so she could squeeze in. Her coat was the problem. It was a rich, black fur, not exactly made for a comfortable roll in the snow. There was barely room in the toboggan for her, much less the coat. She stood by the sled, still wavering. Then the young man must have shifted the weight of his body, by accident, for the toboggan started to plunge, leaving the woman in the fur behind.

She was a dead ringer for Norma Shearer; she was that lovely—though many women then were aping the stars, penciling their eyebrows, extending their lipstick slightly above the upper lip to capture the bee-stung look. Her hair glistened, like obsidian. She wore no hat. Neither did I. Perhaps hers had blown away. I was a renegade hatless male in those days. The woman I eventually married made up for my breach in etiquette. The woman on the hill, however, did wear a long white cashmere scarf that flapped behind her, like a banner of defeat. Some people who were lucky enough to be unaffected by the Depression continued to maintain an air of chirpiness, of brittle gaiety; a postponed pleasure was the gravest disappointment imaginable. This woman looked both plucky and vulnerable. Were she to have stepped off the edge or slipped, her coat might have saved her, though a mink-lined ride to oblivion might be no less bumpy than any other.

Sometimes I ask myself: Eric, if you had it to do all over again, that one move in particular, would you? But I know the question is academic, absurd. I had no choice. She was wary when I offered her the front seat in my chariot. "I shouldn't," she said. "Of course you shouldn't," I remember saying to her. "But it's no fun if you shouldn't. Who wants to ride alone? or die alone?" She needn't have fretted about being thrust into sudden physical intimacy. Her coat would obtrude sufficiently. But that barrier was also comfortable, and could allow me the illusion that she was snuggling against me as we descended. She did not shriek once as we plummeted; she was quite composed. And I swore that I could smell violets, that they were hiding somewhere under her coat or beneath her skin. On the way down I tasted her cashmere scarf. She had doubled it around her neck so it wouldn't fly off or get caught under the toboggan. But one free end flew in my face and nearly upset my steering. Were I predisposed towards the prophetic, I might have read some special significance then in the fact that our first encounter was a plunge, that it was absolutely thrilling and that I was clearly blind. The trouble with prophecies, however, is that they're way too neat; and they flatter too much those who believe in ulterior motives.

Her name was Dory. Not a nickname for Dorothy, but just Dory, like the boat. She was barely twenty, seven years younger than I. She lived, she told me, on the South Side of Chicago. Her father was dead. Her mother was sick, an invalid; and Dory spent much of her time at home, taking care of her, escaping only occasionally for an afternoon's or early evening's entertainment. She liked rides, she said. She needed something "to make the blood race." She never permitted me to phone her, refused even to give me her telephone number. I never met the mother, nor learned exactly where they lived. Her expensive fur coat, as well as her porcelain profile, assured her the freedom, obviously, to move from the lacquered world of tea dances to the more rough-and-tumble world of sledding. The evening we met, I asked her if she might like to join me for a late supper. But she refused. She was going out for hot chocolate with her friends. We rode down the hill once more, and she seemed more relaxed the second time. Then she rejoined the people she'd come with, who resembled so many of the wealthy paper dolls whose mug shots kept turning up in the society pages. The man, I recall, showed a lot of pin-striped vest and watch fob. He could have been a young bank clerk still horse-blindered enough to believe the crash was over, or a shirt salesman hanging on for dear life to his counter at Marshall Field. The other women were lesser beauties compared with Dory.

I was no libertine. I'd had, at most, but a few, short-lived entanglements, and those with women who had been private patrons of mine and who assumed that, as an artisan, I would always be in debt, and that my financial livelihood depended solely on them. They always disengaged themselves expeditiously, but only after I had coughed up what they most wanted—a matched pair of living-room chairs in shagreen or antelope skin, a dressing table made of palissandre and inlaid *coquille d'oeuf*. We lived at a time then when too many women preferred to be decorative objects, indistinguishable from the sofas they reclined on so glamorously. The inventive furniture I designed often proved far more complicated and engaging than my patrons. What drew me to Dory was a certain edginess beneath the shimmering exterior. The way she dressed, the way she stared at you, the disconcerting perfume she wore created a sort of rush; but beneath all of that was this deliberate withdrawal. Some part of her always hung back. She was like a feather boa dangling on a crucifix. How well I understand that now, as I hide out here, like some ancient Greek monk on top of Meteora, while my eyes gorge on these blackberry lilies from Timor, these Indonesian canderawasihs.

She did not go tobogganing the week after I met her. But she did the next week, and she came with different friends. When she noticed me there, waiting for her at the top of the slide, I think her surprise was both feigned and genuine. What I know she most skillfully feigned to her companions was enough prior knowledge of me to allow her to come tobogganing with me. They were, she told me on the way down, friends of a friend. She did not rejoin them afterwards. Instead, the three of us—Dory, the toboggan, and I—went out for hot chocolate. With marshmallows.

I'm not sure what one would call this relationship we had in the weeks, the months that followed. Not a relationship, really. More like a prelude to one. We never touched one another. Sometimes she would take my arm when we walked, but that happened only when the wind got too blowy on Michigan Avenue. Though she knew where I lived in Lincoln Park, she never visited me or called me there. She would call at the studio instead, where there were always other designers at work and where intimacy over the phone was disrupted not only by that but by the constant noise of tools punching through metal.

I would meet her frequently at Kranz's on State Street, where we'd sit at one of those onyx tables and down chocolate sodas in tandem. Like my father, I'd fallen in love with Chicago's extravagant architecture, and so I would always ask her to meet me at a place like the lobby of the Rookery, or in front of the Masonic Temple, or at a window table in Henrici's. Chicago girl that she was, she'd taken the city for granted, hadn't noticed the elaborate, three-tiered facades on Michigan Avenue or been inside these snazzy club rooms and foyers. One afternoon I took her to the Oriental, not to view the movie but to look at the lobby, a glut of amusing Victoriana. The elephant chairs banked against one wall were the sort of stuff Richard Halliburton might have brought back from his adventures abroad when he was playing at being Hannibal.

She could never stay more than an hour when we met, nor could I. Her mother got angry when she was left alone for too long. And unfinished pieces were always calling me. Tables aching for more veneer, mirror glass begging to be wed to chrome.

Her serious passions, I could only guess at; I knew very little. She seemed to drink in mine instead, the same way she would consume a cup of hot chocolate or a soda—almost to the bottom but not quite. She was by no means empty, even though she hadn't been to college. She was hungry, I think. But there were limits to that hunger. She would never go overboard with me in anything. Not that I ever tried to encourage that. I always felt that she knew something I didn't, and it was that that she held on to. Then, for several weeks during that spring of '31, she did not call at all. And I assumed, like all hungers, this one she'd had with me—surely not for me—had been fed, sated, and replaced by some other. I would see violets now in florists' windows. And I would sometimes buy them, stick them in a tiny vase in my studio, and from a distance I could smell them while I worked.

I was asleep the night she rang my doorbell, the first and only night she ever entered my apartment. As I turned on the lamps and showed her in, I hoped she might see beyond my own personal disarray and notice a few of the things I'd made, like the bird screen and lacquered boudoir chairs, things I was proud of. I loved rooms then. Splendid and striking furniture transforms a room. What are memories after all but furniture? They fill the rooms inside our heads. We can be choosy even there, discard or keep the pieces that have gone out of style.

She did not take off her coat. She was dressed, I could see, in a way that precluded the very possibility of her undressing. A fox-head stole encircled her neck. "Pack, Eric," she said to me. "Just the things you need." I obeyed her then as though I'd been hypnotized. I dressed, hurriedly; I bundled a suit, a sport jacket, two pair of pants, and some shirts, along with toiletries, underwear, socks, and a few ties, into a gladstone whose buckles were as unreliable as dentures. I sensed she was in trouble, but only she could put a name to it. "Where are we going?" I asked, as if that mattered. I must have also known then that we were not running away for just a weekend, and that I would have calls to make, eventually, from somewhere, in order to account for my absence. Mrs. Corbin's immense desk in Macassar ebony and steel would have to remain on hold. And indeed it did. For it was I who held on to it, finally, since Mrs. Corbin found its conflicting textures too radical. It is the desk I have sat at for years, sturdier than anything else I ever made, roomy enough so that I can open all my stamp albums at once and spread them out comfortably.

We were driving to Florida, she said. To my home. If I smiled then in order to hide my confusion, I am sure the smile vanished as soon as I saw her car. I was still jostled by Dory's midnight appearance, still woozy from my interrupted sleep. I lived on a quiet street where the street lamps were outnumbered by trees, and the new foliage each spring would block or diffuse the light. But even in the furry green light and darkness, I could see this was no ordinary car. Its blue was neither Prussian nor cerulean but a kind of slatey indigo. It was a Duesenberg, a convertible sedan. In the backseat, along with her suitcases, was a child's rocking horse. The horse was lucky, she told me. When she'd ridden it as a girl, she could always escape, she said. She sat in the driver's seat, so I had no other choice but to ride beside her. She did not want me to drive. I never drove, in fact, the entire way down, until we crossed the state line in Florida. You're tired, she said. Get some shut-eye. Trust me.

I did, although I wondered whether the car was actually Dory's or her mother's. Dory said a good friend was taking care of her mother now, she could relax. But I couldn't.

I have never forgotten that night, and the long, spooky ride down Halsted Street past dark speakeasies, mute dime stores, the stern granite facades of banks, their Doric columns proclaiming ruin in this century. She drove all night, I thought, though by early morning we were still in Illinois, an Illinois that was more like the Deep South. Dory must have pulled off the road—there were barely any shoulders on the roads then—some time after two in the morning, shortly after we passed Watseka. I'd already fallen asleep. When I awoke, near dawn, she was slicing breakfast for the two of us. This girl who wore violets and furs had made a rhubarb pie before we'd left, and packed it along with some pork sandwiches. "I haven't slept for days," she said, after she'd eaten. "Let me snooze awhile."

She'd parked on the edge of a cornfield. She'd also mowed down a patch of young stalks. I knew that farmers would be up by then, so I got out of the car and walked down the road a ways to make sure no tractors were coming. There was little traffic at that hour, only an occasional roadster. A man in a tractor, however, would do more than just gape at a Duesenberg stuck in a cornfield, especially if the Duesenberg was chewing up his corn.

Her car wasn't that far from the last two signs of a Burma-Shave jingle. Because I liked to guess the punchlines, I walked further ahead, so that when I turned around and headed back I could read the signs in order, make my guess. Which I did; and I was on target. *Shaving Brushes. You'll Soon See 'Em. On the Shelf. In Some. Museum. Burma-Shave.* What drivel stays lodged in the grey matter. When I die, the last thing on my mind may not be sorrow or my children or relief, but only Burma-Shave.

Something besides impishness dictated my next move— which was to uproot every one of those signs and cart them back to the car. I know Dory in her own way followed suit, then and years later. We weren't just acquiring curios, souvenirs. We were wresting something from this unpredictable trip, from this grizzled, gamy earth in which we lived, with an eye towards hoarding. Hoarding for what was bound to come ahead. Loss of memory, loss of everything.

We could hardly malinger for long in the alien corn, not after my pillage which only compounded hers. Dory awoke, refreshed, alert. She ate another slice of pie; then we continued our way down old U.S. 41. Though I cannot drive now, and have not wished to drive for years, I pity car drivers today who are so inured to these cheerless expressways. They hate billboards. A digital dashboard has more appeal to them than a neon diner sign. They couldn't imagine a road without a Holiday Inn. The sky is supposed to open up sumptuous queen-sized beds for them at their command.

Back then, there were only auto camps to service the tourists, if that's what we were. But Dory was too unnerved by the gypsies to even consider an auto camp. Occasionally, a motor court with its tacky little cabins would pop into view—but we happened on them during the day instead of at night, when I would have consented to a bed anywhere. Money wasn't the problem. Dory was simply loath to unwind in a comfortable, Main Street hotel. The car gave me the jitters at night. I considered it quite unsafe to sleep in, and was baffled by Dory's reluctance to stretch out on something that might resemble a mattress. The front seat, in which we both slept, had all the appeal of a three-quarters-sawed-off Murphy bed. We never rubbed up against one another while we were in that car, though I would sometimes rub the kinks out of her shoulders while she drove. She was a good driver. Nonetheless, I was apprehensive and often feared we would die together. At times a narrow road would shrink to one terribly skimpy lane over a rickety wooden bridge; and I was certain the bulk of the car would shear off the railings and the weight of the car would collapse the bridge. But Dory sped past these hurdles with astonishing blitheness. I understand my paranoia now: before they'd even occurred, I had car accidents on the brain.

I have never played golf, though I live in a city where men my age, if they can still walk, do nothing but. I see them, whenever Denis takes me for a drive, waddling across the greens at The Breakers, wearing pants the color of either the inside or the outside of a watermelon. You eat colors like those; you shouldn't wear them. My father, who never played golf either, always wore cream-colored trousers.

But I played miniature golf with Dory that spring, when we fled whatever it was she was fleeing, in Chattanooga. The fad was already dying. The Depression was killing even the cheapest forms of entertainment. But there, right on the main street, in a vacant lot, a miniature golf course was fighting for its life. Dory took to the golf course with the same unflinching intensity that had gripped her on the toboggan ride. When she putted her ball into the whale's nose instead of its mouth, a spout of water shot from the whale's head and doused her. "I want it to happen again," she said. That was often the way I felt too, especially after she left me.

She was unable to walk off with her putting iron, though I figured by the year's end the golf course would be in tatters, the hazards occupied by hungry gophers. Still, we did not leave Chattanooga without acquiring more gimcracks for what I thought of as her, or our, grab-bag hope chest. In a secondhand store cluttered with chifforobes and fraying Confederate soldier uniforms, she headed straight for the beehive of colored feathers, which turned out to be two tangled-up warbonnets. She also found a peace pipe. "For Halloween," she said of the former. "For when I lose my cigarette lighter," she said of the latter. She acted, sometimes, like a child who preferred to shop at the homeliest dime store rather than at the toy counters at Marshall Field, and who could always find the one distinctive object buried in the cheap debris. She knew how to indulge herself at little expense, probably because she could afford a pearl necklace when she wanted. I should have been more watchful, feared for her more than I did—this expensive girl, this child, driving an incredibly expensive car with a boyfriend who was not a boyfriend at all and who was simply following her cues. We would have been easy pickings for the dangerously hard-up. But when we pulled into some weather-beaten lunch stand calling itself the Dew Drop Inn, Dory refused to regard such a place, or the disgruntled people who worked there, with any measure of alarm or disdain. In so many ways she was absolutely without vanity or affectation. She would lean across the counter and instead of purring for a black-and-white soda, she would politely ask for lemonade, pay a dime, then leave a quarter tip.

The pies, the further south we drove, at last began to vary. Occasionally a berry or a butterscotch pie would surface, to offset the cherry and the apple.

How delicious peaches were then. I remember that Dory would regularly stop at those desolate fruit stands in Georgia and buy two large peaches, one for each of us. A peach, to her, was as exotic as her violet perfume was, to me. When she bit into one, she would attack it, and the juice would gallop down her chin. She always ate the peach outside the car, oblivious to the man or woman who had sold it to her. That fruit peddler might not have looked quite as hopeless as his or her counterpart selling apples in the city. But I knew, whenever one of them eyed that car of Dory's, that Dory's small cries of pleasure while she ate only deepened the chasm.

I suppose I saw more of the poverty than Dory did, because it was she who was always driving. Though I also sensed she knew exactly what she was avoiding, how to spare herself pain, unpleasantness. To drive through Georgia was to witness an interminable flat despair everywhere you looked: tar-paper shacks too flimsy even to be called that, baking under the cruel sunlight; hunched-over sharecroppers attacking weeds in the cotton fields. Sometimes, near creek beds that seemed more dusty than wet, I would glimpse black women washing their clothes in cast-iron vats, then beating at them with sticks that looked like flattened baseball bats. One needs a weapon now, I know, to survive. One needed tools or weapons there in Georgia, to thrash the weeds out of the dirt, then the dirt out of one's clothes. But all of them—the men who worked the shovel plows, the women who boiled clothes—were beating a stick at the wrong thing. The enemy wasn't the weeds, or the weevil, or the stains that would never lift, or even the rich and indifferent car that shot past them, the way dreams do. We were all scrabbling in a godforsaken, hardscrabble world. Some of us just had a little more mobility. What I wouldn't give for some of that locomotion now, now that I've become the weeder, pruning postage stamps.

Only once was Dory ever really jangled; and that happened in Tennessee, not Georgia—the Sunday afternoon we left Nashville. We'd been forced to travel at a snail's pace, because the street out of town was clogged with what looked like Bible salesmen. Saleswomen too. Some men had taken to standing on car hoods, brandishing Bibles and hollering at each other. Dory tried in vain to turn the car around. One of the hecklers pointed in our direction and shouted, "Jeremiah!" I assumed he was trying to shut up or shut down one of his competitors; but then he started to rave about being "full of the fury of the Lord," and his finger, like a quivering compass needle, aimed right for Dory. I should have known. Jeremiah had to be one of those sick prophets in the Old Testament; their names all ended in *iah*. Dory was mumbling curses. I had never heard her swear before. Her forehead had begun to sweat. When I saw her foot was about to press down hard on the gas pedal, I used mine as a sort of doorstop. She could have easily mowed down a good third of that crowd. They weren't salesmen, of course; they were itinerant preachers, out for a congregation as well as a scarce Depression sawbuck. The churches are packed with them now: Saviour-pumping Pentecostal crazies. What a plague they are, as feisty and brazen as roaches. After we'd finally escaped from Nashville, Dory kept stopping the car every so often, and would ask me to get out and check the roof. She'd heard footsteps, seething voices, shouting; she wanted to make sure no lunatic minister was clomping over her head.

When she reached Route 1 and crossed the Florida state line, she let me take the wheel. That her stamina had kept up over so many bad roads and through so much desolation amazed me rather than unsettled me. I did not know then that fearlessness can bespeak the fear of letting go. We stopped that first night at an unprepossessing motor court near Jacksonville, and had dinner at a dismal truck-stop restaurant called The Limelight—which was provided, I recall, by sour-green reflections cast by the shaded lamps above the booths. The restaurant, which was part curio shop, sold live baby alligators. Even back then, Florida prided itself on its tacky, backwater gaudiness. Jessie's worm radio, I realize, fits right in here.

Dory picked at her dinner, barely ate. The fish was leathery; the coffee tasted like brine. Dory nearly fell asleep in the booth. When I asked if there was anything wrong, if she wanted something else to eat, she looked at me and said, "I am so tired of taking care of the things I have to take care of." Fatigue had clearly done her in; she was relinquishing more than just control of the wheel. I put her to bed in the tourist cabin, a real bed at last. Later, years later, I thought about what she'd said. I assumed at first she meant only the incidentals—her car, the godawful roads, the at times frustrating search for gasoline stations, the maddening effort to keep her clothes free of dust. Later I wondered if she didn't also mean me as well. I thought I was assisting her, caring for her. Certainly I loved her. But I was in fact only a passenger on a ride with no easily foreseeable end, unlike a Burma-Shave jingle.

The next day we drove to Palm Beach, and Dory's zest revived en route. The palm trees seemed to stir up the air the way swizzle sticks shake up drinks. A salty breeze would slap us in the face; and then maybe the odor of swamp, or the scent of oranges, pungent and sweet. Dory's fragile perfume couldn't compete. It was too subtle, too evanescent. The only smell strong enough now to arouse me comes from the daily garbage truck. I drove her past my parents' home but did not stop. She was somewhat perplexed, I remember. But my mother would have raised her eyebrows at the notion of Dory's staying on as a houseguest. I pointed out to Dory some of my father's handiwork as we pulled up to the entrance of The Breakers. She was reluctant to get out of the car. "I'm staying here?" she said. "In a hotel?" "But this is *the* hotel," I told her. Dory's surprise may have been equaled by that of the doormen and bellboys, who were not used to unloading shaving-cream signs from their guests' cars. The room was quiet and classy, not overdone. Nothing detracted from that majestic vision of the Atlantic, which seemed to lie within a long arm's reach, just outside the window. Dory sat on the bed. She hadn't yet looked out the window. She said she needed to rest awhile before meeting my parents. She lay back, her legs dangling over the edge of the bed. I remember that her eyes were wide open, and she was gazing at the ceiling, as if that could do just as well as any ocean. I slipped out to let her unwind.

I should have left the car alone. I know that now. Instead, I decided to give my parents a rise of sorts, startle them not only with my out-of-the-blue arrival but also with this blue dream-machine, as I guess such a car might be called today. And, of course, I needed to prepare them for Dory. So I drove it home, honked several times; but no one was there except Felice, who told me my parents had gone for a drive in their new car but were expected for dinner at seven. I wondered how this recent acquisition of theirs would stack up against Dory's indigo monster. There was no competition, as it turned out. Dory's was the tame one, a pussycat. I told Felice to set two extra places for dinner that night, and to tell my parents I was bringing a friend.

Then I drove back to The Breakers to pick up Dory and show her Palm Beach, this hive of wealthy crones and vulpine gigolos. But she was not there. Not in the room, nor in the hotel. A bellboy told me she had left shortly after me, that she'd taken a cab, that he had no idea where she'd gone; and she had left no messages. What she'd left were her suitcases, her clothes, her rocking horse, everything but her purse. I knew what this meant.

I called Felice and told her to subtract one place setting. She grumbled. She didn't need to. I'd spared her one extra trip back and forth to the pantry. I stayed in that hotel room until dinner-time. Then I drove the Duesenberg home, and did not honk. I politely garaged it. Afterwards I dined with my parents, who were just as polite and asked few questions. And two days later I took a more efficacious route back to Chicago, by train. The garage became a stable for the dead—dead hopes, dead horses, dead wood. My parents' car remained there until it and they expired. Likewise the old woody, until the termites discovered it; then Roo took it off our hands. And the car I bought Denis, to cheer him up, is nearly an antique now. But it still shines and hasn't a single dent, unlike Denis.

If one is diligent enough, one can track down nearly any missing stamp. This multicolored Mozambique fish, the fifteen-escudo *Odonus niger*, I obtained from a dealer in Chicago whose specialty was French and Portuguese colonies. Some collectors much prefer a canceled issue to a mint stamp, especially in the higher denominations of a particular set, since those denominations so rarely appear on mail leaving the country. I chase after mint stamps whenever possible—their colors unmuddied, their designs clear, uncrushed. Once they're inserted into the crystal mounts, each becomes a tiny, gemlike painting. The mint *Odonus niger*, though it's by no means the highest denomination amongst the fish or the prettiest of the fish, has turned out to be the most valuable.

Sometimes years can go by; but eventually they all turn up, like flora and fauna that have strayed from the Ark and are now glad to be on board. Perhaps stamps have taken the place of the family I no longer possess, and provide me with what I can no longer obtain from humans: a sense of well-being, completeness. As for those who are missing from my own life and are unrecoverable, I have long ago given up waiting. I have called off the search efforts; I no longer write letters.

My work awaited me once I got back to Chicago. Even though hard times were leaving many of the affluent pinched, my well-heeled clients still coveted dramatically disorienting furniture for their homes. Many were aware of what was transpiring abroad in interior design, as a result of the Paris world's fair, and were thankfully pitching their creaky Eastlake chairs and stodgy Empire sofas into secondhand stores. In the early winter of 1933, nearly two years after Dory had left me, I was delivering to the Edgewater Beach Hotel a four-panel screen I had made of gessoed ebony, for a Mrs. Jarvis. The hotel, a sensuous, yellow-stucco affair that sat near the water's edge, belonged on the Riviera, not Lake Michigan. Mostly permanent residents lived there. I assume it, like every distinctive and grandly out-of-place goliath of a building in America, either already has been or is about to be demolished. I was going to ask the man at the desk to ring Mrs. Jarvis and announce the arrival of her screen, when I saw her enter the elevator, alone. Dory, not Mrs. Jarvis. She had not seen me. She was wearing the same black mink coat. I waited to see what floor the elevator would stop at. Then I left the screen at the desk, and tipped the man well for the two services he had rendered me.

When she answered her door, I gave her no time to prepare an excuse—since there was no need. "So you live here," I remember saying. "In a hotel. Not exactly the South Side." "Yes," she said. "But you can't come in." I'd already barged inside, however, like an obnoxious Fuller Brush salesman. Her living room was a bower of high-style chic. Costly sofas, streamlined drapes, skillfully placed mirrors. "And are you married too?" I asked her. "No," she said, the only word she uttered during those several minutes while I appraised her unerring way with furniture, her slipshod way with men. For by then he had stepped into the room, almost as though he'd been following me, a robust young man, much younger than I, dressed in a dapper, pin-striped suit with a boutonniere, his hair black and thick. "So what's he doing here?" he said. His voice was croaky and raw, like a pubescent boy's. "No," Dory said. "So this is the one," the man said. And again I heard Dory say "No," as though she were some talking doll with a one-word vocabulary. "So you oughta say goodbye," the man said, though it really didn't matter whom he was speaking to, Dory or me, for I was too busy taking note of what he held in his hand while she scurried to his side.

Practitioners of fine etiquette as they were, neither of my parents had ever instructed me as to what to do if a revolver was pointed at my head either directly or at close range. Fear should have unhinged my bowels and bladder, if not my mind. But what I realized then—seeing him in his charcoal pin-striped suit with a yellow carnation tucked in the lapel button, and her pressing hard upon his arm as though he were this too-garish wrap she was trying to stuff back into her closet, seeing the two of them bristle against this backdrop of satin sofas and glossy burled ash and fruitwood chairs and shimmering tables, all of which I could have had a hand in making—was that however much I craved those hard, gleaming surfaces, adored that sculpturally rich, rough, and glamorous city, I did not belong there. I had made a terrible error and was caught, as they say, between a rock and a hard place. What I most longed for—as I eyeballed that revolver—was to be here, listening to the surf, the palms, not the beseeching "No" of a woman who was now a total stranger.

The event that followed I have yet to make sense of. For Dory had grabbed his arm as though it were a slot-machine lever, and now the gun was pointed at my groin, not my head. And at the same time I heard her say "No," I heard the gun go off. I must have moved just far enough to the right, for when the bullet hit I knew my poor thigh had become the unpleasant target.

The man with the gun looked somewhat confused, then irritated. No one had given him a prize. Dory was tugging at his arm, as though she expected quarters to fall out and join me on the floor.

"This is your life, Dory," he said. "Your mess." She still hadn't looked at me. He pocketed his gun. When he opened the door to leave, I could see a few curious residents or guests gathered in the hallway. I was afraid to call her name, for fear he would turn around, shoot me again. When I finally did call out for help, both of them had gone.

The bullet did not wait around either. It had work to do. The initial stun of it had given way to a pain like a hundred throbbing toothaches. In a fit of crazed politeness and concern for the hotel's maids, I lay on my back and wriggled to the door, hoping my blood would not ruin Dory's carpet. Better to bleed on the doormat—though it seemed unlikely that either of them would be returning to the Edgewater Beach to take up residence again.

Today, a shooting or a murder in a hotel is no big deal. You almost need one to pep up a dreary floor show. Some hotels in New York and Miami are virtual shooting galleries. You're charged for your last night on earth. In Chicago, a bloodbath was not exactly a rara avis. Nonetheless, I felt some shame at having caused such a disturbance in a lovely old hotel. And one maid did have to wring out several bloody towels under cold water.

Chicago hospitals, of course, were used to shooting victims. The wound healed in good time. The doctor told me I might limp were I to stay in a cold climate. But I had no intention of staying. I did not hear from Dory at all while I was in the hospital until my last day there. The nurse who'd been tending to me brought into my room a small white vase the size of a sno-globe. Tucked inside was a bouquet of violets. The card read: *Wait for me. D.*

I gave the violets to the nurse. I doubted that Dory would be waiting for me downstairs or at my apartment or anywhere. Before the week was out I had packed up everything in my apartment and had it all trucked down to Florida—and I left Chicago for good. Had I stayed, Dory's friend might have found me a nice Chicago overcoat to wear, just my size.

Sometimes, when I'm holding one of my stamps up to the light so that I can relish its colors—bistre, deep Venetian red, brown rose—I will see the grey and slowly moving shape of a boat, far beyond the lawn, the palms, the beach, perhaps a tanker or a garbage scow. And I will watch for however long it takes that ship to move across the horizon and then disappear from sight. I remember the *Ile de France* then. It was sunk, I believe, long after the war at the behest of some film director who needed it as the central character in some disaster movie called *The Last Voyage*, which I never saw. The title, though, is apropos. It was the only boat we ever sailed on together, though we were both boat-crazy, or pretended to be.

When she returned to me, she was much older, as was I. The tenseness in her had been replaced by a kind of steeliness. She was less vulnerable, or less noticeably vulnerable. There was vigor to her stride, though that is required of anyone trying to outwit desperation, maintain a gaudy heartiness. Her recklessness might have been tempered, but not so much that it couldn't yank me out of my life and bind me to her again. Other things hadn't changed: her bold lipstick, the smell of crushed flowers—violets, sometimes sweet william. She was far more beautiful than I remembered, and now more driven. Having made herself over, she wanted to do the same for me.

Andy, her racketeer, was dead, she told me while we were on the train to New York, only days before we boarded the boat. He had been wiped out by some other mobster. He'd left her comfortable, though. She'd had no children. She was afraid if she had, they would turn into monsters when they grew up, gun down their mother.

That spring, on the *Ile de France*, there seemed to be more dogs than children. Topcoated men, women in furs like Dory's, perambulated up and down deck with their setters and collies and springer spaniels and Pomeranians, occasionally stopping to let them use either the lamppost or hydrant which had been ingeniously installed for that purpose. We kept mostly to ourselves. Skeet ball, bingo, or a rubber of bridge did not rank high on my list of major temptations. The crêpes suzette so frequently served at dinner turned out to be far more appetizing than our assigned dinner companions. We'd had little time to purchase much of a wardrobe for me in New York, so even if I'd wanted to strike a convincing pose as gadabout, I couldn't. The writing room was where we liked to curl up most, even though neither of us wrote a letter. The room still smacked of the thirties—with its ceiling lamps like illuminated chessboards, its windows like jigsaw dominoes.

Rectangles and squares. They dominated my life then; they dominate it still. Only once did I try seriously to break away. Only once.

That spring and into the summer, we lived on the fourth floor of a not-too-dressy apartment building near the boulevard Saint-Germain. The facade, like so many others, was pocked with the occasional bullet hole. Scars from the war remained as well on haggard Parisian faces. We had no icebox or refrigerator. Few people did then. Mme Richoux, our landlady, told us we would have to make do with the *garde-manger* and trust that the lower temperatures at night would keep eggs and cheese and a liter of milk cool enough. Nor could a decent mattress be found anywhere. Ours was stuffed with straw and flimsy cotton, and crinkled under our bodies, stabbing us in the back when the straw poked through. Dory could not have realized when we boarded the boat how doubly fortunate she was in having brought with her that enormous fur coat of hers. It kept her warm on deck, and it became our mattress cover. Were we either timid or frigid lovers, we would have felt pressed to move as little as possible, conscious of not only the creak and jiggle of the bed but also the crunching noise of the mattress. But I remember only laughter, and Dory whispering, "Is that mice?" every time our jouncing stirred up the straw.

I shared a studio, of sorts, with a *ferronnier*-turned-sculptor whom I met one day when we were combing the same junkyard for oddly shaped pieces of scrap metal. Till then I had wheeled them back to the apartment in one of those cumbersome French baby carriages and simply stored them in our bedroom, hammering and welding and soldering them only in my imagination. Dory must have thought me crazy then, a clochard who stuffed his bags with scraps of iron, not grimy clothes. I remember how upset she was when I first showed up with that baby carriage. Perhaps I did entertain, for a moment, the notion of some other use for it besides a munitions transport. She, I know, had no such notions, and was relieved when the carriage took up regular lodging in the studio. Théodore, the former ironworker, had stumbled upon a wineshop that had gone under during the occupation, and had occupied it himself. He slept on the first floor—with mostly his cats and occasionally a baker named Gertrude who worked in the nearby boulangerie—and then rode the *monte-charge* down to the former wine cellar, now a cavernous studio littered with slabs of metal. When the lights grew too dim or he was out of coal, he would pile his work and his tools onto the *monte-charge*, ascend, and continue hammering in his apartment. The floor, the tables and chairs, the sheets on his bed were always dusted with fine metal shavings. The cats didn't mind; Gertrude did. He allowed me to share his basement space, for which I paid him well. And it was he who steered me away from pursuing "beautility," who made me see that what I'd really been doing all those years without knowing it was sculpting.

He was a burly fellow, Théodore; the shapes he felt most comfortable working with, the pieces he finally produced, took after his body—chunks of steel that were massive as his chest. They were nothing like Brancusi's birds. I worked with slender rods, corroded scraps, and wire that was tensile and strong and almost invisible. Before, I might have stroked these shapes into perverse, elongated figures, animals—recognizable iconographs. But now I let space and air direct my hands, choose the textures and shapes; and what would emerge would be this bruised, skeletal not-quite-flower, not-quite-face. Théodore made up a word for me then: *l'aérofil*, a sort of air-and-wire artist. Jessie's analogous word for such a man today is brusquer, maybe truer: "airhead." None of those works survive. The few I kept I later destroyed. No doubt Théodore scrapped the rest of them when I abruptly left Paris, or melted them down for his own work. Compacted, they would probably resemble a dozen black eggs or doorknobs. Only one thing, apart from my life, did I manage to preserve and send back and keep mostly intact.

In my twenties, when I looked as young as I felt, I would sometimes be swept up by a feeling of ownership that only young men can have. Everywhere I turned in Chicago, every hotel lobby or apartment I set foot in, every furniture showroom was stamped with the presence of an exciting, new, streamlined grace. And I liked thinking that I'd played a small role in that, that somewhere, angled against a wall, was a bronze screen of mine, or perhaps a decorative chair made of coromandel and shagreen; and that feeling, no doubt illusion, of pride in one's craft and one's craftiness was all the more enhanced by the presence of that young woman by my side, her hard green eyes glowing like agates, her voice growling for hot chocolate in the winter, lemonade in the spring.

And now I had that feeling again, years later, in Paris. Had the city's liberation worked on her like a benign osmosis? Or was she simply free of her racketeer, free from her past? Or was I willfully, blissfully myopic? One is never free from the past. The ghost of the daughter who has not stepped inside this house in more than twenty years will still bound onto my lap, showing me a clay turtle she's made. Sometimes I awaken from a nightmare and see my parents burning. As Dana paces the halls relentlessly, she drags behind her like an unsheddable weight this albatross of unhappiness and disappointment. Maybe only Denis is free from the past. For him time has stopped altogether.

On the weekends Dory and I would ramble through the city parks or idle at cafés—I trying in vain to teach Dory not to *accent-aigu* every *e*. Once, in the Tuileries, we saw a middle-aged woman out for a stroll with her monkey. The monkey was outfitted more dashingly than most Parisians. Given black-market prices for good clothes, only a suit that could fit a monkey was affordable. When we passed by stores in Saint-Germain-des-Prés, some of which had begun to fill up with lovely clothes that had been hidden during the war, Dory window-shopped with abandon. She purchased little, though, except for a clasp or two, or a *sautoir*. She could have bought smashing jewels; instead, she bought jujubes, pastilles. Some of the clothes she'd brought with her to Paris predated the war. A few even had dropped waists. At times she looked like a

woman who had both survived the war and bypassed it totally—
by simply turning back the clock. Her French was atrocious. Yet
waiters at bistros were kind to her. I always thought that was due
less to her beauty than to some neediness imprisoned behind that
steely gaze of hers. I see that look in Dana's eyes. It makes me
quail.

Evenings, we would seek out cafés in Montparnasse, dine on
pain et fromage, listen—or pretend to listen, as was the case with
Dory—to writers and painters snipe and rail at one another or
curse de Gaulle. We went to the Opéra once that spring, to see
a new ballet by Cocteau called *Le Jeune Homme et la mort*. An odd,
lugubrious spectacle, in which a young man falls in love with a
woman, hangs himself, then dances off with the same woman,
who turns out to be Death itself. We saw as well *La Folle de
Chaillot*, Giraudoux's last play, about a madwoman and her zany
friends who do in a band of corrupt politicians by locking them
in the underground sewer. One of those zanies was a young man
who had almost drowned. Time—all it is is fluid mischief.

Was I ever lonely for what I'd left behind? Guilt-ridden?
What I had abandoned I could almost imagine for a while had
never existed. I threw myself into my work as though I had jumped
into a volcano. The fire and pain of it absorbed me wholly. And
when I returned home each night to Dory, it was as though we
had never left Chicago and as though there never were a Chicago.
For while I was sculpting, she was creating some other world in
that apartment on the *troisième étage*. In the Marché aux Puces she
would find these stuffed animal heads—an impala, an ocelot, a
pangolin—and hang them on the wall like Balinese masks, like
Fauve paintings. They were always creatures from exotic countries
we planned to visit. And if we could not board a prahu to North
Borneo yet, or a thamakau to Fiji, if we could not snare a mangabey
in Cameroon, or a touraco or an angwantibo, we could breathe
them into being in our apartment—by stroking animal fur, each
other's fur, by plunging into the only boat we had now, which
was Dory, Dory, Dory.

The young cannot imagine how a liver-spotted, arthritic old mantis shape could ever have made love. They see the sunken eyeballs only, the wizened fingers like stripped chicken bones—and, in truth, that really is all there is to see, but for memory. I know a fifty-year-old body is buried but still alive in me, likewise a thirty-year-old, also a sixteen-year-old. My cheeks are sinkholes, cobwebbed with wrinkles. But in Paris this body knew nothing but the sweetest dissolution. No other woman could have been as canny in bed as Dory. Such talents, I realize now, come easily to those who believe themselves damned. There's no need to hold back. The yawning pit has already chosen you.

Still, we played with time, Dory and I, played for time. On another lazy Sunday jaunt we came upon a corset mannequin propped in an alley like a dismembered corpse. "Aren't I dummy enough for you?" she said, laughing, as I tucked it under my arm. I told her I planned to dismantle it, reuse the wires; but I lied. I had in mind something more imaginative. I carted it off to the studio the next morning, where it became the ribcage and guts of the thing I most enjoyed making—my feeble but inspirited homage to Dadaism, I suppose I'd call it now. Through Théodore, who knew an artist who worked in a glass factory, I was able to obtain fragments of leaded glass in colors ranging from deep purple to jonquil. I hadn't worked with stained glass in nearly fifteen years; but difficult crafts, once mastered, remain at or in one's fingertips, so long as one puts up a fight against quickly fading things, the sort one can see for an eternity on television. The face I fashioned out of crushed-glass paste and chips of pale lavender, deep vermilion and smaragdine, was a Dory that looked like a Pre-Raphaelite lamia, a siren that would swoon while she shed her skin, then strike. Dory's pale skin never tanned, and seldom burned. Instead of opting for the pale, frosted white glass, I chose the rosy tones to give the face a flushed, feverish look. I braced the head with saddle bars, soldered it securely to the torso. Then I attached her new lead-and-stained-glass arms: one hand raised, as though to pledge allegiance; the other extended, as though to throw crumbs to pigeons. There were to be no legs, only the pole stand with its castors. But I wanted the suggestion of apparel, something peculiar, something there and not there, something that hinted at the weird bones beneath everything that breathes and blooms—like those in a bat's wing. So I patinated thirteen bronze rods until they were encrusted with verdigris, then twisted each one differently and soldered them to the waist of the mannequin so that they flared out like the remains of some rusty ball gown that had been torched.

The heart of it, the motor and wires, I disguised as visible entrails. Only the switch in her navel announced the presence of some secret machinery. But even that I had played with too, taking my lead from the Song of Solomon. I'd turned the toggle switch into a tiny goblet that tipped when it was pressed; then I'd painted it red as a blood-red ruby.

It took me weeks to engineer all the movements precisely; and still it would behave unpredictably, like a music box that suddenly decided to change its tune. But when I was through, I had it the way I wanted it: dancing. It would glide towards you slowly, those eyes sizing up its prey, and then it would whirl clockwise, three times, pause, whirl counterclockwise, then resume its frontal assault. Théodore called her *La Sirène affreuse*. I called her Delphine.

She was my birthday present to Dory, on a terribly hot night in July, a week before Bastille Day, at a time when there were no ration coupons for Julys. And Dory embraced Delphine the way I knew she would, energetically, adoringly: she asked Delphine, of course, for the first dance.

I know this above all, the closer I approach the end of my life. I know that time is forever stopping. I know that those moments when the body was lithe and vibrant and dancing are as quicksilver—they run through the fingers, unrecapturable. And yet, in spite of age and decrepitude, they are somehow still there, balled in the palms of arthritic hands. And when memory fastens on them, battens on them almost, the real world unspools like a rush of confetti. I am nearly eighty-five, a no-longer-hardy, much-ruined man, glued to my chair at the window. With these tongs in my right hand I hold an austere but elegant thirty-five-year-old stamp from Nyasaland, marveling at the handsomeness of both the leopard, which rises on its haunches, and the cameo profile of King George VI, wondering if anyone Jessie's age knows that Malawi was once Nyasaland, or that there was a Nyasaland—not that Jessie could find either on a globe, or would want to. It is two o'clock, the aquamarine sky has turned nearly white, the sun has hours to go before it sets. The leopard cannot leap. Nor can I. Yet it is also twilight, and I am naked, in our Parisian apartment, and our black-market gramophone is playing a scratchy 78 of Harry James's "Ciribiribin," and I am bowing before a swirling, stained-glass robot, dancing a stuttery waltz with her, and then I watch Dory, who has rouged her face to match Delphine's, who has also painted circles around her nipples in blue paint as though she were some Babylonian fertility goddess, dance in quick circles around her counterpart, outspinning her, and then—as the doll tires and her figure eights grow lazier and sluggish—Dory laces the long white scarf she wore when I first met her on the toboggan slide around Delphine's arms, and applauds. Each is the other's oda-lisque. When I stare at Dory's navel I see a red jewel. She has lodged it there, in honor of her graven image. I never danced like that again. Nor did she.

Tout s'évanouit. One evening I returned home to find her somewhat unhinged, hysterical. Her mother, she said, had written her. "I am going to hell," Dory told me. "We're all going to hell. She said she heard it from God's mouth pressing against her ear." I had no idea Dory was corresponding with her mother, that her mother knew how to find us. I thought she had left all that behind, as had I. I cradled her in my arms, I rocked her like my own child, but all she kept saying was "I'm going to hell, I'm going to hell." The next morning she wouldn't eat or speak. I stayed home with her. Then, that afternoon, she dragged me to countless churches in Paris so that she could light candles and pray. The sight of her on her knees before a prie-dieu made my own knees jelly. She was not some religious fool, a Calvinist maniac; she was as godless as I, and far steelier. What was she doing? For whom was she atoning—if this could even be called atoning? Us? We two—or three, including Delphine?

Now, whenever I came home, apprehension met me at the door. Would she be there, or would she have gone out to brood in some church, talk to some priest? Would she be gloating over some African mask she had transported to our flat of geographic exotica? Or would her eyes be glassy and dead as paperweights?

My angst, I see, prepared me then to be what I am today, a landlord for the bewildered—though with one major difference. I feel companionable with the dreams that govern the boy who is fixated on trains, the young woman who glories in animal droppings, the poor polo player who has only one horse left to ride in this life, and that's the horse out of this life. I never need to open their doors, inspect their lives. Even were I to do so, I know that whatever I'd find inside those rooms would not be frightening.

Their dreams are not misshapen; life is.

The day before Dory left me I found her on the floor, at dinnertime, pushing a tray with an empty demitasse cup and a rusk of baguette. "I have to feed my mother," she said. I picked her up, carried her to bed, and asked her if she wanted me to call a doctor. "Call my mother, tell her it's you who are keeping me here," she said. Did she want to leave Paris? Would she marry me? She didn't answer, except to say that I had left one wife behind already. I fed her thimblefuls of cassis that night, in the hopes she would pass out, that only sweet visions would afflict her.

I came home early from the studio the following day, and she had not expected that. She was strikingly dressed, in a crepe blouse and velveteen skirt. Her hair gleamed as though it had just been dyed. She was wearing a new hat with a veil. She belonged, suddenly, to the time she lived in. And beside her was a small suitcase.

When you are old, and running home movies in your head, those special films reserved for an audience of one, you already know beforehand what the most terrible moment will be and where it occurs, which is why you are running the film in the first place. Because you also know you will stop the camera just before that worst thing happens—for only a few minutes, so you can review the options, though there aren't any. You can't rewind the film. You can only go forwards. Perhaps you wish you had been someone else then, or been with someone else. But deep down, you know you don't wish that at all. Memory is mean. With your taste buds gone and your olfactory nerves dead, it sneers, all you can savor now is your bad choices.

She had brought with her from Chicago—I could see—not only her dated clothes and her heavy black fur but also something else just as old, which she held shakily in her hand as she or he had so many years ago. It was the same gun, surely. I realized too then that perhaps her racketeer had died as a result of it. Why else the sudden flight from Chicago to Florida to New York, the ship abroad? I was her last anchor, and a lightweight one at that. "Put the gun down," I told her, but I knew she wouldn't. "My aunt is with my mother now," she said. "They've told me if I don't feed them God is coming after me with his dogs, his Doberman pinschers, to tear me up." What does one do, what does one ever do, in the presence of madness? I did then as I would do twenty years later, when I confronted another crazy person, only to lose sight of my daughter for twenty-two years. For a second or two I refused to flinch, and then I buckled. Her aim was high, but she came far closer to my heart than he had. She was gone with her baggage by the time Mme Richoux, who had heard the shot, came to my door. It must have been as much a struggle for her to climb those flights of stairs as it was for me to crawl to the door. *"Mais Monsieur, vous êtes blessé,"* she said. *"Vraiment, Madame,"* I said. *"C'est joli, n'est-ce pas?"*

The surgeons in Paris were as capable as those in Chicago fifteen years before. They'd seen many like me already: war victims. They told me I would have trouble lifting things for a while, to go easy with my left arm.

I did not leave Paris as hurriedly as I'd fled Chicago. I tramped around the city for days, until my feet ached, as though only through leg cramps could I both memorize the city and grow weary of it. I never returned to the studio. The day before I sailed back to the States I climbed up the tower in Notre-Dame and rested my elbows on the parapet, right next to the grumpiest of the gargoyles, and morosely surveyed the city below. "A frightening place, isn't it?" I remember saying to the gargoyle. And could he talk, I am sure he would have said in return, "Scares the shit out of me. That's why I stay up here."

I never saw nor heard from Dory again.

A muffled train whistle bleats from the nearest bedroom. One so rarely hears trains anymore, only the grumble of planes as they hack through the sky. Perhaps I let that broken-down young man erect those bygone train sets so I could hear, occasionally, that plaintive whistle. Like me, he is in love with things that no longer exist. But I know, or at least pray, that he will find the strength eventually to crawl out of his boxcar cocoon and put his feet back on earth. He is too young to go round in circles forever. Were he to do that, he would wind up like my son, who is no longer young.

The afternoon, I can feel, is already dying. Slowly and quietly, like all my afternoons. Soon Denis will cease his mowing, retreat to his room as though he were one of my boarders, and turn on his phonograph. Sad music soothes him; but sometimes I wonder if it isn't sweet poison too, killing him as well as his pain. Then I remember: he is beyond harm, beyond being hurt anymore, simply beyond.

Perhaps he is lucky after all.

The rap at my door must be Jessie's. Though she's a loud child and though that toxic radio of hers always murders the stillness in the hallway, her knock is softer than Dana's. She has opened the door only far enough to poke her head into my room.

"It's teatime, Gramps. Mom wants to know if you'd like a treat or something."

"Some kind of snack, you mean?"

"Yeah. Or something liquid. Mom's snacks are always liquid."

"Not right now, Jessie. But tell your mother thank you for the offer."

As soon as the door is shut, she turns on that cursed radio, drowning out the train whistle. She is a queer, grating child, quite self-absorbed; and I fear she resembles me.

What she lacks, like her mother, is what these stamps of mine have never stinted on: colorfulness. Dana's sad photographs, Jessie's morbid clothes—they stem from a grey palette, an even greyer vision. But not these tiny squares and rectangles and occasional triangles. Red lilac, rose lake, slate purple, yellow bistre, orange buff, vermilion greenish yellow—the very names of the colors are passwords to some other life, another way of seeing things. Lydia never understood. How could she? Her eyes were rooted to unreal flowers, to roses that never bloomed until she was dead. As I slide these multicolored fish from Mozambique in and out of their crystal mounts, I remember a similar though much harder task, performed in a dark wine cellar in Paris forty years ago by a sculptor manqué, who lifted out fragments of violet-colored glass from U-shaped leaden channels, only to try some other color.

Sarawak.

Tristan da Cunha.

Seychelles.

Dahomey.

These Mandara women from Cameroon, these Gambian elephants and whydahs.

We dreamed of such creatures, such places, such colors as we lay on that crackling mattress.

The only perfume left me is these stamps, these names. I turn the pages of my albums, I open the stoppered bottles, I smell the flowers of paradise. I touch it, that other country—with my tongs.

Is this love? Or is this all that I am capable of in the absence of love? In my eighties I know no more about love, really, than I did when I was thirty, or fifty. Except that without it, life is a sorry place. And yet with it, life is even sadder. And when it goes, we find out that everything in life is a phantom.

Do I regret love? No. My regrets are few. But they are like so many of my stamps: uncanceled. I regret that a daughter I worshiped dearly has not spoken to me in over twenty years and, I know, will never set foot in this house until I am gone. Dana is wrong. She won't call. And I regret that my son was cut down too soon, that he has known nothing of love, that his fingers have touched only spiny plants and begonias.

I was not a good parent, I fear, nor a good grandparent.

Apart from Jessie, whom I at best tolerate, and Trevor, whom I have never met, I cannot even remember the names of my other grandchildren.

She began hallucinating about forty minutes after she'd had breakfast in the Palm Court of the Plaza Hotel. Dana had told her to go on downstairs without her, she was still too hung over to crawl out from under the covers; their mother, likewise, wasn't ready to descend, not having awakened yet. So Roo had eaten alone, leisurely, dawdling over her coffee and cinnamon toast. She'd picked at her eggs but couldn't eat them. She should never have ordered them. They'd been given the expensive-hotel treatment, whisked and fluffed into some alien egginess. They looked like air; they tasted like soggy pillow. The young waiter, whose studied imperiousness couldn't quite squelch his fear of receiving either a rebuke or a crummy tip, asked her if there was anything wrong. "Life," she'd shot back. "I'd like a little more coffee, please." His lips lifted in a smile of faint but unmistakable resentment. He disappeared with her empty coffee-pot and returned shortly with another that was steaming hot. "Thank you," she said. But she didn't look at him. There were more complicated things on her mind now than the overzealous-ness of some worried waiter. She was remembering the conver-sation she'd had last night with Dana in the hotel bar, and how much Dana didn't want to talk about her personal life, and how much Dana was drinking in order not to talk about it. Dana's life had come to resemble a sinkhole.

The day ahead promised to be dreary, certainly surpriseless. One more of her mother's hallowed, four-times-a-year shopping jaunts with both daughters in tow, and with bribes extended to each to make sure they coddled her. The two hundred-dollar bills her mother had tucked into her palm last night she was not going to waste on new clothes. Dana, on the other hand, needed to blow hers on clothes; if she didn't, Leon would snatch the money from her and feed it to his antiwar kitty. In fact, Roo hoped her mother would splurge a little more on Dana, who was too pretty to be looking so down in the mouth. "I've an Audrey Hepburn who prefers to wear sackcloth instead of Givenchy," her mother had said to Dana, disparagingly. "Why can't you dress more like your sister? Even when her scarves are too loud she still looks fresh, interesting. But you . . ." Roo had chuckled with Dana over that line last night while they sat in the bar. "Join me for a late-night romp down Canal Street," she'd said to Dana. "I find all my designer scarves there—in bins. Sold by the gypsies." "I have no desire to shop," Dana had huffed. "Not with the war." "I know. But Mother needs her entertainment. What else is there in her life? You could do with a frivolous indulgence or two." "There's a war on, Roo." "I know, Dana. I know."

But there was another war on as well, thought Roo. Otherwise Dana wouldn't have been killing off so many scotch mists. Maybe her mother's stubborn insistence on spending money would make Dana bend a little, so long as her mother didn't dictate the purchases. Dana had enough dictators running her life already. At least she and Dana had long ago pronounced themselves hat free. Never would they let their mother strap them into ridiculous bonnets the way she used to. Hats were never far from her mind. "Why must I keep coming to New York for my hats? Why are the hats in Florida never quite as splendid? Why won't you let me treat you girls to a spring hat—for old times' sake?"

It was probably a good thing that Roo had left the two of them asleep upstairs, her mother exhausted from the late flight, her sister wiped out from drinking. When they were finally ready for breakfast, Roo already would have skipped out and later could plead guilty to an excess of early-morning energy, a ravenous desire to take to the streets alone. She knew they would waste no time waiting for her to return; she knew her mother's priorities—Bonwit Teller, Saks, Lord & Taylor—and how they took a backseat to no one. Were the lifeboat too heavy, the daughters would be dumped first; then, reluctantly, the hat from Mr. John. Roo preferred to spend the morning her own way, mostly checking out whatever adventurous jewelry, if any, was turning up in the flossy and not-so-flossy stores, to see if any designers were coming anywhere close to what she was doing, in plastic. If her mother ever guessed that those hundred-dollar bills were going to land in the hands of a plastic-trinket merchant on Canal Street, she'd be off the parental dole for good. Mr. Zucker had told her that new pieces in more unusual precut shapes were arriving by the barrel load on Monday morning, and in the Nevelson colors she loved—milky white, silver, and black. She could hardly wait.

She still had a half hour to kill before stores opened. No matter; she could dally by the windows at Bergdorf's, then Bonwit's. The lazy walk down Fifth Avenue would give her more time to be with herself. The weather, for early May, was surprisingly warm. She had no need to scoot back to the hotel and borrow a light sweater from Dana. Besides, if she really needed one, she could hop the subway back to Frederick's loft and pick one up there. She knew he never stayed home those nights when her mother came to New York to visit. At first she thought it ridiculous to stay in a pricey hotel room for a weekend when she lived less than fifteen minutes away in the same city. But as she got older she accustomed herself to the absurdity. She and Dana seemed to see much less of each other now. It took her mother's hat-buying sprees, plus the annual get-togethers in Florida in July, to bring the two of them together. And even then she had to maneuver around the wedgelike presence of her mother, to say nothing of the hats. Whenever she tried to lure Dana into New York by offering to pay her way from Boston, Dana always begged off. The phone visit was safer. Dana could keep her at a convenient distance, thanks to Ma Bell and Leon and the other mother. Roo could never have lived like that, cut off from everyone. Frederick made rules as infrequently as he made the bed. He liked her to be around when he brought home clients—artists whose muddled paintings he was showing in the gallery, gullible buyers about to be chiseled out of big bucks. She didn't mind; she could keep up with the shop talk. She had her own work, her jewelry making, and she worked there at home, in the loft. She'd already assumed she was not in this relationship for the long run, as she hadn't been for the last four or five relationships. One too-tidy husband and one very messy divorce were enough to kill her interest in another marriage. Nor did she mind, really, that Frederick took occasional nights off at other times, quite apart from her mother's visits. Clients were always courting him. She understood the loose definition of "an appraisal," "a look-see."

Another rug store on Fifth was closing down, or pretending to close down. She was certain some consortium of merchants was making a bundle off these eternally vacating stores which periodically switched storefronts but simply reshuffled the same merchandise—thick stacks of maroon and tomato-red rugs, ready-made for hotel lobbies and middle-class dining rooms. She'd had no particular fondness for even the finer and slightly tatty Orientals in her parents' living room, in fact had come to hate all Oriental rugs ever since that day Dana had called her up, years ago, weeping, telling her that she'd just been dumped by Tyler. She could not shake from her head that image of her sister, alone on the sidewalk, like some ditched Cleopatra, shackled to a rug while the man made his escape. The word *Markdown*, blazoned across one of the windows facing her, was apparently melting. The letters, which must have been freshly painted, were drooling down the glass. The paint had begun as a bright fire-engine red, but as the letters elongated, the paint began to alter too. The red became a Schiaparelli pink, then a very pale pink, then orange, then a flaming yellow-orange, then citrine. She blinked her eyes, then looked at just one letter, the *o*. It was spinning and changing colors as it spun. First it was bright yellow, then a dusky green, and then chartreuse. Slowly she began to realize she hadn't moved for maybe five minutes, maybe ten, maybe a half-hour. She'd been glued to the window. The colors had sucked her in, like a whirlpool. When she pulled herself away, she bumped into someone. "I'm so sorry," Roo said. The woman glared at her. A pink antenna was poking out of her forehead like a gigantic golf tee. One of her ears was larger than an elephant's. It flapped back and forth like a loose sail. When she opened her mouth, her teeth played ragtime. "Fuck off," said the woman, brushing Roo aside.

Roo kept on walking, trying to keep calm. The men she passed were all totally bald, their faces chalk white. Each of them was wearing a checkerboard madras suit. And squares of plaid kept hopping from one suit to the next. Now the women were wearing identical madras outfits. They had dyed their hair in outrageous colors—tangerine, lime, shocking maroon. Clusters of honeybees whirred around the tall beehives of hair. Then the hair dye started to ooze out of the hives, dribble down their necks, bleed into the bleeding madras. She watched women leaving behind paisley pools of menstrual blood on the sidewalks. Honeybees, like kamikaze pilots, dived into the pools.

She spun her way fast through a revolving door and into a Chock Full o' Nuts. Maybe she was hypoglycemic; maybe her blood sugar was low. She ordered a whole-wheat donut and black coffee. The waitress brought her blue coffee and a madras donut. She could not look at the waitress. She closed her eyes, ate the donut. When she opened them, the coffee had turned into a glistening orange light. The waitress brought back her change. A large nose protruded from the crevice between her breasts. Two golf tees were jitterbugging on the tip of it.

She knew what was happening now, and what must have happened earlier. The waiter at breakfast. The way he'd smiled. Her coffee. He had slipped something into the coffeepot. Acid. LSD. A tab of whatever it was. And whatever it was, she had never wanted to try it, any of it. She was still square that way; she couldn't forgo her need for control. And so here she was, a prisoner of some alien chemical, freaking out on Saturday morning on Fifth Avenue, with no one to help her.

By noon the visions had become far more grotesque. She had done nothing but walk—in and out of stores, up and down Fifth and Madison—as if this were some kind of hangover that could be ground up under her feet, pounded away. But her feet belonged to someone else, a crazy lady. Everyone she saw now on the street was mutilated. Ears sprouted out of men's necks. Some men had but one eye, glowing where their mouths should have been. When she looked at her own reflection in the window glass she saw a monster, something that belonged in a painting by Redon or Goya or Bacon. Whenever she heard sirens she was terrified. She knew they were coming for her.

Once, when she'd actually thought she'd outwitted the visions, she shut herself inside a phone booth and called Frederick at work. "I need help," she told him. "I'm being attacked. By pink bees. Thousands of them." Then she started laughing uncontrollably. "Jesus, Roo, I thought it was your sister who was the lush, not you." She hung up. The bees were coating the glass. They had left their hives, the other women; they wanted her. From inside, the phone booth looked as though it were smothered by thousands of tiny pink carnations.

She made her decision when she opened the door. She would fly with them, buzz with them, ride with the colors that sang. She walked into a clothing store full of spinning golf tees. She bought a floating blouse, even though its colors kept changing and she was not sure whether she had settled for pale lavender or pale green. When the saleslady's piano teeth started playing Scott Joplin, Roo hummed along and accompanied her.

By midafternoon the spells had diminished to infrequent shotgun bursts. She was exhausted, pulverized. It had been like riding a barrel over the falls all day long. She was lucky to be alive, functioning. When she got back to the hotel room she fell asleep, praying amnesia would bunk down with her. By the time her sister and mother returned, she was awake, though still in bed. Her head had cleared now. Whatever cord it was that had been plugged into some deranged Inner Light source in her brain had at last been shorted, pulled.

That night the three of them ate dinner in the hotel. Somewhat reluctantly Roo had followed her mother and Dana to the table. She had hoped they would eat elsewhere, but she had made no protest the night before when her mother, still unwinding from her late flight into New York, had rigorously laid out the agenda for the following day before retiring: heavy shopping from ten-thirty to oneish, with a pleasant but speedy lunch to follow; then more heavy shopping, though each would be on her own until fiveish; then a quiet, relaxed, early dinner together in a place unruffled by noise, preferably a restaurant that resembled a safety deposit vault. Her mother had always regarded fine hotels as second homes, sanctuaries. After dinner, if the old routine still held, they would all retreat to their mother's bedroom and watch television— or, if her mother was daring enough, they might take in a movie across the street, where the ushers were indistinguishable from the hotel bellboys. Only if their mother entered one of her Garbo moods and wanted to be alone did the two of them stand a chance of eluding her, getting out, catching up on their lives.

She'd said nothing to either her mother or Dana when they found her late that afternoon stretched out on her bed with her eyes focused on the ceiling light fixture except that she'd had a tiring day. While the two of them unloaded shopping bags, then bathed and prepared themselves for dinner, Roo opened and closed her eyes, testing them as though they were shutter buttons on a new camera. They worked; nothing jammed. Each click revealed the same blank space of ceiling, the same stupid lamp.

Now she was reading the menu, grateful that no words were leaking onto the tablecloth, that the braised sweetbreads she'd glimpsed on a neighboring table had not turned into dirigibles, the hearts of palm into green toadstools.

"Roo dear, do you know what you'll have?"

She shook her head no. Her mother's reading glasses had slid down her nose and hovered there like a dragonfly.

"I don't know about you, but the veal française looks tempting. Roo?"

"Mom, she's pretty done in. So am I, for that matter. So are we all. Give her a little more time."

"I'm not rushing her, Dana. I'm only suggesting. What are you in the mood for, then, while Roo decides?"

"I'm famished. Suprêmes de volaille for me. I'd also like some wine."

"Fine. I guess we're ready. Roo dear, you are looking flushed. Do you have a fever? Why don't you let me order for you. Something cool, light, not quite so rich. Something healthy. Something which won't give any of us food poisoning."

Roo nodded, smiled. She pretended to acknowledge their concern, appear agreeable; but she was, in fact, looking beyond her mother's shoulder, checking out the waiters to make certain the one who'd served her this morning was nowhere around. I've already been quite poisoned, thanks, she thought.

"Has Denis seen any other doctors?" asked Dana. "Someone new?"

"What about the jellied consommé? I haven't had that in ages. Not since either of you were girls. It suits the veal too."

Roo studied the waiter who had just now materialized by the table and who was quite eye-catching. She saw only his ear, because that was all that rose above his neck. His face was all mollusk. Lilac-colored butterflies fluttered around the lobe, occasionally alighting. She could hear her mother ordering a litany of dishes. The ear shriveled and was borne away by the butterflies.

"Mom, I asked you about Denis."

"I heard you, Dana. Nothing has changed. Your father still

gamely corresponds with neurologists and what have you when he's not writing away for postage stamps. His passions. I am tired of his passions. They are all the same. Thin, self-absorbing, pointless. But he would call them, of course, 'colorful.' "

"You can't give up on him."

"I did. Twenty years ago, to be exact."

"I mean Denis. You can't give up hope."

"I can't, or you can't? That seems to me precisely what you've already done. You never finished college, you've never followed through on anything. Your marriage was a disaster. And this latest arrangement of yours, which I consider a marriage, is just as disastrous. You cannot blame me for what has happened to Denis. Don't you think my heart breaks every day I see him? My beautiful son? I live with him—you don't. I'm even surprised you seem to be so concerned about him now. You never used to. You were always jealous of him."

"That's not true."

"Yes it is. Because he was a boy. And he was as beautiful as you, and could have been far more ambitious. He wasn't as selfish as either you or me. Money mattered less to him. You pretend it doesn't matter; you're giving it all away and trying so hard to look poor. But money matters."

"I disagree."

"Let's not disagree, and let's also stop being disagreeable."

"You claim I've forgotten about him, and I haven't."

"You never write to him the way your sister does."

"Mother, let's not kid ourselves why you fly up here so often; it's not just for clothes. You could buy as many designer dresses and hats on Worth Avenue if you wanted. You fly up here to forget too."

"If only I could forget. That's why death will be wonderful, of course, when it happens. No more hair appointments, no more searching for clothes to accommodate a figure whose flesh has turned to porridge, no more struggling to extract just one unmurdered rosebud from my foolish garden, just one. And no more remembering. Ah, our appetizers."

The mollusk deposited a small dish in front of Roo. She stared at the cold asparagus. The three slender spears looked like pieces of severed intestine, or severed something else.

"This asparagus is pink," she said.

"Is something wrong?" asked her mother. "Did you say 'pink'?"

"It's just the light, Mother. The reflections in here, or something. Roo, are you OK?"

She could not tell yet what her voice was going to do, only that she could see her voice, see the cave of her mouth where this shuddering quake of noise was starting to forklift her tongue and pry open her lips. The luminescence of the words she was about to speak glowed more pinkly now than even the asparagus.

"I'm leaving."

"You don't feel well, do you?" said her mother. "I was right. I knew it. Maybe you should go upstairs, lie down again. We can call room service for you later."

"No," Roo said. Her voice sounded ghostly to her, like it came from a tomb. "I'm not leaving the table, that's not what I meant. I mean, I'm leaving. Leaving the city."

"The city?"

"I'm leaving Frederick. I'm leaving New York. I'm going."

"Where?" Dana asked.

She could see vowels leapfrogging on her tongue, hear the hiss of *s*'s. They asked to be unjumbled, made into words.

"San Francisco."

"You're not serious," her mother said. "You're simply tired. You should never have gone out on your own this morning. You should have waited for Dana and me."

"I live here," said Roo. "I go out on my own all the time. No, that's not really true. I haven't gone out on my own, ever. I've only been pretending. That's why I'm going."

"When did you decide this?"

"Five minutes ago."

"We'll talk about this later," said her mother. "Look. The consommé. What a lovely amber."

"I'm not hungry after all," said Roo. "I think I will go upstairs and rest."

The next three hours were all fog and shifting colors. Dana had rushed in and out, grabbing a sweater as she ran, mentioning something about a ballet. Her mother had checked in on her to see if she was hungry or wanted a glass of cool something, anything—before she herself settled down to reading *The Bell Jar* and watching television.

By eleven o'clock that night the ceiling had finally shut up. Moldings no longer frugged. The overhead light ceased to be a stripper popping out of a wedding cake. Roo sat up in bed, eyed the reflection in the mirror opposite her. No fluegelhorns sprouted from her ears. No butterflies waltzed. Her hair was sandy again, not purple. She looked like herself, a nearly thirty-year-old woman, disappointed, perplexed, angry, too freckly, not terribly pretty, · certainly not as good-looking as her brother and sister, but not a washout either, stuck in a stuffy archaic hotel room by herself and ready to skip out now, for good, if she could just find her shoes first, then her purse, and then—in time—everything else that was missing in her life.

The only shaky images around were on the television. She must have switched the set on some time earlier in the evening but turned off the volume. Vietnam footage was flashing before her now as it did almost every night, Rorschach blots of jungle and foot patrols, helicopters and mortar fire. The cameraman out in the field had had no easy time of it. The film kept jiggling, as though the camera were some machine gun gone berserk. Just then Dana returned. When she saw what was on the late news, she turned up the volume.

"How was the ballet?"

"Wait."

"It's just more DMZ, NLF, LBJ, LSD. We can't talk anymore in this country so we use acronyms."

"You've come out of your coma, I see."

From the one downstairs, yes, Roo thought. *But not the one I've been in for most of my life. I've seen something, Dana. I've seen something.*

A newsman was reporting from what looked like timber country in Oregon, except there were no trees left. They'd been chopped down. It wasn't Oregon; it was Khe Sanh. A mouthwash commercial interrupted the interview.

"I don't understand you, Roo. You pay no attention to the war or what's happening to the country. We have an obscene cowboy for President who's drafting thousands of innocent men to fight in some godforsaken swamp, and all you care about right now is plastic sculpture."

"Jewelry. Couldn't you turn down the volume just a little?"

"This day has been odious from the moment I woke up. You weren't here when Mother and I finally got around to breakfast, so I had to accompany her to Saks afterwards while she tried on hundreds of hats and then forced me to try on dresses. Then, after I consented to let her buy me two dresses, we found ourselves entrammeled in a major demonstration outside the store, which made the two hours I'd spent with Mother seem more unforgivable. A prowar rally was being staged on Fifth Avenue by these sneering angry longshoremen who were brandishing the usual hate placards. Kill the Viet Cong. It's their own sons who are being slaughtered right and left and they don't even know it, they're so bullheaded and dumb. Then Mother took me out to lunch, thinking an artichoke and endive salad would calm me down, but I was furious with those men, with her, and with myself most of all."

"I've stopped listening to war rhetoric, or any rhetoric. It all sounds the same."

"It's not. There are differences. Important differences."

"At least don't waste your rage on Mother. She can't change.

You didn't have to 'let' her buy you a dress, you know. You could have said no, or you could have used your own money. If you still had any."

"It's tied up."

"I know. Every antiwar organization in the country will be beholden to you. Not that they'd ever know or even give a damn."

"Are you really going to leave Frederick?"

"Yes. He doesn't know it yet, but yes. He'll find some other struggling madcap artist to provide gusto for his life, only this one will be about to turn twenty instead of thirty."

"What happened to you today? What was wrong with you? Were you just nervous about telling us you're leaving?"

"I was tripping out, Dana. I guess that's what the teeny-boppers call it. I was on acid."

"You're kidding."

"No. Somebody slipped it into something I ate or drank. Maybe my coffee. Anyway, that trip is over."

"Were you frightened?"

"Yes. I thought I'd gone crazy. I thought I was going under. Now I view the entire day as a sign, telling me that other things were going under, were meant to go under. Like Frederick and my life in New York."

"You can't walk away from a life that easily."

Yes I can, thought Roo. *The man I married at twenty-one, my Renaissance art professor, I left a year later. He was medieval in bed. And the others I didn't marry—the sculptor, the disk jockey, the stage-set designer, the funny-hat-and-party-favor designer—I left them too. Frederick's no different. Only noisier.*

"I see you've been shopping also," said Dana. "Hmm, Korvettes. Class, Roo."

Roo could not remember going into Korvettes or buying anything. Dana reached into the green shopping bag.

"What's this? Expecting, are we?"

Dangling from Dana's hand was a toddler's pink pajama suit.

"Oh God," Roo groaned.

"Shhh," said Dana, "you'll wake up Mother. Are you sure you're not hungry?"

No, she wasn't hungry. That afternoon she'd devoured two blue donuts, a madras hamburger at Hamburger Heaven, and a rainbow-colored bratwurst.

"You want to sneak downstairs to the bar and have a drink?" asked Dana.

"All right," said Roo. "I assume the war news, though not the war, is over."

"Yes. I don't always think about war."

"I imagine it was the last thing on your mind at the ballet. How was it? The ballet."

"It made me wistful. It always does. That's why I seldom go."

"Why don't you put on some lipstick before we go down? We can pretend to be girls again."

"No. I'm fine without it."

None of us is fine right now, thought Roo. *None of us.* And Dana was wrong—about her not caring a whit about the war. She would have spared nothing, neither violence nor money, to protect the one sweet boy in her life, the only man whom she loved unconditionally, from being destroyed. But he'd already been mown down in a battle even more absurd, where he'd had no weapons at all, where the enemy was well beyond the reach of mortars. No other wars and no other men mattered now.

Roo and Dana slid into a comfortable booth near the bar.

"A lovely amber, this Chivas," said Dana, laughing, as the bartender handed her her drink.

Yes, Roo thought. *But not as lovely as what I rode all afternoon. Niagaras of color. Multitudinous. Unstoppable.*

I'm through with black and white.

■ ■   ■ ■   ■ ■

It was the lemon tree in the postage-stamp-sized garden in back that sold her on the house, that and the exuberant gingerbread facade. When she thought of lemons in Manhattan, all she could see were garnishes for Frederick's iced vodkas, tiny yellow footballs awaiting the crush of his hand. She'd nearly forgotten lemons grew on trees, that the trees blossomed. And there'd been nothing like gingerbread either outside or inside his loft near Canal Street, unless one considered ceiling ducts some architect's vision of florid excessiveness.

Unlike many of the houses in the Haight, this one had escaped the psychedelic-rainbow paint job on the exterior, probably because the woman who'd most recently owned it was too old, too hobbled by cataracts and too exhausted to deal with any more visual disturbances. The young hippies who lived next door volunteered to paint it paisley for Roo, if she wanted, but she begged off. They'd turned their house into a commune. The men, or boys, looked like Appalachian bootleggers with their long dusky beards and handlebar moustaches and corncob pipes. But two were from Newark and the rest were native Californians. Only one man, the youngest, was beardless. He wore his long blond hair in a ponytail and painted Day-Glo corsages on his bare chest. He'd also painted the van parked in front of their house. The swirling crests of pink and fuchsia turned the van into an Art Nouveau wet dream. When he offered to do the same to her old wooden station wagon, only in different colors, she was tempted. Her father had more or less given her the car. It had been rotting away in the Florida garage with that other behemoth he never used, as well as that Ford he'd bought a few years ago for Denis, which Denis mostly ignored. But she knew that were she ever to drive the wagon back to Florida coated with Day-Glo and Make Love Not War slogans, her father would find her version of artfully hand-painted wood incoherent and garish.

None of the men appeared to have jobs, unlike the women whom she'd see emerge at regular intervals in the morning and return later in the afternoon. The women wore peasant skirts and fringed piano shawls and with their frizzy hair could have passed for Pre-Raphaelites, except for their nose rings. At night Roo could hear them all laughing and dancing, and then there would be only the sound of a record playing or some instrument, like a lute or a zither. She figured they were getting stoned then, or making love, or both. Sometimes one of the women knocked on her door, offered her a platter of their leftover ratatouille, and then asked her if she wanted to join them. They were dropping acid. But again, she begged off. She didn't mind getting slightly high now. In fact, she figured she had already come under the influence just by walking down Haight Street. But she'd not forgotten that day in New York when her brain had melted, so she preferred to play it safe. The women were sweet, though, considerate, at ease with a slightly square neighbor, helpful. And so were the men, especially when she needed help unloading crates and furniture from her station wagon.

She'd taken nothing with her from New York except her clothes and fifteen or more buckets full of pieces of colored plastic. Mr. Zucker had promised her before she left that the warehouse would ship new pieces to her whenever she needed them, though she was sure she could find all she needed in San Francisco. Everything serious and hulking and heavy-duty—her walnut commode, the sideboard her mother had given her, the man she'd been doing time with for the past three years—had been left behind, none of it worth the price of storage.

She wanted only lightweight furniture now. The house was already steeped in history and turn-of-the-century embellishments. Plaster rosettes festooned each of the high ceilings. They were lovely, but they reminded her too much of wedding-cake tops. What had been so riveting about the outside of the house was its jazzy geometry, its jigsawed layers, so like her jewelry. But inside there was a surfeit of gooeyness. Even the marble fireplaces looked too heavy and rich, like slabs of Brie. So she spent days pruning the excess, scraping off the flowered wallpaper while she listened to the Doors and the Four Tops. When she was finished, she was too tired to paint the mottled ancient plaster beneath. So she left it like that—pebbled, pocked with liver spots. She turned the dining room into her studio and made a worktable out of an old Victorian door which she nailed securely to three sawhorses. The recessed panels on the door she used for troughs to hold art supplies. She dissolved the distinction between her workroom and her living room by keeping the sliding pocket doors buried inside the walls. Instead of ormolu and mahogany side tables she bought Korean dowry chests; instead of a sofa and wing chairs—huge, stuffed floor pillows. She scattered Navajo blankets on the floor as rugs. The large but unpretentious cachepots she'd judiciously placed in both rooms she filled with variegated cacti. In the glass bowls on her kitchen windowsill she planted calla lilies. She bought a large fish tank for her kitchen, then turned it into a terrarium. In the second-floor bedroom there was nothing but a mattress on the floor, an old blue-and-white checkerboard quilt she'd dug up at a church sale, a television set, and a ficus tree. She hid all her clothes in the closet on hangers and built-in shelves. Her one extravagant purchase for her bedroom was an ancient Japanese scroll which had the same color and texture as the wall—a musty, sandpapery beige.

She did not know what to do with the third floor, so she left it empty. In the morning the sunlight shone on nothing up there but bare, scruffy plaster and ochre floorboards. The emptiness soothed her; it was a hard, bright emptiness. When she meditated there she felt strangely close to her father. He had always needed a room of his own. "For dreaminess," he said. "For a way out."

She was in no hurry to have the phone connected. Her mother would only harass her into flying back east soon, to go shopping again, to join in the search for some wild and as yet uncaptured hat. She was sick of hat safaris. Dana, whenever she called, would reverse the charges, then chat her up for money. And Frederick would probably phone first—so he could call her a coward and a slut and a manipulator, all of which terms were more applicable to him. The one person she wanted to talk to she, of course, couldn't. She thought he might like it here: the exotic plants, the cypresses, the eucalyptus; the smell of magnolia incense; the colors, the purple fog, the startling light. But the music was different— sometimes raspy and steely, sometimes loose and demented, not at all like the three-minute ballads that worked on him like tranquilizers. She wrote him postcards regularly, telling him she was all right and that she missed him, and that San Francisco was almost as beautiful as Florida.

The city had disoriented her at first. The bizarre visions she had seen in New York that one day she now saw every day, and they weren't visions. They were her next-door neighbors, the boys and girls with painted faces who roamed the streets and the parks. It was she who was the hallucination, some alien from an even freakier world of unhipness, uptightness. There was no way she could pepper her face with Day-Glo hearts or pointillistic microdots. No makeup at all was as far as she was ever able to go in terms of radical face alteration. But to give up on lipstick entirely was close to impossible. She would have looked like a vampire victim, like Dana. Her dye-splattered blouses, at least, made her blend in, feel less out of it. She'd ditched her Peck & Peck wardrobe right after the art professor. Her jewelry was certainly as colorful as what the hippies wore and much more outré, better made as well. Gradually she began to recognize some of the more outlandishly garbed women who got high in the streets every night as the same people who were working as salesgirls at small boutiques. The straight and not-so-straight lines were continually blurring. Most of the nine-to-five women, the ones who weren't hippies, were also wearing miniskirts and chandelier earrings and looked like tarts—so that they passed, just as Roo, in her own way, started to pass. She had no idea how the hippie men supported themselves, though. Maybe as janitors or dishwashers, safe from too much public scrutiny. They no doubt toted hairnets in their back pockets along with tabs of acid.

It took her less than two weeks to flesh out the interior of her house. She'd worked speedily and methodically, so she could have the security of her house to fall back on before easing herself into the city, a hive of craziness. In the mornings now, before she started working on her jewelry, she would walk to the Japanese Tea Garden in Golden Gate Park and study the graceful zaniness of the bonsai trees. Then she'd stroll past a meadow where hippies lounged and got stoned all day. If she wanted to hear music, she had only to walk to the polo fields nearby. Then, sated with images and smells and sounds, she would head back home and start sketching new designs for her necklaces. She was bored with the chunky and rectangular pieces she'd made in New York. The shapes she jigsawed out of plastic now were as curvy as those Dairy Queen swirls on the van painted by the young hippie next door or the lavish scrolls in those posters for the Fillmore that were plastered all over the Haight. Her pendants swelled now with a richer density, their moony surfaces studded with tiny crescents and hemispheres.

On weekends tourists would swarm through the Haight, poking their heads out of car windows, eyeing suspiciously the braless girls, the barefoot boys in bowlers and weskits, the long-haired men and women quietly rocking on their front-porch chairs. She avoided that circus of tension by staying inside on Saturdays and working. Whenever she got too lonely at night she would walk to the Regency and take in a movie, until either the film or the smell of grass made her too sleepy.

On Sunday mornings she would make lemon muffins, leave a tray of them on the rear porch next door, then pack the remaining few and take them with her to the Palace of Fine Arts. A water-colorist she'd met in the Japanese Tea Garden had told her about the Palace her first week in San Francisco. She finally walked there one afternoon, expecting to find some turreted confection straight out of Disneyland. Instead, she found a lagoon where swans clustered like miniature gondolas, and an enormous, ochre-colored Greek temple and colonnade that belonged in a painting by Poussin. Now, every Sunday, she would sit by the edge of the lagoon and toss the swans crumbs of lemon muffin, hoping the sea gulls wouldn't beat them to it, though they always did. She was often alone then, except for a flute player whom she could hear but couldn't see. The jazzy flute riff that seemed to be coming from the colonnade always ceased whenever the swans stopped paddling, almost as though the lagoon were some weird music box and the swans mechanical toys, illusions keyed into motion by a flute song. Before she would leave, she would throw her last handful of crumbs into the water with a grand gesture, as if they were gold coins, as if she were somehow tipping the invisible musician. She belonged, at last. The East was a morgue. So was Florida. *I'm alive. I'm here. Picking lemons. Making my bread, my jewelry. Hearing this flute. Breathing. Being.*

Years later, when her son asked her if he could learn an instrument, something you blew, a horn or one of those funny whistles with lots of holes, she took a deep breath but did not miss a beat, then said he should wait until all his permanent teeth came in and his hands got a little bigger and stronger, and she was very grateful the next year when he decided that a pocket calculator might be a good deal more fun to play with.

■■　■■　■■

The day after she had the phone connected, Frederick called her, just as she'd predicted. It was late in the evening in New York, and he was drunk.

"Do you want the photographs?" he asked.

"What photographs?"

"You don't. The ones of us. A deux. In Florence. At Quogue. Laughing. Cavorting. Looking like we were, you know, tight."

"If you want them, keep them."

"I don't. I tossed them, jettisoned everything. There's nothing left of you here."

"You've had too much to drink. You're being too mean."

"You bet. So is Nicole. She's up here now. She's a Pop Tartist.

I mean, Op Artist. Hear the glass breaking? That's Nicole punching through all the framed photographs of the two of us with her spike heels, grinding away. Go, Nicole. More, more."

She hung up.

Two days later her mother called.

"I thought you were dead," she said.

"I'm not," said Roo.

"If it hadn't been for the postcards you've sent Denis, we wouldn't know what you've been up to."

"I'm up to here with too much already."

"We want you to know, your father and I, that you're still expected."

"Expected?"

"For the Fourth. July is still more than a month away, I know, but I need to make plans. Have you spoken with Dana recently?"

"Mother, the phone was just installed a few days ago."

"You need a man, and she needs to get rid of hers."

"Right now I'm fine being alone."

"Everything I read about this city you're living in depresses me. The country is falling apart at the seams, and all the flower children out there think love is the answer. Love is the answer to nothing. Were I to choose between love and a nice begonia for the front lawn, I'd take the begonia."

"How's Dad? Where is he?"

"With his newest love. Some packet of stamps from New Caledonia, wherever that is."

"May I say hi?"

"He's busy now. Don't forget about the Fourth. We'll send you a plane ticket, so let us know how long you want to stay. Do call Dana too, now that you're somewhat settled. And Roo, I hope you're not thinking about living there permanently. You don't belong there. Frederick, I daresay, has more to offer you than those flower children."

"Frederick is also a child, Mother. A *puer aeternus*. Milton Berle trying to be Andy Warhol."

"Even your father's postage stamps manage to stay hinged longer than you can stick to any man. You're always coming unglued. What's wrong with you?"

"Nothing that a great lay wouldn't cure, Mom, but you wouldn't know about that either."

"Roo?"

She hung up. The phone rang. She didn't answer it. Then the house was still, as though all lines had been cut, as though someone had died. But the one person in the house was flat on her back and alive, and still waiting. *I'm lonely,* she thought.

The next day she did not work on her jewelry. She went to Chinatown instead. She had figured out what she needed for the third floor. Maybe it was because of the flute music she kept hearing on Sunday mornings, or because of the harshness that rang in her ears after the recent phone calls. She bought twenty of them, from nearly as many different shops. And each of them differed in small but precise ways. Some looked like carousels with dangling trapezes, others like fancy girandoles.

She hung all the wind chimes from the third-floor ceiling, then opened the windows at both ends of the room. Then she took off her clothes, made a small pillow out of her pants and blouse, placed it on the floor, and walked slowly under the chimes, rippling them with her fingers until they all sang. For the rest of the day she lay there on the floor and listened to the chimes rustle and tinkle, her brain a blank white space, an empty well into which the glass notes fell and broke.

■ ■   ■ ■   ■ ■

"I see your aura! You have a fantastic aura!"

Roo had been feeding the swans at the lagoon, somewhat irked that the sea gulls were once again horning in on the free meal, somewhat disappointed too that the flute player hadn't showed up this Sunday. And now this girl, who'd been dancing by herself under the trees and was probably stoned out of her gourd, was suddenly kneeling before her, gushing about auras. She wore a scoop-necked peasant dress, and her breasts were freckled and monumental. Baby fat bloated her cheeks. She stared at Roo like some overgrown chipmunk begging for nibblies. Roo was not about to give her the remaining crumbs from her muffins.

"What about my aura?"

"Let me do my cards," she said.

She couldn't have been all that stoned, thought Roo. For the girl had swiftly pulled out a deck of tarot cards from a pocket in her skirt as though she were a professional gambler or a magician or both. Roo knew nothing about tarot cards, though she had seen them in the head shops and boutiques and thought them pretty to look at. They reminded her of the old animal lotto cards she and her brother used to play with when they were kids.

The girl gave the deck to Roo to shuffle. "Cut them in three piles," she said. Her arms gave off this green shimmer. Roo thought at first it was some reflection cast up by the nearby water. But no, it was a light all to its own.

"This is a good sign," said the girl as she crossed two cards.

"What are these cards?"

"The King. The Ace of Cups. That means you're questing for joy. In your art or something. You're an artist, aren't you?"

The cup looked like a sprinkler on the fritz; the king, like some porky nerd. The card that appeared next was an auburn-haired woman embracing a metallic lobster.

"This is some woman you know," said the girl. "Someone who's very beautiful, maybe weirded out too, a little kinky. I see her dancing."

"My sister," Roo said.

"Don't talk yet," said the girl. "Let me play it out."

The next card was a blindfolded woman marooned in a swamp of swords and tied to a sword. The card that followed was just as unappealing. Three more swords were skewering a fat pincushion of a heart.

"You're there."

"Where?"

"The jabber. That's you. You're cutting off three important things in your life. Maybe lovers. Who knows?"

The jabber, Roo thought, was what was coming out of the girl's mouth. Cards kept flipping over. The time for a good marriage was apparently gone. Roo shrugged. She was nearly thirty anyway, well on her way to ruin and untrustworthiness if she was to believe the hippies. Wands and swords and cups skidded by her like tiddlywinks.

"This one is it," said the girl. "The most important card. Your future."

It was a man in a beautiful gold lamé tunic, holding a flower. A dog frisked at his feet. The man should have been gazing up at the sun, but the card had been dealt upside down. He was dangling like a bat now, in midair. Still, he looked like a frolicsome knave, someone you'd want to cartwheel with in a meadow.

"That's the Fool," the girl said. "He's about to walk off a cliff. But don't worry. I deal myself the Fool all the time. I think he's great, even though he's supposed to be a real bummer, disaster city. You know Shakespeare's fools, right? They're wild, they're madmen, they're way out there. So you can love a fool. This is the first time I ever dealt him upside down, though. Say, where'd you get that necklace? It's really far out."

"Wait," said Roo. "This upside-down fool. What does it mean?"

"It means you're going to make a choice in the future which will be all wrong, really awful, a bummer."

"And then?"

"That's it. Emptiness. The void. Sans teeth, sans eyes, sans taste, sans everything. Like Shakespeare. Wow." The girl laughed. "See? I told you you had an aura. That'll be five dollars. Because

I gave you a special reading. Unless you want to give me the necklace instead."

Roo pulled out a ten-dollar bill from her purse.

"I have nothing smaller."

"No problem. You were intense. Intensity always costs a little more anyway. Just hold on to your aura, because it's a really special aura."

Before Roo could insist on a five back, the girl had already dashed off, in search of other quarry, and in less than a minute was out of sight. *What a con job,* thought Roo. *And what a jerk I was.*

That green luminescence still remained, though, there in the distance, like a cape flung on a tree branch. Maybe she was suffering from eyestrain. The stoical swans relinquished their turf. Her last crumbs were gobbled by the gulls.

Years later, after she too had begun to give readings, after the swords had shattered and the cups were all smashed and the wands broken, she wished she could turn the clock back and run after that not-so-silly girl and hand her the necklace, tell her there were things far more terrible in life than emptiness, far more terrible.

■■　■■　■■

She had more reasons to leave the city after that encounter with the tarot card girl.

She began seeing auras herself. Glowing sheaths of color that clung to people like luminescent Saran Wrap. At first she thought she was freaking out again, that maybe the hippies next door had laced the casserole leftovers they'd been dropping off at her house with hallucinogens. But no—these colors weren't psychedelic, they were hot and a little foggy and they burned steadily, like neon. Furthermore, not everyone she saw in a crowd or on the street gleamed like that. Sometimes it would be just one person—a fat woman in a muumuu singing to herself in a laundromat; a teenage boy in a buckskin vest and granny glasses, tinkering with his motorcycle. When she approached these people more closely—and it was impossible not to, because the colors were pulling her, sticking to her like flypaper—she could also see numbers and letters and sometimes words spinning around their heads like tickertape halos.

Once she started deciphering the halos, she thought she'd truly gone over the edge. For she could no longer control her urge to talk to these people, especially when the readings she was getting from the halos were dire, unpleasant. And they always were. She was bundling Bing cherries into a plastic bag in Cala Foods one afternoon when a middle-aged woman nearby stopped to squeeze a cantaloupe. Roo dropped the cherries.

"Go home," she said, clutching the woman's arm. "This can wait. Go home immediately. Your mother's dying. She needs you. Please. Go home. Call your mother now."

The woman's face twitched, then grew ashen.

"What? Who are you? What are you saying? What? What?"

"Go home," said Roo. The woman started to cry and backed off.

"Oh God," said Roo. "I'm sorry, I'm sorry."

She fled the grocery store.

The following day she was sketching in the Japanese Tea Garden when a young woman in a grey summer suit walked past her.

"Liliane," called Roo.

The woman stopped.

"Yes?"

"You're Liliane?" Roo had no idea how the name had come to her. She had never seen this woman before in her life. The woman's suit was no longer grey but on fire.

"Who are you?" said the woman. "How did you know my name?"

"Your son, André—I can see him. He's wearing his red

sleeveless sweater, the one his grandmother made for him. Don't let him out of your sight tonight. He'll need you. He'll want to know where his father's gone."

"My husband has not gone anywhere. I don't know what you're talking about, but you're very rude. And don't let me catch you spying on my house or my child again, do you hear? That goes for my mother too."

The woman turned and walked away quickly.

Roo fled again.

Before the week was over she had spoken to eight more people, people she didn't know from Adam, and delivered eight more letter bombs. Then the halos and their hieroglyphic messages started fading. If they were still there, they didn't let on. Perhaps because now when Roo saw people who were encased in those gaudy cocoons of light, she no longer approached them but turned away.

She threw out the delicious leftovers her neighbors continued to deposit on her doorstep. She began to scrutinize fanatically all the food that she bought. She switched from coffee to herbal tea.

The colors were omnipresent, though, inescapable. She saw them now in the pendants she made, and the bracelets. The jewels rippled, glowed, like underwater neon. They gave off auras. Cautiously, she began to stud the surfaces of her work with tiny chips of dazzle, mysterious bas-reliefs, friezes made of quartz diamonds, numbers, letters.

■■　■■　■■

"When are you leaving San Francisco?"

"I'm not. When are you leaving Trotsky?"

"I wish you wouldn't call him that. You needn't be nasty."

"I'm sorry, Dana. Frederick has called twice the past week, and he's been bitter and drunk both times. I'm sick of men right now. They're bone-and-spirit-crushers."

"And you think I'm living with one."

Roo had not spoken to Dana since she'd moved west. When her mother last called she had informed Roo that Dana was "door-matting herself" more than necessary. But Roo had avoided calling her, knowing that Leon would listen in and then whisper into Dana's ear, reminding her to tap into her sister's money if at all possible. Dana already had handed over her entire trust fund to him, an act that still appalled Roo, depressed her mother, and outraged her father. He hated Leon, and called him Boss Tweed when Dana was out of earshot. Roo was helpless to change anything or intercede. All she kept thinking whenever Dana called was: *How did my beautiful sister become so powerless? How?*

"I think you'd be better off living with just your kids."

"I couldn't afford it. Not now."

"If you wanted to, you could."

"I don't know if I could stand the loneliness."

"There are far worse things than living alone. Living with someone who makes you feel even lonelier is one of them."

"Aren't you lonely?"

"Yes. Sometimes. But I don't think about it. I have my work."

"How is your work? How's the jewelry business?"

She couldn't tell if Dana was being slightly cruel or not.

"I hope to have a clientele that's made up of more than street people, if that's what you mean."

"No. I meant are you selling anything?"

"I've sold a few things," she said. She could afford to tell at least one lie. "Nothing to write home about."

"Tell me about the city, your life there. Mother's been her usual parsimonious self about dishing out details."

You could have called me, Roo thought. *Or I, you.* But there was this wedge now. She'd followed in her sister's shoes, she'd done everything her sister had except drop out of college. She'd been married, divorced, then lived with a man. A number of men, in fact. But now she'd broken loose. She knew where she was, but not where she and Dana were—except at opposite ends of a continent, which she sensed said everything about their relationship now. She would have liked to tell Dana about the strange lights she had seen, the unsettling psychic powers humming beneath her skin, but she was nervous.

"Being here's like living in a kaleidoscope. The moment I step outside, the colors are everywhere, dancing, just like the hippies. I'm bombarded by colors and sensations, constantly. And they're having a really powerful effect on my jewelry, on everything. I'm too old to be a hippie, I know that. And sometimes I think there's too much drift out here, too many lost people. I'm more into worry beads than love beads. But I blend in, I take whatever's happening out here inside me, and then release it, in my jewels. I feel comfortable here. Dana?"

"I'm still here."

"I've been meeting people. People who have this shining light on their skin. I don't know how to explain this, but I see unusual lights sometimes. Shimmering colors."

"Are you stoned?"

"No."

"Maybe you should have your eyes checked."

"You sound like Mother. My eyes are fine."

"You're sure you're not stoned? You sound like you did in New York."

"No. Forget it. All I can say about my life right now is this: being alone doesn't scare me. I leave my windows open at night. No one's going to climb in. I listen to wind chimes and Jim Morrison and my next-door neighbors laughing. The noise, raucous as it is, is often comforting. I have my own space. Dad, I think, would love it. Denis too."

"I don't suppose you could lend me a little cash, could you?"

"Dana, I've just bought a house, and have had to shell out for furniture as well as art supplies. I'm on a tight budget too."

"But you still have some of Daddy's money left, don't you?"

"Yes. Unlike you."

"I'm running really low. All the time."

"Then wring some more out of Mother or Dad. I can't be filling Trotsky's coffers too."

"But it's not for him, Roo, it's for me, it's—"

"My God, Dana, don't you remember how you yearned to be a ballet dancer, how you wanted to do something exciting with your life? What's happened to you? What's happened? You've turned into a sponge as well as a sponger."

Roo hung up the phone angrily, then wept, then blew up again. Dana didn't call back. The air was so still not even the wind chimes tinkled. The phone sat on the floor like a dead turtle. All she really wanted to do was smooth out, make a cup of jasmine tea, put on an old Shirelles album. But she did not move.

Years later she wondered if she shouldn't have walked out then, on the house, her art, her fraudulent new life—especially then, when not a single wind chime stirred, when not a single note of music twittered through those vacant rooms.

■■   ■■   ■■

"It's not that they aren't good," said the woman who was the buyer in Gump's. "They are, they are. They're radiant in a way, without pandering, you know, well, to the psychedelic." When she spoke the last word, her upper lip twisted, as though some insect had just landed there for refueling. At the same moment, she removed her appraising fingers from the perfume bottles, those weirdly beautiful cones and pyramids Roo had sweated over, dyed and glued and buffed. They too, apparently, were as welcome as houseflies.

"It's just that they're, well—"

"Plastic," said Roo.

"Exactly."

"But this is my medium," said Roo.

"Oh, I know," said the woman. "You're doing marvelous things here, and who knows? You could be the Kandinsky of plastic. I've seen nothing quite like these before, nothing. But the risk—well, it's just too great right now. We wouldn't be doing justice to your work, we wouldn't."

"I take it you won't be too interested in the jewelry either."

"Unless you're using real stones, no. Have you thought of mixing your media? Some of these bottles have an almost fire-opal luminosity. What if you tried, you know, a sort of radical wedding of real gems with these gemlike configurations? Have you thought of that?"

Roo had slipped the perfume bottles back into their tiny felt coverlets.

"You've been very kind," she said. "Perhaps when I've cooked up some new configurations, I'll stop by again."

"Oh, do," said the woman.

As soon as she stepped out of air-conditioned Gump's, the heat walloped her. She smothered, but barely, the impulse to strip off her clothes and toss her wares into the nearest trash barrel. She should have known better; her jewelry was either too bizarre or just not good enough. She'd be better off making pot holders or salt and pepper shakers. Those, people could use. What she wanted now was a numbingly cool drink, something on the order of a nepenthe frappe.

A sunflower head was walking towards her, one of the many freaks who had long ago forgone haircuts. A tall, frightfully thin young man whose shirt was so transparent she could see his ribs beneath it. His hair shot out in all directions, like blond fire. He was smiling at her. "The swans thank you," he said as he passed by. "And so do I."

"What?"

She turned around, but he didn't.

"You feed all of us," he shouted back.

She watched him not quite disappear in the sidewalk traffic, his head borne aloft above the other pedestrians like John the Baptist's on a tray. Then he turned the corner and was gone.

The heat now was making her dizzy, sick. She wobbled into

a decent bar and ordered a glass of soda with lime. Two businessmen were hunkering down over their gin and tonics. "She's like a killer," one of them said to the other. "Putting your cock in her would be like screwing an electric pencil sharpener. She thought her tits were Pinkerton safes."

She left before the drink arrived. Back home, she dumped her bottles and jewels on her bed, undressed, and embraced the cool white sheets. When the phone rang she wondered who it would be. Maybe the woman she'd talked to in the Japanese Tea Garden, Liliane. Maybe the boy in the street with the white fireball hair. Maybe God, telling her to give up.

It was none of them.

"Hi, bitch," said Frederick. "Are you ever going to—"

She left the phone off the hook after she'd exterminated him. Then she walked calmly to the kitchen, opened the fridge, and drank from a pitcher of ice water. Then she poured the water on her breasts until she was shaking. She buried her face in a bowl of grapes, smelled them, felt them bump against her forehead like icy marbles. *I need to be fed. Somehow I need to be fed.*

And now she knew how.

■■   ■■   ■■

She was not sleepwalking, though she knew if anyone else but he were staring at her she would most likely resemble some drugged zombie in a white sundress, walking across wet grass, water, air, scattering birds, crumbs, the last of her reserve. He was waiting for her in the shade of the colonnade, the steamy shade, as it turned out, for she was perspiring heavily, and when he started to play "Bibbidi-Bobbidi-Boo" she laughed a laugh as silver as his flute. "You're nuts," she said, "absolutely." "No, I'm Sky." "You're what?" "I told you. Sky." "Sky who?" "Just Sky. As in diver, scraper, rocket." "You've made it up." "Of course. Nothing's real unless it's made up. Who wants to be unreal?" "You need a decent breakfast. Something more than crumbs. How about a whole lemon muffin? Or two muffins? Or three." "Lady, hey. What are you? Gone, are you?

Absolutely gone?" "Yes. But the muffins are real. Believe me. I made them up." "Who'll feed the swans?" "Somebody. Some other fool."

■■   ■■   ■■

That he slid into her house and her life so effortlessly, that she fell goofily in love with him—and so painlessly—told her she'd been right to ignore the predictions of the tarot card girl.

Some things about him puzzled her, but she assumed in time there would be answers. His quirks were more amusing than infuriating. He refused to tell her where he worked. He would steal out of the house early in the morning and be back by suppertime. He always took his flute with him. She asked him once if he was in a band or rehearsing, but she already knew the answer. Bands played at night, and he was always home at night. If he rehearsed all day, he'd not be making money—and he was. He persisted in buying the groceries each week, unwilling to let her support him. Occasionally she wondered if he took his flute with him every day because he wanted to be prepared—in case he decided some afternoon that he was sick of her and wanted to cut out immediately. "Do you need your flute at work?" she asked. "I always need it," he said. "At work, in the john, in bed. Hey, you never know. Guess it's my Linus blanket." She had stopped entreating him to think seriously of auditioning for a jazz club somewhere. Every time she'd tried he bristled. "Jazz?" he'd say. "You gotta be kidding. In this town? There's no jazz here. Nobody listens to jazz. It's all Beatles and Jefferson Airplane. 'White Rabbit' shit. And who's gonna shell out bread for a flutist? Come on. I mean, the flute is not exactly your hot instrument right now, is it?" No matter that runaway kids in Golden Gate Park were playing recorders. "Oh, the 'recorder,' " he'd say, smirking. "Too low and mopey for me. Recorders are for snake charmers. The moron's clarinet." And then he would squat on the floor in a lotus position, blowing the lowest notes he could out of his flute. And she would crack up. Then, moments later, after he'd smoked a joint or two and was high, he would play something so fanciful and hypnotic that she would shiver, as though the notes were raining cold drops of mercury on her skin.

She bent to his love of whimsicality. She had been with too many men who loved seriousness and who took everything seriously but her. Sky treated her as though she were nearly as valuable as his flute, but treated life as though all things of value were destined to go up in smoke—one of the reasons why he got high so often. "It keeps my mind on the pleasantness of things passing," he said. "Disappearance is too depressing otherwise."

He never told her his real name, or his age. After that first night, he moved in with her, emptied his duffel-bag wardrobe and stowed his few clothes neatly on one shelf in her closet, then just as neatly piled his only other possessions next to her stereo —the used classical and jazz albums that he'd bought from discount bins. Sometimes he'd accompany Bach. Other times, he'd sit in with the Modern Jazz Quartet or Stan Getz. He said he'd gotten hooked on jazzy reeds and horns when he was a teenager—and that the only thing missing from those records was a flute.

No laundryman had stamped initials in the collars of his shirts. While he was out one day, she combed through his meager belongings, searching for papers—a Social Security card, a driver's license. There was nothing. All he'd told her was that he'd grown up in Kansas and had left with his sister. She assumed his parents were dead. He'd burned everything, torched the past as well as his draft card.

That he hated shoes pleased her in a perverse way. Sky could survive in the world without cordovans. He was nearly always barefoot. He'd loop a pair of sandals around his belt in the morning, but she doubted he ever wore them during the day. When he got home the first thing he did was soak the soles of his feet in the old Victorian tub. He was surprisingly clean, she thought, given the way he must have been living before she'd arrived. He'd been a capable panhandler when he was desperate, he'd told her. His flute had served him well. And someone always had a spare bed to flop down in at night. He'd lived with a girl two years ago, for about three months. Then cops had awakened them and hauled them both down to the station. She'd broken her parole, they told him. She'd been in jail for assault and robbery. He'd never known. From prison she'd mail him letters begging him to take her back when she was released. The letters, he said, looked as though they'd been written by a child. What he loved about her was the child in her. He'd simply never seen how she was all child, and sometimes a very disturbed one at that. When she finally got out of prison, she attacked a sixty-year-old woman with a pipe and got sent back for fifteen more years.

He would tell Roo these minimal stories while he scrubbed his feet, and then gently rubbed her legs with those same feet as they bathed together. The men she'd known back east had been born with ankle-length black socks which they never took off. Sky was all prehensile digits, his feet another set of hands.

He never spoke about his body's other peculiarity, the tiny dents on his back and stomach, as though nickels and quarters had lain there once and left their expensive impressions forever.

He knew when to leave her alone. But occasionally he would leave her too much alone, disappear, drop off the face of the earth, it seemed. And she would freak out, like a mother who'd somehow let her child wander away from her in a department store. This happened frequently on the weekends she would drive the two of them to Sausalito or to Carmel, where she would try to hustle some of her jewelry into the boutiques, with little success. Afterward they would retire for a long lunch in a cove off Pfeiffer Beach, she to meditate on her failure, he to wolf down plums before taking off. He had asked her that first time if she would mind his borrowing her car for a short drive, while she soaked up the sun. "But you don't have a license," she'd said. "Do you think I'm a bad driver?" he asked. "I don't know." "You think I'll buzz down to L.A., hock your car, and then fly to New York? Maybe get a real job at the Café Au Go-Go?" "No. Be serious." "If I'm arrested I'll call you." "Where?" "Here. On the beach. I'll dial, and you pick up any conch shell and listen." "Then go. Go, go. But come back soon." When he didn't come back soon, she knew for certain that all men were versions of Frederick. He was totally untrustworthy, she thought. He was crazy. And she was frantic. Then, when she was just about ready to give up on him and start hitching back to the city, the old woody would rumble down the path to the beach. And he'd be grinning, as though fooling her, upsetting her, getting her to walk the edge was part of the plan. And she knew what he'd probably been doing: getting high, flying on wheels. His smile was his giveaway.

He would unsettle her even more in bed, but she did not mind that. He would make love to her in startling ways. Some nights he would bring a basket of fruit to their bed, tell her to close her eyes, ask her to guess. She would feel his supple lips pressing against hers, and taste him first, then the sweet gush of Bing cherry, or grape, or plum, whatever he'd hidden inside his mouth before gashing it with his teeth. Once, after they'd showered, he had asked her to lie on the floor like a virgin strapped to a cross. Around her body he placed tiny brass urns filled with cones of incense—patchouli, wisteria, sandalwood, lotus—and lit them. "Only our hips can move. Or else we'll get burned." Then he arched over her, slid into her, using only his fingers and toes to suspend himself. She could not tell if it was the odors of incense or his cock which drew her upwards, forcing her to levitate. Her thighs were burning, but the fire was all inside. He was like a searing fuse in her that wouldn't go out. And she could hear a voice crooning, *Burn, witch, burn.* The voice was hers.

■ ■　　■ ■　　■ ■

She decided one foggy morning to work some of the shops near Berkeley. She was getting tired of showing her new work—her rings like tiny Mayan temples, her glowy neon bracelets—to the woman at Gump's, who kept rebuffing her. The girls who passed themselves off as buyers in the head shops in the Haight were even more disheartening. They had funky but rubbishy taste. All they were really into now were cheap pendants from Afghanistan, necklaces strung out of Indian corn, and earrings made of old baby spoons and salad forks.

The fog refused to lift that morning. It drifted through the streets like long, dirty wedding veils. She parked near the campus and then headed up Bancroft Street. Under the nearby trees a dozen or more students were snake-dancing and chanting. In the fog they seemed more like nymphs in a Botticelli painting than stoned college kids. As she moved closer she could see the lead dancer break away and enter the center of the ring. Her face was a deep red mahogany. She looked a little like Cher, that singer on "Hullabaloo" with the incredibly long hair. "Feel the sprinkle," she was saying to the dancers. "Get into that sprinkly feeling, feel the sprinkle." The dancers raised their arms and fluttered their fingers. They were turning themselves into shower nozzles or sprinkling cans.

Then Roo heard the flute. From somewhere up ahead. And she knew it was Sky's. She kept walking. Wherever he was, he was not playing for the dancers. They had dissolved behind her in the grey-green mist. Ahead of her was another cluster of students, each of them angling for a position closer to a small white truck. The sides of the truck were painted in psychedelic swirls that looked like flaming sno-cones.

She stayed back. She hid behind a tree. She could see him but dimly as he dispensed what must have been ice cream sandwiches and ice cream bars. When he finished he picked up his flute again and played a fragment of melody that was like no song that had ever come from an Eskimo Pie truck, sounds that seemed to take their cue from the fog itself—moody and low and skittery. Before he'd finished she had already begun running back to her station wagon.

She followed him. Cautiously. All day. Carefully maintaining her distance from him lest she be seen in his rearview mirror. She wondered where the truck had come from, who owned it, who'd painted it. She'd never seen one in the city before. Eskimo Pies, Popsicles—they belonged in sleepy suburbs, not here. But most of all she wondered how the two of them had gotten together. Not she and Sky, but Sky and the truck.

Whenever she heard snatches of flute music she would pull over quickly, double-park, and listen. The truck snaked through the city, skillfully avoiding heavy congestion. It knew precisely what intersections were magnets for the flute-and-ice-cream-starved. Sometimes she could see his arm shoot out the window, his hand extending packets in white wrappers, cool treats. By late afternoon he had found his way into the Mission District. She seldom drove through here. The poverty saddened and scared her. The houses, most of them painted a dull ochre, had a scrunched and scabby look to them. There were no lawns, only scrawny plants struggling to eke out a life from the cracks in the sidewalk. Most of the faces she saw were Hispanic. The children looked doleful and trapped. Ice cream was probably the only affordable luxury. But she could see glowing colors here that had nothing to do with her visions. Middle-aged women in pink and orange and turquoise housedresses. Children in shirts and blouses brighter than orchids. They made all the Day-Glo hippies seem crumbly as chalk.

The kids were following the truck now. He hadn't even stopped to trill on his flute yet, but they must have known he'd be here. They could hear him, smell him, the way a cat could sense its owner coming home long before footsteps sounded at the door. The truck finally halted near a small park. She backed up the station wagon and parked it in the shadow of one of the few trees. Twenty or more children had gathered around the truck. Some were teenagers. She could hear them whistling and laughing. They were clearly there for more than ice cream.

What she heard next, though, was unreal—a flute that

sounded like castanets. Sky was teasing one or two notes, then stopping, then teasing them again until you could almost hear them clicking. And then she heard a drum. One of the kids must have joined in. The others swiveled and swayed like flamenco dancers to whatever it was—rumba or samba or bolero. Sky was completely invisible to her. But his flute—she could see the notes fire-dance out of the cool white truck, flames licking under each one. When he was through, some of the kids whistled even louder and clapped. Then the truck pulled away and disappeared.

She was drenched with sweat and shaking. She had melted into the car seat. Her brain had been blasted by more than music. She could barely start the ignition. Once she did, she drove home immediately.

When he returned around dinnertime she was in bed, listening to her pulse. When he took off his clothes she could see a sheath of silver flames coating his body. "I'm in a good mood tonight," he said, smirking. "I want to get smashed and then I want to get laid."

He snuggled into her body and the flames slithered over her belly like copperheads. She could not hear the genial banter in his voice. His mockery of barbarousness was itself a barbarous thing, because it was one more mask of his, and the masks never ended. She was all masks now too, hiding things from him she couldn't hide from herself. She was sad, she was depressed, even while the fire kept nicking and nibbling at her. She knew without it ever being said that he was the finer artist of the two of them, even if neither became much of a success. Yet he was all the more successful than she because he didn't care about it. And she was hurt and a little angry too, knowing that he would always keep hidden from her the best of him, and the worst. *What do I have in my arms?* she thought, listening now to two unsyncopated heartbeats.

The flames danced out of control from her toes to her hair. When she stared at his face, she saw it was melting, like tallow.

When he took her at last in all his white fire, she screamed and did not stop screaming.

■■   ■■   ■■

For the next two weeks she was consumed with fever, could work only an hour each day at the most, then spent the remainder of the day in bed. Sky often came home early and made her a chilled fruit salad and soup, then entertained her by playing ragtime on his flute. Sometimes the television was on, though the volume was turned off. Always there were clips from the battlefront. Helicopters twitching, then diving down into some nameless jungle or wasteland. She saw it all as a silent horror movie, giant insects raiding the landscape, scouting for prey.

"Doesn't it get to you?" he said one night. "The war?"

"No. I've seen enough battles already."

She had not yet told him about Denis. One broken man in her life was enough to care about.

"Don't you worry?" she asked. "You're still draftable."

"How can they find me? I have no address. I'm nameless. When I was nine I ceased to exist. Or I ceased living on one plane." He sucked in a deep breath. When he let it out he sounded like an expired balloon. "Anyway, I have two tough feet. I can still run. So can you."

She begged him to sleep in the living room, so he would not catch her fever. But frequently, when she woke during the night, she found him curled around her body, cocooning it. His flesh, surprisingly, cooled her.

Sometimes the fridge was bereft of fruit, if they had over-indulged the night before. Woozy, in the middle of the afternoon, she would struggle out to Cala Foods, unable to wait for Sky to make his nightly grocery run, then collapse once she got back, the fruit tumbling out of her hands, scattering like billiard balls. And she would have to crawl across the floor to fetch the renegade apples, the slippery grapes. Sky would promise that night to overload the fridge the next day, but he always made those promises when he was high or spacey or about to surrender himself to his flute, a greater passion. Sometimes he would forget.

One afternoon she thought she would collapse while she was standing in line at Cala Foods, holding in one hand two crumpled dollar bills and in the other four Santa Rosa plums. She wore nothing but a flimsy shift and even flimsier sandals, yet she could feel her face turning scarlet from the heat, the sweat boiling out of her forehead. She wasn't moving. She couldn't tell if the line was moving or not. She knew if she took one more step she would dissolve into a puddle on the floor, like molten pudding.

Then she felt an arm clutching hers, and heard someone whisper in her ear, "Thank you."

Roo turned. The woman by her side, supporting her, was middle-aged, with a turnipy nose, somebody's mother, nobody she knew.

"You were right, you know," said the woman. "I'm so glad I called. She died the very next day, would you believe? I flew home to New Jersey the day I called, the day I met you, she was in the hospital already. And we had such a good talk, we did, we did, before she went. If I hadn't called, I just don't know what. You're sweating awfully. Are you all right?"

"I think so."

The woman took a Kleenex from her purse and wiped Roo's brow.

"Do you have a card?" the woman asked. "I'd love a card."

"A card?"

"For another reading."

"I'm sorry. I have no cards."

"No matter. I'm sure you'll see me again, like you did before."

Then she disappeared down the vegetable aisle. When Roo got to the cash register she realized juice was running down her leg like blood. She paid for her bruised plums. She ate them while she walked home. She would have fainted if she hadn't. She staggered up her front stairs. Her shift was stained. Her hands dripped red. *I look like a vampire.*

She was calmer by the time Sky returned. That night he looked somber, almost worried. He'd bought some pears, and sliced one for her, very neatly; he did not smoke.

"They're talking about a march to the Pentagon," he said. "They want to levitate the Pentagon."

"Who?"

"The perfectibles. Everybody here who believes in the perfectibility of man."

"Hush. We shouldn't make fun of perfection. Perhaps it exists."

"I don't make fun of it. I'm just not one of them. I don't believe anything changes things for the better. Least of all war."

"Play something for me. Make me feel better, even if we can't change."

"It's dying, you know. Already. The Haight. Everything here in San Francisco. Everything happy."

She shivered. She hoped he did not mean everything that was there in that bedroom.

"You don't see it," he said, "because you're older, and your work is, well, different. And you stay inside. And you don't really get stoned. But the Mafia's here already. It's more a business now, the drug scene. Heavy drugs, and big business. You want to stay here, really?"

"You mean here, in this house?"

"I mean San Francisco."

"Something is keeping me here." She wanted to say, *You, you keep me here.* But he was in too hard a mood.

"Would you want to raise your kids here?"

"I told you before, Sky. I can't have children. Something's wrong with me down there, or wrong with my head. I don't spend much time thinking about kids."

"Could you imagine fourth-graders, or first-graders, dropping acid?"

"No. That will never happen."

"It may. Maybe it already is happening." He left the room. She knew he was heading for the kitchen—to slit another pear, to light up. Her belly still felt empty. But nowhere near as empty as her womb. Kids. She couldn't succeed there either. No wonder she mostly ignored them. The only children she'd remembered paying any attention to were those Spanish kids who bought the ice cream bars and listened to—

"Sky?"

He stood in the doorway, a joint dangling from his lips. Then he knelt down beside her and began to rub her feet. He smelled of reefer and pear juice.

"How was your day?" he asked.

"Sick. Why were you asking me all those questions about drugs and kids?"

"I won't let it happen," he said. Then he kissed her feet.

"What?"

"Maybe I'll take some time off." He lay down beside her. "I've been lucky so far, haven't I? You know, not getting your fever. You're right, maybe I could get a job in a club somewhere, with a good drummer, a bassist. You'd like that, wouldn't you. But then, what about the angels? They're all a hoax anyway. He tricked me, didn't he. He messed me up. But not as bad as the dog pound. No sir, not as bad. I'm no angel but I'm no devil either. I should drink vino. Out of a goblet, out of a shoe, but there are no shoes. Vino, Sister Stephen. Let me kiss your feet. I never could, you know, though I always wanted to. Why didn't I? Zounds. Sister Zounds. Divino vino. Coward. You should have."

"Sky?"

"I'm too stoned, I'm asleep. I'm gone. There are too many cars in my head. Too many cars."

She put out his joint. And then she saw it, rippling over his body—a phosphorescence like blue magma. And the number 4— it was pirouetting on his forehead like a music-box ballerina. Then it cracked, broke into four little slivers useless as burnt matchsticks. The hot blue light ferried them away. Then the magma disappeared, became what it in fact was, her old blue quilt. Her fever was gone. She was staring at his eyelashes, shut as tight as Venus's flytraps, at his lips that barely moved while he slept. This was the music man she loved perhaps as much as she could love anyone, the crazyboy.

And she had never felt more at home, or more at sea.

■ ■   ■ ■   ■ ■

He had asked her once if her name was short for something. "You mean like Reubena?" she'd answered. "Or Rutilia? Ruby Tuesday?" He'd smirked, then started to sing. "Roo, roo, roo your boat, gently down the stream." He knew better than to pursue the question. He did not want the shoe on the other foot.

When she was two her father had put a stop to her name. "I can't stand it anymore, Liddie, I can't," he said to her mother. "I rue the day we named her, Liddie, I rue it." "What's wrong with Enid?" "Enid. How about Peanuts? Or Penis? Enid. Enamel. Enzyme. Enema. Enough. Name me a lovely word beginning with e-n, name it." "If you rue it so much, then call her Rue."

So she was no longer Enid. She was Rue. But it was Dana who taught her how to spell her name. R-O-O. That was Dana's nasty joke on her. "Your name is full of zeroes," she said, guiding Roo's hands as she spelled. "Because you're a big zero."

She kept it that way. When she eventually learned what "rue" meant, in fourth grade, she was glad she'd kept it that way, without the u and the e. A cheery "roo," as in "rooster, root beer, room service."

Years later she regretted that no one had corrected her cute spelling error, that no one had punished Dana. Years later she wished she had told the story of her name to the one man whose name was like hers, the only man apart from her brother who knew what zero really meant.

■ ■   ■ ■   ■ ■

The night was muggy, ungodly hot, the stillness in the air a killer. The ocean rumbled but stingily withheld any breezes. She felt patches of sweat suck at her body like leeches.

Too many sticky things had surfaced at dinner, or threatened to surface, only to be submerged under the familiar slick of politeness. They had all feasted from a table set in quicksand. Now that it was quite dark, she hoped a drunken neighbor would be daring enough to set off a skyrocket or two from a front lawn or the beach; the sky wouldn't balk at being festooned with something sparkly and noisy. Yachtsmen could always be counted on to launch an illegal burst of fireworks, unless they were too pie-eyed to light a match. Since the late afternoon, though, she had seen no pleasure boats offshore. Coming home had been even more of a downer this time. She wasn't sure how long either she or Sky could put up with it, and they weren't scheduled to return to San Francisco until Sunday.

Her mother had calmed down at least, though she'd retired to bed rather early. Felice's cooking sometimes set everybody's stomach on edge. Roo thought the fish somewhat oddly flavored. The pale slices of pompano smelled of both licorice and walnuts. She knew how her mother abhorred all things spicy and offbeat, in cuisine as well as elsewhere. The exotic fish sauce had probably done her in for the evening.

The major difficulties she predicted she'd have with her mother had, thank God, been dealt with already, on the phone while she was still in California. *Yes, Mother, his name is Sky. Does he have a last name? No, Mother. But what am I supposed to call him then—Mr. Sky? No, Mother, call him Sky the way you call me Roo. He sounds like a character on some children's television show. Yes, Mother, "Sky King."* The only remaining hurdle she knew her mother would put him through was saved for dinner, the artichoke test. But that he passed easily. Of course he knew how to peel the leaves properly to get to the heart. What else did they live on in San Francisco but fruits and vegetables? Harder for Sky, she knew, would be keeping his sandals on during dinner. But the shoe rule had been broken by others. Dana wore nothing but muumuus and spent the entire day barefoot. Probably because she could make less noise traipsing to the liquor cabinet. Denis was always barefoot too, and had never once stepped on a bumblebee while working on the lawn. Only her mother continued to perform well in the dumb show of propriety, her legs encased in nylons in July, her feet clamped into size six low-heeled pumps. Even her father's loafer-shod feet, she had noticed, were sockless.

But it was her father whose behavior at dinner she'd found the most disconcerting. He seemed withdrawn or tired, was far less talkative than anyone else. And the more he withheld himself, the more she felt he was silently judging her. Sky's questions were never innocent gambits to ignite a conversation. "So what do you think about the war thus far?" was hardly a suitable query to be thrust at her father, who probably knew what kinds of hardwood were produced in Vietnam or what the postage stamps looked like but who, like her, cared little or nothing about the war. Both men were daunted by each other, she figured, but her father more so. Sky, she knew, had never been inside a house so carelessly opulent, nor had he ever been with people who took such wealth for granted. Even she had sometimes felt puny and inconsequential here, bouncing from room to room like some token on a Monopoly board. When she was younger she thought each room was either Park Place or Boardwalk. Now she was sure every room was Jail.

Though Sky had assumed as relaxed a position as he could in his stiff-backed dining-room chair, his bare feet occasionally nudging hers, she suspected there was tension coiled beneath his laid-back manner. Her father no doubt found that manner unnerving, languor being solely the right of those who'd grown up with privileges. Maybe he saw in Sky the wild young man he himself had never been, she thought. Someone who had a racy, unconventional woman at his side, a woman so unlike her mother. Maybe the heat the two of them generated made the dining room all the more uncomfortable, since it was so hot inside already. Her father's brow, unlike hers, was dry as talc. When he sweated, if ever, he sweated from within. His staccato answers to Sky's questions—"Yes," "No," "Not much," "Not often"—befitted her mother, not him. Perhaps it was that, his ungivingness, rather than Felice's fish, that had unseated her mother, caused her to exit from the table early. They were now all quite used to dinners where long spells of silence periodically welled up, since one of the persons at that table had not spoken a word in five years. For once, Roo wished that Dana hadn't left her dreadful daughters behind in Boston. The twins were always testy and fidgety whenever they visited; but their no-holds-barred belligerence, their noise might have been welcome tonight. "Could anything tempt an older person to grow his hair really long, sir? I mean it, truly. Anything?" Why had Sky continued that fruitless parrying with her father, why? It was like tossing a hatchet into pudding or tomato aspic. Her father quivered, but just barely; the hatchet sank and disappeared.

Dana had been no help at all. She could have risen to the bait easily, fenced with Sky all night long about Vietnam. The two of them were alike, politically, except Dana's role as a protester was simply that, a role. She wasn't a draftee; she hadn't the least notion what it would be like to be a young man whose days were numbered. But tonight Dana had seemed to regard the war as a gigantic bore. She'd held down the drinking at dinner, because she was loaded already. Roo had not seen Dana let go of the tumbler in her hand once all afternoon. Her parents, she realized, were probably more startled by Sky's hair than by the fact that their elder daughter had become an alcoholic. At least her father had complimented Sky on his flute-playing. Dana had said nothing. Maybe because the house was still filled with scratchy echoes of *Swan Lake.*

Only Denis was totally smitten with Sky. She knew he would be. The bittersweet songs that Denis listened to were nothing like the manic and jazzy solos Sky played. But for two hours or more that afternoon she had heard Sky's flute dancing lightly over gloomy saxophones and low trombones and Sinatra's dusky voice. Something more than lamentation poured out of the record player. Denis would not let Sky even attempt to disassemble his flute. It was as though he wanted to install the two of them in his downstairs bedroom forever, within easy reach, right next to the record player. Permanent as furniture, permanent as his unspoken grief.

She could hear booming and sputtering noises from somewhere now. The night was not utterly shorn of color. She could also hear someone approaching her from the darkened room behind her, hear him step past the French windows, feel his arms slide around her chest.

"We're the only ones up," he said.

"Up is not exactly how I feel."

"Your sister's hard as nails," he said. "What's wrong with her? And I don't mean the bottle. We all need to get high a little."

"She never gets high," said Roo. "She only gets low. What's wrong with her is the man she's living with, the life she's leading. Things haven't worked out well for her."

"She's better off than your brother."

"I'm not so sure."

"Why were you afraid to tell me about him?"

"I don't know. I guess he needs protecting."

"Maybe not. He's sturdy enough to mow lawns."

"My brother is, or was, the best thing this family ever had to offer."

"And you're just a gnawed-up artichoke leaf. Sure, babe, sure. Listen. Why don't we sleep out here? Fuck the bedrooms. They're steambaths. We can move some of this lawn furniture, sleep on the chaise-lounge pillows, sleep on the grass."

"The pillows," she said. "And kiddo—it's chaise longue."

"Chaise who?"

She lay beneath him. They fit into each other as comfortably as if they were at Pfeiffer Beach, their panting timed to the gush of waves. *Better than sparklers,* she thought, *better than skyrockets.* When he was finally still, his head buried against her neck, she had an unblocked view of one side of the house, dark as a curtain, shutting down on the helpless lives inside. And she knew there was nothing she could do to rescue any of them. None of them saw a way out of pain. They were locked in the shadows, pressed behind glass. They were no different from all those mounted animal heads in the attic.

She fell asleep, embracing another kind of darkness, one warmer and more shapely, though her sleep did not last more than an hour. The curtain had moved. She was awake, she had seen it. And now she saw another dark shape, standing there between the French windows, like a muffled butler or bellboy. It was her father. She could also recognize what he was carrying in his hands. Duffel bags. Hers and Sky's. He had not yet stepped past the windows onto the verandah. It was as though he were trying to maintain his last foothold on discretion. She was wide awake now, embarrassed and angry.

"I've called The Breakers," he said quietly. "They're holding a room for both of you. A cab should be here soon."

"What?"

"You must go. Please. There's no time. There never has been."

She felt Sky stir against her. He knew the strange voice he'd heard wasn't hers. "What?" he muttered. "Oh shit." When he leaped up she felt cold all of a sudden and clasped her arms around her chest. Then, as though she were some adolescent girl caught with her boyfriend, she started to pick up what clothes she could see and put them back on. She didn't scramble; she was seething. Her father had backed away from the windows. He'd retreated once Sky stalked past him, naked. She could hear Sky rummaging through the living room, cursing. No one had turned on a light. She was glad she'd been wearing so little. She found her sandals last, but her watch had disappeared. She was not going to crawl around on her hands and knees and feel for it like a blind person. What was wrong with her father? Was he just hopelessly old-fashioned? How could he be so rude, so mean?

A flash of silver guided her into the living room. Sky was brandishing his flute like a shillelagh, but there was nothing to bash at but shadows. Her father had retreated still further, to the front door.

"I can't find my fucking flute case!"

Sky's voice sounded like a fire alarm.

"Leave it," she said. "We'll get another."

She knew she didn't belong here anymore. *I haven't even protested,* she thought. *I've said nothing.* Inchoate rage kept her moving, but she felt as though what was happening were an extension of some dream that had seized her an hour ago, or maybe years ago, a dream she was still having.

At the front door she faced her father, took her duffel bag from him. *Is vacation over? Am I going back to college? Is the cab here?* This was no different; this was terribly different. Anger or pain stiffened for a moment his sagging face; but she sensed it would melt or crumble the moment she turned her back on him. And she was torn then. She wanted to slam the door in his face; she also wanted to take that face in her hands, prop it up, support him, press out the fury with her strong fingers. Sky had already gone out. She'd seen him in the driveway, only half-dressed, his back to her, waiting for whatever was to happen next. She'd noticed he was shivering, but the night was still a scorcher and she was sweating. She heard a cab pull into the driveway.

Her father touched her arm, almost as if to show her how to use a paintbrush.

"I know you can't understand this, Roo. Neither can I. I wish I could."

His formality, his sheepishness, his plaintive gibberish made her boil now.

"I understand perfectly. But Mother wouldn't let you get away with—"

"She's asleep. Please, go now. With your young man. I will call you tomorrow morning. Everything's been paid for. You needn't—"

She did not look back once. She knew the moment she got into the cab that she had said goodbye forever to that house, and that she and Sky would find a flight out of Florida that very morning. His teeth were chattering. "The Breakers," she said to the cabdriver.

Sky's arms were shaking. The cab might as well have been an electric chair with the juice turned on.

"He booted me out, like a dog."

"And me too," she said. "But he's old and ruined and doesn't know what he's doing."

"He beat me like a dog too. With the buckle end. Every day, every night."

"Sky?"

"I wore an iron collar around my neck. He chained me to a pole in the basement, on a metal leash. And I had to run around like a dog and I could never get out. And the leash got shorter and shorter the more I ran around the pole so I couldn't escape him. The buckle felt like a hundred bee stings, each time he hit me. He'd let me out for school and then chain me up at night, and I wasn't strong, I wasn't strong enough to break the chain or get out of the collar, and the pole was too big, too fat. And he was fucking my sister, I know it, I know it. And then one night when it was cold he dragged me out of the basement and he padlocked the chain to an old icebox in the backyard and he let me freeze there, and I would've died. But that was the night my sister got him really drunk, and she came outside with the pliers and she cut the chain, and then we stole his car and she drove and she drove and she drove. Some man who made horseshoes broke the collar around my neck, somewhere in Colorado. We just kept driving, and driving. My sister got us money, doing what Daddy'd taught her to do so well. She's nowhere now, she's gone. I'm never going back there. I'm never going back there. I'm never going back there."

"Neither am I," she whispered, though she knew his "there" was not hers. She could feel his body slump and unwind as it pressed next to hers. "Lay your head on my lap," she said. "Rest till we find a bed." She told the cabdriver to drive them to West Palm Beach instead, to any decent motel near the airport. She did not want to be awakened by her father's phone call. His behavior was unpardonable now, his banishment of them far more than an act of benighted conservatism. He'd been stupid, mean, picayune. And she had nothing to fear from the darkness in that house. The shadows were only shadows, easily dispelled by the sunlight. The shadowboxer on her lap had known a darkness she would never know.

The cabdriver hummed "Estrellita." If he'd seen the bogey-man too, his face didn't show it. He'd surely heard every word of Sky's wail. Perhaps he was used to it. Perhaps that's what cabs were sometimes for. A safe place to detonate a bomb in the brain, to open Pandora's box. The cabs never exploded; the nightmares blew out the window. Maybe the drunks coming out of the bars now, the middle-aged couples tucked away in their beds, the barefoot boys dreaming of endless beaches, uninterrupted sunlight, maybe everyone in the world was Sky, tamping down the terrors. The world had never seemed so tough to her, and so frightening.

At ten in the morning they were able to board a flight back to San Francisco. When her father called that night, she hung up. In the months that followed she changed her phone number frequently. She kept it listed, though, in case of an emergency.

She never spoke to him again, though Dana and her mother kept her informed as to his health, both physical and mental. As she forgot him more and more, she no longer felt guilty about not forgiving him. Sometimes, though, when she went into trances, she could hear him talk to her, moaning, wailing. His face, she could see it, was as tormented as Masaccio's Eve. Had she wanted to speak, she might have said, *It was yourself you exiled, Daddy*. But she did not think he would ever hear.

■■ ■■ ■■

When she answered the phone and heard the woman speak, she assumed it was another wrong number. Roo knew nobody named Oren Yonkers or Yunkers. Last week someone had called, asking for a Honeychild Gutterballer. She figured it was a prank. No mother would allow a child to go through life with such a name. That week she'd also had to deal with a belligerent man who kept calling "about the shirts." And Roo had to explain three times that she wasn't a laundry.

"I'm sorry," she said, "there's no one here by that name."

"Excuse me. You don't understand," said the woman. "I'm not calling for Mr. Youngquist, I'm calling about him. He's here. At St. Luke's."

"I don't understand."

"Is this Miss Downer? He said Miss Downer would know him. Claire? What's Mr. Youngquist's first name again? No, his nickname. Guy? Kai?"

"Oh my God. Sky."

"Yes. That's it. You'd better come to the hospital. He's had an accident."

"My God, is he all right? What's happened? Tell me what's happened!"

"It'd be better for you to come down first. We don't know if we can admit him officially, of course. He says he hasn't any insurance."

"Jesus Christ, I'll pay for everything. Just admit him. Don't waste time over the insurance. Now what's happened to him? Goddamnit, what's happened?"

"You needn't swear at me, Miss Downer. It's his hand. It's been damaged. You can ask for me or Wendy Chin at the emergency room. I'm Ruth Kirkpatrick, the head nurse."

"I'll be right there."

It was happening all over again. The call from the hospital. The shattering call. *Oh God, no.*

She drove like a maniac, cursing the stoplights, talking to herself, praying to a God who she knew didn't exist. She parked in the lot reserved for doctors. She didn't bother locking the car door. She ran to the emergency room.

Nurse Kirkpatrick looked like Olive Oyl's twin sister—spindly and slightly buck-toothed, her bangs glistening under her white cap. Her eyes, though, were small and stingy. She sat Roo down at a desk as though she were about to interview her for a job.

"He's lost two fingers," she said. "He almost lost another, but that one should heal."

"Fingers? Two fingers?"

"On his right hand."

"The right?"

"Fortunately, they weren't the thumb and the index finger."

"You said fingers. Two of them."

"The ring finger and the little finger."

"What happened?"

"A freak accident, apparently. A brick fell on his hand."

"Where?"

"I told you. His right hand."

"No. I mean, where was he? Where did this happen?"

"I believe he said near some construction site. He said he was making deliveries when the brick fell. That happens, you know. A flowerpot can fall off a windowsill and kill someone instantly. Sometimes the object is no bigger than an ashtray. Nobody should leave loose objects like that on a windowsill."

"How did he get here? In his truck? Could he still drive?"

"I know nothing about a truck. Some young people found him bleeding by the side of the road and brought him here."

"May I see him?"

"You'll have to sign these forms first."

She handed Roo a clipboard. Roo stared at the name for the first time. Oren Youngquist. The Social Security number that came afterwards was a blur. But not his date of birth. He was older than she thought. Twenty-four, not twenty-one. But still too young to lose his grip on the world, like Denis.

Another nurse directed her to the elevator. The whiteness of everything—walls, curtains, uniforms, faces—depressed her no end. If there was anyone who needed her foolish jewelry now, it was these people—the grey-haired ruin in her gunnysack of a johnny, plopped in a wheelchair in the hallway; the head nurse she'd just dealt with, all bib and starch, her outfit as cold and clipped as her voice.

At the second-floor nurses' station a Nurse Williams asked her more questions, then escorted her down a long hallway that smelled of alcohol swabs and old people. "He's asleep," she said as she led Roo toward the furthest bed in the four-bed ward. "We gave him some Demerol. For the pain."

His hair was tangled, lifeless. She brushed her hand through it, softly. He was too deep in slumber to stir. He looked like a sunflower that had been felled by a hatchet. One hand was encased in a cocoon of bandages.

"You can visit him tomorrow if you'd like. He won't need to be here for more than four or five days, depending on the therapy."

"You can't depend on anything," said Roo.

As she passed the nurses' station on her way out, she heard someone calling her. "Miss? Oh, Miss?"

A young nurse approached, holding a shiny black box.

"He wouldn't let go of it at first," she said to Roo. "I told him I'd keep an eye on it for him. He's very nice."

"Yes. He is. Very."

"I'm so sorry. About his hand."

"Yes. So am I." She took the flute from the nurse. *And this is the unspeakable loss.*

She sat on a bench outside for a few moments before returning to her car. The sky was cloudless, a brilliant aquamarine. She wondered what had become of his fingers. Had he carried them with him, hoping they could be sewn back on? Or had he known better and tossed them, the way she used to throw crumbs to the swans? She could not imagine his little finger doing anything else but leapfrogging at the end of a flute. How could it happen? How could you stroll out the door one morning, fine-tuned and fit, and then return several hours later mangled? Why a falling brick? How could a brick do this?

None of the pieces fit. It was all a dumb hopscotch. You had to keep jumping even though there was no place to land. If you hadn't a rabbit's foot or a keychain to pitch at an empty square, you tossed in your fingers instead—and kept on jumping. No wonder he loved that stupid song from the Disney movie. He knew already what you always got when you put the pieces together, or tried to. Nonsense. Bibbidi-Bobbidi-Boo.

■■　■■　■■

She found the key by accident. The night she took the flute home with her, instead of him.

She'd opened the case, just to make sure the flute was safe, all there, though she could not imagine him ever wanting to look at it again. The pieces of flute lay there quietly in their new velvet coffin—sturdy as pipes, fragile as candy canes. When she closed the case, the key fell out.

The next morning she walked to the central post office, inserted the key in box 1605, and removed the mail, which consisted of one letter addressed to Oren Youngquist. *Forgive me, Sky, but I must know.* She used a nail file to unseal it, unfolded the letter, and read it. The letterhead was from a detective agency in Los Angeles.

Dear Mr. Youngquist:

Enclosed is the bill for last month's work. Thought I had a lead on your sister in Chula Vista but no dice. So am still checking city halls, vagrancy lists, boarding houses, whorehouses, and morgues. I don't think she's in this state anymore, even if she's alive, but am still looking.

A. Ryder

The bill was a low four-digit figure. She tucked it back in the envelope. She would reseal it with glue, bring it back later, then return the key to his flute case. She wondered how many such bills had come his way, how many years he'd been looking, and paying. She thought she knew now how he paid for it all. That day she'd first seen him, near Gump's, he was probably en route to pick up his mail.

Outside the post office a mother was fighting with her young daughter, pulling her tiny arm while the girl screamed. "I'm tired and I'm cranky!" shouted the woman. "And you're coming with me, whether you want to or not!" The girl howled and struggled, as though she were being led off to witness the end of the world.

You can't run away now, Roo thought, *but in time you will, you will*.

She did not know she was whispering the charm for herself as well.

■ ■   ■ ■   ■ ■

"Tell me the truth," she said to him his last night in the hospital. "Were you dealing? You know, dealing. Did this happen because you were dealing?"

He would not let her hold his wounded hand. His arms were folded across his chest as though he were a mummy case.

"No," he said. "No more. Not now. Maybe once. But hey, I can't deal for shit now. Because I have been dealt. Man, I have been dealt. Almost makes me believe in the Big Guy. The Big Lopper."

The night nurse appeared, waving a thermometer as though it were a magic wand. The patient next to Sky asked to have his bedpan removed. "When can I have a raspberry danish?" he said. "You can't," said the nurse, "you're a diabetic now." "But I'm hungry!" "You can't."

Sky had closed his eyes, as though he were hypnotized by the nurse's voice, as though he'd consented to everything spoken and unspoken. You can't, you can't, you can't.

Roo, along with the visiting hours, dissolved.

■ ■   ■ ■   ■ ■

"I miss being able to drive," he said to her one afternoon. "Hey, not that I drove a hell of a lot. Even after you showed up. But I miss it, you know? Why else would I get involved with you anyway, except for your old clunker."

"You can still drive. You don't need all your fingers to work a steering wheel," she said, knowing it wasn't driving he was missing, knowing too that he had to struggle now to be droll—about the two of them. She could sometimes see that other worry in his eyes, the fear that he had become one of them, the layabouts next door, a hippie boy dependent upon his breadwinning girl-friend.

He was stretched out on the floor beneath her, naked except for his frayed, shredded jeans. The gleam on the floor took all the sheen from him. His long, waxy white toes could have passed for their limp counterparts on any crucifix; all that was lacking were the nail holes. He'd not been out of the house in two weeks, not since he'd been released from the hospital.

That he lied to her still about how much he'd driven didn't bother her, only made her sad. She had never told him about that foggy, surreal day when she had followed him on his rounds. Maybe he'd seen her in his rearview mirror, maybe he'd even played that manic flute bolero in part for her. Yet he'd said nothing. Now the ice cream truck, wherever it was, would have to make do with a tinkly bell like the one Miss Frances rang on "Ding Dong School," and with some other driver as well.

In the morning he listened to either classical music or the Modern Jazz Quartet, watered the spider plants, fished from the barrels of plastic the pieces she needed so she didn't have to lean down and break her concentration. Every so often he would attempt a few chin-ups on the bar in the kitchen doorway, but only when he thought she was too absorbed to watch him. She could see his shadow, though, especially in the late afternoon, and his arms did not appear to move lopsidedly at all. He had the agility of a three-toed sloth. He had strength, he could still hang on.

In the afternoon he read—books like *The Seven Pillars of Wisdom, Tess of the d'Urbervilles, Memoirs of a Midget*—and then meditated upstairs in the chime room, or daydreamed on the workroom floor, quietly getting stoned.

"About the wheel," he said. "The steering wheel. It just doesn't feel right. You know?"

"I know."

"When you're asleep I sometimes sneak outside and sit in the car for a while. Try the wheel. Imagine."

"That I didn't know. You could go outside in the daytime. Try it then. Get some of the glow of the sunshine on you. You wouldn't have to sneak anymore."

"Something's missing. I don't mean my fingers."

"I'm still here."

"My hand is full of tingly ghosts. But so's my head. I wish they'd shove off, let go of me, stop dangling."

Her pliers slipped. The smoke rings he'd been blowing floated closer her way, each one a mine field. She would have to move her stool a little to the left if she wanted to keep her head steady, her hands working.

"Roo, would you do me a favor?"

"What?"

"Will you take me for a ride? Now?"

"What kind of ride?"

"How about a quasi-metaphysical joyride?"

"We could have that right here when I'm through with this. Right here on the floor. Even without what you're smoking."

They'd made love but once these past weeks, and one-sidedly at that. He had refused to caress her with either hand, as though she too had become as unplayable as his flute.

"No, I don't mean that," he said. "This is different. Very different. I have to show you something. Where I was, what I've been, where I can't go anymore, except this once. I have to see them again. I have to."

He was kneeling in front of her. His eyes were iridescent.

"Did you really believe when I ran off with your car all those times at the beach that I was just racking up miles on your odom, cruising around and getting high, tumbling along with the tumbling tumbleweed, going nowhere? Don't you want to see where I come from?"

"You come from Kansas."

"No. I come from where you're going to take me now."

She put down the chain she was working on. "You need a shirt. A sweater," she said. She got up, went into the kitchen, ran the tap, and splashed her face savagely with cold water. *No more surprises. Dear God. No more betrayals.* She ran her dripping fingers through her hair, dried her face with a dishcloth, and then stared at the lemons on the windowsill, as though to memorize their shapes before the knife destroyed them.

When she emerged she saw him waiting for her in the front hallway, still shirtless, though his tatty fisherman's sweater was wrapped around his bad hand like a muff. The good hand held his flute case. She went upstairs and fetched her shawl and purse from the bedroom. By the time she'd come down he'd managed to open the front door and was standing out on the porch landing.

He was flinching a little, as though the sun were shooting darts at him.

"Do you need sunglasses?"

"No. I'm fine."

She locked the front door.

"So you lied to me about Kansas, about your father." *And about everything else too*, she thought.

"No. I never lied to you about that. Maybe about other things, but not that. Everything happened exactly like I told you. Except that my sister kept on driving. Without me. She dumped me too. Maybe she went back to Kansas, but I doubt it. Maybe she got knocked up, or got married. I don't know. I don't know where she is or what she is. She disappeared on me, and I never saw her again. She left me howling on the door stoop too."

Roo wiped the sweat from his forehead.

"You're feverish. You're hot."

"No. It feels good. The sunshine. You were right."

"I won't leave you howling. You must know that. I won't leave you, period."

She wished he would grab hold of her now, use her as a crutch, a pillow. But both his hands were occupied. And even if they weren't, she knew how wary he was of support, and comfort.

"Sky. Where are we going?"

"To hell," he said, then laughed. "But first to Carmel."

Only when she got in the car and started fishing for the car keys did she realize she hadn't tucked her espadrilles into her purse. *My God, I am stoned. I am in no shape to drive.*

"I need shoes," she said. "So do you. Where are your sandals?"

"No we don't. We're perfect. As is. Barefoot is perfect. Believe me."

She relented.

"Promise me," she said. "No smoking in the car."

"I promise."

"One of us needs a clear head."

"No head is clearer than mine, Roo. No one's."

As they drove towards Carmel she asked him more questions—about his sister, his father, the past. But most of them he skillfully deflected. She was asking about things he had put to sleep years ago and dreaded resurrecting. So she listened instead to the roar of Austin-Healys gusting past her, and to the occasional thunderclaps overhead. Even with the windows open the car was still overpoweringly hot. She could feel some of that heat coming from Sky. His skin was phosphorescent. His hair, like an explosion of white fire. Letters were starting to form on the inside of her forehead, her eyeballs—*f*'s and *l*'s—but she was in no mood to decipher them. They reared up, like telephone poles planted in the middle of the highway, but she played Dodg'em and refused to slow down.

"You can turn off here," he said.

"But we're not in Carmel yet."

"I know. But it's shorter this way. Trust me."

Trust you. How can I trust you, or the world, or anything? Look what a stone, or a wooden pole, or a lake did to my brother. For the first time, she saw the two of them, her lover and her brother, converge, like falling stars in the lonesome sky. Each of them grappling with unspeakable mutilation, each of them courting music for solace. But that solace was as frail as the skin on their bones, as crackable as an old 78 or the slender stem of a flute. When the body breaks, the soul shrivels. The *f*'s were whistling and flying now; the *l*'s did flips and cartwheels. Then they picked up some *a*'s and danced on top of the dashboard like a conga line: *la la, fa fa, fa la la, fa la la.*

Cliffs and oceans had given way long ago to trees, valleys, arroyos, lavender vistas. The road meandered without end, and the car simply followed the groove, like a marble in a runnel. Occasionally, a patch of vineyard would rise up from the side of the road, or a two-pump gas station. Or sometimes a town no bigger than four city blocks, gathering dust but outwitting disintegration. The only sentient things for miles around were clumps of cattle, stupidly dozing.

She could not imagine where he was taking her. But she could imagine Dana at that moment, walled inside a stuffy townhouse, shredding iceberg lettuce and slicing cucumbers, preparing a cool supper for four people, none of whom she liked much. She could see her mother, still on her hands and knees in the garden, at dusk, driving holes into the earth and seeding them with roses that would never bloom. She would never see her father again, not while either of them lived, but she could imagine him as well, in his bedroom, poring over postage stamps with his magnifying glass. He had never needed glasses before to see anything. His eyes had always been as keen as a bird's, and so blue, like Sky's. Maybe he too was in mourning. Mourning the fact that he'd given up as an artist, that his fingers at play could lift only specks of paper—not iron, not wood. But she would never see him again. What was unimaginable to all of them, she knew, was she herself and precisely where she was now—driving barefoot, through barren gullies of lavender and burnt umber, a landscape that half belonged to John Steinbeck, half to Georgia O'Keeffe, with a man whose hair was a ball of white fire, both of them gunning toward some invisible point in the visible world, some hell, some oasis, where dreams dried up, where ruin blossomed like an atomic rose.

Unimaginable to everyone but her brother, whom she could see now too, handsome as Icarus, falling through an ocean of sky.

Denis. Denis.

"We're almost there," said Sky. "Go slow."

The tiny town they were driving through belonged to no fixed time or place, a patchwork of buildings culled from the jumble of history. An ancient Amoco station nestled alongside a pastelería. The pharmacy window display was composed of nothing but old apothecary jars. A poster of Jimi Hendrix hung beneath the awning of the five-and-dime. Some of the old wooden houses had antebellum verandahs; other homes were made of stucco or clay and looked Mexican or Pueblan. Yucca plants shot up in some yards, rhododendrons in others. A rack on the sidewalk in front of the corner bakery still cradled a few wreaths of braided bread. Prosperity had bypassed the town. The Depression, or some other sad, squalid time, had sapped and flattened it, left it patched and scaly. Only the town's diehards could have kept it going, along with their broods. Somebody was buying rock posters and Carter's Little Liver Pills.

"There it is," he said. "You can park out front. They won't mind."

Were it not for the bell tower, the building might have passed for a large loaf of Spam. The setting sun cast an oily sheen on the pinkish walls, though the wetness, she knew, was an illusion. The walls were as crumbly as everything else here.

"Is this some mission?"

"What we're on? Or what we're about to go in?"

"Don't josh with me, Sky. Not now."

"It's a convent. For Carmelites. The Sisters of Charity used to run it when I was here. Now it's a dumb show, sort of. Come on. I want you to see it."

As they walked closer she could see a small building directly behind the convent and off to the side, partially hidden by the trees.

"They sleep back there. There used to be another building too, the orphanage. But that burned down several years after I left. Some crazy farmer torched it, said God had told him to burn all the orphans, turn them into toasties. But most of the orphans had left by then. And the bright nuns, the singers and talkers— they were starting to leave too, leave the order for good. Wear minis instead. Become hippies. Like me."

The door to the chapel was open. She could see wood that glowed like dark honey.

"It's OK. We can go in," he said.

"But we're barefoot."

He slipped on his sweater. He'd left his flute behind in the car. She followed him, sat beside him in the last pew. His hands were clasped together as though he were packing a snowball. The stumps of his fingers slid across the top of his unsmashed hand. He did not look at her at all while he talked.

"She left me right here, in this pew, when I was nine years old. My sister. And she told me, 'You wait here and don't move. I'll be right back.' Then she turned around and left. And when I heard her start up the car she'd stolen from Dad, I knew what she was going to do. So I ran outside, bawling and howling, but she'd already split, flown the coop. And then they showed up, Sister Marguerite and Sister Anna Maria, and they took me into the orphanage. The other boys were mostly runaways, kids nobody wanted. Some were Mexicans. I stayed there until I was a teenager and could get some work in town. You know, feeding mules, fence building. Helping farmers. I wanted to clear out, but then again, I didn't want to—because of the sisters. They'd taken good care of me, and I guess I owed them something. One of them, Sister Stephen, could play the guitar and piano. Not bad for a nun either. She taught me what she could, but then I figured out how to play by ear and didn't really need her.

"I've never told you about the flute, how I got it. There were some nights here, after my sister left, when I was so unhappy I wanted to die. I didn't talk to the other boys much. Some of them couldn't speak English. Some were just quiet, like me. Mostly we played softball together, out in the fields in back. Sister Stephen could pitch too. And not bad for a nun. I was a lousy ball player. I was lousy at everything but being alone. Every night I went to bed I'd pull the blankets over my head and pray I'd never have to wake up again. I'd curl myself up into a tight little ball, hard as a jawbreaker, then I'd beg the darkness to swallow me. One of those nights I decided to run away. So I waited until the other boys were asleep, sneaked out the bathroom window, and then hustled my little ass into town. It was dark out, but I wasn't scared. The Hacienda bar was still open, and a few drunks were reeling along the sidewalk, talking to the moon. But they were harmless. There's nothing to do in a town like this anyway when you get old except drink and curse the moon. They were far too gone to notice this pipsqueak who was roaming down Main Street and trying hard not to fall asleep.

"And then I heard this voice saying, 'Angel. Come here, angel.' I didn't think it was calling me, but it was. 'Angel,' the voice said. And I saw this big blue moon of a face leaning out of a car window. The car was huge. A metal balloon. It looked like one of those tortoises in the Galápagos. So did he. He was huge too, and had eyes like a turtle's. If I'd known any better then, I wouldn't have walked up to a strange man in a car. But nobody ever told me about men like that, if that's even what he was. I'd had too many doors slammed in my face. So if anyone actually opened a car door for me, any kind of door, I'd have walked right in. 'I've got something for you, angel,' he said. 'Pennies from heaven, angel.' What a nut case. But I raced up to that car like some starving cat. And you know what he did then? He poured poker chips into my hands. Poker chips. He must have had some case full of chips sitting on his lap. For he'd reach down and pull up one stackful of chips after another, red ones, blue ones, yellow ones, and then drop them in my hands like they were gum balls. He'd drop them slowly sometimes, and then fast. My hands started to hurt. I thought it was a kind of crummy trick. All these stupid chips. I couldn't survive on poker chips. I'd have rather had pennies, though they probably wouldn't have gotten me very far either. And then he said, 'Angel, you want a kazoo?' And that's when he gave me this black box. I had no idea what it was. He'd pulled it out from the backseat of his car. The entire backseat was piled high with stuff, like a flea market on wheels.

"I knew he was crazy. Totally wacko. You know those things when you're a kid. You know them even better then. And who knows what else he had hidden in that backseat? Hacksaws, knives, kiddie thumbscrews. Maybe he should've opened that door. Maybe I would have gone with him. Maybe it'd be all over by now. But all he showed me was that big, smiley, crazy moonface. I've never forgotten what he did next. He blew me a kiss, and then he said, 'Play for all the pretty angels like you.' His car sounded like a motorcycle when he drove off. It had muffler problems. So there I was, coughing from his exhaust fumes, with a giant puddle of poker chips pooling around my shoes. And this thing in my hands, which turned out to be a first-class flute instead of a kazoo.

"I went back to the orphanage that night. I felt calmer, less lonely. Like maybe I could survive after all. I scooped up as many poker chips as I could and hid them from the nuns. We could gamble now at night when we played five-card draw. When the nuns were around we played only rummy. The nuns let me keep the flute. They knew I hadn't stolen it. It was just what a depressed kid like me needed—an instrument that sounded like birds sailing through the trees. It was made for me. Then four years later Sister Marguerite and Sister Stephen left or got transferred, and a new mother superior took over, a sourpuss, a real crank. So I split too, got a room in town. I was too old to stick around much longer anyway. But I still played for the other nuns, and the ones who came after. The unfortunates. With Sister Stephen gone, they had no music. I missed them when I left. When I'd get stoned in the Palace I could see them sometimes, and I'd play for them. But I knew they couldn't hear.

"So that's why I'd run off with your car. To come back here, and whistle a little, the way I used to. Now I'm one of them."

She heard a quiet pattering from behind, a rustling. Then she saw them filing down the aisle next to her. Their grey smocks were as drab as hospital johnnies. Their faces were homely too, but tranquil, focused. Except for the nuns bringing up the rear of the procession. Their eyes wobbled. Their foreheads were pinched, wizened. They looked like colicky babies. Then she realized they were slightly retarded, simpleminded. Defectives. Their lips moved to some unheard music, a holy gibberish only they could understand. And they were all barefoot.

"They're discalced nuns," he said. "The slow ones don't do much. Make the host, clean the altar. Simple things that don't require a brain. But do require two hands."

His fists unclenched. His hands settled to his knees.

"Let's go," he said. "I can do nothing for them now." She squirmed out of the pew. He had already beaten her to the door and was on his way to the car.

"I figured I'd leave my flute there," he said, once they were back on the road. "You know, ashes to ashes, dust to dust. In the end is my beginning or whatever. They could maybe pass it on to some other lost kid. But hell, I know that'll never happen. They can't manage. Nobody ever stops there but tourists who run out of gas. And kids leave that town as soon as they learn how to thumb. I don't want some fucking asshole to walk off with this flute. I've got a much better idea how to put this baby to sleep."

The sun was dying. The moon was nowhere. She was grateful its face hadn't shown up yet. Could she see it in her rearview mirror, it would be howling at her. And not like a wolf.

■■   ■■   ■■

They'd left the car behind, parked it on the rise before the bridge. A stupid move, she knew. They should have driven right across the bridge, gone home and put on warmer clothing, then come back later. Her bare feet were cold and hurting. But Sky was probably much colder. The walk, he said, would do her good. Back in Sausalito, where they'd wound up after the trip to the convent, she had been unable to keep her dinner down, had to keep hiking back to the grungy bathroom. Without shoes they'd had to settle for a fish shack geared towards surfers and hippies. The lemon tea had finally steadied her a little. But now she was shivering again, and feeling a tinge of returning nausea. She knew what he was going to do with his flute, and knew she couldn't stop him. It was his, to do with as he pleased.

"I love this bridge," he said. "It's like a parachute that dropped from heaven. When it goes I bet you anything the Great String Puller will haul it back upstairs, where it belongs."

"Aren't you freezing?" she asked.

"I feel nothing," he said. The guardrail, taller than both of them, kept some of the darkness at bay. But she felt unsafe. The bridge was like some interminable and flimsy stockade, trapping the two of them like dumb animals, and barely shielding them from the creatures uncoiling below. Then she saw one, a beast, a grizzly as tall as Coit Tower, bounding across the car roofs, a party hat on its head, a champagne glass in its paw.

"Sky, I'm spacing out. I feel awful."

"It's nothing. Relax. Everything's easy now. We're on a roll, we've just begun. Relax, Roo, relax."

She stopped, and clutched his arm more tightly.

"What's happening?"

"Ecstasy. Paradise. Forever's happening."

"What have you done? What have you done to me?"

"Transformed you. Transfigured you. I gave you the holy wafer."

"Wafer?"

"In your tea."

"Oh God, no. You promised me, you promised. Oh Jesus. Not again. No! No!" She grabbed him by the shoulders, forced him to look at her. "I am not going to freak out here all by myself, do you understand? Don't you dare trip out on me now, don't you dare let go of me. I need you to be strong, do you hear me? I can't go through this again, I can't, I can't." But steadiness now was about as impossible to retrieve as his missing fingers. The flashing headlamps shot past her like billiard balls. If she misstepped but once, she'd drop into the pocket.

"What do you see, Roo? Where are we?"

Spider webs. Jewels. Crayons, salmon and blue and magenta. The lights were punching her like sequined snowballs, but she couldn't feel them. They sped right through her, leaving her skin peppered with holes. She could still walk, but she was as lightweight as a paper doll, a sieve. She looked at Sky. Orange plumes shot out of his hair.

"You're on fire," she said. "Your skin's on fire."

"Then we're in hell, just like I said. And this is the desert, isn't it? And God's a big scorpion. Twang your magic stinger, Big Boy. Here comes the Lone Ranger, and he's going to mow you down. Hiyo, Silver."

The arm she'd been holding on to had turned into leather, a box. The flute was out of her grasp, was nearly out of his. It rose from the stump of his hand like a silver rattler. Then she saw him grip it by the head with his good hand, and fling it into the sky.

"Close your eyes," he whispered, "and listen."

She did as he told her. And she could hear it, even above the roar of the traffic—a doleful peeping, an intermittent wail as the chill wind whistled through the holes of the flute. *Make it stop, please. Don't let it stop.*

When she opened her eyes, he was gone, but not quite. His bare feet still perched on the metal rail, but his arms had unfolded now, and as he flew off the bridge, pursuing the echoes, she saw fingers of silver, twirling like tiny batons in the darkness, one, two, racing after the third and the fourth, and the mournful wail, the howl, she realized was coming not from the flute, and not from the falling boy, not even from the banshee sirens and alarms bearing down hard on her.

■■   ■■   ■■

Years later, after she'd had a series of breakdowns and lost her Inner Light source for a while and then moved to L.A., after she'd started a small antiques store specializing in Mission furniture and saw it take off when the real estate boom overtook California and the lust for chrome tube chairs and flokati rugs turned into an even more unruly passion for old wooden desks and oak headboards, after her Light Source finally clicked on again and she had this vision on her thirty-fourth birthday that she would meet a man who was "an eruption of brilliance" in a Szechuan restaurant and she did indeed and he turned out to be a lava lamp and hi-fi-a-go-go lamp salesman named Chaney La Flamme, after she'd married him and became pregnant at last and gave birth to a boy whom they named Trevor (because gold and green shone, in French, in the scrambled letters of his name), after she'd fully recovered as a psychic and taken stress-reduction courses and set her spiritual house in order, after she'd gone through one of her annual throw-out-all-that's-throwable spells one day in the basement of her nonfigurative house and finally attacked the long-forgotten and no-longer-played-with toys that were rusting away in her adolescent son's abandoned toy box, she found one of those metal sparklers her husband must have given him, a tiny pinwheel that sizzled and shot off sparks when you pressed the lever, and the faster you pumped the brighter and louder the sizzle.

And she sat there on the basement floor in a not-quite-lotus position, as she had sat so long ago on the wet summer grass near the Palace, and she listened to the crackle and watched the pinwheel flash like a halo of electric knives, and a head made of sunlight and scorching silver rolled into her lap as though it had dropped from a guillotine, and she picked it up, rocked it against her breast like a broken doll while it burned and whispered, *My name is Oren, I'm made of gold too,* and all the flutes of the world leered and whistled, *Hey hey, hot stuff, play for the pretty lady, play.* And she remembered.

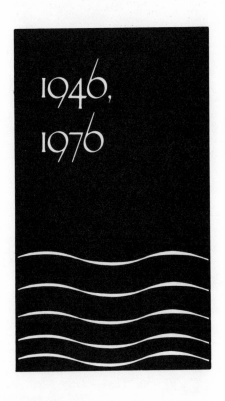

1946,
1976

When she walked into our dining room that April evening—it was the twenty-fourth, a day I shall never forget, and "strutted" is perhaps a more accurate way to put it than "walked" or even "sauntered," and our casual open-door policy, especially regarding the front door, most assuredly ceased from that day forward—I did not know then quite what I know now: that I died that day. The surprise of her intrusion, the very boldness of it—I had no idea who she was then, and to some extent I believe I never really shall know—kept at bay the terrible thump that was to knock against my breast as soon as she left, a thump as harsh and loud as that of a clapper battering inside a bell, which I, of course, could hear but no one else, telling me that I had come face to face with tragedy. Not hers (she looked far too jaunty to have ever known tragedy). Not even Eric's (he'd taken his parents' death with an almost unnatural calm, his pursuit of the decadent precluding all things tragic). But mine. My tragedy. Mine.

I had raised my children well, I thought. I was, in fact, still raising them, for none of them had even reached puberty yet. Surely they knew the ground rules, the basics, how and when to be sensibly cautious. Cosseted as they were, they knew something of life's terrible deviousness, the way life itself could be pulled right out from under you like a slippery carpet. Beware, I had taught them, beware—of nearly everything. Beware the puddles on the floor when you clamber out of the bathtub, and never, never turn on a light or the radio or anything electrical while you're still wet. Beware of strange men who smile at you invitingly and who open their car doors—or whatever—offering you lollipops, jawbreakers. Much finer candy can be found here at home. Look both ways when crossing a street, look again and again and again. A car that creeps like a turtle can turn suddenly into a cheetah. When you carry a pair of scissors, be sure you hold them in front of you with your arm extended, and with the blades of the scissors pointing down, in case you should fall. Beware of unidentifiable liquids, bottles with skulls and crossbones on the labels, germ-riddled cookies on the floor, matchbooks, sparklers. Beware of toothpicks; they can poke your eyes out. Nobody has ever envied Oedipus or Helen Keller. At one time I feared I might have taught them too much fearfulness. Now, knowing what happened in the end, I fear I did not teach them enough. Somehow I believed, wanted to believe, that if they were prepared, on the qui vive, they might avoid being trapped, maimed, as surely I had been—the day I married him—though I did not know that then either. And, of course, what happened was precisely what I had been trying to protect them from: the worst.

But neither of my daughters had yet come down to the table that April evening when she strutted in; only Denis and Eric were seated. Sometimes I've wondered if that was why Roo and Dana were spared, that they had not seen her and Denis had. I had been calling and gently badgering them for five minutes, to no avail. I had finally sent Felice upstairs to see what was detaining them, and she had reported that they were immersed in a game of animal lotto. "Girls," I called much too loudly, "you can return to your game of lotto after dinner." And I remember Roo shouting back at me that she was "waiting for the tapir to turn up." I was more than a little put out by their antics, but also, at times, taken by their wit. The soup—and Felice made good soup, albeit sometimes oversalted—was getting cold. And it was rude for the two of them to keep all of us waiting, especially when there was no immediate end in sight to the game they were playing. Yet just then I was imagining the stir it might create, the sight of it—a bulky grey tapir, a real one, with its queer snout—foraging here in the dining room. Occasionally I could dote on the comic thrust of something unimaginably grotesque—or in this case, something grotesquely imagined. In truth, I was grateful no beasts larger than palmetto bugs ever wedged their way through our doors. They were nightmare and nuisance enough, and I had even more trouble with smaller monsters—the caterpillars that ravaged every floribunda and tea rose I tried to cultivate.

And then she was there. I had not heard her come in. I had no idea where she'd come from, who she was. She did not see me, nor did she see Denis. She looked only at Eric. And she said to him, "I'm free. I've come. It's time." Her sentences were so snipped, so simple she might have been reciting from a first-grade primer, from *Dick and Jane*. Eric appeared dazed at first, then color flooded his face. And it was not—as I came to surmise later—a flush that stemmed from shame or fear or guilt. He rose from the table, without even having tasted Felice's soup. He bent over and kissed Denis on the forehead and cheek, he passed behind my chair, leaned over and whispered, "Don't worry, dear, I'll be back." And then they left, the two of them, they hurried out the front door. I heard a car, and it must have been hers or perhaps a cab. We had all grown too accustomed now to bicycling, even though the long spell of gas rationing was finally over. And I—I had no time to react, to think, no time whatsoever. For Roo and Dana hurtled down the stairs precisely at that moment, took their seats. And then Roo asked, "Where's Daddy?" I looked at Denis—he was far too young to comprehend what had just transpired, at least I prayed he was too young, I know better now—and then I looked at Roo and said, "He's stepped out. Eat your soup, both of you. It's your favorite. Tomato and dill."

I must have realized then—amid swallows of lukewarm soup—that he had stepped out for good, that he had some other life totally apart from the one at best minimally shared with the four of us and apart as well from that life of his inside his studio, where he frittered away his days, halfheartedly building and then demolishing those outré chairs and lamps that were by no means as solid as the things he'd made fifteen years before, even before we were married.

Who was she? Wallflower though I was and certainly no great lover of gossip, I nonetheless think I was as aware as any of who was who in this tight little beach town, and who wasn't who. New faces, especially young, striking, not yet tattered faces, always made themselves known here, aspiring as they were to be somebody's armpiece, to latch on to some polo player or natty, preferably elderly, bachelor or some yachtsman whose only goal in life was pulling in more sailfish. Then the new faces swiftly became the old, tired faces. The only women I saw with any regularity were fellow DAR members, who met monthly, usually at some member's house (never at ours, though; Eric would not hear of it), and whom I lunched with, infrequently, at the Bath and Tennis Club. But I never felt terribly comfortable there, perhaps because I was not a pretty woman, perhaps because my family had only been modestly, not preposterously, rich. I, of course, passed muster, because my children were beautiful and Eric's money considerably enhanced my own. But Eric never liked me taking them to clubs like this, so I rarely did. "When they rename it 'Wallow and Diddle,' " he said, "then I'll go." His harshness towards clubs, and those men and women who languished there all day like dead pickerel, must have been rooted to some extent in self-loathing; for he was nothing if not a wallower and diddler himself.

This woman, though—she could have never been marooned, or gone to waste. Never had I seen anywhere, either at the clubs or at homes of friends of mine or on the streets of Palm Beach, a woman who looked quite like this. Women, younger women, were wearing their hair long or in pageboys now, like Lauren Bacall and June Allyson, or else wearing it up, like Ann Dvorak. But not this woman. What I remember most was her hair, which was short and defiantly marcelled, as though she were daring anyone to say to her, "You're dated, dearie, you're out of touch." And also the beauty mark that hovered on her lower cheek, below her lips, just like Ilona Massey's. Her suit was grey and severe, perhaps a thin wool, and cut somewhat like a tunic. Her blouse was an ecru crepe de chine. She wore a lilac scarf. And she left behind her the smell of violets. No woman looked like this in Florida then, or smelled like this. She belonged to some other life.

Who was she? How could he have met her? Eric, who so seldom left the house, behaved more like a priest who loved to loll quietly in his monastic solitude than like some smoldering voluptuary on the prowl, even in spite of those times when he would become barbarous, pound on my door fruitlessly until either he or his passion wilted, and his good sense prevailed. The children, after all, were not the soundest sleepers. Had he known her for a long time? She was younger than I, but not by much. How did he know her, where had he met her? Who was she?

I did not ask those questions aloud. How could I? Dr. Swerd- low had not yet come into the picture. Instead I asked the girls why they were playing with Denis's board game when they could be playing a much more grown-up game like gin rummy. Roo said she loved the drawings of the animals on the lotto cards. Dana said that Roo had forced her to play since Roo always lost whenever she played grown-up card games. Dana was always the luckier of the two when it came to game playing. Had I not intervened then, the two of them would have embarked on another nasty quarrel. "I hope," I said, "that you were at least kind enough to ask Denis whether you could play with his game." The two of them pretended to look abashed, and Denis might well have been on the verge of crying, though I knew, if he wept, it would have nothing to do with animal lotto, and I also knew that I had probably uttered my last sentence that would ever begin with the words *I hope*.

I was, and was not, prepared for any of this. This was, I thought, a good year, or was going to be. It was 1946. The war was over. Truman might not be anywhere near as majestic as Roosevelt. He looked, in fact, like what he was—some haberdasher from Kansas City. But no matter. At least thousands of my tax dollars would no longer be spent on guns. I had been grateful that my husband was both too old and too lame to fight, even more grateful that my son was still a child. Never would I consent to his being cannon fodder, never. But I should have listened more closely to my mother, who warned me: the worst always happens. Had she in mind only my gardening skills, I would have almost been grateful for her discouraging and pithy assessment. I planted no vegetables at all during the war, since vegetables were so unsightly. I planted what I called my "Herbert Hoover" roses. Instead of a victory garden I grew a defeat garden. Wives who are friends of mine—even, occasionally, the husbands of those same wives— have had no trouble growing either roses or orchids in Florida, though some said it was a prickly proposition with roses, literally and figuratively. But I had trouble, and struggled year after year with marauding caterpillars and an ever-changing array of bug killers, and the struggle continues. I should consider myself lucky, I suppose, to have witnessed several gardenias bloom while all the roses failed. And I should consider myself lucky that only one of my children got badly broken instead of two or all three—but I do not.

The tunic she wore, if it could be called that, was expensive. Her legs were far slimmer than mine. Her shoes shimmered. I could tell she had never worn a hat, a real hat, in her life and probably detested hats. And there was something greedy about her, it seemed to me too, which I could sense in her lipstick, its fire. Hers was a mouth that would leave only scars behind. What hurt me so, then angered me no end afterwards, was that she had somehow turned her back to me, assumed I wasn't there, was indistinguishable from a saltcellar or a soup spoon. And it was her back, like some impenetrable grey shield between Eric and me, that was all I saw as the two of them left. "Will Daddy be home soon?" Roo asked, as Felice took away the soup bowls. "I'm not sure," I said. "He has something to attend to."

Did they see through me? I have no idea. Years later they must have thought they had. But I was as competent a liar, then, as any. Dana was eleven, and very clever, and much too pretty. Roo was still nine, and probably her daddy's girl more than Dana was. But they had each other, and though I knew they were often at each other's throats, I also knew there would come nights now when they would probably fall asleep in each other's arms, crying bitterly. Still, they were not who I worried about most.

For a father to walk out on his five-year-old son—the dearest of all our children—it was, it is unconscionable. And so though the worst had happened to me—my marriage now as victimized by a marauder as my roses—it would be even more trying for my son, my quiet, polite, and beautiful boy. Who asked no questions that night, who ate sparingly of his chicken breast, for which I did not castigate him (he had good reason, more than one, since Felice had baked the chicken with too much lemon). Only at bedtime, after I had tucked in Denis and kissed him gently on both cheeks, did he ask, "Is Daddy never coming back?"

The "never" is what killed me, the second thing that night that killed me, the first being that grey-and-lavender intruder reeking of violets who so devoured my husband, the dinner table, the room itself with her daunting presence that no meal of perfection to follow could taste of anything but salt and ashes. I did not cry then, nor did I lie to my boy. I simply held him in my arms and said, "Say your prayers now before you fall asleep. Wish for good things. Treats. Elephants with howdahs to carry us all off to India. Stars to fall on your lap. And maybe a tapir to chase around the living room. And Mother's bedtime hugs, which you have in abundance already." I could not tell him bedtime stories. It was Eric who made up stories for him, night after night—stories about butterfly wizards and warrior worms. I could not poach upon his territory. I had no imagination. Had he forgotten that, when he walked out—that his son would be left storyless, starless, kissless? That there would be only I, inadequate in so many ways, to fill in for him? Was it worth it, whatever it was he was doing, fleeing with this marcelled fury, this woman out of silent movies, this interloper who left behind a wake of wildflower scent as though that might sweeten the emptiness?

That dinner, with the head of the table gone for good, that evening was the longest night of my life. For, of course, I prayed, even after the peach cobbler had been polished off and the dessert dishes had been cleared and the children had retired to their bedrooms, that the front door would burst open and Eric would sashay in and say, "Sorry, my pet, just some problem with a downed palm tree next door, with my trust account, with a runaway monkey that belonged to Countess Grabowski-Florscheim. Oh, and that woman? Her? Why, she was just a secretary from the bank, a sculptress I once knew, an interior decorator, a cigarette girl, a clip-joint canary, fill in the blank, Lydia, fill in the blank." I prowled about the living room like some runaway animal myself, trying out one sofa, then another, one chair, then another, unable to settle. Finally I sat down at the escritoire and played solitaire for nearly two hours. And then I turned off all the lamps and simply sank into the shadows of the room, too frightened even to shut the French windows, and for a long time I stared out at the deep purple vastness, listening to the waves rumble. Then I must have drifted off to sleep, one of my rare, dreamless sleeps, the kind that always frustrated Dr. Swerdlow. "Dreams," he would say to me, "I want you to tell me your dreams. I do not mean silly desires or fancies, Lydia. We are both too old for that. I mean dreams. Dreams about your mother, your father, Eric." And had I not given him always the same answer? "I have no dreams. Only nightmares." "Tell me your nightmares, then." He was persistent, unflaggingly so, which is more than I can say for Eric, who was unable to pursue anything to its proper finish: his work, his art; his love, if it was that, for his children; and finally, that woman.

Only the girls asked for their father the following morning, and I told them he had gone on a short business trip, perhaps to obtain art supplies, though I had no idea then that that trip would be anything but short and would take him thousands of miles away. That I found out several days later, after I hired someone to discover where he was, where he was headed, and with whom—and learned he had sailed from New York to Cherbourg en route to Paris. That bitter pill was oddly restorative. But I did not have such a pill then, the morning after he'd left. What I had were three soon-to-be very jangled children. School, I knew, would keep their minds busy, and I thanked the God whom I might have wanted to believe in then but surely could never believe in now, that Denis was in kindergarten. I would have at least a morning and part of the afternoon to figure out where we all went from here—assuming, as I did rightly, that we would be minus someone.

I had not wept yet. I was not a weeper. Nor had I gnashed my teeth and howled like some wronged heroine in a bad novel. A woman out of nowhere strolls into your house—no, struts—and walks off with your husband, and you cannot raise your voice, create a scene, protest, fight for what is your own. Because, of course, nothing belongs to you, and people are only loaned to us, and love—for some men, most men—is only a powerful scent to attract the dogs.

I told no one at first, though I alerted Felice to the fact that although a place setting should be left for him, a glass of water need not be poured. In time, the plate, the silverware, the folded napkin would come to seem superfluous accessories, and then they could be removed, along with the chair as well. I also instructed her to prepare meals for four rather than five. Waste not, want not. My children, like most children then, were well aware of the starving people in China. If Eric did return one evening and found there were no lamb chops waiting for him, no Waldorf salad and hot rolls, for that one night he would have to make do with saltines.

For weeks I created pleasing and silly diversions for all of us. We replayed Easter and dyed several dozen more eggs, and Roo taught Denis how to create an egg that was evenly or almost evenly divided into two colors. After some time I let them know that Daddy had telegrammed me from Paris, that he had been taken on as a protégé at some famous design firm, and that he needed this vacation from us which was not really a vacation at all but a sacrifice—a sacrifice that one had to make for art. Denis, at five, I am sure could neither swallow nor digest these abstractions as he had so easily consumed applesauce when he was a baby. One might as well have eaten buttons or nails. I already had contacted by then a most peripheral acquaintance from college, an Irene Snell, who lived in Paris, and had directed her to mail me packets of unusual postcards and a selection of used French stamps, all of which I put to good use here. Eric could keep us posted then on his Parisian travails, his studies, his most recent piece. "Isn't he awfully old to be studying?" Dana asked me at first. "We are never too old," I told her. Never too old to be chucked to the wolves.

As the days went by without a sign of the real Eric, only missives from "the expatriate artist," I began to develop this peculiar, almost sympathetic bond with the woman in grey. For she had accomplished, in a way, what I myself had set out to do twelve years earlier—assault and seize. Was I less strong now? In some way I believe he still held on to me, and I to him, though maybe what we were holding on to was something else—the family we'd created—and that was it. I doubt seriously he would have had the strength, ever, to walk out had she not appeared, had she not pulled those not-well-hidden strings of his as though she knew he was weak, a handsome marionette without any grit (and he knew it too). And how long would she last, I wondered—until another appeared? Were the two of us, though we seemed so sturdy, in fact weaker than he? And did he know that as well? That was something I indeed felt compelled to talk about at length with Dr. Swerdlow, or should I say affirm, there on that leather couch of his, since I mostly talked at Dr. Swerdlow or to the silence in his office—though he would warm up whenever he spooned me his Freudian goo. The questions he asked, or urged me to ask myself, were finally not to the point. There was only one question that mattered now, the one I must have asked again and again that exhausting, lonely night, a night that would pale years later, before that other, far more terrible night: Why did I marry this man, why?

For it was I, the somewhat dowdy wallflower, still unmarried at twenty-eight and feeling already as though I were relegated to fossildom, who turned out to be the predator, not he. My mother had warned me that men were disappointing creatures, and my two brothers—the "visionaries," as she called them—surely proved it. Both had followed Horace Greeley's advice and gone west, the one to devote his life to devising actuarial tables for whooping-cough victims, the other to develop a chain of donut shops in Hollywood during the Depression. We rarely heard from them once they'd left home. Occasionally my brother Edgar would mail us a postcard telling us to be on the lookout for new movies that featured scenes with donuts. He was especially crazy about an actress named Louise Fazenda who in some film apparently gloated over a plain donut which she'd impaled upon the end of a barbecue fork. We never saw the film. We were happy, at least, that my brothers weren't broke. My father husbanded his money well during the lean years. He owned a company in West Palm Beach which manufactured something called Woodite, which all the architects in Palm Beach were using for the new hotels. It was a wood paneling that could be tinkered with so as to acquire a vermiculated, almost medieval finish. He manufactured fake stone animals as well, and plastery ornaments that looked as though they'd been peeled from the ceilings of ransacked castles in Europe, not jerry-built out of papier-mâché in Florida. It got so whenever I visited people's homes I was no longer sure what was authentic, what fake. The chow dogs on the mantelpiece might be vintage Ming; they might also be vintage Mexican peon employee working at my father's business.

Men reveled in manufacturing deceit, said my mother. In

that way they could pretend deceit was no different from some product made on an assembly line, some ordinary, predictable, unprepossessing thing. Which it never was for women. You did not see or hear of robber baronesses, my mother said. They were too clever. It was the men, the benighted men, who charmed, then robbed you blind and thought nothing of it. My father was not much of a talker, and saved his mouth for drinking. I had only my mother's version of the male universe to work with. And though I saw just how much bitterness governed her view of the opposite sex—how could there not be? she had married a man who regarded her as a piece of furniture—I also think she was right. "Don't marry a hollow man," she told me once. "You'd be better off buying paneling."

But marriage I tried not to think about. I was a moldy young woman, and I let moss grow over the dreams I felt I didn't deserve to dream. I'd been sent away to boarding school as a girl, but I found the East too cold for body and soul. When I finished college I returned to Florida for good and expected to marry some respectable, enterprising young fixture, someone like an umbrella stand—sturdy and to the point. But these fixtures did not come my way—at tea parties, or dances, or soirées. Was my brow always too furrowed? Was I, in spite of myself, unconsciously mimicking my mother? Did I somehow look as though I knew, deep down, that nothing would ever work out well, thereby scaring off every brisk young hopeful, every buffoon of an optimist? Or was I just not pretty enough? Some girls drew boys the way hibiscus blossoms attracted bumblebees. My drawing power was about as riveting as a Fig Newton's. Dr. Swerdlow, I know, was taken by my occasional raised eyebrow, my ironic shadings of all events. He found my manner more fetching, I think, than belligerent. But I always cocked my eye—out of some fundamental distrust, perhaps, but also out of fear.

"Furniture," I suppose, brought Eric and me together, I remember telling Dr. Swerdlow. But I meant that quite without irony. Eric too was something of a lost soul. He was only two years older than I, but I do not recall ever meeting him socially while I was growing up in Palm Beach. So many homes there were like fortresses barricaded by palm trees. And homes, of course, are very much like their inhabitants. Eric's mother, though, belonged to the DAR, as did mine, so perhaps the seeds for an invitation were planted there. I remember my mother prattling on about Mrs. Downer's son, a "handsome recluse," she said, "an architect" who had "lost his way" and was "puttering around the house pining for good company." I could not tell whether my mother's inflections were her own or Mrs. Downer's. "Totally lost his grip on life" and "completely off his hinges" were probably far more accurate assessments. He was not some sweet, straying lamb. I doubt very much he was pining for company, given how much he loved solitude. And good company is hardly how I would have described myself. Chatting up Lydia or cracking walnuts—I saw little difference.

He had floated through Harvard on gentleman C's; then he'd moved to Chicago, and gone to work at a design firm as a furniture maker and craftsman; then, when the firm crashed, along with everything else that year, he lost his job as well as something of his zest and was now down in the doldrums, biding time, collecting himself. All this he told me the first afternoon I met him, in that house which was to become ours all too quickly once his parents were dead. Our mothers drank iced tea out on the front lawn beneath the palms, both of them pretending to be years younger, both of them acting like chaperones for two bashful, gawky teenagers, both of them trying hard to avoid the fact that they had nothing in common, really, except Revolutionary blood. Mrs. Downer tended to look either mildly terrified or distressed most of the time, something which drew me to her. Her composure, however, never cracked. A bear trap might shut on her foot, but she would on no account scream. My mother's face over the years had grown meaner, her pointed features more pinched. It was the face of a woman who had speared too many canapés.

While the mothers talked, the younger dinosaurs toured the

Downer house. Eric at thirty was even more prehistoric than I. Like me, he should have been married years ago. He escorted me through the immense living room, tossing off discouraging remarks about the furniture, most of which was Victorian and much to my liking. "Too baroque," he'd say, about some bombé desk. "Now if this chair were only Gothic instead of Eastlake." Some of his finer points escaped me then, perhaps all of them later—though I would not mistake some lines, like the line of a pearl-grey tunic. Then he led me upstairs—the house was gargantuan—and showed me the room where he worked, not the room that is his bedroom studio now, but another prodigious room the size of a small art gallery. Which was what it was really—a gallery of furniture that looked like sculpture, and sculpture that looked like furniture. I did not know then that many of the pieces there he had constructed several years before, and that in the past year he had built nothing. What I saw, though, was startling. Screens with Japanese motifs hammered out of bronze. Armless chairs with backs made of fluted silver ribs that fanned out like peacock tails. Tables carved in the strangest shapes, and out of the strangest woods. Plants that weren't plants at all but copper fantasies, uncoiling from the floor like baskets of golden cobras. I remember gazing at the objects in that room the way Denis must have peered into those Styrofoam Easter eggs, much later, delighted by such an unexpected vision, such extravagance so unassumingly contained. I liked to think that I saw something of Eric's soul there. For what struck me about him then was that he seemed both flamboyant and monkish, pagan and pristine. Were he more of the former, I realize, we might have had more children. So I am grateful now for that balance, which at first charmed me, then infuriated me. I almost wish now that balance had tipped the other way. Had I stopped at only two children, perhaps, just two . . .

He made no overtures to me that afternoon. Why would he? He had treated me as if I were some tourist in a museum. He was at once voluble and remote. And I spoke very little, though I occasionally carped at some of his assertions, his opinions, which I thought he was often tossing at me like hot potatoes—wondering whether I was bold enough to throw them back, cautious enough to drop them, shrewd enough to know they could be peeled right then and dispensed with. I suppose I saw in him, though, someone who was in part like me. Oh, I was without the jousting passion he had, or once had. I could never whirl my son in the air so freewheelingly as he did. I was always afraid of dropping him, terrified that Eric would drop him as well. Which he, of course, did, later, in another way. I did not know how to build anything, create anything—except, perhaps, a family. I had neither designs on life nor a design for life. I adored flowers. I adored growing them, arranging them. Which was what I had done for years, for my friends, which is all that I had done. A woman who lets moss grow over her does not want for a green thumb or two.

"Come visit again," he said as he deposited me with the two mothers and then disappeared into the house. "Eric," his mother called after him, "won't you have some iced tea?" Clearly he wouldn't. So I sat there, listening to the mothers run on about the ambiguous blessings now bestowed by the end of Prohibition, waiting for the maid to bring out another glass and refill the pitcher, knowing full well what the two of them were really thinking. *My son is eccentric, attractive, impossible, a little crazy. My daughter is not exactly Jean Harlow, can in fact be quite a killjoy—like her mother—but give her time.* After all, if my mother wanted to make dead certain that my own marriage be as shudderingly grim as hers, she would have to pull for me with Mrs. Downer and the son who appeared not in the least to be interested in me.

When I returned for a second visit the next week, I seduced him. That I did so astonishes me, since I know nothing of seduction except from having read Thomas Hardy. But what I did know from that first visit was just how commodious that house was, and how easily one could chart a course to the more isolated bedrooms upstairs, and how Mrs. Downer preferred to spend her afternoons in the cool downstairs, chattering with friends on the telephone or in the flesh, since it was too hot upstairs to get anything done. What we broke through, on one of those anachronistic canopy beds, was more than our mutual reserve. And at least that afternoon—and several others that followed in the years to come, though very few—I felt, unlike my unhappy mother, that I had been touched like something other than a chair or a doorknob. Though I know now that what I should have done was to rise from that bed, leave him spent but happy, and shut the door on him forever.

I do not think 1934 was a very propitious year for marriage. Stuntwomen were wing-walking on airplanes as though hanging upside down were nothing more than some silly game, an afternoon's caper. But that was how I lived, every day with Eric. And that was how he left me, and left all of us—up in the air and perilously dangling. Roosevelt, we assumed, would be slowly turning the country around toward better days—if you believed in better days. But even though Hoovervilles were not exactly snuggling up to Palm Beach, I had heard of, and had endured, enough disasters to last me my young lifetime. That year my father died of liver failure and heat exhaustion, and it was my mother who more or less gave me away in marriage, or "hustled me off" is more like it. My father's death both pleased and enraged her. He keeled over one afternoon when the two of them were playing golf at The Breakers. My mother was just about to birdie on the fourteenth hole when it happened. "If he could have only waited until the last hole," I remember her complaining. It was bad enough, I suppose, for him to have ruined her life, but for him to have spoiled her golf game made her all the more aggrieved.

I cannot say I missed him much at my wedding. Enough merriment was rigged up by others without his having to go off on a private toot with his mouth cozying up to a champagne bottle. I remember too what my mother whispered to me shortly before I walked down the aisle with Eric. "I hope you will make a better arrangement with him than I did with your father," she said. "Just remember, if things don't work out, we're all damaged goods." Then she kissed me and scuttled down the aisle to her seat. Eric's father was not exactly highly visible at the wedding either. Not that he shared my father's liver problem. The heat in the church had simply been too much for him, and he was resting outside in the shade. That the two mothers—one slightly dotty, the other a shrew—should be running the show seemed grimly appropriate to me then. For they both engineered this marriage from start to finish, utterly apart from the one bold maneuver that afternoon in his bedroom, a maneuver I never repeated—though I bore him his children.

Why we enjoyed each other's company so little for so many years I have never really fathomed. He never wanted me, I am convinced now, and so my turning him away so frequently was meant not to hurt him but to protect me. Perhaps the marriage was doomed the moment we returned from Antigua, where we had spent a honeymoon swatting bugs every night in a sweltering bungalow, and then had to bury what was left of his unfortunate parents, who had spent an even more sweltering time being burned alive in their automobile when it suddenly exploded and neither of them could escape. No wonder Eric was so loath to drive. No wonder the cars stayed in the garage all the time. We were practicing gas rationing long before the war.

Out of the frying pan, into the fire, my mother would have said about all this. Whatever it is you think you want most, you don't—as soon as you get it. So I stayed inside and raised my children, trapped in this hearse of a marriage. Sometimes I wished it too would go up in flames. But I did nothing to fan or even start a blaze. We burned in bed a few times, until after Denis was born. Then he lost all interest, except for those crazed moments when he would storm my door late at night and I would have to drive him out with a poker. Had he been gentler, just a little less vivid, had it been me he wanted, I might have consented. Although

Dr. Swerdlow was convinced that even then I would never have relented, that there was something cold in me that was too controlling, also something fiery that Eric simply did not know how to ignite. No wonder you garden, Dr. Swerdlow told me, no wonder you adore hats. Each of your hats is a sexual garden. Feast on me, your hats are telling you.

It was my mother, weirdly enough, who found Dr. Swerdlow for me. She had urged me to attend a DAR afternoon while I was moldering in despair following Eric's abrupt departure. I was not up for it. The guest speaker, a Miss Lillian Hollowbourne, was scheduled to deliver a talk on "The Forgotten Women of the American Revolution." No subject could have interested me less at that point, having just recently become the forgotten woman of this century. Nor would tea biscuits and cucumber sandwiches do much to improve my constitution. My mother, immeasurably pleased somehow that her predictions about my future had come true, had wasted no time in informing one of her good friends, a fellow DAR member, that her daughter's marriage had acquired, like the marriage veil itself, several large moth holes. So I was towed along, this moth-eaten presence, to this gathering of postcolonial dames. And there, her good friend impressed upon me the need to see a Dr. Swerdlow, who was one of those fashionable new Freudian analysts and whose office was in Manhattan.

Freud I had never read. I much preferred poetry, and novels that skirted happy endings. I did not at all like reading *The Interpretation of Dreams,* which Dr. Swerdlow foisted upon me. An umbrella for me was, and always will be, an umbrella, not a phallus. My hats were not sexual gardens. They were hats—butterfly-wing hats, broad-brimmed straws, or sequin-dot platters. That spring, the year Eric left, my children and I, along with Felice, made the first of what would be many annual pilgrimages to New York, which I'd schedule to coincide with school vacations. And during those three-to-five-day stays, most of which we spent sightseeing or shopping or feeding animals in the Central Park

Zoo, I would periodically absent myself to consult with Dr. Swerd-low about my damaged life, sessions that continued long after my mother died, long after my children were fully grown. They had been easy to deceive when they were young. Felice would simply take charge of them while "Mother stepped out." And Denis never once feared that his mother would follow his father's suit. Later, when my daughters were much older and living their separate lives, we would still upon occasion meet in New York, and I could still pull the wool, or felt, or straw over their eyes.

At first Dr. Swerdlow would not consent to these shortish visits. He preferred that I move to New York. He wanted my analysis to be everything. But I was adamant. When everything unimaginably disastrous has happened to you, you can cope with no more everythings. I offered instead to pay him well, exceedingly well—and what I did, I can now see, was to extend somewhat the normal two-to-three-year analysis into thirty years, spread out, with comfortable breaks.

His tiny office was located in Gramercy Park. He lived else-where. The most prominent object in his office was that hard leather couch in red Moroccan. Whenever I lay there I always felt as though I were about to be operated on, or about to have my wisdom teeth extracted. What did I talk about? Eric, I suppose, in the beginning. Then myself, and my children.

Detached from them, I could see them now more clearly, see how they distressed me, how they no longer fit together so neatly, how they were but pieces in some larger, incomplete jigsaw puzzle. Even their faces began to seem foreign, alarming. Where Dana and Denis had acquired their looks, I do not know, though Eric was indeed handsome, far prettier than I. Had their faces in some way prepared them for what was to happen? Were all things beautiful destined to be shattered, in different ways? If one could, would one choose a different face in order to face the world? Were some faces safer, like Roo's?

Dr. Swerdlow was always nagging me to hunt for the tiny,

telling details, objects that were like the concealed animals in those picture games for children. I complied, but I did not see the purpose. I remembered the gifts that Eric had brought home for them one day, after one of his rare, whimsical shopping trips. Denis was three then—and Roo and Dana were only seven and nine. He gave Dana an Art Nouveau hand mirror with a matching hairbrush. He gave Roo a box of sixty-four colored crayons, and a tray of pastels. And he gave Denis *A Child's Garden of Verses* by Robert Louis Stevenson. On the jacket of the book a lamplighter stood on the upper rungs of his ladder. The lamp he'd just lighted gave off a blue glow, like a firefly. Denis barely knew what poems were—though I read them to him those nights after Eric had vanished. What did I see in these gifts? I am afraid I saw nothing sexual. What I saw was doom. Roo secretly wanted the mirror and brush. Dana broke on purpose Roo's favorite crayons, the medium-rose violet, the salmon, and the ultramarine. And Denis was far too handsome to become a bookworm at three. If he'd only been more strapping, I told Dr. Swerdlow later. If he could have floated on something less fragile than books, words.

So I would dredge up these scenes, and we would flash them upon the wall like stereopticon slides, and I would try—oh, how I would try—to read the hidden clues, the warning signs, as if I could wrench time backwards and say to this child or that, Stop, take not a step further, once you scowl, once you say what you're about to say, the die will be cast. See? See what has happened while you wrangle? You have left your brother alone, to fend for himself. Can't you see the look of confusion on his face? the pain he is burying? Can't you? Can't you?

Gradually, I learned—learned how to satisfy Dr. Swerdlow. What he wanted was this network of distrust made visible, a slide show of people whose intersecting agonies were unknown to each other, a radar scan of blips of pain which would allow both him and me to play connect-the-dots.

So I gave him what he wanted, scene after scene. But what

I never gave him were those other moments, where the five of us enjoyed something I shall never know again on this earth.

There was one birthday party I remember, when Denis turned ten. It was a lovely May evening, and we were celebrating on the front lawn. Dana had broken up with her high-school boyfriend so, for once, could think of someone other than herself. Roo had just had her braces removed and had been singled out by her art teacher for a polka-dotted still life she'd painted, a clumsy imitation of Seurat. Denis had recently received a prize at school for having read all of Dickens's novels. And Eric? He had spent the entire day with Felice in the kitchen. He would not let us see what they were doing. Felice stood at the kitchen door like Cerberus at the gates of hell. The ovens were hot.

The cake that the two of them rolled out to the lawn was essentially Felice's, a perfect angel food drenched in a sugary vanilla glaze. Though Felice so often went awry with her poultry and game dishes, she never mismanaged desserts. There was no mistaking, however, who had conceived and orchestrated the cake's decorations. Installed inside the well of the angel food, floating on top as though it were part of the crown, was a miniature, one-ring circus—a bicycling clown, a tiger leaping through a hoop of crepe-paper fire, a ringmaster in a top hat, a ballerina perched daintily upon the back of an elephant, and two spangly trapeze artists. And all of them moved. He had designed this rotating stand to work like some fantastic cuckoo clock or music box. And once he nudged the stand from below—the ballerina twirled, the clown pedaled and grinned, the tiger jumped forwards and then backwards through the hoop, the ringmaster prodded them all with his baton, and the trapezes actually swung.

None of us dared to cut the cake, to eat it; none of us wanted to. Whenever a breeze blew out the candles we would relight them. We did not want the show to end, the birthday to be over. When we at last relented—for it was getting dark, and the girls still had homework to do—Eric lowered the cake stand. And that act was more final than dismantling a Christmas tree. Somehow I knew this circus would never return, this cake was a once-in-a-lifetime thing. It was no real disappointment then, afterwards, when both Roo and Dana said the cake tasted funny. Felice had bombarded the batter with too much salt. So much for her perfect record with desserts.

That night Denis told me that when he looked up at the stars now he would always see a circus up there—stars vaulting from trapezes, Cassiopeia astride an elephant instead of shackled to a chair, and Orion flashing his belt like a lion trainer's whip, panthers and tigers at his feet. It was I whom he told that to, not Eric. But what, of course, he was telling me was how much he loved Eric, in spite of everything. In spite of Eric.

That I took him back should have surprised no one. In fact, I had some satisfaction in telling my mother of his return, knowing how she would expect me then to don the mantle of defeat, the mask of perpetual, irreversible dourness—and I would not. I had triumphed in my own way, kept some dignity intact, unsavaged; and I had acquired more than a Germanic or Francophilic sounding board in Dr. Swerdlow. One man on this earth found me worth listening to, was attentive to me, notwithstanding the infrequency of my visits or his exorbitant fees, the considerably exorbitant fees. My children in my hour of need had rallied around me as the sole remaining head of the house. The girls were no longer so combative and obstreperous. Denis, my handsomest, would gladly ride on my back as he had Eric's, when I was exhausted from gardening but not too exhausted for horseplay.

He came back at dinnertime, as though he had not been gone for five months, as though he had indeed just "stepped out." I had never expected to see him again at all. Then later, once I realized how weak he had become, I was surprised he could have lasted away from home for even that long. He had been gone for the spring and the summer. He came back in the fall, at the end of September, as though it were time to return for school and he had played hooky for several weeks.

The girls bounded out of their chairs to greet him. Denis did not budge. Perhaps he was afraid his father was an apparition, a bogeyman who'd slithered out of the pantry to make off with either him or the desserts. "Denis, my love," I said to him, "look who's back. Aren't you going to kiss Daddy hello?" I more than half expected he wouldn't. But before he could get out of the chair Eric was already by his side. He kissed Denis soundly, again and again, lifted him up and whirled him around, and then stopped, suddenly. He must have pulled a muscle or something, for he groaned. Then he smiled, wanly, but he still looked baffled. I shuddered. He had no business doing this in the dining room. I was not sure he had any business in the dining room, period. He noticed then the missing chair and silver. I called Felice and told her to set another place. He stood there, awkwardly, like some poor vagrant left out in the cold, wondering if he'd ever sleep in a warm bed again. The girls were back in their chairs, shrieking, "How was Paris, Daddy? Tell us about Paris!" "Paris?" Eric asked. "The postcards," I said to him. "They were so delightful. Each time one arrived, we immediately shared it. How good of you to write to each of us, to think of us all." I hoped he had enough sense to carry it from there. At least he realized now that I and the children knew something, and had always known—the full extent of what we knew, however, we would never reveal to him. I took some satisfaction in that too.

In time I think he actually came to forget that that brutal break in our lives had ever occurred, wherein we had all become displaced people. Maybe the girls forgot as well. I am not so sure about Denis. I know I never forgot, never.

Years later, Dana told me on one of our get-togethers in New York that she thought her father had spoiled her for boyfriends later on, that she was forever searching for intense willfulness in the other sex, accompanied by flights of free-spiritedness. She had certainly passed on the latter. The trouble with her marriages, I told her—if the second was to even be called that—was that she had failed to marry a thrilling man. "Yes," she replied, "and you did, and look what happened to yours." Only as she got older did I sense that her unspoiled admiration for her father had possibly waned. Roo, at nine, at nineteen, at twenty-nine, was still proudly showing to her father the things she had made, those lopsided clay pots and ridiculous, toothpicky sculptures her father always enthusiastically praised. Until she stopped talking to him and showing him anything, and I suppose I am partly responsible for that—that may have been the one wicked thing I did in this life, but he deserved it. Eric finally melted the ice in Denis, but it melted slowly. Wouldn't you know, it was then that Eric hatched his plan for a swimming pool in the back of the house—so his girls could throw festive parties there, so he could teach his son how to swim. When he found he could not teach him, he discovered—I fear, I hope—a much deeper emptiness than could be contained by a swimming pool. And though the pool remained intact but empty for years (so as to remind him constantly of his failure, his uselessness, his dereliction), it would only be rendered completely dysfunctional once the second worst thing happened, far, far worse than the first. So it is no wonder that I thought of dying nearly every day after that, my handsome son now turned into Humpty Dumpty, and he, my husband, somehow as unfazed by that as he was when he walked out on me. And Dr. Swerdlow then was no help at all, his ministrations pointless. I could tell him nothing of my bottomless grief, though he must have seen that in my eyes, my face, if he were looking closely through some other lens besides the eye. Oh, I was broken too.

We had stopped by then our family reunions at Thanksgiving. I found the holiday a torture, a misnomer. I could give thanks to no one. And so we would gather now on the Fourth of July, a somewhat less cruel parody of a holiday. For none of us were independent. Or if we were, like me, it was what we least wanted. Eric was always slavishly dependent on his women, and Dana equally dependent upon her men. Eric could no longer count on art to absorb or uplift him. His very last pieces—the ones he'd shipped back from Paris—he swiftly dismantled, except for one. They were far flimsier than his previous work. They reminded me of Roo's Tinkertoy disasters. I'm not even sure he made them himself. Soon he abandoned sculpture and wood carving for other, more sedentary crutches.

And Denis—Denis was now dependent on us forever.

So when Roo arrived that Fourth of July with that unkempt young man in tow—so unlike Denis, so uncivilized, so ill-bred—and pronounced him her live-in, her virtual husband, I knew my mother was laughing at me from her grave and inviting me to join her. She knew that Roo would have been better off killing herself or going back to Frederick than staying with that vagabond, that loser.

I couldn't watch another life be—as Eric might have sportily put it—"pissed away." And I daresay I was jealous too. An exhilarating sex life was one thing neither Roo nor her boyfriend surely wanted for.

I was tired. Tired of ruin, unhappiness. I had thought the thirties not a particularly euphoric moment in time, but neither were the sixties. And Denis and I had been destroyed, each of us, in the time between—so there was no good time at all, anywhere. And it seemed to me wrong, terribly wrong, that Eric should have been able to glide so blithely through it all, alighting on all these tragic events as though he were Tinker Bell.

When I went upstairs to my bedroom that night, after bowing out of dinner, I was still not certain I could do it. So I fell asleep, for several hours. And dreamed of what it would be like, the exploratory scrape of the razor's edge against my wrist, almost the way my trowel would poke and stab at the earth, until resistance crumbled and the loosened ground gave way and the trowel plunged, and one knew what would emerge. Wet, and wormy. My rose-killers. My aborted blossoms.

The blood was poppy-red. The pain was ungodly. So I fortified myself with Empirin, one-handedly, as if that could help, chewing the pills like hard candy. It was just past midnight. I grasped my bleeding wrist with the palm of my other hand, walked from the bathroom, through the bedroom, down the hall to Eric's bedroom, and then opened the door just slightly. He was not a heavy sleeper. "Eric," I said, "could you please come to my bedroom? You needn't turn on the light."

When he did, he found me standing at the door to my bathroom. "Close the bedroom door," I said, "but do not come near me." I would not dupe him into thinking I was preparing for some other sort of visitation from him. Then I switched on the light in the bathroom so he could see what I'd been doing to my wrist. My nightgown was grandly speckled with blood. Even cold water might not redeem all of it. He rushed towards me, as I knew he would, but I had locked myself behind the bathroom door by then. "Liddie," he shouted, "open this door!"

"Don't shout," I hissed. "And don't make a scene. You have exactly ten minutes. Ten minutes from now to remove that ridiculous man from our daughter's bedroom and to usher him out of this house. If he is not gone, then I will be gone. And don't you dare dream of lying to me. You have lied far too long. I am going to save at least one of my daughters from a stupid man. At least one of them. You had better go now. I'm not playing games here. This is your blood as well as mine."

Was I deranged then? Undoubtedly. Deranged and confused and hurt. I could hear him dialing a cab company, then a hotel. When he hung up the phone I let him know he had used up nearly five minutes with those calls. I heard him leave the room quickly. I had stanched the wound with a towel, using it as a compress. The blood, I knew, would stop, unlike either my anger or grief. I was a better gardener than I was a suicide. He behaved far more kindly to me than he had in years, once I emerged from the bathroom, erect, in command of my senses. Roo and her friend had cleared out. The next call he made was to our doctor, describing my "accident." Our doctor was no dummy. He was also discreet.

Neither Dana nor Denis took any note of this brouhaha, Dana having drunk herself into a coma—and Denis, he had simply learned to shut out the world in too many ways. No wonder he listened to only that maudlin music of his, songs in which pain could be stroked away by violins.

Eric, I presume, returned to his uneasy sleep in his easy bed. Roo, I know, ceased from that night to ever speak to him again. Did I feel guilty? Had I committed a dreadful wrong, was it really I who was responsible for this breach between the two of them? No. They were too much alike already, too wayward and obsessive, competing with one another without their even knowing it. The rupture between the two would have occurred whether I'd been the one to shed blood, or Roo, or Eric. I, of course, continued to see both my daughters, who remained good friends in spite of their differences. Perhaps not close friends, but close enough. Roo, I felt, was always so much more dependent on Dana, needed her too much. Dana was the level-headed one, the one with goals— until she met Leon. How he sank her, how her beauty toppled once she was under his thumb and stomach. Nothing, really, could save her—but then I had long ago given up on anyone being saved. Still, out of some dogged attachment to the myth that we were an intact family, the three of us continued to reunite in New York—and shop, and sup, the way we used to when Roo was living on the East Coast near Dana. And I would visit with Dr. Swerdlow while the two of them went off to be by themselves. I was grateful when my younger daughter finally remarried, though he too, like Leon, was not the sort of man I would have imagined for a daughter of mine. Her marrying someone who had a last name, however, relieved me no end. Her sister would probably never be released from her jailer lover and would suffer as had I— in a house no different from a mausoleum.

I am a selfish woman. I know that. Selfish, because I fled from unbearable despair, a despair that would have left me no reason to live at all, and indulged instead my need to lash out at the world by bemoaning my daughters, who—even had they learned from my grievous errors—still would have chosen desperate circumstances for their lives and desperate men, the inevitability of those destinies ironically comforting me. For I could then say to myself, and to them: Though the shape of your future seemed to be in my hands, it was really out of my hands entirely. There was no other choice. You had no choice. The fate that befell you— it could not have not happened.

But if I were to think the reverse, ever—that it might not have happened this way—then I could not go on living, or accept what had happened to my son, whom I loved more dearly than my daughters, far more. For he was the one most deeply betrayed.

Years ago my mother gave me a book called *Poems by Emily Dickinson*. Read them, she said to me, they're like poisoned pills, you'll like them. I remember one poem very well, called "Parting." I learned it by heart because it made me so sad at first, and then later, so angry.

> My life closed twice before its close;
> It yet remains to see
> If Immortality unveil
> A third event to me,
>
> So huge, so hopeless to conceive,
> As these that twice befell.
> Parting is all we know of heaven,
> And all we need of hell.

She had not cornered the market on grief. My life had closed twice too. But I would have liked to slap Miss Dickinson silly. For I wasted no time in brooding over some further disaster. Twice was enough. Even once was enough. And nothing was so huge and so hopeless, so inconceivable, as what happened to my son. Nothing worse could happen, nothing. Parting is easy. Parting is as easy as pressing a razor to one's wrist and opening that flimsy envelope of flesh. Life is nothing but a monotonous round of partings.

But to keep on going when your precious face and even more precious life have been cleaved, halved, to awaken each day shackled like some abominable Siamese twin to what you used to be and can no longer be again and yet is still there, as though beauty were not content to be some utterly vanished ghost, as though it still might rise in piecemeal from the ruins—nothing could be more unendurable, nothing. Parting isn't hell. What is hell is the impossibility of parting, the inability to let go, to relinquish for good the loveliness that so stupidly remains.

But I do not dream of third events. Future losses. Closings. Though Dr. Swerdlow would no doubt contend that the day we two conclude my analysis surely will be such an event, a momentous, long-dreamed-of parting—to be both welcomed and mourned.

For pain, the tiny things suffice, I would tell him or anyone. The smell of violets wilting in a shattered room. A small boy's panicky eyes at bedtime. And the sound of your heart exploding like a bomb—while no one else hears, while the world plays canasta and soup spoons, and the ocean turns on its back and grumbles.

■■　■■　■■

She had outlasted the doorman. When she arrived at that familiar grey building on upper Park Avenue, her home away from home as it were, she saw that he was no longer there, that doorman who was roughly her age, who had been tending that building since he was twenty-four, whose face had come to resemble the lobby in its blank, sallow permanence. The new doorman hovered on the lip of middle age and looked both discontent and resigned.

"I'm here to see Dr. Swerdlow," she said.

"Whom should I say is calling?"

"Who. Miss Hurst."

He pressed a buzzer, then spoke into a phone.

"There's a Miss Hurst to see you." He barely looked at her. She was simply an inconvenience that had to be dealt with, no more worth ogling than a portable ashtray. "You can go up. Apartment 903."

"There used to be another doorman," she said, tentatively.

"He died."

"Oh. How sad."

She walked to the elevator. The elevator man was also new. His face was swarthy, vaguely Spanish. They were everywhere now, she thought. Soon there would be no such thing as WASPs anymore. Inbreeding had given way to outbreeding. Perhaps it was all for the better. Maybe if she'd married an African or a Hindu her life would have been merrier, more colorful, interesting. She could have worn hoops through her nose and necklaces that looked like Slinkies. She could have painted a deep-vermilion dot in the center of her forehead.

He was waiting for her in his usual outfit, slippers and robe. He had had that paisley robe for as long as they had been lovers. Sometimes she feared the silk had worn itself so thin that the very press of her fingers might shred it. But she had never touched it. He always removed it himself and carefully draped it over the back of his favorite armchair before he started work with her. He did most of his work with just his slippers on.

"Ah, *mon charme, ma petite*, you have brought us a new one."

"Bought and brought," she said. Petite she no longer was. She had grown far too ample once she'd tipped forty-five in years and one hundred forty-five in pounds. She noticed he had started to load the Magicubes already. She hated the flash bulbs, even these newer, tinier ones, but she had never told him. She preferred it so much more when she could stand in the late-afternoon light that poured through the French windows and then settled in lop-sided rectangles on the old carpet. But the sky was grey, the day like lead. The last time she'd been here, four months ago, it had been sunny all weekend. The girls had put something of a damper on her spirits then. Roo had been sulky; Dana, depressed. But the glorious weather had made up for that short spell of mopishness, sullenness, plus her visit here.

She took off her clothes in the bathroom. Her breasts sagged like old wine sacks. Loose flesh bunched up in layers below her navel. Her thighs had gone soft as porridge. Little dent marks peppered the skin like thumbprints. She did not want to look in the mirror quite yet, though she would have to, eventually.

She opened the sturdy box that she'd brought in with her, which was nearly the size of a small suitcase. Gingerly she removed the hat. It was a beauty. Lavender silk flowers roller-coastered around the brim. A tiny bouquet of forget-me-nots fluttered on one side of the crown. The hat was both gorgeous and racy, with just enough bounce to make it seem light, even capable of being airborne. She looked at herself in the mirror now as she first freshened her makeup and then pinned on the hat. The light in his bathroom had always been a little too harsh and glarey. For years she had packed in her purse softer bulbs for the bathroom sconces whenever she came. But he always changed them back after she'd gone, she knew. Maybe because his eyes were weaker than hers. Today she'd forgotten to bring them. But neither glare nor softness really mattered anymore. The face was hopeless. Only the hat mattered.

Finally she emerged from the bathroom.

"Lydia, Lydia," he said. "Ah, you are ravishing as ever. A treat for sore eyes, *comme toujours*. Sit there, why don't you, on the settee. Here. Let me arrange your legs."

She watched him rotate her arms and legs as though they were, or had once been, pipe cleaners. She could feel her thick flesh wobble in his hands. Sometimes the poses he engineered strained her considerably, but she did not grimace. In the Gramercy Park office they never touched, barely exchanged glances. He hid behind his charcoal suit and vest while she talked to a ceiling, a shadow.

Her eyes were beginning to smart just a bit. She tried not to show it. Each time the light flashed she smiled. "Here now. Stand by the window. Caress the curtain gently. Pretend it's a smooth, silky cat named Rimbaud who adores you. Pretend it's your lover who will do anything you ask. Anything."

She petted the curtain, paused, petted it again. It felt like a horse blanket. "Now fold it around your heavenly flanks. But leave one breast showing, like a precious love-apple."

She did as she was told. Her breast, she knew, looked no more like an apple than she herself looked like a French tart. He darted around her in his floppy slippers, the Magicubes popping. But she was staring beyond him and his one-man fireworks show, and was appraising instead the living room itself, which she had known now for nearly three decades: the gaudy, too gaudy rococo mirror above the fireplace; the marble obelisks ranged like spear-heads upon the mantel; the faded Persian rug whose complex patterns had melted into a large lavender bruise; the vases full of dried flowers, never fresh ones; the magisterial desk in which he kept all these portraits of his private passion; the mahogany book-cases crammed with fat, unreadable tomes; the few pieces that smacked almost of Victorian bordello, like the méridienne up-holstered in aubergine velvet. It was a room that had never been altered. Yet it bore secret witness to the myriad ways she had altered, as well as her hats, as well as her body. The room would never change. Unlike the doorman downstairs.

"Look dreamy now, my dear. Tip your head to the right just a smidgen. Like that. Now let me see those adorable eyes, that ravishing hat. Sigh for me, Lydia. Sigh."

She sighed. Again. And again. Each time she exhaled she imagined she was letting the air out of the room and out of the illusion too, that the two of them would suddenly sputter and sag to the floor like deflated balloons. All she could hear were the flash cubes, and her breathing.

Then he was holding her tenderly by the waist and leading

her to the bedroom. Her hat did not interfere. She was at least six inches taller than he.

For a small man his bed was enormous. She carefully detached her hat, placed it on top of his dresser, then lay on the bed, waiting for him. The room needed airing, desperately. It smelled of bachelordom and old age. There were no photographs at all in his bedroom—of parents or any other relatives, a wife or a child. Nor were there family portraits of any sort in his museum of a living room. It was as though he'd been hatched from a Platonic egg—forever bald, forever single, forever weird. She had forgotten what he looked like years ago. He had always been sixty to her.

He mounted her, and it was a struggle for both of them. There is no juice left, she thought. Neither in her nor in him. His presence inside her was as tiny and softly intrusive as a pimento's in an olive. Except there was juice in the olive.

Then he died. She felt him detumesce. His eyes were wide open, so was his mouth. She could see the fillings in his ancient, carious teeth. But he did not move. She pushed and rolled him off her, but he simply lay there. She placed her fingers on his chest as though she were testing a cake. Nothing rose. She heard only her own, now rapid breathing.

She groped her way off the bed and got dressed as quickly as a seventy-year-old woman could. Keep calm, she said to herself, pretend as though you have never been here. She cautiously repacked her hat, ensuring that none of the flowers got mussed, then checked the bathroom to see if she'd left any traces of makeup there. Then she got down on her hands and knees and thoroughly explored the carpets in both the bedroom and the living room, searching for flash cubes. She felt like her maid in Florida, scouting under the beds for wayward palmetto bugs. She was used to being on her hands and knees, though. There, in Florida, gardening. Or here, sometimes, doing something else.

After she'd located all the spent flashes, she deposited them in her purse. Then she put on her good pair of spring gloves.

They would get smudged now, she knew, but thank God her mother had raised her to carry gloves with her at all times. She took out the roll of film from his camera, then let it unfurl as though it were a miniature roll of crepe paper. She assumed that even the dull grey light in the room was enough to kill all the exposures. Then she retraced her own movements in the living room, relived her performance, trying to remember all of the objects she might have touched, the clear or hard surfaces, like the wood beneath the scrolled arm of the méridienne, or one of the French windowpanes. She dabbed at all of them with her handkerchief.

Then she checked for hairs on the bed pillow. His eyes, still bright, gawked up at the ceiling, though they were now more like the eyes of some dead fish. When she leaned towards him more closely she could see how unattractive he really was. The tufts of mouse-colored hair that curled out of his ears and nostrils. The hard Adam's apple lodged in his throat like a wee brussels sprout. His waxy skin.

"Why did you never get married, Dr. Swerdlow? Why did you never try to take me away from my husband? What would your mother think if she saw you like this?"

When she had finished cleaning up everything, she sat down at his desk and began the search for the key to the drawers. There was only one thing left to dispose of or take home with her: her past. She knew he wouldn't hide the key too obscurely. People who spent their lives unlocking other people's heads needed all their keys within easy reach.

She found it in less than five minutes, hidden beneath an antique inkwell. She supposed the spot was well chosen. He had been dipping into more than ink, after all, for thirty years.

She had never seen any of the photographs he had taken of her. That had been part of their agreement, the trade-off for those strange and often too short fumblings that occurred on the bed and elsewhere. She never feared blackmail. He was too sweet for that, also too pathetic. Her initial curiosity about the photographs had faded over time, had been consumed by this other bizarre need to indulge herself.

Now, she was afraid. Afraid to see what he had captured with that perverted lens of his. Afraid to see how she either had kept her poise under extraordinarily humiliating circumstances or had dismantled it with one leering smile or wink. Afraid to see how her mortal coil had been shuffling off, slowly but relentlessly, year by year.

She opened the large bottom drawer. It was cavernous. There she was. Right up front. Her name attached to a bulging portfolio neatly tied with a ribbon.

And behind her nearly a dozen more. Glenda Babcock. Alice Dwerlkotte. Courtney Ferringer. Daphne Firkin-Mummsey. Penelope Heyworth. Sister Jerome. Elspeth and Edna McKinney. Portia Schnackenburg. Georgia Steinbugler and assorted pets. Valerie Tutu.

Some of the women were pretty. Far prettier than she. Few, however, had portfolios as thick as hers. She had perhaps outlasted them as well as the doorman, though there were several that were ongoing and relatively new. None of the others, she was grateful, wore hats, except for Sister Jerome, and her head garb never changed. She was surprised at both the size and the kind of animals that doted on Miss Steinbugler. Somehow Dr. Swerdlow's small and meticulous apartment did not seem made for the likes of a Saluki or a howler monkey. A couple of photographs made her laugh in spite of herself. Mostly they made her bitter.

She left all the packets there except for hers, locked the drawer and replaced the key.

Slowly she pored through those images of her he had battened on, thirty years' worth. The hats themselves told their own history, ranging from cloches to turbans to boaters to snoods to bird hats to even an occasional pillbox. Mostly, though, she had preferred the wide-brimmed hats with small crowns and floral rims. Some of the photographs had been doctored to resemble old sepia post-cards. She looked like a French tart after all, in those.

She had good carriage, for a long time, she could see that. And even a smile that belied despair until around 1962, when she saw some of the light die a little in her face. She was fifty-six then, and her body had begun to thicken and shift some, and menopause had struck the year before. But that was not what had struck her down then.

The ways he had posed her had changed very little. The reclining positions on the méridienne and the carpet. The standing positions near the window. Those tilting shots in which she seemed to be languishing over something that had died.

She had expected to be moved—shaken or saddened by the accumulating weight of lost years, discarded guises. But she wasn't. If she flicked rapidly through all the photographs, she knew she would be both bored and frustrated, her life but a tiresome blue movie that was all promise, no delivery.

She decided to keep one of the shots, one of the sepia cards in which she looked jaunty, almost lewd, her breasts nearly as perky as the flowers on her hat, her skin aglow with a kind of hearty creaminess.

She burned the rest, one by one, in his fireplace, along with the exposed film, slowly at first because she wasn't sure the flue was still open. It took over an hour to burn them all. Then she swept up the ashes in a dustpan and flushed them down the toilet.

Before she left she went into the bedroom for one last time. She sat beside him, at the edge of the bed, and held one of his stiff hands. "Goodbye, Dr. Swerdlow. May you have lush and wonderful dreams about Sister Jerome and Miss Steinbugler and her delectable menagerie, and may the devil then analyze them for you. You frightful man, you." She made the bed over him, pulled the sheet up to his chin, then at the last moment decided to cover his entire face with the sheet.

No trace of her remained. She shut a final door on him and

on New York forever. She would need no more hats. The hundreds she had would have to make do. If the doorman were asked who had seen Dr. Swerdlow last, he might remember a Miss Hurst. But that was not her real name. It was the name of a very bad novelist whom she hated. And people did not look closely at old faces. Old faces were interchangeable walnuts to the young, even the middle-aged. The doorman was too worried about his own disillusionment with life anyway to be that upset about some dead man upstairs. Everybody died. Dr. Swerdlow would probably linger up there, undiscovered, for a few days at least, until Valerie of the many tutus perhaps got worried and started calling.

At the street corner a block away, she hailed a cab. She asked the driver to detour through Central Park on her way back to the hotel. It was still light out. She wanted to see trees, bicyclists, roller skaters, nannies walking baby carriages, young lovers, the bright green forest of the living. In Florida there was nothing green and wild but the Everglades. And everyone in Florida was like herself—old.

"It's beautiful here, isn't it?" she said to the cabdriver.

"Not at night, lady. Not at night."

She clutched her purse. She would take care to hide the photograph where no one could find it, once she got home. Maybe in one of the hatboxes, maybe in a drawer somewhere, like his, under lock and key. She knew there would come moments, of a late afternoon, when the house was still and suffocating, when Eric would be hibernating inside his room and Denis would be mowing the lawn or listening to his music, moments when she could steal into that locked drawer or that hatbox in her closet and behold this *ravissante*, not-yet-corpulent siren with eyes flashing beneath a cockade of silken roses—and realize she had had another life.

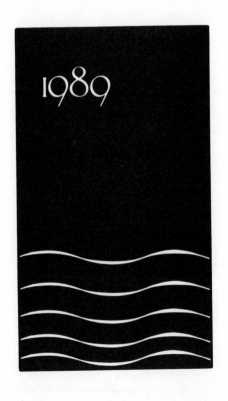

1989

This place was a zoo, I told Trevor, long before this. Probably long before I was born and maybe longer. Sure as hell long before these turkeys from the church started waddling in here to chow down and scarf up a few drinkie-poos, on the house. We were standing around like coatracks on the second floor, trying to look innocuous and invisible. Help them off with their wraps, said Mother, show them where the powder rooms are. Sure, Mom, sure. Trevor had put in a good half hour trying to take the coat off one old babe. She was like some ancient pretzel. One crunch, and her arm'd come off. Some of the walking dead were spackling up there in the nearest bedroom, powdering their faces maggot-white, poking little dots of rouge in the gullies. Clowns on their way to the morgue, I whispered to Trevor. Since we were the walking coatracks and weren't any too thrilled about that, and since most of the closets up here were already stuffed, we wound up dumping the coats on one of the moldy big beds that nobody was using. The bed now looked like a chinchilla ranch. Why these old dolls wore fur coats in the summer I sure didn't know, except maybe the layered look was good for tired blood. I hated touching their spindly little arms. So did Trevor. They felt like cold chicken bones. There were so many veins you could read the arms like maps.

Their husbands had enough sense to stay put downstairs. Mostly because they were too pooped out to climb any more stairs. The stairs at church plus the boring service had done them in already. Also because downstairs was where the liquor was. They'd been snoring so loudly in church that if I'd been a nurse I'd've fed them all morphine cocktails instantly, put 'em out for good. Some people here were under seventy—Mom, Aunt Roo, Trevor, Half-and-Half, the kitchen help, the boarders and some of their friends—but that was it. My half-sisters never showed, and Mom was truly pissed. They couldn't leave their families on short notice, they didn't like Gramps anyway, they'd never planned to celebrate his birthday with us, and now that the birthday had turned into a funeral they were even less interested. They were just like my dad, and like their dad too. Cold-blooded. Bitches. Bastards. Mom sure had crummy luck with her men and her children. She spawned newts when she was eighteen. Then at forty-one she hatched me. The weasel. I was smarter than my sisters, but so what? We were all monsters from the same womb. I probably hated my mother as much as they did.

"Is that the dress you had on yesterday?" Trevor asked.

"No, Trevor. It's not. It's a totally different dress. Totally."

"I'm sorry, I'm sorry. You were wearing black yesterday. I just asked. This dress looks a lot like the other one."

"Trevor, I wear black every day. Black is my color. Mother hates it, but I love it. She says I'm always dressed for a funeral, and I say, be prepared. I'm my own funeral."

"You're disturbed, Jessie."

"Better disturbed than a dweeb."

Trevor was the only other kid here. He was a year older than me, fourteen, and an artsy-fartsy technoid. Unfortunately, he was also cute, but I don't think he'd caught on to that yet. Sometimes he could be funny in a mean-spirited way. That ran in our family. He was a whole lot smarter than the nerds on "Jeopardy!" but he wasn't too smart about stuff that was real. He and his mom would fly to New York once a year from L.A. and visit for a few days. They always left the Lava behind, thank God. I should be calling him Blabber now, but I can't. He was always Lava to me. He'd be somewhere out on the road in California hawking those stupid things while Mom and Aunt Roo lathered up their faces with mint slime in some health spa on Fifth Avenue and shelled out hundreds of dollars for that and for the lunch afterwards, which amounted to two prunes, a glass of Poland Spring water, and a tea-leaf reading from some gypsy con-artist wearing a Hermès babushka. Trevor and I spent most of those afternoons then in my room at home, arguing about my taste in posters and music. He was into that zithery Japanese shit, Kitaro or whatever, music that sounded like dying canaries trilling their last cheep while somebody beat them to death with chopsticks. I was into the Cure and Depeche Mode and INXS and Sinéad O'Connor and Billy Idol. His mother probably foisted Kitaro on him. Music for the marshmallowheads of the eighties. My mom and his mom could have come from two different planets. Mom went to seminars on Diane Arbus. Aunt Roo went to séances. Mom was up on every fringe movement in the photography world. Aunt Roo believed in the fringe movement of large floor pillows. Mom worshiped art, even though I wasn't all that impressed with her photographs. They were so tiny you needed a magnifying glass to see what was going on in them. And nothing was, but pinheads dancing with each other and looking gaga. Mongoloid pinups is all I saw. But Mom says they're strongly influenced by Persian miniatures, whatever they are. Aunt Roo thought art was origami party favors. The strongest influence on Aunt Roo is Shirley MacLaine. She and the Shit Artist, one of Gramps's boarders, would get on great.

I'd been counting the purses some of the fossils had left behind, thinking bad thoughts. What I wanted right now wouldn't be in any of them. But what was maybe in some of them was the means to that end. While Trevor pried off another pretzel's coat, I could feel my empty fingers dancing. I knew what they were itching for. Lycra slinked out of the smaller powder room, hiking up her nonexistent breasts. Her real name was Vivienne, with a heavy accent on the *enne*, but I called her Lycra. She was about forty trying to look twenty and flunking. Gramps let her stay on because she didn't cost much to feed and because she could work up low-impact aerobic routines for the fossil set. Gramps tended to sit a lot. She was trying to sell real estate on the side. What was low-impact was her brain, plus her boobs. Every time you ran into her she was wearing one of those Lycra wet suits that made her look like four blue Popsicles jammed into a magenta skyrocket. I thought she'd show up at church in shiny black leotards, maybe doing her crunches in the pew when she got bored. Instead she was wearing this flecky green dress that looked like it was shedding worms. She'd been in the bathroom nearly a half hour. Trying to inflate her boobs was like blowing up a flat tire with your mouth.

"How are we doing, you two?" Lycra asked, smiling.

"We're doing fine," I said. "We're just dying to be eighty, we can hardly wait. Aren't they all hot stuff up here? Aren't they in great shape? Has Jane Fonda made a tape for when we're dead? If I do enough crunches in my coffin, will somebody still want to jump my bones? Hubba hubba hubba."

Lycra gave me a sour look and scooted downstairs. Trevor grinned.

"How long has he had these boarders?"

Trevor had never been to the Florida house. I guess there'd been some falling out between Aunt Roo and Gramps years ago. Trevor didn't talk about it, because he didn't know. I hadn't come down here all that often either, but whenever Mom flew down, like once a year, so did I. She had to keep me on a tight leash. She knew what I'd been into since I was ten. But not all of it.

"These boarders?" I said. "Or boarders in general?"

"Both."

"This crew wasn't on the boat last year. Last year there was a woman who made necklaces out of chunks of lacquered fruitcake, I kid you not, and some old guy with bad teeth who was designing musical toothbrushes. Artists, Gramps's favorites. Mom said the place started to go zooey after Gramma died, and Gramps was stuck here alone with Half-and-Half."

Trevor laughed.

"You're mean, Jessie," he said. "You're so mean."

"Yeah, right. And what do you call him?"

"Who?"

"Half-and-Half."

"You mean Droopy?" he said. "See? I'm much kinder than you."

We both cackled. Once I got his mean side working, Trevor was almost bearable. I could see him as a movie, *The Three Faces of Trev*. One-third megadweeb, one-third wise-ass cutie, and then the one-third gushy dufus who probably got his rocks off riding an escalator. I figured he was a virgin. I also figured he'd go along with me only so far on some things. Mostly because he knew I was scary, and he knew he wasn't. I had my plans. I always had plans. If I didn't I'd be a basket case.

We were both getting pretty fed up with having to stay inside all the time. I'd walked down to the beach about several hundred times this week, just to get away from Mom and because I was bored. But after five minutes on the beach I'd OD'd on sand and prickly heat and dead jellyfish, and was moaning for a joint and MTV. There weren't any TVs in Gramps's house. And Mom had found the dime bag I'd brought with me from New York and flushed it down the toilet. As soon as Aunt Roo and Trevor flew down here yesterday, the beachcombing episodes got canceled. Trevor and I had to stick around the grown-ups like sponges, mopping up their tears. And they weren't even crying about Gramps. I don't know what they were so sad and angry about, but a lot of it had to do with Half-and-Half, who'd found himself a lawyer, they said, and who, it turns out now, could talk after all. Twenty-five years of drifting around the house like a mute, and now he finally jabbers and drools. Mom and Aunt Roo were plenty pissed when they learned they weren't going to ride first-class on Gramps's gravy train. They weren't even riding the caboose. I didn't much care. Or I cared, but what good would that do? Even if Mom had inherited something she'd blow it all on contact sheets and zoom lenses, and then hire pinheads by the hour to pose for her so she didn't have to scavenge retard homes and SROs and the state bins. She could set up an escort agency for the handicapped: Date a Pinhead. She could start a Diane Arbus newsletter. Have Aunt Roo summon up Diane in one of her séances, ask her how good Mom's chances were of getting arrested in the near future for near forgery.

Still, it did seem kind of crummy and mean of Gramps to leave everything to a halfwit. Mom told Aunt Roo she was "very cross" with Denis, not just because she got screwed out of Gramps's money but because she had to call up the caterers and do all the major legwork for the big funeral lunch. On the phone Half-and-Half probably sounds like Marlon Brando in *The Godfather*. Mom wasn't cross, though. She was boiling. She'd been cross with me ever since I was born. "Cross" meant angry as hell. "Very cross" meant "I'll-blow-your-fucking-head-off-with-a-Magnum."

At least Trevor and I got to escape for a half hour yesterday and go sightseeing on Worth Avenue. Aunt Roo was totally fixated on finding some gourmet shop that sold seaweed, since she's on some new Korean diet. There was plenty of seaweed on Gramps's beach, I told her. Why didn't she just stroll down there with a big spoon? But she was determined, so I knew she wouldn't luck out. Determined people wound up like my mother: determined to lose. There was nothing on Worth Avenue but jewelry stores selling stickpins only a jillionaire could afford, and women's clothing stores full of hideous evening gowns nobody would be caught dead in except the living dead in Palm Beach, and boutiques that were jam-packed with Oriental rugs and rattan hippos and giraffes and reminded me of that movie *The Fly*, only here the Ralph Lauren den from Bloomie's got crossed with an outlet from Pier 1.

A few more old crullers and pretzels wobbled out of the bedroom. From what I knew of Gramps I didn't think he ever got into town or even had any friends, but just stayed inside, licking stamp hinges and keeping tabs on Half-and-Half. Mom's convinced they're all spongers, and that most of them read about the funeral in *The Shiny Sheet* and decided to trot along for the free booze and lunch. They probably ate like sparrows anyway, so the caterers didn't need to fret about running out of food. Nobody but Aunt Roo would be diving into the seaweed tarts.

A man in a rush swooped up the stairs and dodged past the old dolls who weren't even halfway down yet. It was Lionel. A breakdown in a tunnel, no doubt. Maybe a collapsed trestle bridge. Or a mouse hopping a ride in one of the boxcars and derailing the whole shebang.

"He's the one with the trains," I told Trevor.

"When can we see them?"

"We can't. He's a hermit. Like Gramps. He always locks his door."

"How many does he have?"

"Two. On two different platforms. I've only seen them once. There's no place to stand in his room. The floor's a railway yard. He lives on his bed."

"Are they original Lionels?"

"How should I know? He's a total wasteland, a loser, like everyone else who lives here. Would somebody normal lock himself in his room all day so he could play choo-choo with a pair of dumb toy trains?"

"Depends, Jess. If they were the originals, I might. At least for part of a day. I've never seen a really old Lionel train. When'd he show them to you?"

"He didn't. I borrowed his keys. He leaves them lying around sometimes along with his brains. Mom thinks he's a local college student who's gone off the deep end."

"How does he pay rent?"

"How do they all pay rent, Trevor? Do you think some museum is going to shower big bucks on the Shit Artist, the soon-to-be-famous sculptress? 'Yes, we must have the Buffalo Chip, we absolutely must. Only fifty thousand dollars? A bargain. Sold. And what about that other little treasure, what's it called? Alaskan Moose Nugget? Oh, it's a honey, a real gem, what every gallery wants now.' Listen, for all we know it's been Gramps who's been buying her art supplies. And Old Yeller, old Prep downstairs, must have cost Gramps about a million in liquor bills. His wastebaskets are always full of empties. All five wastebaskets. His room's the glass menagerie."

"He asked me in church if I played," said Trevor.

"What?"

"Polo."

"Oh, Jesus."

"I told him I didn't play polo, I wore Polo." He laughed.

"See, you are for sure as mean as I am," I said.

"No. You just bring it out of me."

"Let's go up to the attic. I'm bored here. If any of these old farts collapse, they'll have to crawl around on the floor the way Joan Crawford did in *Baby Jane*. I can't pick them up. I'm sick of old people."

We walked past Gramps's room. His door was shut. We weren't supposed to go in there until the police were through. Two doors down we could hear the steam whistles and the chugging. Trevor wanted to listen by the door but I pulled him away. The second floor was like the furniture floor in Bloomie's. One monstrous overstuffed room spawning another. The ceilings were so high Godzilla would have felt like a gerbil in here. Around the corner were the bedrooms where Mom and I slept. Our doors were shut, but the door to the Shit Artist's studio was wide open. The only furniture in there was a worktable, a bunch of pedestals made out of old orange crates, and a small refrigerator. She'd ditched the bed. She told Mom she slept on the floor because mattresses robbed her of visions. Since she was getting plastered downstairs on champagne, I figured she'd be flat out soon, visions or no visions, so we could snoop around safely.

I couldn't see much difference between one of her pieces and another. She'd doused them all in polyurethane or Lemon Pledge or something so that they gleamed. To me they looked like bad vegetables drowning in vinaigrette. Each one had a different name, though. Platypus Chip. Zebra Chip. Trevor was fondling one of them.

"They're made of wood!"

"Well, what did you think they'd be made of? The real stuff and some shellac?"

"Jessie, somebody will buy these," he said. "I mean it. They're really good. She's serious, she's a serious artist."

"So's my mother with her mini-coneheads."

"Yeah. And isn't your mother finally starting to show?"

"You bet. She's showing wear and tear and meanness and menopause. But major thrill—her admirers are buying her peanut-sized photos of peanut brains. I'm tired of my mother. Come on. To the attic."

"I'm thirsty."

"Check out her fridge, then."

"We shouldn't. It's not ours."

"Listen. She's a wino, just like Old Yeller. Gramps had Half-and-Half keeping the liquor cabinets filled every day, so that Lapdog and Nevelturd here could ransack at will."

I opened the fridge, pulled out a bottle of pissy-looking wine that had already been opened, and sniffed it.

"Pure gold, Trevor," I said. "Bristling. Tannic."

"Toxic."

"Scintillating. Suave."

"*Soave*. It sucks."

"So does life, Trev. Come on."

You could only get to the attic through a hall closet. A stepladder descended when you pulled the chain that opened the trap door. We both took a few swallows of wine before climbing up.

"What's the big deal about this attic?"

"You'll see."

"No, I won't. My glasses are steamed up. It's sweltering here."

After I made it to the top and was in, I reached down and took the bottle from Trevor, then helped him up the rest of the way. Trevor had that gaga look, like Mom's pinheads.

"Jesus, Jessie, it's like Xanadu! It's like that scene in *Citizen Kane* when you find out about Rosebud. Whose toboggan is this anyway? Oh, wow. A toboggan in Florida. Is that a *Kane* touch or what?"

"I don't know *Citizen Kane*. You're the total filmo."

"This is amazing. What's going to happen to this stuff?"

"Nothing. It all belongs to Half-and-Half. He can drool away up here, talk to the animals."

The amount of crap in the attic really was awesome, humongous. Empty dollhouses, stuffed animal heads that had gone bald, hundreds of prehistoric hatboxes piled up like stacks of Big Macs, a cruddy-looking rocking chair in need of paint, a wicker baby carriage, bicycles out of the Dark Ages, a battered red sign advertising Burma-Shave, whatever that was, antique chairs with all the springs and stuffing poking out of them, an old-fashioned radio as big as a jukebox, card tables loaded with ancient board games I'd never heard of, floor lamps with tassels and moldy shades, a birdcage, two Indian headdresses with ratty old feathers hanging on a coatrack along with a tuxedo that had lost all its sheen, a glass bowl full of old matchbooks, a sewing-machine table, a grimy-looking flute that turned out to be an Indian peace pipe, a saxophone case but with no saxophone, empty picture frames, a typewriter that must have been made around the time of the Civil War, some ugly china vases nearly as big as me, dozens of clodhoppery wooden shoe trees, two bags of ancient golf clubs, a batch of wooden tennis rackets in terrible shape. And that wasn't the half of it. Ten or more steamer trunks were lying around like coffins. And a few more were leaning against the wall like mummy cases. Vampires would have loved it up here.

"Did you bring the stakes?" I asked Trevor.

"Steaks? What steaks? I'm nearly fainting from the heat up here, and you want steaks? Isn't wine enough?"

That was the trouble with technoids like Trevor. Wax in the ears. Still, he had cute ears.

"Look, Jessie. A croquet set. Too bad we can't play. Maybe if the front lawn weren't full of mourners."

"Why don't we play? Now. Here."

"Don't be absurd. It's too hot. Besides, I don't think the wickets are going to sink into the floorboards like candles in a cake."

"Forget about wickets. We'll just go after each other's balls."

"Not mine you won't. Watch where you aim that thing."

I'd picked out a mallet already, and gave one of the balls a nice sock so that it scooted right between the old radio and one of the steamer trunks and managed to stay out of sight. Then Trevor hit his so that it snaked past the dollhouses and tried to come up on mine from behind. As soon as I saw it, I attacked. But I missed, damn it. Even though mine was still on the run, Trevor, the lucky bastard, nicked it with his.

"Scumbag," I said.

"I'm not through, Jessie. Now I get to send you."

This looked like fun. Even if he sent my ball hard, it couldn't go very far because there were too many obstacles on the floor. I could pounce after his fast and nail him.

"I am calling this croquet shot," he said. "My ball will stay under my shoe. Your pathetic ball will bank off the third green steamer trunk, narrowly missing the birdcage, and then disappear into the dusty Xanadu depths beyond the tuxedo."

"Hit it, Trev, okay?"

He swung the mallet back fiercely and, wouldn't you know, banged it into the wall, ruining his shot. I laughed. Plaster crumbled to the floor, and there was an ugly hole in the attic wall now. Then something fell on the floor. Trevor picked it up. It was a spoon, with a beautiful handle, an antique silver spoon. I stared at the hole. I heard a noise like rattling, like mice scurrying. Then a fork fell out. It was just as old, just as beautiful.

I took my mallet and hammered away at the hole until more plaster cracked. What was coming out was amazing. A Niagara of forks and knives and spoons. The wall had turned into a silverware slot machine. I reached into the hole and felt something like a beanbag. As I pulled it out the cloth ripped. What dribbled down my arms now was another kind of silver. Jewelry. Old dangly earrings with little red stones, some bracelets and pins and rings with the same kind of stones in them, a cameo ring, and a necklace that looked as though it were a piece of chain mail inlaid with dark purple stones as big as beetles. My God, I heard Trevor say, over and over. My God, my God, my God.

I wasn't dreaming. I hadn't spaced out. A wall had coughed up this loot.

And I knew exactly what we had to do, exactly. I trusted my fingers. My fingers were always right. They hadn't been itching this past hour for nothing.

"We need a fence," I said. "You know any vowels?"

Trevor looked like a wall. He didn't get it. Cute, but hollow.

"Vowels, Trevor. Luigi? Mario? Cocaine-O? Capisco?"

"Oh."

"A friendly gangster, a local connection, that's what we need, and fat chance we'll find him here. Trevor, Trevorino, we have to unload this stuff, all of it. I can't sneak any of it back with me on the plane, no way José, not with my snoop of a mother."

"Jessie, it's not ours."

"Yep. It's the wall's. Listen, Trev. Has anyone here been missing this stuff? Do you think Half-and-Half's been moping around the house all this time in secret mourning? 'Where's my missing flatware? where's my cameo brooch?' He's been missing for so long he doesn't miss anything. You know that. And Gramps has corked off. So he's not going to be grieving over the loss of a few soup spoons. Are you worried about the mice, Trevor? Have they been eating off fine sterling for the past century? Are we going to muck up their dinner parties now by running off with their place settings? Spiders, Trevor. You know any spiders who wear diamonds?"

"Shut up, Jessie. You've made your point. I'm not a feeb."

"No, just another mouse. The feebs are all downstairs. And most of them are on their way to the Alzheimer's ward. So why don't we hustle this stuff out of the house right now and cash it in while we can, while they're getting bombed?"

"Jessie, come off it. No store on Worth Avenue's going to open its doors to some thirteen-year-old girl carting in return merchandise like this. Do you honestly think some nice man at Van Cleef and Arpels is going to beam his eyes at you and say, 'Oh, I'm so sorry your poor mother has passed away and yes, oh yes, I see you're in charge of her estate and you want to sell some of her trinkets and spoons, because the stones are a little too dark for your complexion, and you prefer eating with your fingers, and of course I believe you, a foul-mouthed ninth-grader with a bag full of Victorian jewels and sterling silver, oh goodie, I'll write you a handsome check for them right now.' "

I liked Trevor when he talked like that. He got this gnarly, nasty look in his eyes. And his voice did a mean little dance, sort of glidey and stabbing. Like Michael Jackson. Like me.

"No, cutie," I said. "We're not going to P.B. We're going to West P.B."

"For what?"

"To play chess."

He got that wall look again.

"Pawns, Trevor. Pawnshops."

"I've never been in a pawnshop."

"Neither have I. You can tell me all about it after you've turned the silver into gold. My cousin the alchemist."

"Unh-unh, Jess. I'm not doing it. This is your idea."

"Oh yes you will do it. You're right, you know. I'm too young looking to get away with it. You aren't."

"I am too. I'm not even fifteen."

"You were growing a moustache already when you were eleven. And your voice changed at twelve. You look almost twenty right now. Over the hill. You must have been hot stuff back then, all that testosterone pumping away in sixth grade."

"You don't know anything."

"I know lots. Try me. Later. First things first. Now let's pack this dinnerware into something tidy and portable."

I had him under control. Separately we poked through the stockpile of Gramps's garbage. The trunks and suitcases were much too big and too heavy. We'd never pull off a smooth exit toting one of those out the house. We'd look like some scene from *I Dismember Mama*. The birdcage wouldn't do either. Its bottom had rotted out. The hatboxes weren't strong enough. The saxophone case was a possibility, but then we'd look like a scene from *The Untouchables*, and if Mom saw us she'd know something was up. I pried open one of the trunks, hoping there'd be some kind of strong, shoeboxy container inside. But there was only a stack of old curtains or lace tablecloths. A tiny grey spider beat a fast retreat as soon as it saw my hands. The trunk smelled weird, like mold and stale perfume at the same time. I pulled the top tablecloth out, shook it, and discovered it wasn't a tablecloth at all but a dress. Only some dippy southern girl could have gotten away with wearing it. Sleeves thin as tissue paper, a lacy top that looked like some dumb old doily, and hundreds of squashed little ribbons that stuck to the skirt like dead moths. It must have been a hundred years old at least. I was amazed it didn't disintegrate in my hands.

"Hey, Trevor. Take a look at this. 'White Wedding.' "

I held the dress up over my black number.

"Dream on, Jessie. The closest you'll ever get to Billy Idol is the poster in your bedroom."

"Fuck off, Trevor."

"Don't look so hurt. You're bulletproof. Hey, will this do?"

"What's the bottom like?"

"Intact. But I wouldn't try punching it with a croquet mallet."

The picnic basket Trevor had dug up had a flip top but no buckles or straps to hold any silverware or plates. A real Dark Age basket.

"The silverware'll clink," said Trevor.

"I'm aware of that. We can use Scarlett O'Hara's nightgown here to cushion the basket."

I stacked the large serving spoons together neatly, then the smaller ones, then the knives and forks, tucking them in between the folds of the dress so they wouldn't jiggle and slide around too much. Boys can't do anything like that gracefully, so I told Trevor to back off. I was probably a jerk to think he could be a smooth operator and sweet-talk some guy in a pawnshop. But then men were such bullshitters when they talked to each other about anything, maybe I didn't need to worry. Half-and-Half must have figured that out years ago, so that's why he closed down early. I folded the lacier half of the dress over the silverware and began arranging the jewelry on top of that.

"They really are beautiful," said Trevor. "Especially the necklace. Go on, Jessie. Try it on. Just this once. No one's going to know except us mice. Us spiders."

He smirked, like I was some dirty joke. I scowled at him.

"It's old-maid jewelry. I'm not an old maid like some people I know."

I stuck the rest of the jewelry in without looking at it. I didn't want to. What I wanted was to break Trevor's bones, all of them, and then jump them.

I picked up the basket, carefully, then jiggled it a little to see if anything rattled. It was heavier than I thought.

"Good bottom," I said to Trevor. "Like yours."

"Let's get this over with, Jessie. Now what? How are we

getting to West Palm Beach? Do we call a friendly cab providing pawnshop tours for out-of-towners or what?"

"We'll drive, bimbo."

"I can't drive. I don't know how. I don't even have a learner's permit yet."

"I can."

"You don't have a permit either, and you're way too young. When'd you learn how to drive?"

"This year. A boy taught me."

"Jesus. Does your mother know?"

"No. My mother is dumb. So is yours, Trevor. So are all mothers. Now let's go. Gramps has two or three cars in the garage. And he keeps duplicate keys to them and everything else on the pegboard in the kitchen."

"But someone downstairs might see us."

"Trevor, you are such a wimp, such a superween. Of course we'll bump into somebody, even in the kitchen. But we have business in the kitchen, you and I. We're going on a picnic, loading up the basket, leaving the grown-ups to moan and groan and mourn and guzzle. Just chill out, relax."

We made our way down from the attic, past the second-floor bedrooms, then down the main stairs. Trevor carried the basket but had to keep shifting it. It really was heavy.

"You're switching hands a lot, wimpo, my little vowel," I whispered.

"We're doing something crazy, Jessie. Wrong."

"Yes, I know. Why bother living if we don't? Besides, you love it, only you're too scared to admit it."

Some of the gloomy geriatrics were snoring upright on the sofas in the living room. I guess when you're eighty everything you sit on turns into a bed. I still couldn't get over Gramps's living room. It was about five times as big as our entire apartment in New York and maybe twice as large as our old place in Boston. Two fireplaces, three chandeliers, five sofas and about three times as many tables and chairs. The chairs were all French antiques with seats like whoopee cushions. The sort of chairs fat women always wanted to sit on and always wound up breaking. Some younger couples were picking up those tiny Chinese bowls that sat on the tables like ashtrays and were inspecting the bottoms. Probably deciding which ones to filch while the old farts dozed. Most of the guests were out on the front lawn, guzzling away, real bucketheads. Champagne for breakfast, for dinner, for weddings and now funerals. Life just gets pissed away anyway, so you might as well get high.

Trevor was heading the wrong way to the kitchen.

"This way," I said.

"No, I'm hungry."

He was already in the dining room before I could stop him. The caterers, I could see, had gone the whole nine yards. It was quite a spread. The food, though, had a slimy look to it. Salmon mousse, quivery gelatins, slabs of pâté, pasta salads that looked like mounds of yellow worms drowning in glue. Trevor was spearing breadsticks into the mousse.

"Come on, Trevor, we can eat later."

"I'm girding my loins, Jessie. I'm feeding literal hunger here, then we can feed your hunger for excitement. Just a few more breadsticks."

"I should have locked you in one of those trunks up there. No one would miss you the way no one misses Gramps."

Trevor's mom walked in through the kitchen door.

"What are you doing?" she asked. "We're not ready to serve yet. Trevor! My God, you've mussed up the mousse."

I giggled. It was hard not to. What a ditz she was.

"We're going to picnic on the beach," I said, ramming some breadsticks and rolls into the basket. Trevor's arm was wobbling. "We thought the grown-ups would want to be alone."

"Then why don't you come into the kitchen instead, and have one of the caterers wrap up some food for you instead of ruining the presentation."

She was smoothing down the salmon mound with a tiny knife.

"We will," I said. "We're on our way."

"Oh, Trevor," she said. Trevor gave me the basket. It weighed a ton. The breadsticks and rolls might as well have been dumbbells. I knew why Trevor had done this. He was daring me to hold on. He was hoping the basket would collapse or that I'd drop it.

"If I'm not here when you get back," she said, "I'll be at the Aqua Retreat Center."

"What's that?"

"It's where you go when you're feeling like I'm feeling now."

"Aqua Retreat?" said Trevor. "You mean you'll be in the shower."

She gave him that same look I'd given him up in the attic.

"Trevor, an Aqua Retreat is primarily a spiritual, not a liquid, oasis. I sit inside a large, dark, comfy cylinder which happens to be full of warm, soothing water, I listen to an audio which tells me how to erase my present difficulties, my grief as well as my anxieties. I am hypnotized, Trevor, and I become calm, as calm as I surely must have been before I came into this world howling. This is not, young man, quite the same thing as lounging by the swimming pool back home while listening to one's Sony Walkman tapes."

My arm was aching. Just then my mother walked in. Oh God, I had to set the basket down, had to.

She stared at the basket.

"Where are you going?"

"A picnic," I said.

"On the beach," said Trevor.

"Why?" asked my mother.

To get away. From this house, from you, from all of it.

"Why did he do this to us? What was the point? If you've lived as long as he has, why end it now? Why?"

She didn't see me. I was the trash can. She was yapping at Aunt Roo.

"We're not in our eighties yet, Dana. Maybe when we're his

age we'll feel exactly the same way. Tired, bored, addled, more willing to give in to the dark omega self. But I hope not. If he hadn't been so stubborn about his unwillingness to find peace while he was alive, I could have helped him. With crystals, or readings. Something."

"This happens precisely when I've begun to feel really good about myself again. He does this now. Just when I've started to succeed at something, to sell my work. Mother may have been right, you know. You remember how she said he'd destroyed Denis."

"By his not being there."

"Yes. And he's not here now."

"Dana, even when he was here he was never here. Something happened, something we know nothing about. He was never in touch with himself, or in touch the way we are."

"I will not allow Denis to have this house, I won't."

"You have no choice. Neither do I. Denis receives everything."

"He can't manage. He can barely talk, he's half-here."

"Half-here is more here than Father ever was. And Denis can talk, at last. Be grateful."

"I'll sue if I have to. I will, I will."

"You need to relax with me at Aqua Retreat."

Mother looked at me then, as though she finally remembered I was here, as though she were accusing me of having disappeared too. I had. I didn't know what she and my aunt meant about Gramps and Denis in the past. I didn't want to know. Trevor picked up the basket. Maybe he saw I needed rescuing.

"We'll be back soon," he said. "Come on, Jess."

"Do you have everything? Do you need silver?" his mother asked.

"No," said Trevor. "We have silver already."

Trevor steered me towards the kitchen. The caterers were stamping out rounds of bread, squeezing squiggles of cream cheese on each one, adding dollops of caviar, olives, pimentos. "The keys, Jess," Trevor whispered to me, "the keys." They dangled on the pegboard near the freezer like fishing lures. I flicked through them slowly, then took the two sets that were the most likely. I was coming back to my senses. I'd lost it a little, listening to my mother yammer. I'd fallen into a hole she dug. A black hole, an emptiness. I often did that. She asked too many "why" questions. Sometimes she asked them until she was bawling. And then she'd slap me around as though I was the reason things weren't working out for her.

We stepped around one of Gramps's boarders, the sculptress, on our way out the backyard. She was either drunk or asleep or lawn channeling. She'd find more inspiration in the living room. Old poops galore in there. We passed the swimming pool that was no longer a swimming pool. Gramps had dumped dirt into it, years ago, before I was born, then covered it with flagstones. I never knew why. Now it looked like the patio in "Father Knows Best." The diving board had been turned into a bench. A few pots of cornball geraniums were sitting there, gathering lizards.

The garage was a joy. Cool, cool at last. Why Gramps never air-conditioned the house was just another mystery.

"Will you look at that car!" said Trevor.

"What about it?"

"It's a Mustang."

"So what?"

"I think it's a '65. The primo year. God, it looks totally pristine. Pristine as in virginal."

"I bet. Let's see how far around the track it's gone."

I tried the first set of keys. None of them worked.

"It's too valuable to drive, Jessie. It's an antique now, a classic."

"Ah, Trevor, right. Too valuable. We'd better find a wheelbarrow instead, or something like a wheelbarrow, maybe that toboggan in the attic, to transport all this Tupperware we found.

Would you rather go in the other car? The one back there, behind you?"

He'd been so gaga over the Mustang he'd missed the other. Even I was scared of that one. It was as big as a stagecoach. Blue-grey, with big swoopy fenders. Otherworldly. Like something out of a Stephen King movie.

"What is it? A Packard?"

"You're the Trivial Pursuit freak, Trev. Come on, get in the 'stang."

"What's it doing there, Jess? Whose is it?"

"I don't know. Get in the 'stang."

"This garage needs airing out, Jess. Something smells in here."

"Get in the car!"

"Right."

As soon as we pulled out of the driveway, I checked the odometer.

"Hymen is missing," I said.

"Hyman who?"

"Sweet stuff, the car has been had. Eight thousand miles. We just don't know how many have had her."

"On a twenty-five-year-old car? Only eight thousand miles? Didn't Gramps ever drive a lot when he was younger? How did he get away with so little mileage? What did he do?"

"Lick hinges. If you're in the fast philately lane, you lick a lot of hinges. I don't think Gramps was ever fast, the other way. Who knows? Maybe Half-and-Half did all the driving."

We crawled through Palm Beach, which must be the only town in America where the dead are allowed to drive, so I didn't think any cop would make a stink out of a thirteen-year-old without a license. At least I could see, read stop signs, and reach the brake pedal in less than five minutes, unlike the ninety-year-old crock ahead of me. Stop signs were no different from go signs around here anyway, since the maximum speed was about two miles an hour. One thing about Palm Beach: it was clean. There wasn't a single trash barrel in sight anywhere. They were probably masquerading as fake baby palm trees sprouting along the sidewalk. Palm Beach was nothing but golf-crazy mummies, and squeaky-clean streets, and stuccoey white houses, whiter than powdered sugar or milk or death. Haciendas for millionaires on walkers.

Clean and superwhite. Where we were going was neither.

West Palm Beach looked like every trailer camp in America set end-to-end. Ratty scrunty houses with metal awnings and chicken-coop gardens. Dog-shitty hair salons, laundromats, scuzzy Greek restaurants, furniture stores full of lighting fixtures only lower-class vowels would buy, colon-irrigation clinics. While I drove, Trevor scouted the windows for pawnshop signs.

"I want us to hit a store where the pawnbroker's black," I said.

"Why?" said Trevor.

"Because he'll give you less trouble."

"You don't think much of me, do you? Even though I'm the one who got us out of the house. You don't think I can carry the load from my end at all, do you?"

"Yes I do. Only you'll be less scared of blowing it if I can make sure you're scared shitless for some other reason."

"So I'm both a chicken and a racist. Thank you kindly."

"We're all a little chickenshit and racist, Trev. There's one. You weren't watching. I'll park up there. You don't need to wear out your arm with the basket. Just check out the personnel."

He was back in a jiffy. "Sorry," he said. "Nothing but Archie Bunkers."

We stopped by two more. They didn't look right either. Trevor was in and out in a flash. I was starting to have doubts now about the whole venture. I also wanted to look at that necklace more closely, here, in the sunlight. No way would my mother leave me anything like that when she corked off. She hadn't worn lipstick in over four years now, and she never wore any jewelry. Except for that dumb turquoise wedding ring, which she should have pitched when she got rid of Daddy.

The next pawnshop was right on the mark. Trevor said the pawnbroker looked like Denzel Washington and talked like Clint Eastwood. There was only one customer in the store, an old geezer pawning a chain saw.

"Our day is made," I said.

"Yes," said Trevor. "We're about to be massacred."

"Now remember, whatever his first offer is, tell him no dice, no way. Bargain, ask for more. Tell him it's not enough. Tell him you have a growing family, mouths to feed. A five-year-old dweeb of a son, just like his daddy, who wants a computer for Christmas. Feed him a line, Trevor."

"Wisemouth, you do this. You're the dealer, you're the pusher."

"Come on, Trev. We're going to be rich for a day, and with no sweat, no wheel to spin, no geeky trivia questions to ask. I bet we walk off with a thousand dollars. Easily. These are heirlooms, family heirlooms. They have to be worth something—why would they have been walled up? Forget about how weak you are. Try being tough. Pretend you're Rambo. You look more like him than I do. I'm the one who's the shrimp."

"Jessie, let's drive home. This is crazy. You're crazy."

"Trevor, you look at me. You look at me now. You're no different from me, really. No different at all. Look at us, look at this family. You've got a father who sells joke-shop crap for a living and a mother who sits in some giant soup can full of hot water and talks to her navel. I've got a father who should be locked up in either jail or a nuthouse and a mother who photographs pinheads and calls her work 'ground-breaking, seismic.' Wake up, Trevor. The earthquake's over. Long over. They didn't even hear it. But it happened. And we're the ones that fell through the cracks and got squashed. Just like Half-and-Half."

He seized the basket and got out of the car. He was halfway to the pawnshop when I remembered.

"Trevor!" I shouted. "The necklace. Take it out."

I saw him fish it out of the basket.

"Put it in your pocket. Hold on to it."

"Why?" he shouted back.

"You're right. It's too nice."

He slid it into his pocket.

"Step lively, handsome. Score one for Miss Jessie."

I saw him grin. There was an imp in Trev. Maybe the quake hadn't totally creamed us. Once he saw how much fun this was I could maybe turn him into a thief for real, if he'd stay here longer.

In a few hours the afternoon would be dead. So would my freedom. Then it was back to Mama, back on the leash.

Trevor'd been gone now for some time. I was getting depressed again. The car was starting to piss me off. It was a great car, and I wondered who in my family was going to luck out and get it. Half-and-Half didn't deserve everything.

Then I saw Trev coming down the sidewalk, swinging the picnic basket around his head. It was obviously lighter.

"How much?" I asked him when he got in the car.

"Good enough."

"How much?"

"I thought he'd kill me. I told him I had this terrific stuff to pawn, and then the first things I pulled out were the damn breadsticks."

"How much, Trevor?"

"Two hundred. He wouldn't take the dress."

"You hopeless loser. You were always a loser."

"Don't you believe me?"

"Let me see. Give."

He handed over the bills.

"Nice, Trevor. Nice. Fifty-dollar bills. So easy to change in any drugstore."

I unbuttoned the front of my dress, stuffed the money in my brassiere, then pulled back out onto Dixie Highway.

"This car really is old, Jess. No air-conditioning. Where are we going?"

"You'll see. I'm running the show now."

Two hundred dollars. I could've lifted that from the purses back at Gramps's.

"We should get back, Jessie. Someone might miss the car."

"Don't worry. My mother's probably scouting the guests for exciting new deformities she can photograph. And yours is in a hot tub somewhere hearing voices."

I was looking for a video arcade. There had to be one. This stretch of Dixie was nothing but discount stores and crappo fast-food joints like Arby's. The bad kids had to go somewhere besides the shiny new malls. Then I spotted one, and parked.

"This time I'm going in."

"What for? What are you getting?"

"High, Trevor. Very high, after this sudden nickel-and-dime low. You just sit tight."

"Jessie!"

He stayed in the car. I saw some black dudes in spandex racing shorts hanging out in the parking lot behind the arcade. Next to the arcade was a boarded-up Pizza Hut and beside that a runty shack penned in by a cyclone fence, like it was some rabid outhouse. Florida, the jungle paradise, the new Eden. This place looked about as good as any to cop a bag.

There were the usual wasteland types at the machines, studs in their ears, popcorn for brains, feeding nonstop quarters to Donkey Kong. There weren't any girls. I was looking for someone who wasn't with anyone, someone totally alone. He'd have his eyes on the stoners, sort of, but he wouldn't be obvious. You could always find them, though, because of that look. Their clothes never gave them away. Only the look.

The one I drew a bead on was leaning against the dollar-changing machine near the rear door. He was white and skinny. He needed a tan. He looked a little dumb and more than a little mean. I could tell that from his T-shirt. It was black and had "fuck" phrases printed all over it. Fuck Fast Food. Fuck Therapy. Fuck Girl Scout Cookies.

"What do you have?" I asked him.

"Dime bag, nickel bag, mesc, acid, crack."

"How about some really excellent grass?"

"Sure. But it costs. A hundred bucks, two ounces. That's two, babe, not two and a half."

"I'll take two bags. That's four ounces. I can add."

"Let's see the money."

I knew why I'd turned my bra into a change purse and had left the top of my dress unbuttoned. Trevor didn't. The creep managed to sneak a look while I fished for the bills.

"Here," I said. I pulled out the money.

"Lemme see."

"No," I said. "Not until I see what you have."

I smiled a little. His complexion was terrible. He had a face like a termite colony. I figured some tough flirting, though, would speed things up.

"Wait here," he said.

A rendezvous, no doubt, with one of the cars in the back lot. Then maybe a hit and some high-fiving with the clients back there. I waited. When he came back he gave me two wadded-up sandwich bags. Inside each was a fat green cigar.

"Don't tuck 'em in the same place now," he said. "Not much room left in there."

"I haven't any choice."

He folded the bills neatly and stuck them in his rear pants pocket. Then he followed me back to the car. I could see Trevor didn't know whether he should roll up the car window or start screaming.

"Trevor," I said, "meet Prince Alexis Du Merde."

I got into the car. The creep leaned over Trevor's window. Trevor was trying to melt into his seat.

"You her pimp?" the guy said, and laughed.

"We're late, Jessie."

"Hey, Jessie," said the guy, "is your car for sale too? Or is it your daddy's?"

"My uncle's," I said. I started the motor.

"Looks real cherry to me. Real cherry. Hey, if you want to sell it, come on back. I got a buyer. You know who I am now. Ask for Billy Raw." He winked at me. Too bad his complexion was the pits. "Here's a little something for you and your pimp." Two vials with orange caps landed in Trevor's lap. Trevor looked as if his cock had just been bitten by a tarantula.

I knew what they were.

"Fantastic car, Jessie. Fan-tas-tic. Bye, Jessie."

After I U-turned I could see him in my rearview mirror, scuttling away like a cockroach.

"Give them to me," I said to Trevor, before he threw them out the window.

They joined the sandwich bags. I'd become the picnic basket now.

"What'd you do?"

"I paid through the nose, but it looks good."

"How much money is left?"

"*Rien,* Trevor. *Nada.*"

"You bitch. Half of that was my money. I'm the one who got that money for us."

At the next stoplight I stared him down.

"Trevor," I said, "I'm a junkie. I like grass. A lot. I don't like life. You get to fly back west tomorrow or the next day, but I'm stuck down here for at least another week with my mother, and living with her is murder. She's a walking downer. She didn't used to be, but she sure is now. I hope I never wind up like her, never. My father was king of the rats, for sure, and I'm so fucking glad he's no longer around. But when he got booted she turned into this depressed zombie bitch. It's depressing down here, Trev. I don't happen to like death very much either, or mommies who are angry because they've gotten the shaft. I got shafted long before Mommy, and so this is how I deal with it. I drink. I steal things. I drive somebody else's car. I lie. And I get stoned out of my mind."

Trevor shut up. When we got back to Gramps's it was as though we'd never left. The driveway was still choked with cars. Nobody wanted to walk out on all that free champagne and salmon glop, even if it was somebody's funeral. Trevor was right about the garage. It stank. Probably some dead squirrel in there somewhere.

We snuck back through the kitchen so I could rummage up some matches and something for papers. Through the dining room window I could see Mom out on the front lawn. She was standing apart from the others, staring at the ocean, waving her champagne glass around as though she were directing some orchestra in the sky. She didn't look drunk. She looked sad and lost. The old farts in the living room had departed. Maybe they'd fallen asleep in their limos, or else had called cabs to cart them off to beddy-bye. Or maybe hearses, so they could get in a dry run.

"This is where it happened," I told Trevor. We weren't supposed to go in his bedroom, but what the hell. Nobody'd locked the door.

The weird furniture in Gramps's room wasn't at all like the horsehair stuff downstairs. There was a goofy lamp on the table near the bed that looked like a bouquet of stained-glass toadstools. Gramps's bed sure wouldn't win over the futon crowd. The headboard and foot were these slabs of shiny yellow wood in the shape of gravestones, or pancakes sawed in half. The wood had a sticky gleam to it, like it had been dunked in maple syrup. The bedspread was some sort of speckled animal skin. Most of the wood in the room was orangy, cantaloupe colored. Gramps's desk—where he did it, Mom said—had an ebony top shaped like a spread-out fan, but its legs were totally oddball, sort of like wrought-iron bicycle wheels or hula hoops. Most of the metal chairs and side tables were things some lunatic orthodontist might have dreamed up. There was a folding screen with silhouettes of cranes or ostriches or some giraffe-necky birds carved out of bronze, but you could see right through them. The stupid screen had no backing. It would have looked a whole lot better laid out flat on a sidewalk, like a fancy subway grate. Too bad there weren't any subways in Florida. The weirdest thing in the room was this tacky sculpture that was half stained glass, half rusty pipes, as though the artist had gotten bored halfway through the piece and decided to finish it off fast with whatever junk was lying around. I'd call it *Woman in Dingy Hoopskirt, Raising Her Arm Like Midtown Traffic Cop*. She was wearing a string of pearls around her waist instead of a billy club. Too bad we hadn't stopped in here before. The pearls were probably detachable. Trevor could have bartered them for a licorice stick.

"Wow," said Trevor. "This is like a set from a Fred Astaire movie."

"Gramps never danced in his life."

"Jessie, these things are worth a whole lot more than what we just pawned, believe me. This is all Art Deco. Real Art Deco."

"Oh yeah? And do you think Billy Raw could help us unload a really hot table lamp and this chair that looks like melted coat hangers? Art Deco, Art Drecko. Let's go get high."

I shooed him out the bedroom door and we headed back up to the attic. I dug the stuff out of my bra, knelt on the floor, and rolled some joints while Trevor was wiping off his glasses. Then I took off my dress and wrapped everything in it, including the vials.

"Jesus, Jessie, what are you doing?"

"I'm hot, Trevor. It's hot up here. You make me hot. Here."

I passed him a lighted joint. He coughed at first, then relaxed.

"Take off your clothes," I said.

"What for?"

"You know why."

I'd shucked my shoes, bra, and panties.

"It's dirty up here."

"There are old curtains and things in one of those trunks. Don't worry."

"Jessie, I'm your cousin."

"And you're a virgin."

He started laughing. Good, I knew it was great stuff. I could tell after just two tokes.

"Let me help you."

He barely moved while I undressed him. He still had his glasses on. I shook out one of the old tablecloths that had been packed in that trunk I'd opened, laid it on the floor, took off his glasses, and then drew him down on top of me.

"Am I in?"

"Like Flynn, as my mother says, whatever that means."

His eyes went a little buggy. He laughed some more, then became very intense, not at all nerdy. Something almost happened in me, but not quite. When it was over he put on his underwear.

"You were, weren't you?" I said.

"So? You aren't, but so what? I'm not going to get anything, am I?"

"No. The only other guy I've slept with was safe. He made sure. Though his wife didn't."

"He was married?"

"Yes, Trevor. Then he left his wife, and I was thrilled. Because I knew he'd have to leave me too."

"Oh Christ, Jessie, why didn't you stop him? Why didn't you scream or something?"

"And wake up Mother?"

He'd stopped laughing. He was nearly all dressed except for his shoes. The high hadn't lasted very long for me either. Maybe we'd been gypped.

"Where's the basket, Trevor? Where's that old dress?"

He scooted it across the floor. I pulled out the dress. I thought at first it would be too small for me, but it wasn't. I could feel its crepeyness, the open eyelets on my skin, the moth holes. It felt ghostly.

"Where's the necklace, Trevor? Let me wear the necklace now."

He'd moved away from me. He was standing near the attic door.

"I don't have it."

"What do you mean?"

"I pawned it," he said. "And it's a good thing I did. You spent my share of the other money and squandered it, like the dope fiend you are, like the dope you are."

"You crumb, you shithead. What'd he give you?"

"Enough. I even threw in the breadsticks since he was so generous."

"I wanted that necklace."

"No you didn't. You just want to mess around and get stoned and die."

"Go jump off a bridge, Trevor. Please go jump off a bridge and drown."

The attic door slammed shut. I started to cry. He wasn't any fun anymore, none of it was any fun anymore. I was just like my mother after all. Crying over nothing, over everything, a real loser. Men were going to walk out on me too. I looked like Emily Dickinson in this dumb dress, another real loser.

I wiggled out of it, tossed it back in the trunk. Then I smoked another joint to calm down. I wondered if the rocking horse would hold my weight. It looked so forlorn, so out of it up here. There weren't any children anymore in this house. There weren't any children anywhere. They were all like me. Daddy's girls at eight, potheads at ten. I tried on one of the Indian headdresses. The feathers were in really bad shape. I didn't care. I hoped the pipe still worked. I emptied one of the vials, tamped the little rock into the pipe, and lit up. The rocking horse smiled. Giddyap, it said, giddyap, I can go fast as the wind if you trust me. I settled into its lap, into all the ghosts in the attic. I rode the horse like I was Lady Godiva. It didn't really go fast, but I was speeding now so it didn't matter, nothing mattered. Tomorrow I'd sell the Mustang to Billy Raw and nobody would know. Tomorrow I'd buy back that necklace from the pawnbroker, and *screw Trevor*, but I'd never do that again. Tomorrow and tomorrow and tomorrow were going to be crackerjack days for sure.

Giddyap.

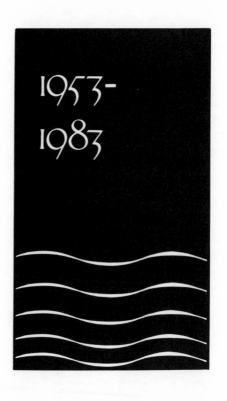

1953-
1983

"**N**o," he said. "No. I just can't."

She lay there naked, like Goya's Duchess of Alba, stretched out upon John's old davenport which he'd covered with a pink woolen blanket and then a sheet—but she could still feel the springs beneath her, threatening to lurch through the fabric and jab. She was all of nineteen.

He took the canvas off the easel.

"You're very beautiful, Dana, and we both know it. But I want you to come back to me when you're forty. I want to paint you then. Then you will own your bones, your face. When you've become whatever it is you're meant to be. Besides, I might treat you unkindly now. Turn you into a de Kooning hag."

"You wouldn't," she said, putting her slip back on.

"No. But I'd make you harder than you really are."

And now she was nearly forty, and every time she thought of "now" she saw the letters switch places, turn into "own," and she no longer knew what she owned anymore—certainly not money, certainly not her children—but whatever it was she'd once had had shrunk, the way the letters in "own" could shrink to two letters, one word, to "no," to all the things she'd said no to, and to all the things she should have said no to but didn't.

Though there was still, at forty, time.

To say no to no.

∎∎ ∎∎ ∎∎

She had been bounced from college at eighteen and had been too stunned by her dismissal to even protest. Her freshman-year roommate, a glum, overweight science major named Penelope whose major thrills were provided by larvae, had gossiped mightily and wrongly to the dean about Dana and her French professor. She had seen the French professor bending too closely towards Dana when the two talked in the halls. Their shoulders sometimes touched. The professor had even taken Dana's arm occasionally, when they walked across campus. She knew that Dana visited the professor often at home, and that professors didn't usually hold office hours at home. The professor's name was Ariadne Meyer; she was a handsome woman, in her mid-forties, given to wearing tweed suits in heather tones. When Dana looked back at that *coup de foudre* in her life, she realized that Dr. Ari probably had been interested in her in another way. But all Dana had been worked up about was French literature, especially *les poètes maudits*. When she visited with Dr. Ari, it was only to pick her brain, to plead for further *explications de texte*. No sooner had she finished what she thought was a triumphant essay on Rimbaud than she was hauled in before the dean and told that the university did not countenance lesbian affairs and that she would have to pack her bags. Dr. Ari resigned the next day, though she apologized to Dana for the harm she had caused. But Dana felt far more concern for Dr. Ari than for herself. After all, she was only eighteen, and her future had yet to take shape, was still an endless vista of terraces to climb. Dr. Ari's academic career had been leveled, as well as perhaps her other life. "Well, I understand Rimbaud a lot better now," Dana told her. "His *long, immense et raisonné dérèglement de tous les sens*. His disorder at least paid off for him."

The dean informed her parents that there had been "boy trouble" and promised Dana that nothing on her academic record would attest to the real reason for her departure. But Dana didn't believe her. When she told her parents, she acceded to the dean's polite lie. Her father tried to cheer her by telling her that life was never so crushing as when you were young. Her mother moaned a little about ruined hopes and reiterated her warning that men were to be as little trusted as women. Dana wept once—after she'd packed most of her clothes and books in the steamer trunk. The day after she'd shipped them to Florida she left college for good, but not without exacting a little revenge. She waited until her roommate had gone out to dinner. Then she ripped up her roommate's first major term paper for history plus all her lab reports, burned them in a wastebasket in the bathroom, and sprinkled the ashes over her roommate's sheets. "Ashes to ashes" she wrote in lipstick on the pillow slip.

She'd told her parents she planned to spend a few days by herself, saying goodbye to friends before she returned to Florida. What she actually did was hop a cab to mid-Manhattan with her one small suitcase of clothes, check in at the Biltmore Hotel, bathe and change into a little black dress and choker, and then take a taxi over to an apartment on Sutton Place so she could attend a party where a few other Barnard girls she knew would probably show up.

She got very high on martinis. The party had clearly moved from cocktail hour to dinner hour with no change in the menu. Few of the men were leaving. She assumed the older ones, the ones in their thirties or forties, were married. She told one handsome man with greying temples that she'd been out of college a year and was job-hunting. He gave her his card and told her to call him, but she could tell he'd had even more to drink than she. He kept calling her Diane. She didn't have to worry about lying. None of her friends had turned up after all. Most of the women seemed to be glorified file clerks or glorified receptionists or both. She would move from one cluster of people to another, using an empty glass as the prop to extricate herself if she got bored. Sometimes she would just stare out the windows at the mother lode of city lights, the midnight star food.

"My God, you're pretty."

The man who spoke to her was a dazzler. His slick black hair gleamed. His white shirt was almost lustrous, metallic. He wore a crisp blue suit and a dusky red tie with tiny polka dots.

"Who are you?" he asked.

"Don't you know?" she said. "I'm a lesbian."

"I don't believe it."

"Neither do I."

By the time Tyler Morrison pulled her away from the martinis and took her out to dinner, she had already figured out she would not be sleeping at the Biltmore that night. By the time she announced to him a month later that although she wasn't a lesbian she was indeed very much pregnant, she had also figured out he would probably marry her. By then she had owned up to her age and her aborted year at college. She had also owned up to her trust fund.

Tyler was not hungry for her money, only for her. He had never gone out with someone quite so raffish and gorgeous, nor with anyone who could give terrific blow jobs. Well-connected, sharp-tongued, ambitious, he'd landed a copyediting job at Random House his first year out of Yale and knew that, in time, that would lead to a job where he'd be choosing the copy, not red-penciling it. His parents were not exactly overjoyed by his choice of bride. Her mother, at least, was relieved that her grandchild would have a last name. The wedding was held under a canopy tent in Connecticut rather than Florida. Tyler was the one with friends, not Dana. What she remembered most from the wedding were the excesses: the pummeling of rice, kernels of which lodged in her ear; her mother's outrageous hat, which had no competition save for the canopy tent; and the playful but not so genial taunt she tossed at her sister. "The only way you can one-up me now is to elope at sixteen."

Tyler was loath at first to give up his one-bedroom apartment on Fifty-second Street. Dana had to convince him that a bassinet might not sit well on top of his rolltop desk. She preferred to live near the Village, where she could walk to coffeehouses, listen to poetry like Rimbaud's. So he found a much larger apartment on Perry Street—only it was a sixth-floor walk-up. But once she gave birth not to one child but to identical twin daughters, she found the last thing she wanted to do was feed two howling babies while sipping espresso.

When she was six she had told her mother she wanted to be a ballerina. When she was ten she gave a performance for just her family in the cavernous living room in Florida. Her father and mother and the maid had moved all the antique sofas and chairs out of the way, all of the tables and vases, so she could do grands jetés. The marble floor was as slick as a mirror. She could see reflections from the chandeliers sparkling under her feet. Roo made fun of Dana's tutu, and tried to get Denis to laugh with her, until her father quieted both of them. And then she danced—for nearly eight minutes—to both sides of her mother's 78 of "Selections from *Swan Lake*," until one of her toe shoes cracked and she tumbled. She expected Roo to laugh, but she didn't. Only Denis giggled. Her mother raced over to help her up. Her ankle ached. Her father then carried her to one of the sofas. "That was a lovely, lovely dance," he said. "Just marvelous." She was crying, but not because of her ankle. She had forgotten what it was like to be held by her father, forgotten if her father had ever held her like that before. It was Denis who had swung in his arms for the past four years.

At thirteen she knew that what she'd wanted at six she wanted now even more. She had seen *The Red Shoes*. She was in love with Moira Shearer. She wanted to be just as good, if not better. Her teacher, Mrs. Roumanski, had once danced in Europe but now lived in Florida because of her emphysema. "Never give up, never give up," she rasped to Dana. "Once you give up the dream, once you ever stop dancing, these toe shoes—they will lance your heart. They will be like ice picks in your eyes. Believe me, dearest."

Now, at nineteen, she was a mother, trotting, not dancing, up five flights of stairs several times daily, carrying babies that were as heavy as water jugs. Sometimes, in the early morning, after Tyler had gone to work, after she'd dressed the girls and then put on their tiny pink booties, she would poke through the bottom drawer of her dresser, and pull out her crinkled toe shoes and stare at them, and wonder what had happened to her plans, knowing that what had happened was life, that humdrum dream-killer—and then she would tuck the shoes back under the jumble in the drawer, the way she'd pressed roses from her bridal bouquet between the pages of Baudelaire, knowing there might come a time, thirty, forty years hence, when she would pull them out by accident and not at all remember having put them there, or what they were doing there or in her life, or had ever done, and would ask, in all honesty and confusion: *What are these?*

■■　■■　■■

By the time she was twenty-one their marriage was like their record player: no longer working well. Instead of bringing his work home with him, he would stay at the office. She could no longer tell whether it was her he wanted to avoid or his daughters. Sometimes she fantasized the girls did not belong to her, that she'd never hatched them, that they were someone else's. Soon after the howling stage, they had settled into an abnormal quiet. She would catch them playing with stubby pencils, as though they were trying to get a leg up on their father, preparing already to be junior editors. They even resembled him physically far more than they did her. Occasionally he'd play with them, tap his fingers on their bellies as though he were testing cakes. But he left the major drudgery for her. When she wasn't walking or changing or patrolling them, she would read, burying herself in novels like *Jean-Christophe* and *Le Rouge et le noir*.

Probably he was seeing other women, though she had swum off all the extra weight she'd put on when she was pregnant, though she still gave Audrey Hepburn a run for her money in the looks department. But it was the Oriental carpet that did in her marriage, not the other women. She had entreated him to go shopping with her one Saturday, to help her pick out a large rug for their living room. The throw rugs weren't enough; both girls had gotten splinters from crawling around the mostly bare floors. She could afford the rug, she wanted it. In a Fifth Avenue emporium they watched, patiently, while rug after rug was unrolled. Finally, Tyler pointed to one he liked—invariably blue and red—and two men in the store neatly wrapped it up for them and carted it to the door. "Now what do we do?" said Tyler. "I guess we should have them deliver it," said Dana. One of the men told her the store didn't make Saturday deliveries. "Oh, great," said Tyler. "Am I supposed to carry this home on the subway?" He dragged the rug out to the sidewalk. Pedestrians awkwardly dodged the rug, him, Dana, the girls in their stroller. "It's heavier than a corpse, and it's going to kill me carrying it. Great, great, great. Jesus—I've married a beautiful dummy, and now I've got this beautiful dumb rug on my hands." He glowered at Dana. "This was your idea. This is your rug. I can't stand this. You take care of it." "Tyler!" she screamed. But he'd already vanished. She screamed again; she didn't care if she looked like some crazy woman. She was stuck now, stranded in the middle of the sidewalk, with an immovable rug and two sullen kids. Cab drivers looked right through her or shook their heads no. Fortunately, there was a phone booth ahead of her. She wheeled the stroller up about a yard, parked it, then kept her eye on it while she dragged the rug up to the stroller. No one stopped to help her, but she understood that. That was New York. When she got to the phone booth, she planted one foot on the rug, one hand on the stroller, and called John, praying he was home. He was; he told her he'd borrow a car from a friend and come for her. She kept hoping Tyler would float back into sight, ashamed, remorseful, so she could punch him, spit at him. Then she called her sister at college and reversed the charges. "You sound hysterical," Roo said. "What's wrong?" "I am hysterical," said Dana. "Tyler's left me, and you won't believe where or how." "Are you going to go after him?" "Impossible." "Well, don't be an idiot and roll out the red carpet for him when he comes back. You'll get into worse trouble. Like Mom." "You needn't worry

about that. The carpet's rolled up, and besides, it's mostly blue."
Then she burst into both laughter and tears.

John stuffed the rug into the backseat of the borrowed car.
The stroller took up most of the front seat. She sat in the rear, on
the rug, with the girls. When they got back to the Village, she
parked the girls in the lobby and helped John lug the rug upstairs.
"Don't you want to take the girls upstairs first?" he said. "Someone
might take them." "I don't care," said Dana. "Let them be kid-
napped. Whoever wants them is welcome to them." When the
rug was finally in place and the girls were straitjacketed in their
cribs, she asked John the other, harder question: Could she stay
with him, for a few days, until she found a lawyer? The divorce
turned out to be rocky and took a year. She retained custody of
the children; Tyler retained custody of the rug. She never wore
the black dress and choker again. She never wanted to live in New
York again. On her last day in the city she sat in a Bleecker Street
coffeehouse and listened to a bad beat poet read while his girlfriend,
who looked like a vampire, strummed a guitar and screeched. For
once she did not mind that her children were with her. Someone
else's howl had surpassed theirs.

■■   ■■   ■■

A year later, in September, on a beach in Wellfleet, she met Leon.
The money her father had tucked away for her until she was twenty,
nearly ninety thousand dollars, had allowed her to drift and would
continue to sustain her and her kids, even without Tyler's hit-or-
miss child-support-payment checks. Yet she did not want to count
on it too much. She knew it would eventually run out, if she
didn't get a job of some sort. And she didn't want to be one of
those drifty, feather-duster girls, now or ten years down the line,
one of those trust-fund babies who puttered at floral and place-
card arrangements in their twenties, only to putt golf balls in their
sixties.

She could count on very little these days; all the goodness in life seemed to have caved in like a fallen cake. Tyler was being a bastard about visiting the girls, but Tyler had nothing to do with the malaise she was feeling. There was no one to talk to. Roo was absorbed in some honors project on Goya and had no time for sympathy. Denis was too young.

She had rented a cottage from the daughter of one of her mother's Palm Beach cronies, who'd decided to acquire her tan that summer in Marbella rather than Wellfleet. The beach was relatively private, confined to the owners, houseguests, and renters occupying the nearby cottages and large homes. Once in a while, someone on a horse would canter by, stirring up the surf, conjuring up Errol Flynn fantasies in the middle-aged women who squirmed like marooned porpoises in their rickety lounge chairs. Then the horseman would dismount, and the fantasy would die fast. Just another middle-aged granite-face, far less handsome than the horse. She read a lot, hoping she would tire of reading and that her fatigue would bestir her into action. It hadn't happened. When she wasn't reading for the pleasure of numbing herself, she was reading to the girls; it passed the time, and maybe a few new words got kicked into their skulls. She was no good at making sand castles. Her father had been so extraordinarily adept at sand castles that she had done nothing but watch, unwilling to risk adding a parapet even when he urged her to, for fear the castle would collapse. It was clumsy Roo who always found some way to upheave a crucial wall by accident. Those differences between her and Roo had often led to contentiousness. And that contentious blood, she feared, had been passed down to her girls. They constantly yammered at each other and fought. Sometimes they'd chase each other on the beach, shrieking, threatening to drop hermit crabs down each other's swimsuits. When their screams were too shrill, she would have to haul them from the water's edge and plant shovels in their hands. When she thought seriously of what the next two years would be like, the next five, picking them up all the time and picking up after them all the time and watching them conspire against her as a team nearly every minute, she could see nothing ahead but a weighty, endless sadness, bleak and turbulent as the ocean.

The beach was slightly less populated now that August had died. She noticed fewer of the grizzled-looking men with the spindly shanks, and their female counterparts, taut as clothespins. The bulky people continued to bring down their beach chairs, picnic baskets, and miniature larders. She'd noticed one couple all summer long who did not fit into either group. The man, who was probably in his early forties, was decently built, though a little soft around the belly. He had a beard and moustache which masked half of his face but which made him look somewhat magisterial, as if, from neck above, he were grooming himself for a portrait. The woman was considerably older. She looked like Ethel Barrymore, especially around the eyes. She had a puffy, valentine face, but the stern forehead and the lips that were much too thin canceled out any impression of sweetness. Dana assumed they were just one more of those couples where the older woman had the man by the balls. He, at least, still had the balls. She could see them. The woman, she figured, had the money.

When she walked past them again on what must have been her two hundredth retrieve-the-wagons-by-the-surf trip, the man finally spoke to her.

"Why don't you sit down with us?" he said. "The wagons won't run away. And you look as if you've lost your best friend."

"I haven't," she said.

"Sit, sit," said the older woman. "Tell us all about yourself. We want to know everything, everything. Your children are a pleasure to behold, like my son's. Only they, unlike my son's, are in need of far more control in their lives. Reasonable limits can be apprehended, even at such a young age. They can, they can."

His name was Leon Arpee. His mother urged her to call her by her first name, Florence. He was an American-history professor at Northeastern in Boston. "And the only Marxist critic whom they did not dare deny tenure to," added Florence. His children, an eight-year-old boy and a six-year-old girl, were spending the summer with their mother, whose family had a farm in Vermont.

Dana told them she was divorced and vacationing. She did not tell them she had been vacationing for over a year. Florence had poured her a glass of what looked like red Kool-Aid. For months Dana had been making Kool-Aid for the girls and was sick of it. The cranberry cooler, or whatever it was she was now drinking, wasn't much better, even though it was tart.

"I suppose most people have left now because school's begun," said Dana.

"Oh, no," said Florence. "The patients are calling—they are so angry, so helpless, they cannot function, cannot grow unless they are shrunk."

"Shrunk?"

"The psychiatrists," said Leon. "They always vacate their offices in the city come August, then retire to their summer homes down here."

"And analyze each other from their lounge chairs. They are like cannibals, believe me, aren't they, Leon? Or like goats. They will eat anything. Money, especially, they love to eat."

"Quite true. They're an unappetizing bunch. Too overweening for my taste, too garrulous as well. And often downright stupid. You will have to forgive Florence. A Veblenesque gorge always rises to her throat whenever they hover too near us."

"What do you mean—Veblenesque?"

"Dear," said Florence, "where did you go to school?"

"I didn't," said Dana. "I was thrown out. For inciting too much arousal."

"I see," said Florence. "Better arousal, certainly, than boredom. Do we have a copy of Veblen in the cottage, Leon?"

"Thorstein Veblen's *The Theory of the Leisure Class*. It's one of the classic texts. A first-rate critique of the excesses of the rich, by one of the shrewdest minds I know. An apocalyptic book for its time, too. I'll see that a copy's in your hands tomorrow. We've noticed that you read a great deal."

"I just finished rereading *Madame Bovary*," she said. She actually had, only that was three weeks ago. She was not sure she wanted to broadcast her reading assignments for the past few weeks. *Peyton Place*. The new, unexpurgated version of *Lady Chatterley's Lover*. And a trashy paperback about vampires called *I Am Legend*.

"Flaubert may fool some critics into thinking he is no 'Decadent,' " said Florence, "but he does not fool me. You know, of course, that he would allow his servant to speak to him only once a week and to say only one thing: '*Monsieur, c'est dimanche.*' The degree to which one starves one's workers is the degree to which one feeds one's own excessive vanity, is that not so, Leon?"

"Empty stomachs, empty heart."

"Words, words—Flaubert robs his servant even of words. Only on Sunday does he not go starving."

"In a manner of speaking."

"Emma Bovary. Now Mr. Veblen would have something to say about her, wouldn't he?"

She let the two of them natter on, occasionally interjecting a remark, careful to avoid any allusions to eating. When she saw the girls about to embark on a shovel-throwing duel, she made her apologies, told them it was nice chatting, and took off to drag the girls back home and muzzle them. Near dinnertime she realized they'd once again left their wagons on the beach, so she went back to retrieve them. Leon was still there, packing up his larder. She could see his mother, waist-deep in the water, wobbling like a bowling pin.

"Is your mother safe out there?" she asked.

"She's a capable swimmer."

"Capabilities she isn't short on, that's for sure."

She thought he might frown, but instead he was smiling.

"I've been watching you a lot this summer," he said.

"Why didn't you say something before?"

"I was nervous. Cautious. Maybe uncertain of my own capabilities. You're quite beautiful. You know who you resemble, in fact?"

"Yes, I know. Audrey Hepburn. Except not in the boob department."

"Why do you wear makeup?"

"I just do. Why do you ask?"

"Because you don't need it. You shouldn't wear it. Promise me that when you go back to your cottage you'll wash it off."

"Why should I?"

"Because I've told you something about yourself you haven't known before, and because I expect you're as curious about yourself as you are about me. Also—because I'd like to see you."

"I can't imagine what it would be like to sleep with a man who lives with his mother. Or maybe I can imagine—and that's worse."

"In our home in Boston, she has a floor entirely to herself. She never intrudes into my study or bedroom, nor I into hers."

"Well, then, whom do we chloroform? Your mother or my children?"

He laughed. "I don't believe you're as merciless as your wit."

"I'm not," she said. "Only I've had a very difficult last two years, and I feel like a squashed punching bag, and I'm not certain I want to begin something right now with a man, and I'm not that interested in one-nighters. I'm also way too vulnerable right now for a one-nighter, and as inadequate as I'm feeling, I feel even more inadequate because I don't know who Thorstein Veblen is."

"You will know, before you're through with me. That I promise."

He was surprisingly good that night in bed, or else she had simply been without sex for so long that she was grateful to forgo Metalious and Lawrence and to feast on anything that could pass for the real thing. Curiously, he did not like to kiss her much while they were making love, and he was loath to linger with her for any length of time before entering her. But when he did enter her, she cried out in pleasure from the sharp jolt of it, a cry her soundly sleeping daughters did not hear. Afterwards, her hands combed through the thick mat of hair on his chest.

"What do you look like without a beard?" she asked him.

"Ordinary," he said. "Does my beard bother you?"

"No," she said. "It's not uncomfortable. I find it sexy. Would you ever shave it off for me?"

"I doubt you'd ask me to."

"Even though you asked me to take off all my makeup, which I did."

"Yes. Because all the things I will ask of you can only benefit you, and will strip you of nothing."

She knew precisely what day the following week he had told his mother of not only his sudden new relationship but also his future plans for such a relationship. The eyes in that reddened, puffy face gleamed a little more brightly, and more coldly. Dana felt as though a lobster were about to explore her private parts. There was no way to ease the tension or probing. *She's a jealous old woman,* thought Dana. *Your own mother might have acted the same way if someone had made a move on your father.* Florence would now dunk queries into the casual beach talk as though she were planting mines. "You've heard of Jessie Weston, haven't you, Dana?" "She's some jazz singer, isn't she?" "Hardly." Dana rather relished delivering these naive replies. That she was hopelessly stupid about intellectual trivia worked to her advantage. Only when Florence began to catch on that Dana was returning the bait did she stop casting lines. Florence assented, albeit grudgingly, to the new routine that shaped their remaining days on the beach, because she had no choice. Now, when the afternoons petered away, Leon would accompany his mother back to their cottage, dine with her one night, then with Dana the next, lunch with them both; and the nights themselves were seldom spent in his cottage.

He asked her if she would marry him. She told him she never

wished to be married again. He kept asking. As a compromise she agreed to live with him. It beat drifting.

The town house he and his mother owned in Boston's South End was several thousand steps above what an average teacher could afford. A gorge, she realized, would have risen in Thorstein Veblen's throat had he ever dropped in. Florence's taste in furniture was on a par with her mother's—heavy on preening period pieces and stuffed chairs, stingy on comfort. She could see nothing of Leon in the house, except for books. There was a grand piano in the living room, but nobody played. The Bechstein was an antique that had belonged to Florence's mother.

She did not feel like a stranger at all in the new surroundings. In fact, she kept expecting to find her father somewhere in the house, behind one of the many doors, chiseling and sawing away at some bizarre object that would turn out to be half sculpture, half bar stool, merrily undermining the regime of petrified wing chairs. The house, she decided, needed to be pruned, if not of Florence herself, certainly of Florence's taste.

But that project had to be put on the back burner. Now there were four children to raise and two spitfire exes to deal with: Leon's former wife, who always looked as though she had just snapped the necks of forty chickens and was aching to do in one more, and her own ex-husband, on one of his dutiful jaunts to Boston, who would drive off with his daughters for a weekend as though he were heading to prison. Florence daily comported herself like the jilted lover of her son, the still secret lover of her son, and the mother Dana ought to have had, had she been wisely engendered. Her favorite meal, astonishingly, was spaghetti, which Leon and his kids also adored, and which Dana had to torment into at least a hundred different versions. Dana did nothing now, that year they started to live together and for the next six, but read the books that were assigned to her by Leon rather than the books she used to pluck from the shelves on her own, and type up the scholarly articles that Leon wrote, which she found both fascinating and boring. Since she did nothing else but raise children and design spaghetti treats and try to cram two thousand or more years' worth of learning into her spongy skull, she had of course felt miserably selfish, then guilty, when she'd backed off at first from Leon's most startling request early on in the game. "Why don't you let me invest your money in the right causes? I've a friend who's doing that for people who think the way we do. Your money could be used for neighborhood organizations, education projects, civil rights projects. Why don't you do something useful with your money, Dana, instead of letting it feed on itself? You do believe in Veblen, don't you?"

She had no idea what she believed in, except French symbolist poetry. But she sensed her life might move up a notch on the totem of purposefulness, just so long as Florence occasionally put down her hatchet. So she signed away her trust to some foundation in Boston. Her father threatened to sue Leon. Her mother prayed she would marry Leon. And Florence must have hoped Dana would expire from incurable ignorance, leaving Leon to his better half.

But Dana was somehow able to steel herself or blind herself or both for seven years, calling her life "knotty and colorful," "full of contrasting textures." Leon kept asking her to marry him, and she kept refusing—until she finally realized what she'd been doing on her own for all those years: saying no to the rising gorge.

She kept it down. Because she could hear her mother whispering to her under her breath: *Never, never make a mess. That is for men to do. But who am I to give advice? Look at the mess that has befallen me, befallen all of us. Nothing can straighten it. Nothing.*

Only once, three years ago, had she been able to step out of her own misery, and into another's. She had felt so spooked then— so fragile, so undeservedly lucky. It was as though the sorrowful tragedy that had struck down Denis could have been lying in wait for her as well. Sometimes at night, alone, she would stare in the mirror, blink her eyes, touch her cheeks, her lips, make sure she was all there, that everything moved, that her face had not slid off and dissolved in the darkness.

■■ ■■ ■■

Her responsibilities seemed to be increasing exponentially by the time she hit thirty, although one variable never changed. She was not only mother and stepmother now; she was also den mother to boot. Leon had turned their home into a meeting ground for talkathons with other radical professors, all of whom were outraged by the war and President Johnson and the enforced drafting of everyone but the privileged, all of whom also happened to be quite privileged themselves and were living off trust funds that supported them while they taught. Dana wasn't cynical enough to believe that every socialist secretly pined to be a capitalist, or that Leon's friends weren't really guilt-ridden about their wealth. But she was nonplussed by how little their lives seemed to square with their principles, by how much of a luxury their fireside chats were and how the talk accomplished nothing. Money was finally what was most instrumental for changing the world; but she doubted any of them in that room had given what she had given, though there were times when she regretted having been so extravagantly generous, so impulsive. Several of the professors who came to chow down were women, and everything about them proclaimed they were from Cambridge: their peasant skirts, their sandals, their faces that looked like bad supermarket vegetables. Florence was always bestowed a seat at center stage, in her peacock chair next to the fireplace; she was as angry as the rest of them, and her voice would dip into its sepulchral lower register in order to acquire a Cassandra-like patina. It was one of Florence's numerous affectations that Dana detested.

Dana kept the coffee steaming and the coffee cakes warm. She could have joined in those heated sessions if she'd wanted to, except the room was always too hot for her, physically, and she couldn't stand sitting near two of the women who always stinted on deodorant. Like Leon's colleagues, she thought the war dreadful, the politicians immoral, the world immeasurably corrupt. But she said nothing. Instead, she would rail at her mother and sister whenever she had them on the phone or saw them in New York, both of whom were far less politically engaged than she. Though even then, when she would castigate them for giving so little of their time or money to the resistance effort, she wondered if it was really she who was venting or some puppet of Leon's. Sometimes the issue of the war, the talk about it seemed pointless—and all that mattered really were the simple, stupid things: laughing with one's sister, enduring and forgiving one's mother. After those nights of heavy, antiwar dialogue, Leon was so exhausted he couldn't function in bed. His libido had been yakked off.

She felt guilty now when she had to ask Leon for money for things that were not Thoreauvian essentials. Not that she yearned for new clothes, not that she wore anything other than jeans, corduroys, or fishermen's sweaters. The dresses her mother bought her she could hardly wear around the house, especially if the guests were members of RESIST. But there were times when she wanted to buy something, own something for the sheer pleasure of it. She finally did splurge one afternoon, and with money she'd squirreled away she treated herself to an expensive camera. More than just whim had governed her purchase, though she would have been hard put to explain exactly why she'd bought it. For some time she'd been seeing outré and disturbing photographs in the newspapers; and she was far more conscious now of violence, and the aesthetics of violence, as a result of the daily pounding of Vietnam footage on television. Photographs, she realized, had the power to startle deeply. If she could do nothing very provocative or productive in the house except devise a new spaghetti dish, she could maybe become something other than a limp noodle once she armed herself with a camera. She recruited her girls, who were none too happy. In the dead of winter she would force both of them to huddle near a broken iron gate or a grubby alleyway, cloaked in heavy overcoats so that they looked like gnomes in mourning. The girls hated standing motionless, hated looking ridiculous. They begged their mother never to show those terrible photographs to anyone, never to tell any of their friends. One evening Dana lucked upon three broken mannequins which had been stuffed inside a garbage bin. She dragged them home, arranged them on the wing chairs and the sofa, then photographed the girls nestling close to the lopsided dummies. After that the girls absolutely refused to model for her. Dana's interest similarly began to flag, once she saw the money at hand could not be stretched to keep her developing supplies replenished. Every time she broached the subject of money with her sister, Roo would always shut the door in her face before she could even tell her what she needed it for. Leon was doling money out to her stingily, as though she were some spendthrift who was about to hand it all over to gypsies. His money was virtually hers anyway, even though all of hers was being invested by some consortium of Red millionaires, so she could not understand his parsimony. Eventually, she hung up her camera along with her ballet slippers and her forsaken college education, consoling herself with the stern probability that all any of those vocations would have amounted to was a useless, expensive hobby.

She'd grown tired of reading. Leon's son, now a senior at Buckingham Browne & Nichols, kept thrusting new books at her which she "ought to read," solely because they'd received his imprimatur. R. D. Laing's *The Politics of Experience*. A ponderous autobiography by an American Indian called *Black Elk Speaks*. She still thought Rimbaud better than any of them, though it had been fifteen years since she'd read Rimbaud. Leon's son had turned into a junior version of his father: an intelligent brute with a Pygmalion complex. Leon's daughter, at fifteen, had recently taken to intellectual name-dropping, as though she were a junior Florence. Dana had enough trouble getting down another spaghetti dinner without having to swallow Berdyaev and Unamuno as well. She was grateful her own daughters were dutiful plodders, who fantasized far more about marrying Art Garfunkel than about making the world safe for socialism. Their breasts were beginning to draw them unwanted attention from fifteen-year-old boys; but they preferred not to talk about that or Unamuno. Dana counted her few lucky stars that none of them, neither her kids nor Leon's, had gone off the deep end, yet. Most children of academics, she knew, wound up being eggheads themselves or else ski bums, bartenders, or short-order cooks. Since she could masquerade as an "academic, sort of" now, she trusted her very straight daughters would remain straight and not pursue Simon and Garfunkel to the ends of the earth like brain-dead groupies. Leon's kids tapped into wildness a little more aggressively—through their hair, which they let grow long but not unkempt, and their music, which boomed through the ceilings: Jefferson Airplane, the Grateful Dead. Dana wished the noise could take a hint from the last names of the bands, and depart early or expire. When the house was still, the stereos gagged, she would try to remember fragments of melody from the songs that Denis loved, music that belonged to the dinosaurs now—but she couldn't.

She continued to type up Leon's newest articles for *Studies on the Left*; she continued to help out Leon's son with the tougher analogy problems in his SAT Practice Book while coaching her own daughters for the SSATs, and a year later assisted Leon's daughter in getting a head start on those same godawful analogy problems, knowing she would have to do it all over again for her own daughters in another two years; she continued to put off any major spiritual housecleaning so that she could avoid confronting all that she'd stuffed in her closet or bottom drawers and labeled unwearable, unusable, not hers at all. By the time she hit thirty-three, she thought Christ had probably gotten off easy.

■■　■■　■■

When she turned thirty-seven, she began to fear she'd missed the boat completely. She had missed out on the most essential thing— her life. That cry of anguish and ecstasy which she could still remember from Rimbaud's "The Drunken Boat" came back to haunt her: *O que ma quille éclate! O que j'aille à la mer!* She would say the line over and over again to herself, while she made herself drinks. She was drinking way too much, but Leon said nothing, perhaps because he was drinking just as heavily. Florence was too self-absorbed to notice the rapidly emptying scotch and vodka bottles. She never emptied the garbage anyway.

The house was still crammed with people, all demanding something. No sooner had the two girls been packed off to Bard than replacements arrived to fill up the empty beds. Leon's daughter, who'd taken a year off from college, had just returned from an archaeological dig in Turkey. Leon's son wanted a quieter place than the graduate dorm to prepare for his M.A. exams. What they all wanted, Dana realized, was home-cooked meals and service and an occasional reaction to let them know their lofty opinions were not knocking blindly against a dumb wall. Florence, all ninety pounds of her now, would sit in her peacock chair like a bag of old bones, in her glory once more as grandmotherly matriarch. "Dana," she said to them at their first dinner together, "is thinking about returning to college." "Oh, really," said Leon's son. "Where?" "Here at the state university," said Florence. "Good for you," said Leon's daughter. Then they all applauded her, as though she were a performing seal.

She did not know what else to do. There was nothing at home for her but proofreading Leon's articles, combing Florence's hair when she was sick, reading books she couldn't talk about with anyone, and drinking on the sly. Sometimes she wondered if her father was responsible for this, whether it was something in the genes. She seemed as marooned and without goals as he, except he was the better dilettante.

"Are you still taking photographs?" asked Leon's son.

"She's given that up for the worthier calling," said Florence. "Though I always told her, if she put her mind to it she could be good, a genius. Who knows? Look. Look how well you two are doing. You are pursuing your passions."

"I haven't passed my exams yet, Gram."

Dana excused herself. They were soiling her future, annihilating it. The daughter would probably stay for three weeks, maybe a month, then zoom off to forage for pottery shards and bottle caps in Baalbek, Machu Picchu, Afghanistan. Florence would get the flu or pneumonia and need a constant live-in nurse. When she was better, Leon would get sick. And then the son—who would leave in two months, only to be followed by the arrival of her own daughters wanting help with their term papers. Then one of Leon's Marxist friends would fly in from California, needing a place to stay. Leon's daughter would return—with a mummified crocodile, a petrified goat turd, which she would study closely for six months, at the house. Her only escapes from the jail were those sporadic trips to New York—to shop with her mother, to visit with Roo and John. But seeing John's paintings always made her feel as though she were mired in cement, unable to move a finger or toe. And Roo's stabs at art made her feel the pain of an unaccomplished life all the more.

Her keel had splintered.

She had been engulfed by the sea.

■■　　■■　　■■

One afternoon, when she was at loose ends, when Leon was at the library, when Florence had actually left the house for a geriatric lunch somewhere, Dana pulled out of the bookshelves her old Garnier paperback of Baudelaire's *Les Fleurs du mal*. She could still make sense of some of the notes she'd scribbled in French in the margin. *"Un attrait pour ce qui c'est victime, exclu."* But when she skimmed through the poems, she was too frequently baffled, stopped short by beautiful, now untranslatable words. What did *"fêlée"* mean? And *"boudeur"*? *"hydropique"*? She remembered he'd written an elegant, extraordinarily sexy sonnet about cats, one of her favorite poems then—"Les Chats." But she could not decipher the last stanza now. The cat's fecund loins were full of *"étincelles magiques."* Magic tinsel she knew it wasn't.

How ashamed Dr. Ari would have been of such a botched

translation. She wondered where Dr. Ari was, what had become of her. She would be in her sixties, maybe still teaching French, or maybe retired, living abroad.

As she riffled through the book, furious with her ignorance, in despair at how much her brain had withered, crushed flower petals sprinkled to the floor, relics from her wedding twenty years ago.

■ ■　　■ ■　　■ ■

She felt as out of place in college at age thirty-eight as she did being a wife at eighteen. Some of her professors were a good deal younger than she; so were most of the students, though some looked to be in their mid-to-late twenties. All of them had steady jobs and were moonlighting as students.

The loneliness at college was no different from that at home. She sat at metal tablet desks and did not move for hours. She seldom commented on anything that had been said in class; she mostly listened. There was little time to make friends with anyone at lunch.

The only good thing that happened to her that first year was the visit to the amusement park near Newport. She and another student had been saddled with a joint project for their sociology course—a study of some segment of American culture, preferably off the beaten track. Her partner, a twenty-two-year-old English major, thought the crowds who attended amusement parks might lead to—as he put it—"riveting epiphanies." He was right, though not in a way he could have foreseen.

She had not used her camera since the girls had gone to high school. The heft of it, the bite of the strap around her neck took getting used to again. While the jerky English major was but-tonholing the people standing in line for rides and interviewing them, she roamed on her own through the park. She had never taken the twins to an amusement park, or been in one herself, unless one counted the carousel ride in Central Park.

Then she saw them, ambling past the concessions, smiling vacantly, their heads bobbing. Microcephalics. Clusters of them. Families. Parents with tiny heads, and their pinheaded children. Nobody was chaperoning them. They didn't seem to need any help. A few people stared, but everyone else was far more intent on buying tickets and cotton candy.

They moved slowly, in a wobbly column, like exotic kiwis. Dana followed them. She used up three rolls of film. Then, feeling guilty for having abandoned her fellow epiphany tracker, she retraced her steps and spent the remainder of the day photographing goons munching on caramel corn, and teenage Neanderthals with tattoos who were dragging their shrieking girlfriends onto the roller coaster.

Back in Boston, she started to focus on people who were jarring to look at, people who were damaged on the inside or the outside. She signed up for an upper-level photography course the next semester. She could see now what so many of her photographs had in common, even those early photographs of her girls: a cruel beauty.

They scared her. She wondered if she ever again could view the world as anything other than worm-eaten.

■■　　■■　　■■

She did not, on her fortieth birthday, call up John and announce she was ready to be rendered on canvas. The face she owned seemed both more solid now and more riven. Wrinkles circled her eyes like tiny doilies; grooves lined her forehead; but her hair was still long and dark, and her eyes still burned. She was a more beautiful woman than most at her age—though she knew that nothing necessarily followed from that fact. It was just a fact. Like the fact of her daughters' both marrying actuaries. Like the fact of the tufts of grey hair that poked out of the ears of men Leon's age, and that always needed to be trimmed. Like the fact of the eerie brightness in Florence's eyes, the futile fight against decrepitude. Anyway, John had long ago given up portraits.

She had hoped at least one of her daughters might call that morning to wish her happy birthday; but no calls came. The cards they'd sent were Hallmarks at their worst. The book Leon had given her was wrapped without frills. She left it in the kitchen, unopened. She went to her afternoon classes, but her mind was not on Gothic rose windows or La Follette and the Grange movement. She had decided that before the afternoon was over she would know, once and for all, whether her photographs had any commercial appeal. The spectres who ran the galleries on Newbury Street were too intimidating to confront. But perhaps an art director or some photographer who worked at the city magazine was approachable. If she waited until shortly before five o'clock, her chances of talking to someone without distractions might be enhanced. On the other hand, the editors and directors might have trooped off early to the nearest bar. Still, the risk was worth taking.

She'd expected a big-city magazine office to resemble the newsroom in *His Girl Friday*: scores of desks bumping up against each other; telephones ringing hectically; whirlwinds of flying paper; and incessant jabber. Instead, she found herself on the tenth floor of a downtown corporate office building, unable to hear a single footfall or a voice other than the receptionist's. The corridors were plushly carpeted. The inner offices were metallic cubicles with slits for doors. She felt as though she had come to pick up someone's cremains.

"Could you tell me where the art director's office is?"

The receptionist picked up a ringing phone.

"*Boston Magazine.* . . . Yes. . . . No, no we don't. . . . Yes. Excuse me a moment." She pointed to the hallway Dana had just left. "Walk back out," she said. "It's the first door on your left. No, your right." She went back to her call. "That's right. You'll want to speak with Gail. She did the piece on designer bidets. . . . No. No. That's Suzanne."

Dana knew now this was a mistake. Nonetheless, she headed back to the hallway and opened the first door on the right. This lobby looked crazy, not dead. Rubbery Halloween masks dangled from a hat rack. The carpet here was green and bristly. Someone had taken a poster from *Jaws* and wired the shark's teeth with braces. An old Cosmo fold-out of Burt Reynolds nude had been turned into a dartboard. Little was left of his crotch. Untampered with was a Berenice Abbott photograph of ruined Penn Station that hung alone on another wall.

A young woman with pencils stuck in her hair had just thrown on her coat.

"Excuse me," said Dana, "but is the art director still here?"

"Hasn't been fired yet," she said. "Yo, Zack. There's someone to see you." The woman plucked the pencils from her head and tossed them on her desktop. "Zacko, you there? I'm taking off. I'll have the Truro-Wellfleet sidebars from Reuben tomorrow. He's behind, but we knew that."

The face that emerged from one of the inner rooms was as arresting as the Halloween masks. Bones slashed through his cheeks like daggers. It was a scary, handsome face. The man looked a little like Jack Palance. His loosened tie was a shocking yellow.

"Steph," he said, "they had better be here tomorrow morning, nine sharp. Or Reuben's ass is grass. We're almost behind production because of him." Then he looked at Dana. "Yes?"

If she were younger she would have simply chickened out, turned around then and left; she would have followed the girl to the elevator, wondering how long pencils could stay in one's hair without becoming a bother. But she was forty. So she stared right back at this man called Zack and tried not to flinch.

"May I see you for a few minutes? If you have the time, which you obviously don't."

"Time," he said. "It makes cowards of some but it makes a deranged man out of me. I never have time. And I imagine you don't either. Time has us all by the short hairs. Sure—come in.

I'm going to be here all night anyway. We're down to the wire."

His office would have given a maid nightmares. Newspaper clippings and photographs from magazines were thumbtacked to every wall, in layers. The desks and easels were inundated with what looked like instrumental scores. Cryptic scribblings littered each page. With his plastic ruler still jittering in his hand, he resembled a frustrated or lunatic conductor, baffled by his missing musicians. Though he also looked as if he'd have no problem making music without them. His eyes hadn't drifted much from hers.

"I apologize for the disorder. My apartment's a similar mess. Now, tell me. Why are you here? Who are you? I'm two months late with my Master Charge bill, so I hope you're not a collector."

"No," she said. She didn't know whether to smile or not. She didn't know if he was being humorous or serious. She pulled the black folder out of her tote bag and handed it to him.

"I was hoping you might look at these."

Some of the curiosity departed from his face. He probably dealt with hundreds like her.

"Sit," he said. There was only one chair. He now towered over her until he cleared off the edge of his desk, perched himself there, and began flipping through her work.

"Why do you get them processed half-size?"

"For intensity. It's the way I see things," she said. "Why do you ask?"

"Oh, sometimes people shoot half-size because they're afraid flaws will show up if they print larger. That's not a problem here."

He studied a few of them for more than ten seconds. She couldn't tell which ones.

"You should print eight-by-tens," he said. "They make a portfolio look more professional."

"I'm a four-by-six professional."

"I know. Don't make them any smaller. We can't use thumbnails."

He handed them back to her. Five minutes, she thought. Maybe six at the most. A fast man.

"The problem's not with you," he said. "It's with me. Or with the magazine, I should say. I like them. Your four-by-six vision is very pungent. Mean, too. Most of them are nicely moody. But that's the problem. This magazine gears itself towards an audience that's upscale and upbeat. I happen to be a little of the former and not much of the latter. But every time I sneak in one or two moody, offbeat shots—and I can, on occasion, get away with it—I have to chop off a finger to do it. And this year I don't have many fingers left."

The ten he had, she noticed, looked quite sturdy. There was no ring on either ring finger.

"That's OK. That wasn't my reason for coming. Thank you. You've told me what I needed to hear."

"I didn't say no, mind you. I meant right now, for the next three or four months, we're booked up. I'll tell you what, though— I'd like to see more."

Again, she wasn't sure how to read him.

"When I have more," she said. "Thank you again."

"You're welcome."

She stood up, shook his hand. He was eyeing her as though there just might be some other purpose for her stopping by. She was afraid to smile.

"You're part Indian, aren't you?"

"Not my better half. My mother was Penobscot. The bad blood's on her side. And you? What are you?"

"I'm forty years old. Today."

She left before he said anything else. She had not even told him her name. She got home just before dinner, hoping they all might eat out tonight. But Leon was feeling flu-ish and out of sorts, and that meant Florence would contract the bug, or whatever it was, within the hour, by spiritual osmosis. The two of them were more like twins than her own daughters.

She made herself a tall drink for dinner, but before she downed it the phone rang. It was the fussbudget daughter.

"Mom, I'm getting into Greyhound at two-thirty tomorrow afternoon."

"What?"

"I'm having problems with Noah. It's like, marriage is weirding me out, and I need a break. Maybe I'm having a breakdown, who knows?"

"Maybe you need another hobby besides watching soap operas."

"He buries himself all the time in his graphs and statistics. I mean, when we go shopping, like we did last Saturday when we got the barbecue grill, he graphs out the route from one shopping mall to the next, he can't just make a list of places to shop. I'm having these weird dreams where I wake up and find out I'm married to a slide rule. He doesn't focus on any of my needs. I mean, I have needs."

"You and about a million other women."

"So I thought I'd stay with you until I get my head together."

"Lovely. We can sit around here, eat a little leftover birthday cake."

"How was it? Your birthday."

"It is."

"Oh, great. Happy birthday. Sorry, I've lost track of time, I've been so pissed at Noah."

After another five minutes of listening to sentence after sentence beginning with "I," Dana pleaded a headache and eased herself off the phone. She walked back into the kitchen, picked up her drink, then turned it over like a dice cup and emptied it into the sink. "I'm going out," she called upstairs, not very loudly.

Feeling morose and masochistic, she stopped at Burger King and had a Whopper for dinner. Ten minutes later she threw it up in the Burger King bathroom. An ice cream cone soothed the rawness of her throat, though not the other rawness.

It was almost nine o'clock when she arrived at the stone fortress she'd left earlier that day. The revolving doors did not turn; all the doors were locked. She knocked until a night watchman materialized.

He was middle-aged, like her, and grumpy looking. He could have done with the drink she'd jettisoned earlier.

"My house keys," she said as he unlocked the door. "They're upstairs."

"Elevator six," he muttered. "Nothing else runs." He wandered back to his chair and his bag of Doritos.

The tenth floor was as it had been hours ago—funereal. Only now the lights were muffled as well as her footsteps. It wasn't a place for a woman alone or without purpose. She hoped he would still be there, if only to escort her out of the building safely.

His outer office door was partly open, and the lights were on. So was a radio. She could hear talk-show babble; then she heard him laugh. She slid into the room without knocking.

He was standing in the doorway of his inner sanctum, his face towards her, a pencil behind his ear, staring at photographs laid out in jagged patterns on the lobby floor.

"I told you I'm offbeat," he said. "This only looks like hopscotch. It isn't."

"Do all the people who work in this place wear pencils on their heads?"

"Why are you here?"

"I was rude. I forgot to tell you my name."

"But I know it. It was written on the inside of your portfolio. You haven't answered my question."

"I can't. I've never done this before. Or not since I was eighteen."

"Neither have I."

"I don't believe you."

"Believe me. I told you before. I haven't the time. I mean, hadn't."

She did not know what to do next. The photographs stood between them like treacherous stepping stones.

"Close the door," he said. "Lock it." He picked up the photographs. "I'll have to turn off the lights. Regrettably. People working at night in the other buildings would have quite a view."

"I don't suppose there's anything softer to lie on than this Astroturf."

"How about some dictionaries? Pushpins?"

In the darkness his face was even more alarming. His body was just as scary, a wild, unknown thing. There was no weak flesh on him. He laughed a little as he entered her. "I don't believe this is happening." She thrust against him. The rough carpet, the anonymity of him, the newness of another body—this was what she really wanted. The intimation that some other connection might have yoked them, the thing they shared with their eyes— that was only the excuse that propelled her here.

Yet he went on with her; he had not stopped. She started to moan, then laughed herself. "My God, will someone hear us?"

"The night watchman could do with a thrill or two in his lonely life. So could I."

His breath was hot against her ear. Even when he was spent, he remained rigid in her for a while. And she—she was impaled more than she'd wanted to be. She would have liked to stay the entire night. Neither stirred to get up.

"Are you married?" she asked.

"No."

"Are you gay?"

"These questions you ask—you're very direct, aren't you?"

"Yes. Are you?"

"Direct or gay?"

She could tell he was smiling, but probably more at himself than at her.

"I guess I'm neither," he said.

"You guess."

"Oh, I'm a good guesser. I bet you are too."

"Sometimes too good. What's wrong with you, then?"

"Everything. I talk to photographs. I talk to my plants, though I rarely play hopscotch with them. I let myself be seduced by beautiful, kinky photographers who like to prowl around empty buildings at night. Everything's wrong with me."

"Not everything. Must you get back to work soon?"

"Very soon, to be honest. I wish I could be dishonest."

"It's easy. Believe me. What were you working on?"

"Oh, the usual. Dummies and layouts. Spreads."

"My ex-husband called me all of those."

"Maybe that's why he's your ex."

She rolled over on top of him. She let her hair drift over his face like a curtain. His fingers roved through it, as though he were a loom weaver.

"I'm the one who forgot something," he said.

"What?"

"Happy birthday."

"I'd better go," she said. "But I'd like to see you again."

"You stole my line. My very words. So would I."

"If not married, are you attached? Or is that too forward a question?"

"Nothing's too forward after what we've just done. No. I'm attached only to major ferns and several pots of philodendron. Can I call you?"

"No. I live with a man, who tends to me. Inadequately, the only way he can. I live with him and his mother, and occasionally his children, who bunk down with us, and occasionally my children, who follow suit, and I don't think after I've told you all that that you would even be interested in calling me."

"Don't be too sure. All you're saying is that you are less free than I am. Which may or may not be true."

"I go to school also, so most of my mornings and afternoons are eaten up, though I'm sometimes free in the mornings, when you are probably talking to your photographs or plants, and once in a while I'm free at lunchtime—and I can't say anything definite about my nights. They could just happen—like this one."

"Why do I think I already know you?"

"Because you have hard eyes. Like mine. And I know what it takes to acquire that hardness."

"But you don't know me."

"Yet," she said. "But I will."

They picked themselves off the floor. Each of them groped for clothes in the darkness. When she mistook his sock for her underwear, she giggled. "I've found everything but my own underwear," he said. "Then go without," she said. "Are you presentable enough to risk exposure? Can I switch on the light, wherever it is?" "Behind you, and yes." Once the lights were back on, they both laughed. Drooping over one of the masks on the hat rack was a pair of boxer shorts.

"I'll be grinning a lot tomorrow. No one will know why."

"Thank you," she said. "For the handsome birthday gift."

"I hope you received other presents."

"Yes. A book. No doubt of Marxist poems. I haven't opened it. And there's a frozen cupcake waiting for me in the fridge."

He rode down with her on the elevator. She'd taken out her house keys and was jingling them as the watchman unlocked the door. "Found them," she said. She didn't wave to the other man behind her, but she hoped he had stared at her for more than five seconds, maybe even a full six, as she walked off.

■ ■   ■ ■   ■ ■

He was right about his apartment. It was a jungle—of both potted ferns and magazines, most of the latter rising in teetery stacks on the floor as though they were plant life as well. The tamer ones bore the names of other cities—Chicago, Los Angeles, Philadelphia. Others, like *Zoom*, had splashier covers. Were she eyeing the floor from above, it might have resembled some tropical bower—and he, sleek and naked, some restless predator.

The apartment was, in fact, a spacious loft, located in a homely brick building in the heart of downtown. She could never have imagined such a vast, flowing space existing six floors above an archaic ice cream parlor. From the sidewalk all she could see of the upper stories was rows of tiny, dirty windows. She assumed the nondescript front entrance to the building led only to cubbyhole offices upstairs, rented to invisible weavers and discount fur dealers.

"A mess," he said, apologetically. "I don't think I've made my bed once since I've lived here." "It's a cohesive mess, though," she said. "Unlike my life." She liked his bed, its jumble; though his blankets were rumpled and balled up, his sheets always smelled fresh.

She came to know his bed well. Her bed away from bed, she called it. But he knew what she really meant. "Tell me about your youth," she said. "Nasty, brutish, mean and short," he replied, then laughed. "I'm kidding," he said. "It was cheerful, and sometimes cheerless, as most lives are. And yours?" "Messy," she said. "Entrammeled." She could see him only twice a week for certain. And he arranged his lunch hours on Tuesday and Thursday so that he would have an extra half hour. But he could walk back to his apartment from work in ten minutes. She was at the mercy of either her car or public transportation. The university was stuck out in Dorchester, only a short drive from the city. But it was an ordeal to park in Boston except at weird times like two in the morning. Waiting for the subways, which were always erratic, chopped off precious time just as cruelly. Often she'd arrive at his place and not even talk, simply undress and grapple with him in bed, unwilling to waste another minute—but he might have only twenty left before he had to go back to work. At those times she felt that the two of them were equals, both victims, prisoners of something out of their control. But at other times she felt as though they were not on an equal footing at all. She was the intruder, and he—he was dispensing favors. He did not need to stretch for her, as she did for him.

Once, when she had him spread-eagled on his bed, she asked him what kind of power he believed in.

"I don't think about power much," he said.

"You have to," she said. "We live in a world where power determines everything."

"Power's not one of my favorite words, Dana."

"Zack, I'm serious. Define power for me."

"Define it? The way I am now? Naked, with you on top of me, and nearly manacled? Right now I am perfectly powerless."

"You are not. You could throw me over easily. Both ways, I might add. I'll let you go when you define power."

"All right," he said. "What did we just wolf down here, besides each other? Chocolate-chip cookies, correct? Now what kind of chocolate-chip cookies? Famous Amos. Now, are these the best chocolate-chip cookies, the very best? I don't know. I don't really care. But someone has pronounced them the best, in this silly magazine or that one. Who is this someone, this authority on chocolate-chip cookies? How did this person come to be such an aficionado? How can you tell the difference between two cookies anyway after you've devoured two thousand? I don't know, Dana, and I don't care to know. I've been brainwashed, and that's how power works. And I gladly assent to it, the same way I gladly eat these cookies and gladly make love to you. Now if you can find me a better-tasting cookie—"

"Shut up," she said, stopping his mouth with her lips.

"I can't breathe," he mumbled. She released him. She still had not let go of his hands.

"Don't you see?" he said. "We love being dictated to. We don't really want power. We willingly relinquish the controls to someone who deludes himself or herself into thinking he or she has the power. Then we kindly oblige them by pulling the wool over our eyes."

"Then you're saying power is an illusion."

"Something like that."

"Hitler wasn't an illusion."

"Oh, Dana, can't you lighten up? Shush. Forget about power. When I'm tangling with you like this, all I think about is—"

"Fucking."

"No. More than that. I think about how I'd like to slide under your skin, get inside you completely."

"Then you'll know all about powerlessness," she said.

She knew even more about it after the first month of their affair, after she'd witnessed the first attack. She had been kissing him greedily when he suddenly started to gasp, wheeze. He lunged for his sport coat. She saw him pull out of the inside pocket what appeared to be a nozzle for a garden hose, then ram it into his mouth. His breathing sounded as terrible as the frantic snuffling of some dying animal. She was by his side at once. "What can I do?" she said. He took the pipe from his mouth. "Nothing," he said. "Go lie down, relax." Then he sucked on the pipe. She did not obey him. She sat on the floor next to him, one hand resting lightly on his leg.

When he was through, he put down the nozzle.

"My bronco," he said. "My bronchodilator. I ride it a lot."

"Why didn't you tell me?"

"I don't like to impose on others."

"I'm not an other. Nothing you asked of me would be an imposition."

"Well, now you know. I have asthma. You've not been around, fortunately, when I've had my attacks. They're pretty scary. In just seconds you can run short of breath and then all you hear is your own gasps. Because you're going under. It's like drowning."

"How long have you had it?"

"Since I was twelve. You can see now why I'm not married. Most girls, most women I've known have preferred the company of men without handicaps. Your red-blooded, all-American type is seldom a red man anyway."

"You're being unfair. To women and to yourself."

"Not totally," he said. "I've simply had to wait until a good woman wasn't so choosy, until she'd acquired a few dents too."

"You are sometimes," she said, "one very dumb Indian. I happen to be a very choosy woman. Very."

"But you've chosen wrong—twice."

"At least I've chosen."

She was in one way grateful she had seen him buckled over, in agony. For a while he became more open about his life, his past. His father had worked in a tannery; his mother, in a shoe factory. They knew their son was gifted when he started solving crossword puzzles at four. They knew such gifts came at a price when he became crippled with asthma later. They sweated to send him to private schools and then Dartmouth, knowing they were already exiles in his life. The week before commencement his father collapsed of heart failure; his mother died of lung cancer three years later. After a long stretch of unsatisfying jobs in industrial design, he drifted into the more playful world of designing magazines. But he attributed that decision not to any rampant affection for contemporary art or journalism. He blamed it all on his fixation with crossword puzzles. He was good at filling up blank spaces with words, or photographs, that fit to a tee. He'd not had many serious lovers; but the few he'd had had always left. The responsibility of loving someone ill had been too much for them, he said. So he had fallen back on his work to keep him amused, happy.

Of the people lost to him his grandmother had counted the most.

"She's the one who gave me my secret name," he told her.

"What is it?" she asked. "Tell me."

"I can't. That's the only Indian part of me left. She gave me my name the year after I got sick. She was a spirit woman. She marched me up to Mount Katahdin, burned sweet grass, spun me around and pointed me in every direction, north, east, south, west, and then she named me. Afterwards she and her friends celebrated. But I knew few of her friends. My parents found my grandmother anachronistic, embarrassing. She died soon after she named me. Her friends buried her there on the mountain. She was my last hold on Native American life. When I came down from that mountain, I embraced the other world. The real one. You know— Big Macs, pet rocks, yellow ties, Famous Amos."

"Are you being serious?"

"No. Sometimes. Yes."

"Did you do the right thing?"

"Yes."

He had no car. One day on a lunch hour that could be miraculously extended to two, she drove them both to the Arnold Arboretum. He needed to check out the site for a fall magazine cover coming up in a few months. His wiliest photographer had been plotting some shot that would make the trees look like the nave at Tintern Abbey. What she knew Zack was plotting was some racy coupling under the snoopy eyes of cardinals and wood-peckers. Afterwards, when they were dressed, he tried to coax her into climbing a tree. "Come on, it's a snap," he said. "For you," she said, "not for me. You don't have a family relying on your legs." "You'll be sorry," he said. "We may never come this way again." She watched him ascend the tree, higher and higher, until she couldn't see him anymore. She had to move out into a clearing before she could glimpse him, roosting up there like some flashy tanager. "Come down," she called. But she didn't think he heard her. He was there—and wasn't there. When he finally returned to earth, brushing the smudges of bark from his hands, she was at once grateful, angry, and envious. During the ride back, he asked her the question she had feared. "When are you going to leave him?" "Do you want to live with me?" "Yes. But if you leave him, you have to do it for yourself, not me." "Will you tell me your secret name?" He laughed. "No, ma'am. Will you ever leave Leon?" "I don't know," she said. "But if I do, I'll leave a scalp on your door."

When she deposited him back at his office building, he removed her right hand from the steering wheel and placed something in her palm. It was a turquoise ring. The stone was as fat as a scarab. "I can't take this," she said. "Sure you can," he said. "You know I can't wear it, Zack." "Someday you will." "I can't." "It was my grandmother's. I can't wear it either and it's going to waste in my jewelry box which is full of nothing but broken buttons anyway. Keep it." "But it belongs to your past." "It needs a future more than a past." When she got home, she buried it in the bottom of one of her crumbling toe shoes.

She had become a very accomplished juggler. Living a double life was both complicated and effortless. No one was keeping close tabs on her hours away from home. She could have been doing research for an essay on Kübler-Ross in the downtown library; she could have been drug dealing or peddling her body in the Combat Zone. After those rare late afternoons spent in bed with Zack, she would rush home, breathless, find Leon conferring with spaghetti noodles in the kitchen, rescue him from a chore she knew he hated, and savor her dexterity, this edge of excitement she lived on. If one of his children dropped in unexpectedly for a few days, the additional variable she had to deal with enhanced the pleasure. Now there were three people to hoodwink, or four, or five. She even managed once, while Florence and Leon and Leon's son were dining out in the back garden, to call John and tell him that there was a young man in her life, someone important. "How young?" he asked. "Will you be jailed?" "He's a little younger, but not much." "Do you love him?" "Yes," she said, "but I have to hang up now."

Only Florence, she thought, suspected what was happening. "Sit, sit," she would say, trying to grab Dana's attention, trying to lure her back to the cage where she belonged. "Why are you dressing differently? You've never worn yellow before." "It's more peach than yellow, Florence." "Peach or yellow, it's not your color. Definitely not." In the past Florence would have tried to shear Dana's plumage out of malice or envy. Now, Dana realized, it was out of fear. She could see what Dana was doing to her son—and could neither stop it nor protect him.

The real problem reared its head in bed. Even though Leon was much older, he still made love adequately. Only there was nothing fresh about their lovemaking. And she was reluctant to behave more aggressively, more inventively, to do some of the things Zack had taught her—for fear of spoiling what she had with Zack, for fear of tipping Leon off. So she was left with little choice but to submit to the old ways and to fantasize. But when that became intolerable, she would wind up pushing her own buttons while Leon hurried himself to a climax. And though he might have been confused by the fact that her hands had left his body and were stroking her own, he would have been too much a prisoner of his own orgasm at that moment to suddenly pause, withdraw, and puzzle at her new self-absorption.

During one of her lunchtime sessions with Zack, she was unable to function well. Her loins were bruised, dry. His forever-hard penis knocked on a door that wouldn't open. "I had a rough time with Leon last night," she confessed. "Sex is sometimes difficult for him. And he won't give up, even if he can't ejaculate. That's why I'm sore." He laid his head against her abdomen, while she fondled his hair. "Do you have any regrets about what's happened, what we're doing?" "Yes," he said. "A good many. You have no idea how often I'd like to call you, but I can't. I've dialed your number many times, and then I quickly hang up. I feel like the other woman. You know, the one who spends her entire day waiting for the phone to ring, and it never does. What I regret more is never being able to wake up with you, to spend a night with you, a lot of nights. I'm a prisoner now too."

"We'll escape for a weekend soon. I promise."

"How?"

"I still have one good friend in New York, whom I haven't seen for a while, and who could conveniently be absent, with enough advance warning. Leon would mind some, if I visited him, but not that much. John was never a threat in the bedroom."

Lying, whether outrageous or subtle, had become second nature to her. She disliked herself for it; and she even resented Zack at times for having forced her into this position, since he did not have to lie at all, only lie in wait. Until recently she had concealed only herself from the others who encroached upon her life; now she had to conceal both herself and him.

And the last, perverse, unjust twist was this: she not only had to work her way through this maze of deceptions, she had to keep on building it too.

■ ■   ■ ■   ■ ■

"What does he call these three?"

"Collage paintings. Timepieces."

"No, I meant the titles."

"I told you," she said. "Timepieces. He calls them Time-pieces. *Timepiece #3, Timepiece #9*, et cetera, et cetera."

"I trust he won't let them overpopulate like Bacon's Popes."

"Don't you like them?"

"I like them a lot. They're sort of like one-dimensional Cornell boxes. He's steamrollered all the contents of the box but without sacrificing any of the freaky business. I can see some Rauschenberg in there too. Still, they could become a little gimmicky, if you know what I mean. You should give a series like this a good run and then stop, say, before you tackle number twenty."

"Why twenty?"

"Even numbers are more stale than odd numbers. Less fidgety, less interesting."

"What about a forty-year-old woman?"

"Oh, quite stale," he said, smirking. "Very, very stale."

He moved up close to one of the canvases, as though he were

inspecting it for flaws, then stepped back to reappraise it. They'd both been so exhausted last night when they'd arrived at her friend John's loft that they'd spent no time at all nosing around the paintings and immediately took to bed, where they further exhausted themselves.

"His conception of time is on the money, I'll say that. Time's chaotic. The sort of arclike, circular patterns here keep getting ripped open by something violent."

"You don't think order and disorder marry well?"

"Only if you believe Heraclitus. When did you meet him— John?"

"After I dropped out of Barnard and married Tyler. We lived in the Village then, right above John and his roommate. He didn't have a real studio at the time, only his 'hypothetical studio,' which was what he called the apartment. Tyler and I could have lived elsewhere and a lot more comfortably. But I was in a bohemian phase, and we were slumming, or at least I was. The rents then were incredibly cheap. John, though, really was living hand-to-mouth. I always thought his roommate had been a former boyfriend and that the roommate was financing the arrangement, keeping John in paintbrushes. No one would keep him as a lover. He took me to the wildest parties, while I was married and while I was getting divorced. Sometimes he needed a sporty, pretty woman to hang out with when he was between boyfriends. We went to the ballet together a lot. Once he tried to paint me, but I felt uncomfortable posing for him. It's hard to be naked in front of a man whom you find very attractive and whom you know you can't have. I couldn't get into it. Neither could he. I've always kept in touch with him, though, and think of him as one of my close friends. He knew me before a lot of things got spoiled."

"How's it worked out for him—as a painter? I don't mean to sound crass here, but has he had any measurable success? Has he sold anything?"

"He's had three exhibits. None in a major uptown gallery. That's not much to show, is it, for thirty or more years of hard labor. I happen to find his work very impressive, and undervalued."

She was angry he'd asked her that. But his question wasn't that surprising, given his job. Zack probably didn't trust artists who lacked winning portfolios. He was more upscale than he thought.

"How does he support himself? I assume he's like most of my free-lance artists, who are putting in time in jobs they hate—waiting, housepainting. This isn't a full-time job, is it?"

"It is now. His parents died and left him money. He doesn't need boyfriends for that anymore."

He was making her squirm, and she knew he didn't know it. She hadn't supported herself for more than twenty years, and had even less of a claim to being an artist than John. Was the measure of her worth as a photographer to be judged solely by sales? Was she going to have to succeed that way in order to count in his eyes?

"Too much money can be a bad thing for an artist," said Zack.

"Maybe that's why I got rid of mine," said Dana. "But the fact that he doesn't have to fend for money shouldn't be held against him. He's still painting."

"Has John met Leon?"

"Once. They didn't get along well. Leon likes art only if it makes its points succinctly. Confusion he has never appreciated."

"I'm glad there is only one of these men I have to worry about."

"In what way?"

"You know the way. And I don't mean Leon."

"Then what do you mean?"

"Nothing."

"You're dodging. As usual," she said. She slipped behind him, locked her arms around his waist, nudged her chin against the long groove in his back. She loved the feel of his buttocks against her groin.

"You're jealous, aren't you?" she said.

"A little. I doubt I could paint like this. Lucky for me he's gay."

"What are you thinking?"

"I like the way his images disintegrate, like that string of what looks like umbrellas humping each other. Then at the same time they coalesce—so you're never quite sure whether they're going to break up or come together. If you get my meaning."

"What are you really thinking?"

"That I'm hungry. That I want to smell bacon, which John had better have in his fridge and which is fattening and unhealthy but I don't care. That I don't want to wear any clothes for the rest of the day. That I would like to spend the rest of the day in here, making love to you underneath all of these paintings."

"*Piece #3, Piece #9.*"

"Something like that. Et cetera, et cetera."

When he turned around, his mouth and shoulders swallowed hers. Then they were all over each other on the floor. "Stop, Zack, it's too hard." "It's always too hard." "The floor, silly." "Get on top of me, then." Minutes later she could hear herself say it again, *Stop, stop, stop*, moaning the words like a chant, while she could also hear him beneath her, grunting and whispering, *Never, never, never*.

They made love three times. Then again. The floor was slippery with their sweat. Every time his back lifted from the floor it made a smacking, squelching noise, like the pop of bubble gum.

Then one more time—though he was drained of all juice other than sweat, and his hardness was now wholly an involuntary response, a machine running on empty. Afterwards, while she made them both scrambled eggs, he nestled behind her, stroking her loins while she was at the stove. "I like my bacon crisp," he said. "Not limp." "Nothing about you is limp," she said. He nibbled at her ear. "Go away. If you stay here any longer your eggs will turn into rocks."

She turned the bacon strips again while he pored through the finished canvases that were stacked against the wall. Even naked, he carried himself with a kind of self-possession that could stun her—and then irk her. Was it all a front, she wondered, the firm smoothness of him, his occasional smugness? She had seen him enough times when he was racked with coughs, broken by windlessness, nearly strangling—and yet she felt more helpless at those moments than he. Why had it taken him so long to own up to a little envy? Why did she have to keep badgering him with questions in order to make him show himself? It was like pulling teeth. She drained the bacon on a paper towel. *I am no different,* she thought. *And I am more selfish than he is. Neither of us is an easy nut to crack.*

Zack had turned on the radio, and kept scanning the stations until he found one with slow music. For a moment, she thought of Denis. They ate breakfast on the floor, in a dry place not yet branded by their bodies. Zack opened the bottle of champagne that John had left for the two of them. They drank all of it. When he kissed her, he released in her mouth the last fizzy swallow he'd held back. Then his tongue was everywhere, trailing down her chest, beyond her navel. "Oh yes," she said. She reached for what she could not touch, his face, his shoulders, and found his legs instead, which slid toward her face. "Oh yes," he moaned. When they were through, they simply lay there, stroking each other's legs.

"We should shower," he said. "You can't tell the folks back home you saw nothing in New York but bacon and pubic hair." When he held her up she could barely stand, she felt so woozy. He was just as light-headed. They padded like old people into the bathroom.

In the shower he got down on his knees and laved her feet, her legs, her loins. He stood up, then ran the bar of soap up the crevasse between her buttocks. Soon both their bodies were slithery, foamy. And then she felt him probing with his finger where no man in her life had ever probed. She was too startled, too excited to resist. She just let his finger, then two fingers keep reaching. Tentatively, more assuredly, she began to explore him in the same way. They did nothing else, though their eyes probed one another's nearly as deeply. "Oh God," he said. Slowly, he withdrew his hand. "I want you to," she said. "I want you to do it. Anything. Everything." "I'm afraid," he said. "Don't be," she said. "No," he whispered, almost cooed, "not yet. I'm not ready." He drew her to him so that the water assaulted them both, blinding them. Then he turned off the shower. She felt a terry-cloth towel patting her dry, and hands beneath that terry cloth turning her around as though she were a mannequin. "Done," he said to her, smiling. Then he quickly buffed himself dry, hopped out of the tub, and headed for his clothes. And she knew right at that moment that she was never going to have all of him, that he would go the limit but not quite for fear of losing that last inch of control, that some part of him would always withdraw. And she also realized she was in love with him despite his fears. Of the prisoners who constituted her world, he was the freest. The people waiting for her back home were lifers, mummies.

Most of the afternoon had melted away. So instead of walking, they took a cab to a gallery where she could check out a recent photography exhibit, have something to report about the world of fine art when she got back to Boston. She also wanted to measure her own work against whoever's work was showing, to confirm what she feared Zack was neither brave enough nor candid enough to admit: that she was good but, like him, she could not go the limit; that her ambition was as diminutive as her photographs.

Her fears proved real. The exhibit was both gorgeous and humbling. Foggy scenes of lawn parties like those her parents must have attended when they were young hung there on the walls like black-and-white Impressionist paintings. Next to them were still lifes of eggs poised in simple bowls or against water glasses—eggs that were lustrous as marble, perfect as wombs, and as fragile. Trees, like sea horses, rose from smoky swamps, uncurling eerily.

Abandoned benches waited, in the middle of forests, for the sad arrival of autumn. "Now I know why you brought me here," he said. "His photographs are the same size as yours. Jesus, some of them are even smaller." She'd never heard of the photographer, some obscure Czech artist. He had, of course. The photograph featured in the poster for the exhibit was the one that moved her the most, a lazy summer lawn fête, with three very relaxed men, two of them in boaters, lounging on a bench beside a picnic table, their slouched bodies casting long shadows across the sunlit lawn. The scene reminded her of Florida, her father and Denis, the birthday parties they'd held outside, year after year, until after the accident. "Why are you so smitten with this one?" Zack asked. "Because life ought to be easy. Because it so rarely is." "Is this my passionate politico speaking? Where are the women, by the way, in this photograph? I see only rich and spoiled men, the kind whose wives I design magazines for." "They're there. You're just not looking close. They're wearing cloches, only the cloches look like men's bowlers. My mother's something of a hat freak. She'd appreciate this." "I like the boy, on the other side of the picnic table. He's the only one aware of the photographer, and he's looking straight at him. And he's probably wondering what the photographer sees in him at that very moment, or whether he's stumbled onto his presence by mistake and should look away. Or whether he himself is the one who has all the power, not the photographer. The boy already casts a shadow, only he doesn't know it yet. And you can't see it."

She couldn't budge. The vision gripped her.

"I want one of the posters."

"What you really want is this stillness."

There were no ogres in these landscapes, no one like the gnomes or stunted creatures she was drawn to. There were no old women clawing at the young, no old men extending handcuffs to their lovers like corsages. The women were all upright. And the men were all chair bound, marooned. It was a world in which snappy women could slip out of the men's lives and out of the picture, with no one minding.

"Stillness doesn't last," she said. "Except here. In a four-by-six."

"Nothing lasts," he said. "But we might."

They took a subway to the Village. She wanted to show him where she'd once lived. The old wedge-shaped building on Perry Street hadn't changed much; the paint in the front hallway was still a ghastly, pea-soup green. "Can you believe I carted a stroller and two kids up and down five flights of stairs here, at least twice daily?" "Yep. You're tough. And you have great legs." "I wasn't tough then," she said. "I was too depressed." She stopped in the local liquor store, one she used to know well, and bought a bottle of Valpolicella for dinner. She was swearing off the hard stuff for good, it seemed, ever since Zack had entered her life. "I know a fine place to eat," she said, taking his hand. "Then I'm yours," he said. She liked being able to lead him for once.

In O.G.'s Dining Room all the tablecloths were made of paper—drawing paper for the hungry to doodle on. "You live on an easel," she said. "You might as well eat on one too." They sat in the back near an empty chess table. Stained-glass murals of purple and yellow irises partly shielded them from other customers. He tried to sketch her face, then scribbled over it.

"You didn't let me see."

"It wasn't any good. I have a hard time with shadows."

They munched their way slowly through glorified hamburgers and played tic-tac-toe between bites. Then he switched to Ghosts. She was no good at these word games. When he added a *U* to the *DU*, she snarled.

"There is no such word," she said. "No real word, that is."

"Give up?"

"I have no choice."

"Duumvir. There aren't many words with double *u*'s, but that's one of them."

"Finish eating. I'll draw you instead."

"While I'm chewing? I'll look like a cow."

"Unlikely. Cows aren't as generously equipped."

He was easy to sketch—the forehead like a cliff wall, the hard jaw, and the protruding bones in his cheeks. His eyes, though, were difficult. They were like Baudelaire cat eyes. They pulled her towards him almost against her will—and then left her thrashing in the depths. They were as impenetrable as they were penetrating. She fudged them. Even before she finished, she knew what her drawing would look like: a mug shot. "Mine's no good either," she said, scrawling over it until it was all shadow.

"Do you know how to play chess?"

She looked up. The boy who had spoken was no more than nine or ten. He was removing chess pieces from a small pouch and setting up the board, still waiting for an answer from Zack. He hadn't asked her, she realized, but it didn't matter. The boy was the handsomest child she'd ever seen, a heartbreaker, flawless.

"I haven't played chess in years," said Zack. "But I'll try. What's your name?"

"Amaron."

What a lovely name, thought Dana.

"What does it mean?" asked Zack.

"It doesn't mean anything. It's an Indian name."

She watched Zack's eyes. Nothing registered. He and the boy began to march out their pawns, then their knights and their bishops. "I can take your bishop," Zack said. "That's OK," said the boy. Zack showed him other moves he could have made to save the piece. After a while, as the pieces got whittled away, Zack checkmated the boy. "Do you want to practice just check-mates?" Zack asked. "OK," the boy said. Zack's king now stood alone. The boy had his own king, plus his queen and a rook. After five moves, the boy calmly said, "Checkmate." "Let's do it differently," said Zack. He removed the boy's rook and replaced it with a bishop. He winked at Dana. "You don't mind us boys playing, do you?" he asked. "No," she said, "just so long as you stay away from other girls." The boy kept checkmating Zack, in fewer and fewer moves.

"Is he really winning?"

A blond girl who looked about the same age as Amaron had poked her way into the tournament.

"He is," said Dana. The girl was as pretty as the boy, a freckled Rapunzel. "Are you his sister?"

"I don't believe it. You're letting him win. He never wins at anything."

"What's your name?" asked Dana.

"Rosie," said the boy. "She thinks she's my sister but she isn't."

"I am too your sister."

"I'm nine and she's only six."

"I am not. I'm nine years old, and he's still a baby."

Dana scanned the tables within her view, but she saw no couples who came close to resembling these children. Maybe the parents had chosen to hide behind irises too. And they were probably not blond, and not particularly pretty. She and Tyler had been a very spunky couple for a while, and certainly good looking. But their children had turned out somewhat average looking— bland, hygienic. Rosie was tugging at Amaron's arm. Amaron, Dana could tell, was trying hard to keep Zack playing, keep up his interest. She was disappointed when Zack confessed to the boy that he needed to take a break for a while. Amaron put the chessmen back into his tiny felt bag, one by one. Dana couldn't watch him. She remembered how much it hurt to break apart a completed jigsaw puzzle, and how she would always destroy it quickly, even if Roo shrieked at her. And how the puzzle pieces crumbled between her fingers like oyster crackers. "Thank you for choosing me to be your partner," Zack said to the boy. "You're welcome," said Amaron. Then he and Rosie disappeared behind one of the panels of stained glass.

"So you play chess too," said Dana.

"Not well."

"God, weren't they beautiful children?"

"He should have been named Amaranth. That would go better with Rosie."

"What's an amaranth?" she asked.

"A flower. An imaginary flower. One that never dies."

"Do you want to have a child someday?"

"Are you asking that question in the abstract?"

"I'm simply asking."

"Dana, you know better than that. Simple always means complicated. It's not a simple question. Do you want to have another child?"

"You didn't answer my question."

"Yes. If I were to be honest I would say yes. But if I were to be realistic the yes wouldn't come easily, if at all. I don't consider myself a vessel of great genes. I may not look sickly, but I am. I'd hate to pass that on."

"You don't pass down diseases like that."

"You pass down the predisposition. Oh, I know, good genes do not preclude the possibility of a son becoming a heroin addict or a daughter an axe murderess. But I think you're asking the wrong question. If you were asking me would I marry you, I would probably say yes. Probably. But you're too old to be having children now."

"I'm not too old."

"Haven't you spent the past twenty years raising children? I thought you wanted to be a photographer now. I thought you wanted to do something for you."

"You always manage to turn the inroads I make into exits. Back to me."

"I was raised to think of others first."

"So long as your self-preservation's not threatened."

"I try to consider both myself and others," he said. "So should you. Another child would sink you. Do you in. Besides, I might only desire a child out of vanity. And would be appropriately punished. By having to raise a cretin who hated chess."

When they left O.G.'s, they saw Amaron and Rosie roosting on the banisters outside, like street waifs, still parentless. Zack said goodbye to them. But stairwells now possessed them, not chess. "They won't even remember we were there, who we were," said Zack. "He'll head right back in and start up a game with somebody else, soon as they tire of the stairs."

She pulled him towards her. They leaned against a car fender and kissed. Someone with a loud stereo in the building across the street was playing Connie Francis's *Greatest Hits in Italian*. They both giggled. But she was wondering when, if ever, he would shatter his stoic front and reveal his regrets, knowing that if he did she could never quite reveal to him all of hers—since she had refused to reveal most of them even to herself.

■■   ■■   ■■

On Sunday morning they lazed about in the loft, as they had the morning before, and thrashed about in bed, though not quite as frequently as before. He made breakfast. His eggs had more dash than hers, which both pleased and nettled her. "What'd you do to them, besides adding peas and fried bananas?" "Hmm, not much. A poor man's *huevos motuleños*." "What is there you can't do?" "I can't paint, like your friend John. Nor can I take cruel and cunning photographs, like you. I'm just a gigolo dilettante." "You're too self-sufficient." "I have to be," he said, smiling. "Whenever my breathing goes out of whack, there's no one to rescue me but me. I live with a killer, sweetie." *So do I*, she thought. They listened to an oldies-but-goodies station while they ate. When he'd finished, he lay back on the floor. He looked like a still life at that moment—nude with empty plate and orange-juice glass, and a speck of egg on his upper right cheek. But she saw he was owned by something other than his shapeliness, something that she was almost jealous of, since it would always come between them: his illness. It had made him strong; it had also made him too wary, too contained. Next to him, though, she seemed scattered: a dropout; a mother, and a halfhearted one at that; a halfhearted politico too; a minor-league alcoholic; a depressed case; a college student once more; an artist, but not really; a chameleon who shed vocations the way her mother switched hats. Nothing had come into focus for her except maybe her new photographs, and him, this beautiful, contented and discontented man. Definitely him.

They spent the better part of the afternoon wandering through Central Park near Fifth Avenue. Roller skaters taxied by, as though nothing were more pleasurable than an endless runway with no possibility of a takeoff. Old people puttered on the park benches, reading the *Times* or just watching the cyclists and skaters, basking in the presence of legs that had an easier time of it. "We're not that different from those lawn-party lollygaggers," she said. "Yep. But a romantic photographer might not be too turned on by these mohawk haircuts." "Ah," she said, "then be grateful for the soft-focus lens." "Hard edge, however, is your forte." "Yours too. Though I'd like to soften a few in you." "No you wouldn't," he said. "Without hard edges we're putty. And I don't think you'd want any of yours softened, the same as me." He was right, she knew. Had she her camera here, she would have ignored the sapped, spongy faces on the bench. She would have aimed instead at the boy they'd just passed, who looked as if he had rickets, and whose eyes were beady as a crow's.

Before they returned to the loft to pick up their bags, she coaxed him into stopping at the Museum of Natural History. She had an ulterior motive; and though it was selfish, it wasn't mean. She hadn't seen in years the exhibits of Indian handicraft, and she wanted to see them with him. Perhaps that could make up too for the ring she couldn't wear.

He seemed not at all interested as they roamed past the display cases, not even curious. Most of the objects were either primitive domestic tools or beaded ornaments or ceremonial masks. The colors had turned dingy over time. The woven baskets, chalky and tattered, looked like forsaken wasps' nests. No one was even bothering with this hallway except for the two of them. Maybe Indian culture really was a desiccated, dead thing now, she thought.

They circled the massive cedar tree canoe in the center of the main lobby. Wooden Indian slaves rowed while chiefs in war paint stood watch in the rear. One of the chiefs resembled a Masai warrior—his face a white mask except for the black rings around his eyes. The mouths of some of the slaves hung open. "I hate these carvings," he said. "They look like ghouls from *Night of the Living Dead*. Let's go, Dana. I prefer toxic waste to this."

On the train back to Boston she buried herself in *Jude the Obscure*, but she found it difficult to concentrate. If she gave herself over completely to Hardy, she knew she'd be admitting it was all over—the weekend. He was diligently piecing together the *Times* crossword puzzle, allowing her to read in silence. But there'd been too much silence ever since they'd left the museum. Then he broke it.

"You remember that talk we once had about power?"

"How could I forget?"

"There's a painting that's always haunted me, by Frederic Remington, who was not as pedestrian a painter as people like to think, even though he wasn't a very sympathetic man. It's called *With the Eye of the Mind*. And there are these three Plains Indians, on horseback, who've stopped somewhere out in the middle of Oklahoma or wherever. And they're gazing up at the clouds. And if you look at the clouds as though you were playing that kids' game, find-the-hidden-animal, you can see this blurry outline, almost like a Rorschach blot, of a chief on horseback, wearing a warbonnet. But this one Indian below—he has his hand raised as if he were trying to shoo away some pesky horsefly. I know Remington didn't intend for him to look like that. He wanted the horseman to be awed by the ghost rider, his arm raised in astonishment. But that's not what I see. All those feathers, all that dime-novel pomp and glory, all that power—it's as empty as clouds, an illusion, a trick of the imagination. So it's better for me—for anyone, for that matter—not to look back, not to look up. We're all dispossessed as it is, in this blighted world. I don't need to be reminded of being dispossessed twice."

"But you can't abdicate the past."

"I can, in order to possess a better future. Now, tell me this. What is a six-letter word for peacock-feather spots?"

"You're not being serious. You're avoiding again."

"I am. I am seriously avoiding. Though you should know me well enough to know you can always gauge the level of my seriousness by my lightheartedness. If it hurts, smile. Ocelli."

"What?"

"Peacock-feather spots. Another super-nasty puzzle."

She continued to half-read, half-brood. Every hour or so, the train stopped, the cars grew emptier. Riding next to him, in the deepening silence, she felt more uneasy than comfortable. She could imagine a future with him as somehow being like this train ride. She'd be leaning over her processing trays in her darkroom; he'd be down on the living-room floor rearranging his layouts; they would intersect at mealtimes and in bed; they would develop film and designs rather than their relationship. She would pester him with endless questions. He would answer but a few, and those minimally. Then, months later, he would flesh out a more copious response, after she'd forgotten the question. There would be mornings and early evenings of extraordinary sex, and moments when he would convulse her with laughter—and then these cool, unexpected, but soon predictable periods of hibernation. He had not betrayed his race at all. His sanctuaries were inaccessible, perched on some high ground she could never reach—and the rituals he performed there were always secret. Even the way he filled in the crossword blanks set him apart from her. She did not know these obscure words he knew: *oryx, xebec, dhow*. She did not know him. He seemed worlds removed from a man like Jude the Obscure, who had to pit himself against everything and was always losing. Zack fought only one thing, really—his illness. He was in retreat from all other battles.

Finally, the train pulled into Boston and began its slow, lumbering chug towards South Station.

"I'm going to have to get off before you," she said. "At Back Bay."

She tucked one man, Thomas Hardy, into her purse. The other got up to retrieve her tote bag and poster from the overhead rack. She slid out into the aisle and he followed her to the door. While the train jiggled to a stop, they kissed for a last time.

"Will you call me?"

"Whenever I can," she said. "It's so hard, what with Florence snooping all the time. Picking up the phone when I'm talking. I'm tired of screaming, 'Get off the phone.' "

"When you're not living there, you won't need to."

"Do you care about me?"

"Do you even need to ask?"

"Yes."

"Well, then, yes."

"Bye."

"I had a terrific weekend. You must thank your friend John for me. Monday morning is going to be a real letdown. No picnic."

"I doubt that. As soon as you're back at the drawing table, this will all seem like a dream."

"No. But my lot's easier. I know that. And you're wrong about one thing. I have chosen. Chosen you. You have the tough decision to make. Whether to leave him."

"If I don't get off now the train will—"

"OK. Talk to you soon."

She jumped off the bottom stair; she did not look back or wave. She was feeling rattled and tense, and guilty now—for having betrayed Leon, for leading a double life so badly, so successfully. She'd been mean when she told Zack he'd soon forget. She was the one who would have to forget. What was real was not a day spent licking each other's bodies, lapping up art and food and stray children playing chess and even Thomas Hardy and crossword puzzles. What was real was the three sad people waiting anxiously for her at home, who would never admit they were anxious but who were absolutely dependent on her.

They were all half-watching television when she came in. Florence was in her peacock chair, working on her needlepoint. Leon was slumped on the couch, with an open book resting on his lap. Her daughter, on leave again from her husband, lay on the floor. "Sit, sit, sit," said Florence. "So tell us what's happening. How was New York? What did you see? What did you buy?"

She was too tired to answer. The older Florence got, the more she behaved like an obnoxious child.

"What are you watching?" asked Dana.

"*Notorious*," said her daughter.

"Fair Hitchcock," said Leon. "Though he's stacked the deck against Claude Rains, who's too short for Bergman."

Too old as well, thought Dana. If she remembered rightly, this was the film where Ingrid Bergman was trapped in her husband's house and was being slowly poisoned by her husband's mother. As bright as Florence and Leon were, Dana knew they would miss the connections.

"Show me your print, Mom," said her daughter.

"It's a poster. You wouldn't like it."

"Come on. I want to see it."

Dana removed it from the cylindrical tube and unrolled it.

"It's pretty, Mom."

"Too much like Monet," said Florence. "But if you think art is 'pretty,' then goodness is irrelevant. This isn't you, Dana. This isn't your taste at all. I see only fuzziness, whereas you, your photographs are genius, Dana, genius. What did you say his name was, this photographer?"

Dana had already rolled up the poster and stuck it back in its tube.

"How was your painter friend?" Leon asked.

"John," said Dana. "He's fine."

"I tried calling you last night, to see how you were," he said.

"John took me to a party. If you don't mind, I'm tired and need to get some sleep. I've a paper on Hardy due next week as well as one on that book *Love's Body*."

"Your mother sounds like an overworked college girl," said Florence. Dana looked at her daughter, who had gone back to watching TV. Ingrid Bergman was so weak now she could barely sit up.

"But then you've been there already," said Florence. "So have we all. Even a genius must take her turn on the assembly line."

"Good night," said Dana. Upstairs, she stuck the poster in the bedroom closet. *I can't hang it here*, she thought. *Not with her, not with him*. She undressed, washed her face, put on a nightgown. Leon would try to make love to her after the movie was over, and she would probably resist at first, plead fatigue, and then give in. She felt as though she were some doomed two-headed creature, one head awaiting the guillotine, the other head plotting to pick up an axe and outdo Lizzie Borden. And there was even a third— it had showed its face in New York, whispering, *Everything is possible, life rushes out in concentric circles, like a dance of turquoise rings, any stone can skip across the puddles*.

But she had chopped off that third head the moment she stepped off the train. She did not believe in the possibility of everything, she could not let herself be hoodwinked by some mirage of even flow and smooth ripples, she could only focus on one small thing, a stone as big as a boulder, or certainly as big as the front door, a stone called *getting out*. No Cary Grant was going to come to her aid and dance off with her, drag her away from Leon and

Florence, and Zack wasn't Cary Grant. Did she want to live with Zack, though? Yes. No. She wanted right now to live with no one. Did she love Zack? Yes. No. Did she want another child? Yes. Maybe. Yes—if they did live together. But getting out was so much more important now than getting into something.

Soon she would hear separate footfalls plodding up the stairs. There was a slim chance she could hypnotize herself before that happened, then drift off to sleep. She reached into the already blurred memory of the weekend for one clear, lovely image that would not recede—not the men in their boaters at the lawn party, not the naked man who had lain beside her like a still life, but that street angel, that boy named Amaron who kept losing and losing and losing, and then kept checkmating, checkmating, checkmating. *I want a son*, she thought. *I never want another girl. Never.*

■ ■   ■ ■   ■ ■

The roses of Sharon were still blooming. The approaching fall meant nothing to them yet. The sun had grown no less scorching either. She had been here on the Vineyard for three weeks, alone, in a rented room in Oak Bluffs. School would be starting in two weeks, but she was pretending it was one of many options. She could drop out again, if she wanted. She could fly to L.A. and stay with Roo, until her sister's kookiness drove her bananas. She could drive to Mexico, Nova Scotia, Alaska. During her first week here, when she'd taken to bed rest like a consumptive, she cooked up dozens of plans. Raising nasturtiums, peonies, and tiger lilies in her own nursery. Writing children's stories, being a calligrapher. Making experimental movies. Working on an Indian reservation somewhere, maybe in Utah. Gradually, she consented to the only reasonable option. She picked up her copies of *Hamlet* and *King Lear*, the two books she'd brought with her, and read each of them three times, in order to write a semester-long overdue paper on madness in Shakespeare's heroes. The more she read, the more convinced she was that neither Lear nor Hamlet was mad. Ophelia, though—that was another story.

She had thought herself nearly as unhinged as Ophelia when she'd fled Boston and driven to Hyannis and taken the ferry to Martha's Vineyard. She had told her daughter first that she was leaving Leon, and her daughter had excoriated her. "Here you are, telling me I should patch up my marriage, while you're about to walk out on yours." "But I never married him," she'd said. "That doesn't matter," her daughter huffed. Dana had no idea then what really mattered, except getting out of that house for good. Leon was not surprised when she announced her departure, though she said nothing about Zack. He hadn't pleaded, he hadn't fumed. In his bathrobe and slippers he looked already capsized and defeated, worried only about his own survival. It was Florence who raged while she packed her bags. "Sex is fine for twenty-year-olds," she hissed. "Do you know that in some respects that is what you are? Twenty, only twenty. And twenty-year-olds always throw reason aside. You have these desires and they're foolish, irrational." "I'm not doing this because of sex," she'd snapped back. Florence was the last person she saw as she left the house. While she piled her bags into the car, Florence just stood there, in the front doorway, her face contorted, her thin hands rummaging through her even thinner hair. "Anyone can fuck!" she screamed at Dana.

That line drummed in her head all the way to Hyannis. Everyone thought about sex—at fifteen, at twenty, forty, even seventy. But she did not want, at seventy, to still be obsessed with it, to be gripped by that shrill demand when her body was like Florence's, veiny, wasted, pathetic.

Yet she knew she would be—that the desire to enter or be entered was unquenchable, nagging, tireless.

She had barely stirred her first three days on the Vineyard, except to feed herself. She listened to voices outside her window. She let herself be hypnotized by the flutter of the window-shade pull. The view from the window here was far more gracious than from her study in the city. No scabby roofs, no grey chimneys, no TV antennas. Only puffy clouds, and stars, and the flapping arcs of sea gulls. In Boston the gulls always looked dirty and menacing. Here, the screeching sounded mournful, almost poignant.

She had neither called nor written Zack. The ocean had put even deeper distance between the two of them. It seemed to her now that they had not been lovers at all, only fucking machines. He could never have pried her out of that South End dungeon. Perhaps he was right about himself. He wasn't strong, or not strong enough. She thought of him, though, nearly every day. She'd brought with her the poster of the picnic and had tacked it to the wall. It was the only thing she'd hung in the room, apart from a long panel of lace which she thought looked better as a curtain than the flimsy tablecloth it actually was, one of the room's few ornaments. The room was terribly Spartan. It contained only a bed and dresser, a writing table, a chair, plus her typewriter.

Slowly, as she began to realize she hadn't gone nuts and could focus more clearly on herself in her new surroundings, she started to soften the room, placing seashells on the dresser and windowsills, pitchers of daisies and black-eyed susans on the table. She bought two perfume bottles and placed them ceremoniously on the dresser top, in the center of the space created by her one beautiful necklace which her mother had bought her. She wore no rings.

Once, she tried to call Leon. But when Florence answered the phone she hung up. Florence would know who had tried to call. Or perhaps not. For Zack must have done that too, more times than she'd ever know.

Other times, she would pick up the phone, dial someone— Roo, John, her next-door neighbors in Boston—and then hang up before the call even went through. A week later she figured out what was wrong, what was missing. This room of her own—which she now finally had—was scaring her, not calming her. She had always been alone in the company of others. Now the lack of any company made her feel even more alone. She wondered if what she was in might be a worse prison than what she'd left behind.

One night, when she was sure no one could spy on her through the window, she put on some lipstick. She had not worn lipstick in nearly twenty years. It was apple-blossom pink. She left it on that night. In the morning, traces were still there—on her lips, on the pillow. She made up her lips again.

In the afternoons, after her mornings spent batting out pages of her Shakespeare essay, she would prowl along the beach with her camera, scouting for ruined bodies. A woman in a wheelchair who let herself be photographed seemed much more vulnerable here, since the chair was mired in the wet sand. Reluctantly, Dana was learning to accept why she was drawn to such figures: they were her twins, her kin. She was as trapped as they were.

One afternoon, when she was having a cup of tea in a local snackery, she heard someone call her by her name. At first she thought it was Leon. The man, who'd just walked in, had Leon's salt-and-pepper beard and moustache. Her first instinct was to glower, withdraw and steel herself: why did men hide their faces so? did they think beards made them more powerful, more intimidating? what were they afraid of? But then she saw it was her economics professor from the previous semester; and she wondered if maybe she wasn't making a snap judgment. After all, she'd had an affair recently with a man who was quite clean-shaven and who was scrupulously secretive.

The professor sat down across from her, as though she'd been waiting for him. "You mind?" he said. It wasn't a question. "No," she said. She did not think she liked this man. He had always seemed somewhat shifty to her, a little too clever and knowing. He had the eyes of a ferret. And those eyes, she knew, had paid more attention to her than they should have in class. She'd deserved an A, but he'd given her a B, probably because she didn't enjoy talking in his class, also because she'd made it clear that she wasn't responding to his mating maneuvers.

"What are you doing here?" he asked.

"Drinking tea right now," she said. "Actually, I'm writing. An overdue essay from last spring."

"You with anyone?"

She was not going to lie. The only way to blunt such an obvious ploy was to respond directly.

"No. And what are you doing here? Vacationing? Or working?"

"Neither. I'm getting divorced, and I'm frazzled, and I need a break before my wife's lawyer starts chopping me up."

Dana smiled a little.

"I'm here for the same reason as you, sort of. Though I am writing too."

"How long've you been married?"

"I'm not. We've lived together twenty years."

"That's too long for anything but a mortgage. Who's the guilty party?"

"I suppose I am."

"Someone else, I bet."

"No." She knew she would have left eventually, with or without Zack.

"You having fun on the island? Or just writing."

"I'm content."

"I'm not. The old supply-demand problem. The supply of fine-looking available women is running low here. They're all married or they're still in their training bras—except for one, I see. The demand, sorry to say, isn't elastic. To shrink and accommodate isn't my style."

"That's too bad. I guess you have no choice."

"I don't believe in too anything."

A half hour later he was in her bed. She could not account for it. All she knew was that she felt directionless, and starved, and needed to be either led or fed or both, if only for a few hours. He was swift and efficient, almost brutal. He peeled off her clothes as though he were stripping skin off fruit. When he took her, in a way she'd never expected, a way she had been ready for with Zack, she felt excruciating pain at first, then a sustained and partly pleasurable spasm of yielding and acceptance. It was, she realized, a total stranger, whose canniness and coarseness equally repelled her, who was managing now to lift her from her limbo. When he pulled out of her, he rolled her around to face him. He was grinning foxily. She touched his beard. It was slightly softer than Leon's. "I always wanted you," he said. "You knew it too. And I knew what we both needed was a mean fuck." Yes, she thought. But as she stroked his wiry body, she was thinking of a face in a doorway, hands grasping at a sunken chest, shriveled cheeks, hands raking through wisps of dying hair. *Anyone can fuck.*

He had to return to Boston before her remaining two weeks were up, in order to prepare for his classes. When she returned, she moved in with him. His apartment was not even the size of one floor of the South End town house. Still, he let her turn his cupboard of a second bedroom into a darkroom. The first night she felt firmly settled there, she made dinner for both him and her daughter, who'd decided a suburban lawn in White Plains made up for an arid, actuarial husband. After dinner, while she was cleaning dishes and her daughter was in their bedroom watching television, he nibbled on the small of her neck and said, "You've got a well-stacked daughter. If I'd known the mother had daughters like that, who knows?" He pinched her and chuckled.

The last weekend in September they spent in New York. "So this is the young man you've told me so much about," said John, when he welcomed them to his loft. Dana smiled. Her new man was precisely nine years younger than she. And five years younger than the last. Later, he told her he thought John's paintings were pretty mediocre. She wondered if he was maybe right.

When they were back in Boston she asked him if he wanted to have a baby. "I can't," he said. "Didn't I tell you? I had a vasectomy." She wondered why he'd never mentioned it before.

He must have assumed she was always safe. "Do you think it could be reversed?" she asked.

They visited a doctor, together. She asked most of the questions. The doctor was not totally discouraging. Afterwards, as they sat in a bar and drank white wine, he told her he'd give it a try, but only if she married him. She had told him all about her family, and the money. If more were ever to come to her, this time she would hold on to it, use it to support them, their new family. She knew his motives were cleaner than Leon's.

Her second night off the pill, when she realized she had perhaps been impregnated by the man who lay snoring beside her, she sat up in bed and trembled. It was just past midnight. The room was chilly. "Leon," she whispered. And then it dawned on her. She had finally married him, a younger, colder version of him. Out of guilt or anger she didn't know. Love's body was a ball and chain. You never escaped. It never came off.

It was close to one o'clock when she rang his bell. She was shivering from the light rain. "Who's there?" she heard him call down through the intercom. "It's me," she said. "Dana."

Would he buzz her through? He had every right not to. She noticed she'd left her parking lights on, but there wasn't time to turn them off. They could wait—like the man she'd left sleeping in bed. When she heard the buzz, she pushed through the door and shut it behind her fast, as though someone outside had been pursuing her. She rode up the freight elevator. When she got to his floor, she saw he had not yet come to his door. She knocked.

He'd obviously been asleep. He'd put on a bathrobe, and his hair was disheveled. His apartment looked even scruffier than when she'd last seen it, seen him—months ago. The stacks of magazines that used to teeter precariously had now collapsed. The slick floor was coated with lily pads of color; magazine covers; 8 × 10 photographs of beautiful buildings, beautiful women, flowers, machines; the paste-ups he was working on before he'd gone to bed. The soft blue light from the kitchen lamp made everything swim for a moment—the pillows, the plants, the stools and chairs, her eyes. And he—he seemed to be floating up towards her now from out of the pool, as wet as she, drenched from sleep, like a drugged merman.

"My place is a mess," he said.

"You always say that. I don't care. I've never cared."

"That's for sure. Would you like a drink or something? Coffee?"

"No. May I take off my coat?"

"What choice do I have?"

"I could leave. Right now if you want."

"No. Don't go."

She took off her raincoat, shook her hair dry while he paced around his kitchen, nervously.

"May I use a towel?" she asked.

"Of course."

When she emerged from his bathroom she saw he had poured himself a large drink. She hoped he did not do this every night, the way she'd used to—before she met him.

"Why are you here?" he said. His face was stricken. He looked as though he were about to weep or explode. "Haven't you done enough to me already? What more do you want from me?"

"I just wanted to see you."

"When you disappeared, when you left me, do you have any idea how frantic I was? How bereft? I wanted to marry you. I thought you loved me."

"I did. I do."

"I figured it out a month ago. I thought I was giving you time—to leave him. Then I saw you in the Public Garden one night with whoever he is. What a coward you were. Not to tell me. And me? I'm still walking around with a javelin in my side, trying to navigate through doorways. Have you come here to pull it out for me, or to twist it in deeper?"

She had taken the glass from his fingers, had cupped his face in her hands. And then her body, in spite of all reason, was pressing against his, needily. She unloosened his robe, and before he had time to offer any resistance she was half-undressed herself, then naked.

"Why are you doing this?" he kept moaning. "Why, why?"

"Because I've missed you. Because I'm hurting too."

Though she rode on top of him, she knew it was he who was taking her, angrily. The room was stifling. Sweat gushed off their bodies. She could feel grit on the sheets rubbing against her legs, skin flaking off and balling. When they were finished he did not speak. She had done something terrible. She no longer knew whose seed swam in her, whose leg she was chained to. But the future was beyond her choosing. That was what she had come to believe about everything that happened to her—in the past and the present as well.

She began to put on her clothes. He crawled out of bed and walked into his kitchen. She heard him cracking open an ice tray. He returned, still naked, the tumbler of scotch now choked with ice cubes.

"I don't want to see you again," he said. "I hated the way I made love to you. Bitterly. And I know there will always be that between us now. Don't ring my doorbell again. Please. Don't."

"I'm sorry," she said. She let herself out; she raced down the stairs rather than wait for the elevator. When she got home, she found the man in bed still smoothly snoring.

Shadowy faces on her dresser top stared at her—her parents, her sister and brother, her daughters and their husbands. But, like Denis, none of the photographs talked. The faces were just tiny bubbles, bobbing in an ocean of darkness. They had all jumped ship, rolled off the slick of the earth like barrels—and the only living thing remaining for her in this world was the slumbering beast with the hairy back who was in bed with her.

There, in those photographs, was everyone she'd lost, and everyone she'd loved. Save one. She had no photograph of him.

She had never taken one. She had never imagined that either of them would need preserving.

■ ■   ■ ■   ■ ■

On a drizzly November Saturday, eight years later, she happened to be standing in a crowded elevator in Jordan Marsh, which was stopping at every floor. She had rested her two shopping bags next to her feet. They were as heavy as the children she'd once toted years ago. Her shoulders slumped and relaxed, gathering strength for the ground floor and the trek to the subway. When the elevator stopped on the third floor, she looked up. And there he was. She did not know what floor he'd gotten on. Perhaps he had been there all the time but hadn't seen her until some of the other people had exited. She knew he was as startled as she. He stared at her coldly; then his face turned red. As soon as the elevator stopped again, he squeezed out quickly and vanished.

She tried to quell the jolt he'd given her, but couldn't. When she left the elevator she staggered a little. It was as though he, or someone, had shoved a javelin into her side.

In one of the mirrors looming beside a cosmetics counter she could see her white face, her tired eyes, her faltered looks. She had crossed over—but that, she knew, did not account for his flight.

She had felt this knocked out only once in her life, when she'd found that photograph of her mother the year after she'd died, and realized that her mother was anything but straitlaced, that her father had married some pornographic Betty Grable, some pinup or tart who'd deceived them all.

Now she was seeing herself in a way she could never have imagined.

"Are you the woman who wanted the Chanel atomizer instead of the bottle?" asked the salesgirl.

Dana shook her head.

No, she thought. *I'm the woman whom one man cannot bear to look at.*

1962

Though the solitary window in Mr. Stice's office was wide open, even screenless, no air blew through it. The secretary in the adjoining room typed to the accompaniment of a humming fan atop her desk. But apparently fans were a luxury that Mr. Stice himself could do without. As soon as he'd walked into the Spartan lobby of Chadbourne Academy, Denis sensed this was a place where the creature comforts would be slim. The open window only confirmed it, affording a preview of the natural air-conditioning for the months ahead. Already, he was beginning to seriously sweat through his seersucker jacket. At least the school was surrounded by trees, so maybe at night they provided some coolness.

Like any headmaster's office, this one was fairly easy to decode. The walls were indiscreetly plastered with framed degrees. Most of the file-cabinet drawers were partially open, as though they knew what a waste of time it would be to close them. A vase of straw flowers, a swivel-top pen, and an appointment book did not succeed at humanizing the room. Headmasters, Denis thought, were just another kind of dentist. Mr. Stice looked to be somewhere in his late fifties. Skin had capsized beneath his cheekbones. The creases in his forehead were deep enough to accommodate the edge of a ruler.

"Your recommendations are very good," he said. "Superlative. I'm fortunate indeed to have a candidate applying here from such a good school. Your placement office has responded with surprising promptness, considering. Considering the hastiness of all this, and our position relative to other schools that might rank, shall we say, higher."

"Yes, sir." Then there were other candidates, thought Denis, even for a summer teaching position at this late a date, less than a week before school started.

"Our generally reliable English teacher, Mr. Forester, jumped ship last week. It seems he has heard the siren call of Ayn Rand, and has elected to become one of her proselytizing disciples. Troubled boys in need no longer interest him, only supermen. At any rate, we are rather desperate for a good English teacher."

Mr. Stice was fingering through a folder. What had at first looked like a cigar ash lying next to the swivel-top pen Denis could now see was a dead insect. Its legs had curled over its abdomen. Its body had started to curl up as well. Denis figured the heat had probably done it in. Or else some Nietzschean superbug.

"You've not had that much experience teaching, I notice, even though you've been hired, I see, for a job next fall. Is that true?"

"Yes and no. I've been tutoring students at this small private school in Cambridge, Manter Hall, while finishing up at Harvard. I assume I performed quite well there, since I've been offered a full-time position. That means five or more classes a day."

"Had you not had any other job offers this summer? Or is this something of a last-minute decision on your part?"

The questions had a needling edge to them. But Denis figured he should answer them honestly—or pretend to.

"I'd originally intended to visit my parents in Florida, and spend some time with them after graduation. Then I decided not to. I'd rather teach."

"You understand, don't you, that Chadbourne boys do not usually wind up at schools like Harvard. Given your background, what in fact has drawn you to Chadbourne?"

What could he say? Yes, he preferred to teach at a private

rather than a public school. He was scared of the latter. But he also wanted to teach boys who would not necessarily be guaranteed the sort of stellar education he'd had, the sort he could, in his own way, pass on to others. Which was why he had taken the job at Manter Hall, which was why he was applying here. But how could he say that without seeming to prejudge Chadbourne boys, not even having seen them yet? And the other reason for grabbing at this job did not bear mentioning here: his mind would turn to mold in Florida, his mother would get on his nerves and drive him crazy, and his father's withdrawal would silently blast out the same old scary warning—*Look at me, Denis, if you don't flee, this is what will happen.*

"I thought that Chadbourne might be good for me," he said. "And that I could be of real assistance to your students. A reasonable gamble, to be sure." Denis wiped his wet brow with his hand. "What little I've seen of the campus so far also seems inviting." About that he was lying some. The campus was simply tennis courts, a rambling driveway, and this clunky wooden building marooned in the woods. A housing development had already begun to eat its way into the trees.

"Everything is a gamble these days," said Mr. Stice. "Just staying afloat is a gamble. You won't know that until you're much older. Now your major field, I see, is British literature."

"Yes, sir. But I'm trained as well in American literature."

"I should tell you that our summer school students in English are not likely to warm up to Chaucer or Shakespeare. They will probably need far more instruction in subjects and predicates, and parts of speech. You may not find that particularly challenging or interesting."

"I'm prepared. I can show them how to diagram sentences. They might even find it fun."

"Fun for them is water balloons, Mr. Downer. And stuffing peanut butter into the keyholes of my doors."

A rueful smile drifted across Mr. Stice's face like a passing cloud. Denis was not inclined to return the smile in kind, especially if the headmaster was in fact gently rapping a candidate's knuckles.

"I assume you can coach a water sport," said Mr. Stice.

It was the query he most dreaded.

"I'm not very good in water, sir."

How else could he have put it? If he had confessed to not being able to swim, he was sure he would not be hired. What young man his age couldn't swim? *And why can't you? Because I'm afraid. Then how could you have gotten out of Harvard, how could you have passed the swimming test? I bribed someone to take it for me. The only sin I've committed, ever.*

"The lake that's situated below the campus and to which we have access has always been one of our major drawing cards. Is there some other sport you'd feel more comfortable with?"

Mr. Stice, he could tell, was beginning to weigh in the missing athletic ingredient as a debit.

"I play a fair game of tennis," said Denis. *Or used to.* He'd played second singles in prep school his last two years, and lost only one match; but he'd not kept up his game during college. Reading novels had gotten the better of him. A few days of solid practice, however, would get him back in shape.

Mr. Stice was still perusing Denis's records as though they were troubling stock reports.

"I notice you've taken a good many French courses."

"Yes, sir. I minored in French."

"Would it be imposing too much if I asked you to consider teaching our French III class as well as two English classes? You see, something else unfortunate has occurred, apart from the unexpected flight of our fledgling objectivist, Mr. Forester." Mr. Stice bit off his words as though he were cracking nuts. But Denis heard something else. The job, it appeared, was his. Almost.

"Miss Kroger, our current language teacher, telephoned me yesterday to announce she could not fulfill her summer duties here. She has just learned she has cancer. Many of the boys enrolled here this summer have signed up for either Latin or Spanish I and II and may decide to back out, if I cannot come up with another language teacher. It would be a comfort if I could prevent the handful of boys who've already signed up for French III from abandoning ship too. They're all repeaters, I should add, as are some of the boys who'll be taking English. I'm afraid I can't offer much in the way of extra compensation, since you did not expect to teach French. But then there are also far fewer students who are enthusiastic about tennis. Most of them come for the lake, the water sports."

"*Je comprends*," said Denis. "I mean, I understand."

"Now, Mr. Downer. I should inform you about some of our rules here, though I don't imagine any of them will come as much of a surprise." Stice's voice went on automatic pilot; Denis heard a litany of phrases beginning with "no"—no drinking on campus, no women in the rooms, no smoking except outside in back, no flagrant misbehavior. "You and Mr. Jones, the history teacher, can alternate evening study hall and weekend duties as you see fit. One or both of you will have to ensure that all boys are in bed by lights out. Mr. Jones has taught summer school here for the past six years, so he's considerably experienced. Mr. Ogden, the science and math teacher, lives off campus. Miss Van Pelt likewise. She teaches art. But both of them take their meals here and serve as heads of table. Have you any questions thus far, other than regarding salary? I take it you would accept the position."

"Yes, sir."

"The salary may not seem like much—it's fifty dollars a week. But when you consider that your meals and room and bedding are taken care of, I think it quite fair. After all, you are only a beginning teacher. There's a laundry in town, by the way, that handles dry cleaning."

"The salary's fine, sir."

He could survive well on that. He did not need money from his parents; he had turned it down, in fact, unlike his sisters. *Why is a boy of your means even thinking about teaching?* his mother had said. *Teachers are poor people. They have no choice.*

"The boys will arrive this coming Sunday, most of them in the afternoon, and our first meal together is dinner that night. You should get here before dinner so that you can meet Mr. Jones and the other faculty. I will make sure that the standard textbooks for your courses are dropped off in your room next Sunday either by Mr. Jones or my secretary. The bookstore happens to be closed right now."

"Thank you, sir. Thank you very much."

Denis stood up and extended his hand, but Mr. Stice stayed put in his chair. His hand felt like a damp sock.

"I would show you around the campus now if I could," he said. "But my day, I fear, must be spent on the phone, tracking down Mister or Miss Polylinguist."

"I understand," said Denis. He did not goof and speak French again.

"This used to be an old hotel," said Mr. Stice. He looked distracted, almost glum, as though the building itself, like Miss Kroger, were on the way out. Then he picked up the phone and started dialing.

Denis roamed down the main hallway. The doors to the classrooms and cubbyhole offices were wide open, probably to let the stale air circulate, if it could. Several wooden tablet desks intermingled with the metallic ones of more recent vintage. The tattered maps hanging above the blackboards looked older than Charlemagne. The hallway angled to the left and led to more classrooms and the science labs. Denis retraced his path, passing the headmaster's office, the secretary's, the main lobby and central staircase, and continued to the other end of the hallway. One door there led to an immense kitchen. The set of French doors on the right opened to the even more spacious dining room. He negotiated his way around the herd of long wooden tables. He could see birch trees and pine trees through the windows, as well as patches of slatey blue that he knew weren't sky. For a moment he imagined he was in some lodge, a wilderness camp, not a private school. Just off the dining-room area, through another set of doors, was the common-room area. Lumpy easy chairs, scatter rugs, and a few card tables tried hard to give the room a relaxed look. But the options for relaxation weren't many. One could either flip through the pages of the *Saturday Evening Post* or flip the channels of the old Sylvania TV, if it worked. He figured the channels got more of a workout. There was a library off the common room, but it was woefully small. The only current book on the shelves seemed to be Nicholas Monsarrat's *The Tribe That Lost Its Head*.

Upstairs, the building was all dormitory. Most of the rooms had bunk beds, though there were several that were provided with single beds. He assumed those were for the resident faculty. An electrician was busily rewiring a fire alarm.

The central staircase was the only lovely feature in the entire building. The varnishy slick look had been tempered by time so that the banisters now looked warm and weathered. There were enough stairs so that one could take the descent at a pace brisk enough to propel one through the main door and past the sundial out front almost without breaking stride.

Denis walked around to the back of the building. Garbage cans were stashed in a shed that lurked outside the rear door to the kitchen. The raccoons no doubt were well fed. The trees behind the building had fooled him. They looked securely rooted. But often the base of a tree trunk was invisible. The school was perched on a high bluff; and many of the trees actually sprouted from the cliffside wall, then twisted, like coat hooks, and shot upwards. They were not trees to climb, or hang from. A massive wooden fence, fit together snugly like Lincoln Logs, cordoned off the cliff edge and the trees.

Denis followed the fence. The thick shrubbery and trees could only partly blot the view of the lake below. Where the fence ended, a steep wooden staircase plummeted to what was probably a beach below, though he couldn't be sure. Evergreen branches had formed too dense a canopy over the stairs.

He descended these stairs a little more carefully. When he arrived at the bottom, he noticed the boathouse moldering under the dense pines. Its rickety doors were peppered with tiny holes, the work of termites or marauding woodpeckers. The tiny padlock could have been filched by a toddler. The beach itself was pretty dingy looking, all grey pebbles instead of sand. Under his shoes it felt more like a driveway. The sandier section appeared to be some yards off, near the pier that jutted out on the water. A young woman in an orange bikini was sunning herself at the end of the pier. Probably a lifeguard, thought Denis. The beach, he guessed, was half private, half public; the pier, undoubtedly shared. A few couples slouched contentedly on their folding chairs, soaking up rays. Denis could see no children around, which was why the woman in the bikini could get away with catnapping. She looked like a cat. Her flanks were tawny, hard.

A tiny restaurant or store, he couldn't tell which, called the Snack Box, nearly abutted the boathouse. He was thirsty, so he crossed the invisible dividing line and walked in. A middle-aged woman who could have passed for Margaret Hamilton was brandishing a swatter and chewing out the flies. The floppy screen door brought them in, or else the unreliable screens on the windows. There were a few wooden tables where you could sit and look out at the scuzzy beach through the rips in the screens. A jukebox perched over one of the tables like a tiny accordion.

"You from the school?" the woman asked.

"Yes, ma'am."

"Damn flies. Gotta get that damn door fixed." Denis checked the door, to see if he'd left it partway open. "Don't bother. It won't stay shut. Soon as those schoolboys arrive, it'll be hell— between them and the flies. At least they pay for their food. What'll it be?"

Denis inspected the display case near the cash register. Nothing it offered roused much hunger. A fly was leaping from one slice of pie to another as though to test the springiness of the crust. The only safely wrapped edibles were Twinkies and potato chips. It was too hot to get anything from the grill.

"I'll have a Coke," he said. "You have any Clark bars?"

"Next week. We're short on candy. Third-graders cleaned me out."

"How about a Good Humor bar then?"

"We've got chocolate, coconut, toasted almond."

"Toasted almond."

She batted at the wall with her swatter. "Little bastards. They never run out of replacements. Just like the boys from that school up there. You aren't one of them, are you? You don't look like a high-school kid."

"No, ma'am. I'm a teacher."

"Marietta," said the woman. "She's studying to be a teacher too." The woman was digging around in the freezer. "She's majoring in PE. She'll be able to coach somewhere when she gets out of college. You an athlete?"

"Not much of one."

"Didn't think so. You don't look like one. Believe it or not, I'm out of toasted almond. How about coconut?"

"Coconut's fine."

Just then the girl in the bikini walked in and padded across the floor, leaving huge wet footprints behind. Her hair was wet too. She must have cooled herself off in the lake. She stroked her hair back and went behind the counter.

"Marietta, you want to ring up this sale?"

"I'm hot, Mom."

"This boy's at the school. He teaches."

The girl regarded him as though he were just another Twinkie. She padded to the cash register. "What am I ringing up, Mom?" "A Coke and a Good Humor." "That's thirty-five cents," she said to Denis. He gave her the correct change. The girl's mother was still foraging through the freezer. Denis still had neither his drink nor his ice cream. "Did I say coconut? I was wrong. We're out of Good Humor bars. I can't believe it. How about a Creamsicle?"

"Fine."

She brought him a bottle of Coke which was sweating worse than he, plus the Creamsicle. He took them over to the table near the jukebox. "Marietta? That woman called. From up the hill. The one with the retarded boy. You watching the beach?" "Not now, Mom. Kids don't show up here till after lunch. Are we out of root beer too?" "The truck's coming this afternoon." "I'm sick of orange Nehi." "Then have a Dr. Pepper."

He heard bottles clicking and sloshing. The girl walked past him, a Nehi in her hand. The screen door slammed behind her. Through the window he saw her mount the pier, set down her drink, stretch her arms up high, and then lean down and touch her toes. She was probably performing for herself, no one else.

"You mind if I play the jukebox?" asked Denis.

"No," said the woman. "So long as it isn't Chubby Checker."

He riffled through the selections. Nothing really interested him but one song. He dropped in a dime, and waited. When the song came on, he knew the selections had been mislabeled. "All the Way" had turned into "Duke of Earl." Marietta's mother must have hated Gene Chandler too, buried him under a Sinatra title she figured no one would play.

He finished his Coke and Creamsicle and placed the stick in the ashtray on the table. Just before he left the Snack Box, he noticed the poster tacked above the door, a gory photograph of what looked like some white fish badly hacked up. The poster was a warning urging swimmers to be careful of motorboats.

■■   ■■   ■■

The driveway in front of the academy was chockablock with sedans and station wagons when he arrived by taxi late Sunday afternoon, carrying his one big suitcase and his stereo. He'd decided not to buy a car that summer. After the interview with Mr. Stice and that quick tour through the school, he'd spent another hour casing the main street of the dismal nearby town before catching the bus back to Worcester and then to Cambridge. The town apparently generated its only business allure from the local shoe factory. Every other shop seemed to be a shoe store. Shoes even marched up the stairs of an aluminum ladder stuck in the display window of the hardware store—crepe-soled oxfords called "floaters." The movie theater, the size of a shoebox, was featuring a double bill of *The Horizontal Lieutenant* and *101 Dalmatians*. Only the stationery-and-book store held out a promise of stimulation for the mind. Otherwise, Main Street was nothing but a row of pre-Depression brick garages for parking shoes. Since the drive back and forth to the school took up a good half hour or more anyway, Denis did not think he would be tempted to leave the campus much in search of urban pleasures.

He had no time to unpack. Students were already knocking on his door, asking him, "Sir, where's this, where's that?" He had to steer them to Brad Jones, whom he'd just met in the lobby and who was now upstairs, trying to comfort some kid on the verge of tears. "What a pisser," said Brad, while Denis stood there watching. "The kid's parents dump him here, then drive off with his snorkel and sneakers. Caring folk. And careless kids. Come along, Steve-o. We'll find you some sneaks somewhere." Brad handed Denis a roster from his clipboard which listed the students at his dinner table, and another one which listed students enrolled in his classes. "Don't sweat it," he said. "I'll take care of the screamers. If any of the others have problems, tell them to see me or else put a pillowcase over their heads and breathe deeply. If they hate their roommates already, direct them to the cold showers."

Chatter and banging rocketed through the corridor. The silence of five days ago seemed a mirage. The boys looked like boys anywhere, except a little more catered to, more used to wearing sport coats. Some were comfortable with their fidgety, energetic bodies; others weren't. A few were pudgeballs. Some boys Denis could size up immediately as snobs or smartasses; others appeared diffident and wary. None of them had chosen to spend the summer this way. A few knew their way around the school already, probably the old-timers who'd flunked a course last semester.

Denis ducked into his room and changed from his polo shirt and khakis into a white shirt, rep tie, blue linen blazer, and khakis. He assumed, even though it was summer, that faculty could not dress casually for any meal, least of all dinner. And likewise the boys, though he wasn't sure. Since it was getting close to six already, he went downstairs and checked out which table in the dining room was his. At the head of one a small name card that read DOWNER had been propped against the water glass.

He felt agitated all of a sudden, worried. Could he do this, and do it well? Teach, take charge? Or was he maybe going to flub royally, in spite of his self-assurance, his "background," as Mr. Stice called it. To quell his jitters he backed off for a moment from the encroaching tide of events and hid in the library. No one was there. He calmed himself by perusing the book titles. *The Mayor of Casterbridge. Tess of the d'Urbervilles.* No *Jude the Obscure.* A smattering of Conrad. Lots of Dickens. The selection of British novels was predictable, standard fare. The American novels outnumbered them, oddly. The edition of *The Portrait of a Lady* was the same one he'd read for his American lit course at Harvard. The Modern Library edition. Such a fat book it was. At first he'd thought it only four hundred some pages long. But when he'd gotten past page four hundred and the end was still nowhere in sight, only then had he realized the novel was actually two books, two hefty four-hundred-page chunks. The page numbers had simply started all over again.

He pulled it out of the shelf, and gave himself no more than two minutes out of the five he had left before dinner to locate the deathbed scene with Ralph Touchett and Isabel. It came near the end but was still difficult to find. James was never generous with his dialogue. Most of the pages were densely larded with descriptions and interior reflections, seldom broken by paragraphs.

"What're you reading?"

Denis looked up. A boy, whose blond hair was almost white, stood there inspecting him.

"I'm not really reading. I've read it before. It's a novel."

"About what?"

"A poor girl who becomes very rich, and then makes some very bad choices."

The boy was perhaps sixteen or seventeen. He was startlingly good looking. His eyes were as bold as a blue jay's.

"It looks huge."

"It is. Eight hundred pages or more."

"Wow. It'd take me a century to read a book that big."

"Maybe not. You could read it in a day, if you did nothing else that day."

"A day? You got to be kidding."

The boy hadn't introduced himself. Denis noticed they were the same height. From a distance they might have been taken for twins.

"Does the girl get married?"

"Yes. That's one of the bad choices she makes."

"Does she get divorced?"

"No."

"So there's no happy ending."

"Not exactly."

"Jesus, why would you want to do all that work, read eight hundred pages, and find out everybody's miserable at the end?"

The dinner bell rang.

"My name's Cary," said the boy, holding out his hand. Denis shook it. "Do you water-ski?"

"No," said Denis.

"Too bad. But you can still be my partner. I'll teach you."

"I don't think so," said Denis, as he put back the novel. "It's time for dinner."

"Who are you?"

"Denis. Denis Downer. Mr. Downer," he said.

Boys were charging down the stairs, ricocheting through the hallway. The boy with blond hair had already abandoned Denis and joined the pack ahead. He looked back briefly, then disappeared into the dining room. Some boys who had failed to check the posted roster of dinner-table assignments had gathered around Brad who pointed them toward their respective places. Denis walked to his assigned table and stood behind the head chair. Then Brad was buzzing into his ear. "Assign Miller here as waiter this week. He's an old hand at it." Brad grinned. The boy named Miller, who was standing to the left of Denis, looked quite ticked off. Headmaster Stice raised a small glass dinner bell and tinkled it vigorously until everyone was quiet. "For these and all thy blessings, Lord, let us be truly thankful." Denis had not lowered his head. He did not really believe in prayers. All of the boys at his table had bent their heads down, like docile robots, except for the one at the end of the table. The boy with the blond hair, who was looking straight at him.

Suddenly chairs were pulled out, the newly dragooned waiters exited for the kitchen, and silence was once again overwhelmed by forty or more raucous male voices. Denis noticed three other heads of table apart from himself, Brad, and the headmaster. Mr. Stice must have lucked out and found Señor Cicero. Denis's anxiety about his new stature at the dinner table dissipated as soon as he sat down. He'd always thought the role of head the exclusive purview of much older men. But Brad wasn't that old. And food, not formality, was what was uppermost on the boys' minds. He didn't know yet the idiosyncrasies of Chadbourne etiquette; but he figured all would go well, would have to go well, if he behaved as cordially as his father and was as watchful as his mother.

"You're new here, aren't you?" asked the boy to his immediate right.

"Yes. I'm Mr. Downer. I'm the English and French teacher. I take it you've been here before."

"Yes, sir. I flunked geometry here last semester so that's why I'm back. Too bad there's no new math teacher."

"I thought Ogden was retiring," said another boy.

"Never. When he's six feet under he'll be figuring out the volume of his coffin." A couple of boys snickered. The boy to his left with the clever tongue smirked. Denis assumed he was being tested—to find out just how much leeway he would grant them.

"At least the grave," said Denis, "is a quiet place to get some work done. It may beat evening study hall."

Some of the boys smiled.

"Oh, Mr. Downer," said one, "no problem there. Soon as we hit study hall we're dead already, we can barely lift a book."

The initial reserve had been broken with ease. The boys were quickly defining themselves by their verbal mannerisms, inflections, facial expressions. He trusted he'd have all their names down pat in a day or two. When he asked for their names, they all delivered their first names first—except for the boy at the end of the table, whose first name he already knew. "Tillotson," he said. "Cary Tillotson. Sometimes Mr. Tillotson." Denis wondered if the boy was somehow mocking him, mimicking him. "You sound like a cadet," said Denis. "I went to military school last year, sir," said the boy, "but I flunked out there too." He smiled helplessly. "You're not amongst strangers," said Shoemaker, the one with the tongue. "We've all been shot down either here or somewhere else. By big and not-so-big guns."

Miller, the reluctant waiter, placed a steaming platter of sliced roast beef on the table, then tureens packed with tiny boiled potatoes and what passed for fresh green beans.

"Looks delicious," said Denis.

"Yes," said the boy named Marty to his right. "Miss Gload

always cooks up a feast the first week. That's so nobody'll complain about the food when our parents call, since that's the first question our parents always ask. 'How's the food?' Starting next week you'll see chipped beef, a lot of chipped beef."

"Chipped barf," said Pearson Adams.

"Then shepherd's pie."

"We know why shepherds won't get near it with a ten-foot staff," said Shoemaker.

"Don't forget the tuna dogs, liver, and Welsh rarebit—or rabbit cheese as we call it here—and for dessert, fish eyes in glue."

"Adams, you're a walking menu of disgust," said Shoemaker.

"Let's not ruin our appetites," said Denis. "I'm sure the food is healthy. Anyway, we shouldn't talk about the food. Something unimaginably tasty may turn up and surprise you."

"Grape Jell-O Surprise," said Adams.

"You mean grape jelly," said Shoemaker. Four of the boys started giggling.

Denis wasn't sure how to control this, since their private allusions were sailing over his head. Fortunately, they had to concentrate more on passing their plates back and forth while he served food. The platter of gravied roast beef looked far too messy and unwieldy to be negotiated by the younger boys. "One potato or two?" he would ask. They all wanted two. The breadbaskets were speedily emptied of rolls; Miller trooped back to refill them.

The boys didn't talk much while they ate. The ones who did talk were the returnees. Denis was used to eating fairly leisurely meals at home, and even at college. But here everyone whipped through dinner in less than fifteen minutes. Most of them wanted seconds, so Denis sent Miller back to replenish the meat platter, only to learn there were seconds on potatoes, not meat, and the beans had now been transmogrified into creamed corn. Maybe the disillusioning process had begun early. The roast beef didn't taste as good as it looked. The gravy had achieved only one of its two purposes. It had not kept the meat warm, but it did hide the gristle. Occasionally Denis glanced over at the table far off in the corner where the headmaster and his wife sat. Her face was as American Gothic as his, pursed up and chalky. Her no-color hair was knotted behind in a tight little pincushion. Neither of them talked while they ate. They were rest-home material already.

Dessert turned out to be a jelly roll. "Miss Gload's major goal in life is the promulgation of jelly," Shoemaker explained, to Denis and the other newcomers. "She's as liberal with it as she is with saltpeter."

"What's saltpeter?" asked Murchison, the boy whose voice hadn't changed yet.

"For growing boys," said Shoemaker. "To keep them from growing."

"And we should keep this particular exchange from growing too," said Denis.

"Yes, sir," said Shoemaker, grinning.

The jelly roll was at least easier to chew than the roast beef. Denis felt, though, as if he were eating breakfast rather than a dinner dessert.

"Mr. Shoemaker, would you clue me in on the rule here for dismissing the table after we're all through? I assume we wait for the headmaster and his wife."

"That's right, sir," he said. "And they move like turtles so it can take time."

The boy had a very snappy tongue, and knew it. But Denis did not think it right to chide him then, in front of the others.

"Are you nervous, sir?" asked Marty Conners. "Is this your first time teaching?"

"It's not quite my first time," said Denis. "And yes, I'm a little nervous. But no more nervous than you maybe are, as a student."

"You don't look old enough to be a teacher. I mean, you don't look any older than us." It was the first time the boy with the blond hair had spoken since he'd mentioned he'd flunked. "How old are you, sir?"

The question disconcerted him. It was probably an innocent

question, but it sounded less innocent than the more probing, even nosier question he'd just been asked. Was the boy intentionally putting him on the spot? Was his answer going to sound weak or evasive?

"I'm twenty-one," said Denis.

The chairs at the next table squealed and creaked and bumped. Students bolted for the hallway. The Stices had obviously left. The sudden noise was as loud as a burst of cannon fire. Denis realized what he'd felt like when the Tillotson boy had asked him that question: he'd been waiting to be executed.

"Come on, Murchison," said the boy named Zalinski. "Finish your jelly roll."

"I'm trying to, but I have a big piece and I don't want to eat fast."

"Masticate," said Shoemaker. "That's as close as you'll come to the real jelly roll anyway."

"Mr. Shoemaker," said Denis.

"Sorry, sir."

The boy finally scraped the last bite of dessert off his plate. Before he'd finished swallowing it, the other boys took off. Denis waited for Murchison to wipe his mouth with his napkin. "May I go now, sir?" "Yes, you may." Denis prayed the boy's voice would change overnight.

"It's worse than marriage," said Brad, who'd walked his cup of coffee over to Denis's now-empty table. "A shitload of uncontrollable kids, most of whom you still have to nurse, and they're fucking teenagers, no less. The others you're trying not to kill—and all you come home to at night is an iron cot, an army blanket, and a room that's hotter than a steambath."

"Don't forget the leather meals. The boys didn't complain, but my roast beef bent the fork tines."

"Listen," said Brad. "After we tuck the bastards in bed, and when the coast is clear, we can zip down to the kitchen. Miss Gload keeps the good stuff locked up, and I don't mean jelly rolls.

This first night the boys'll finish unpacking and decide if they can put up with their roommates. Some of them'll switch by tomorrow. Then they'll spend the remainder of the evening passing around smuggled-in copies of *Playboy*, which Stice will want us to confiscate soon as we can. Then one by one the older ones will head to the bathroom to beat their meat—that's when you hear a hundred toilets flushing. Then they'll finally conk out and give us a break."

Denis grinned politely. Brad was about thirty. He was lanky, pale, and scruffy-haired, and looked like he'd played basketball once, a long time ago. His good humor didn't seem to mask entirely his discontent.

"Shit. I'm already tired, and the summer hasn't even started. What a pisser. Want some coffee?"

"No thanks," said Denis. "I should head upstairs and finish unpacking too." Miller had cleared the table and joined the other waiters who hadn't eaten yet and who were sitting on the other side of the room, out of earshot. Before he left, Denis thanked Miller for the good turn he'd done.

A few of the doors upstairs were closed, but most were open. Boys were playing softball with rolled-up socks, pitching them into wastebaskets or dresser drawers. One was stringing a mobile of cardboard minnows to the ceiling light fixture. The dull slate walls were now brightened with hokey reproductions—Dali's melting timepiece, Picasso's malnourished guitar player, the Keanes' saucer-eyed waifs—most of which had been approved by the parents. The bathing-suit pinups and the Playmate foldouts would probably not last beyond tomorrow morning. All the boys had brought radios and stereos; even with the volume turned down low, they made an unpleasant racket. Denis couldn't imagine playing any of his own records with that din in the background.

Once he was inside his room, he shut the door. He arranged his shirts and underwear and socks and handkerchiefs neatly in his dresser, hung up his ties and pants, and stacked his six favorite

Sinatra albums, the only records he'd brought with him from Cambridge, on top of his stereo. Then he piled up the essential books he'd brought with him—Webster's, Roget, vocab books, his French dictionary—so that they rose in a graduated pyramid on one side of his desk. The unfamiliar textbooks he set directly in front of him, in a smaller pile. The neatness wouldn't last long. He, unlike the boys, had homework tonight.

He started to skim through one of the grammar exercise books, but before he'd gotten far someone knocked at his door. "Come in," he said. He assumed it was Brad needing help curtailing the stampede of stereos. And he hoped Brad would understand how he needed time for himself this one night to study these new texts. He'd planned to help out later anyway during lights out. His uneasiness passed once he saw it wasn't Brad. In the doorway stood Cary Tillotson.

"You're not angry with me, are you, sir?"

The caginess in the boy's eyes seemed to have taken a backseat to something else—a look of concern.

"No. Of course not."

"You're sure? You're really not mad at me?"

"Why would I be?"

"It's too bad you can't be my waterskiing partner, isn't it?"

Denis did not know how to answer. The request was so odd. "Yes, I guess so," he said. "But will you please excuse me now? I have to prepare for my classes tomorrow."

"Sure. That's OK. So long as you're not angry."

The boy shut the door as he departed. Denis tried not to think about the boy, who was a puzzle. They were no doubt all puzzles here, kids struggling with too little or too much sophistication, with too many words and equations or too few, with hopes that were not their own and failures that were. All Denis wanted to do was make each of them feel by the end of the summer term a cut above what he was at the start. A modest proposal, he knew. But a good one.

Denis plugged away at his opening remarks for each course

as well as his opening-day lesson plans. The new books no longer scared him. If anything, after three hours of reading, they bored him. He easily roused himself from the gerundive chapter when he heard Brad's voice bellowing from the other end of the hallway. "Into bed, suckers! Kaput with the records and radios. Nighttime, folks." Denis joined the night patrol, but with some reservation. The dorm, after all, wasn't a prison. He suspected that flashlights would click on once the other lights were doused. In the next half hour Brad barged into six rooms where he thought he'd heard suspicious noises. Denis knew what the boys must be thinking: *snoops, fucking busybodies, perverts.* He had gone to a considerably less relaxed prep school, though a finer one; but there they had the good grace to allow you to create your own hell—and if you wanted to stay up all night, you could, so long as you disturbed no one else. And if you flunked your exams the next day as a result of no sleep, tough. So be it.

"Come on," whispered Brad. "Manna awaits."

Denis followed Brad downstairs towards the kitchen.

"Miss Gload will have belted down a few," said Brad. "She always ties one on after dinner. Sometimes before. Steer clear of her breath if you can. After you've had a few snorts, though, it won't matter. We'll all smell the same."

If that was the manna, Denis knew he'd have to go hungry. He'd never been a drinker in college. He didn't like the taste of hard liquor, or even beer. The white window curtains in the kitchen had been drawn so no one could peer in. A tiny lamp glimmered on a table near the back door.

"Over here, boys. Look what I've got."

Miss Gload was standing in front of the pantry, beckoning to them. Her hair was a morass of sausage curls that had broken loose from her hairnet. When she opened her mouth, all Denis could see were snaggleteeth and spaces where teeth should have been. She was probably sixty, or close to it. She reminded Denis of the witch in "Hansel and Gretel."

"This is Denis," said Brad. "The new English teacher."

"You're a young one, aren't you? But I bet you know how to keep secrets too, don't you, just like Brad. See here, boys? The old skinflint doesn't know a thing, doesn't even suspect. I order them specially from London, England. Then I doctor the bills, right here, so Sticey thinks we're buying everything from Welch's. His stupid secretary—she can't even add. Old Sticeybird. Ha." She handed them each a pudgy glass jar full of dark gunk.

"It's red chelly jerry!" she whispered. "Red chelly jerry! He thinks we're ordering rape, but we're not. And I'm ordering more stuff too. Like preserves. The boys are all tired of apple and rape, and so am I. Always the same here, always the same. Grape apple, apple and rape."

Brad hadn't exaggerated about her breath. Denis was almost reeling.

"Terrif, Miss Gload," said Brad. "Now you wouldn't happen to have some more empty jelly glasses, would you? Like the one on the table over there, the one you just emptied?"

"You boys," said Miss Gload. She put back the jars and waddled over to the sink. From a cupboard below she pulled out a bottle that was half full of something amber-colored. Then she fumbled around in the sink, rattling glasses that maybe hadn't been washed yet.

"Just one glass," said Denis. "Nothing for me, thanks."

"No secret vices, huh?" said Miss Gload.

"None yet," he said.

"How about some ice cream?" she said. "Anything's better than that stinky jelly roll."

Denis was soon digging into a cereal bowl full of strawberry ripple while Brad drank bourbon. Miss Gload told them that before she retired she planned on dosing Stice's meat loaf with chili pepper, lots of it. "You've fed him too much saltpeter already," said Brad. "Nothing can get him hot anymore." "Not even the missus?" snickered Miss Gload. Denis wondered what saltpeter looked like, whether it was visible once it was sprinkled on food, and could be scraped off. He trusted he'd never eaten it before, when he was in prep school, but now he couldn't be sure. Miss Gload poured Brad another drink and offered Denis more ice cream. "I'm stuffed," said Denis. "Thanks anyway." "Whenever you boys want the special jerry," she said, "you let the waiters know." "Miss Gload," said Brad, "you can spread red chelly jerry on my toast anytime."

"She's a character," Denis whispered to Brad, later, as the two of them tiptoed back upstairs. "Yeah. And be glad Stice doesn't live here on campus. If he catches her or any of us with booze on our breath, we are out on our collective ass. Soon as things settle down, I'll take you to Waterfront Sally's some weekend. Where we can have some real fun. Miss Gload may be tired of rape, but not me. I wouldn't mind dipping into a little rape jelly right now. G'night, kid."

Denis was still grinning when he got back to his room. But not at anything Brad had said. *Red chelly jerry*. Miss Gload really was a sort of witch. A Joycean, nicens moocow witch. Gransel and Hetel would have nothing to fear.

■ ■   ■ ■   ■ ■

Shoemaker was his saving grace in French III. In fact, Denis could not understand at all how Shoemaker had managed to botch French so badly the previous semester, unless he and the teacher simply hated each other's guts. The four other boys weren't bad either, though they were less equipped with sophisticated vocabulary and less sure-footed with idiomatic expressions. They occasionally made the silliest errors, like turning *la fenêtre* into a masculine noun. A *celui-là* or *celui-ci*, a *lequel* or *laquelle*, could become an Achilles' heel. Shoemaker's sass always pepped up the class; and Denis knew how to stimulate him and keep him on edge by tossing his way exotic, daunting words that would send him scurrying to the dictionary—though he also knew Shoemaker would try to one-up him at that game, just to get his goat.

The boys in English I were dutiful plodders. They wrote paragraphs the same way they held pencils: stiffly. They dawdled through their quizzes as slowly as Murchison picked at his desserts. No wonder this was the only room in the school where Murchison felt unthreatened. He was a role model of near-feverish torpor, out-turtling even Stice. Whenever grammar lessons failed to up the wattage, Denis had *Great Expectations* to fall back on, which the boys were reading at the galloping rate of about two chapters a week. By the time summer school was half over, maybe Pip would have met Estella.

But English II was the worst. None of the boys could distinguish definite from indefinite pronouns; they could barely distinguish nouns from pronouns. Two of the boys were identical twin brothers from Venezuela—Damon and Arnold Ruiz. The third was Cary Tillotson. Denis assigned them a short story a week to read, along with the grammar exercises. But the Venezuelan boys always had problems comprehending the characters' dialogue, and refused to talk about the stories. Discussion, therefore, fell too frequently upon Tillotson's broad shoulders. But he always felt skittish about "finding deep meanings," as he put it. "This is too deep for me," he'd say—about some story whose depth rose no higher than a wading pool's. So then Denis would go back to scrawling sentences on the board again, like *Walking to work can sometimes be very tiring.* And then he would ask all three of them what the gerund was. And Damon and Arnold would shrug and say nothing. Then finally Cary would smile and say, "*Tiring.*" "Nope." "Then *very.*" "Nope. What do gerunds end with?" "I remember. *I-n-g. Walking.*" Even if he led them to the blackboard unblindfolded, with chalk in hand, and steered their hands to the very word, they would miss, the chalk would skitter wide of the mark. It was the one class that disappointed him.

Stice had been right about the turnout for tennis. After study hall in the afternoon, most of the boys piled on down to the beach. Denis escorted the rest of them to the shabby tennis courts near the school entrance. The tennis players, all six of them, included Shoemaker, the pathetic Murchison, the Ruiz twins, Kenny Osborne, and Marty Conners. He would team up Conners and Murchison, both of whom were poor volleyers, and have them play the twins, who were just as incompetent. All of them tended to lob rather than stroke, and few of the balls landed inside the court. Kenny Osborne, who wore a nylon stocking on his head to cover his alopecia, was as unembarrassed by that as by his manic forehand. His first serves were always powerful, and they always overshot. Denis would stick Osborne in one of the three courts with a bushelful of dead tennis balls and have him serve at an invisible player for hours before he let him do battle with Shoemaker. Shoemaker was a mean, muscular player with a lot of fancy moves, but he tended to cheat on his backhand if he could get away with it. Denis usually got a workout when he played singles with Shoemaker. To strengthen all the boys he'd force Osborne and Shoemaker to play doubles with him and one of the lobbers, depending on which of the lobbers was able to manage an imitation of a serve. Osborne could make Shoemaker play with more consistency, less razzle-dazzle. Shoemaker, on the other hand, could temper Osborne's reckless aggressiveness, make him a more thoughtful player.

When Denis himself was wiped out, having outlasted even Shoemaker, he'd call it quits, send the boys back to the dorm, round up whatever stray balls they'd overlooked, and head for the showers. Afterwards, he'd stretch out in his room, reading ahead for his French class, thinking up questions to ask about Lamartine, Victor Hugo. In that laggard hour or so before dinner, the halls were often quieter than they were during evening study hall. Sometimes, though, when he had quizzes and essays to correct, he'd trot down to the Snack Box and grade them over two Clark bars and a Coke. Which never spoiled his dinner, which in fact made up for it. Whenever misplaced modifiers and dangling participles cast too dark a pall, he could lift his eyes from the spiral-notebook pages and stare at the motorboats bouncing across the lake, at the water-skiers who seemed to be walking upon water as they rode into shore—though nearly all of them sank before reaching land, their skis bobbing to the surface like flotsam.

He had seen the vision on the third day of his second week in summer school. He had loped down the long flight of stairs to the beach, still a little dizzy from a grueling set of tennis with Shoemaker. Sweat dripped into his eyes, stinging him. He needed another shower already. If it was this hot now, in mid-June, then August would be murder. The lake had been hammered into a sheet of rippling steel. The sky gaped, like an open furnace. The whiteness scorched his eyes, made him stagger. And then he saw a man who appeared to be gold-plated rise from the blinding water, dip below, then emerge from the shallows and walk toward him, a lopsided cross of spears borne upon his left shoulder. *I am hallucinating*, he thought. It was either Christ or a savage. But it was neither. It was Cary Tillotson, toting his water skis, and shedding water like feathers. He dropped the skis in front of Denis as though they were offerings. Even through blurry eyes, Denis could see what he had never seen before, on anyone. A fine line of gold hair ran straight down the center of Cary's chest; and intersecting with the fine line of muscle beneath his breasts, it formed a gold crucifix. Denis had shut his eyes, seared by this new stinging. When he'd opened them, a towel had been casually slung around the boy's neck, like a boa, obliterating the cross.

When are you coming waterskiing?

I'm not. I can't swim.

You're joking, sir. I don't believe it. Everybody can swim.

I can't. Believe it.

How come?

An accident. When I was young. The swimming pool and I did not hit it off.

Did you have a teacher?

Yes.

He must have been a lousy teacher.

Yes. No.

I could teach you. You'll be swimming in no time. Honest. As good as me even, or almost as good.

Hey, Tillotson, cut the chatter, you skiing again or not?

Yes sir, Mr. Jones, yes sir.

The boy had melted into water. But Denis had seen the unseen thing, or more than one—and that was what brought him down to the Snack Box, at the tail end of the afternoon, day after day after day.

Today he started work on the essays his freshmen had written about the graveyard scene in *Great Expectations*. None of them could spell *cemetery* correctly. As sluggish as their prose was, it was still livelier than the material turned in by the boys in English II. After he'd cleaned up the essays, he tackled the sophomore quizzes, circling the grammar errors in red pen, then correcting them. Damon's was covered with so many red swirls it could pass for an illuminated manuscript. He was almost through Arnold's, which was turning out to be just as gaudy. The screen door kept swooshing open. He kept scribbling. Marietta's mother kept opening and shutting the freezer, usually in time to the flapping of the screen door.

Then he felt water dripping on him.

"How'd I do? Did I pass? Did I do OK?"

Cary sat down opposite him.

"I don't know. I haven't gotten to yours yet. I saved it for last."

"The best for last, huh?"

The boy always knew now when Denis was in the Snack Box, grading. Sometimes Denis managed to leave before he came in. But he was not really trying very hard to avoid him.

"I thought I told you boys to dry off some before you come traipsing in here," said the old woman.

"I did!" protested Cary.

"Look at those footprints. Look pretty wet to me. What do you call those feet anyway? Bear paws?"

"They'll dry," said Cary. "She's such a grump," he whispered. "What does she expect, owning a store on the beach? People get wet here."

He shook his head. Drops of water spattered on the quizzes.

"Oops, sorry, sir. OK if I watch you? You won't mind, will you? I can wait."

"You don't want to watch me correct your work, Cary."

"Because I'll get depressed? I won't, honest. Because I make a lot of mistakes? I know that already. I'm dumb."

"Don't say that. I don't believe that."

"Do you want another Coke? I'll buy you one."

"No thanks. Besides, you're not carrying any money."

"You should meet my sister, Linda. She went to college. In Michigan. She's older than you but not much. She's really pretty too, and bright. She writes. My younger sister's bright too. Everybody in my family is, except me."

"Where does your family live?"

"Ohio. My dad owns a company. He makes brass fittings. He must be a millionaire by now. The only thing he's lost out on is his hair. Hope I don't lose mine when I get older. He's promised me a job when I get out of school."

"Is that what you want to do? Work for him?"

"What I want to do most is get through sophomore year. I've been a sophomore twice now. I'm seventeen. I should almost be graduating, at my age. Instead, I'm a dunce."

"You'll pass, Cary. I guarantee that. But you have to work harder, concentrate more."

"I can't this weekend," he said. "My girlfriend, Nancy, she's coming to visit me here. Her mom's driving her up from Ohio. She's the chaperone."

Denis picked up his pen.

"You'll have Sunday night to study," he said. "Now let me finish these so I can have them done before dinner."

"I can't watch you?"

"No."

"You'd really like my sister," he said. "She's a lot prettier than the girl who works in here."

"Scoot," said Denis. When the boy left, he dropped his pen and pressed the palms of his hands against his face, as though he were donning a gas mask. He breathed deeply and slowly. *The way he breathed after his father had pulled him from the pool, given him artificial respiration. He'd misjudged the depth of the shallow end. He'd jumped, he hadn't waited. But his father was gone. Gone to fetch an inner tube. Gone. He had never forgotten the way water had closed over his eyes. Never.*

My one and only swimming lesson.

And now he was going under again, in some other way. He lifted his face; only part of the darkness fell from his eyes. He picked up the pen. Cary's quiz was a bramblebush of mistakes. He pruned it quickly so he'd have time to wolf down another Coke plus a grilled cheese, and really ruin his appetite—anything to quiet that other, rumbling hunger.

■ ■   ■ ■   ■ ■

That weekend, his third week at Chadbourne, Denis let himself be dragged off to Waterfront Sally's. A number of the boys had gotten special permission to leave campus that weekend, so the dorm was only a little more than half full. Brad had strong-armed the new language teacher into taking over his Saturday-night dorm duty. Denis wasn't all that wild about spending a night in some bar, watching Brad drink; but the loneliness that had assaulted him recently was keen and unnerving. On Friday afternoon he'd seen a lustrous red Bel Air convertible pull up to the school entrance with two women in the front seat: one, middle-aged with flame-red lipstick and a matching windbreaker; the other, a teenage girl who belonged in a Halo shampoo commercial. When the car drove off, he could see a third person in the rear seat. Denis waved to him with his tennis racket, but the boy was too preoccupied with the women to notice. Denis was grateful he'd finished his match with Shoemaker before he'd seen the convertible. Otherwise, Shoemaker might have trounced him.

Waterfront Sally's was less than a mile and a half away, only it took a good ten minutes by car to get there, since the road through the woods was unrelentingly bumpy and serpentine. Brad said you could see Sally's easily from any boat as soon as you got about forty yards from the beach. It looked like a shanty that had been sucked into a cove and left to rot. The surrounding forest as well as the high bluff shielded it from curious eyes. Sally's, unlike the school, straddled the water on its own level. Drunks who were totally sloshed could do-si-do out of the bar and onto the back porch and pitch themselves into the lake. But no one had ever drowned, said Brad. The water sobered them up right away.

Sally's could have survived safely only by avoiding the public glare. In the dark booths middle-aged couples, probably shoe-factory workers and their wives, crouched over beer mugs like conspirators. Mostly there were round little tables, dark and gouged and coated with ring-stained shellac, where the young townies and their girlfriends sat and smoked and drank and razzed the piano player. He was a guy not much older than Brad, but greyer in the face, sadder looking. He was batting out "When Irish Eyes Are Smiling," missing an occasional note due to either a broken string or his own sloppiness. "Sally loses two pianos a year," said Brad. "Some asshole finally gets fed up with the player and rolls him as well as the piano into the drink. Sally's the broad over there, in the crocheted outfit." She'd gotten a running start on Halloween, thought Denis. Saucers of maroon rouge were painted on her bobbling cheeks. Her hair was dyed the same garish maroon color. She was potbellied and wore a baby-doll slip and a fisherman's sweater, both of which barely covered her crotch. She was as tacky as the beaded curtains dripping from most of the doorways.

Sally planted a kiss on Brad and then chucked Denis under

the chin. Up close he could see wens lurking beneath her makeup. She was nearly as old as Miss Gload. "Honey, I bet the girls eat you up," she said. "What do you want?" Brad asked him. "A beer? You can handle that, can't you?"

The piano player had been ushered off his stool or into the lake. A jerky song that sounded like *tocka-tocka-tocka* boomed from the jukebox. Some of the couples who'd started to dance were doing the twist. Others were hunching their shoulders and jumping up and down as though they were on pogo sticks. Brad handed him a foamy mug of beer. "The UT," said Brad. "Big rage around here. Some dumbo dance they do at the University of Tennessee. Jiggle and hop as though a crab's just nabbed your balls." Denis took one sip of his beer; that was enough.

"How long's it been since you've gotten laid?" asked Brad over the noise.

"A while," said Denis. He had no desire to tell Brad the truth. Getting laid—the possibility of its ever happening seemed so remote. Whenever characters in fiction got laid for the first time, they were always disillusioned or disappointed; some of them even died shortly afterwards. He'd never thought much about sex, really. Whenever it happened, if it did, it would happen.

"I may scout up something tonight, so if I do—"

"Don't worry," said Denis. "I can take care of myself." He figured he could always call a cab if Brad needed the backseat of the car later on. Another garbled, unhummable song followed on the heels of *tocka-tocka*. Brad, he noticed, was wedging his way between two laughing brunettes at the bar. Denis set his glass down, then headed for the bathroom. He relieved himself, washed his hands, combed his hair. The bathroom's ugliness rivaled a gas station's. When he came out he dawdled by the cigarette machine, staring through the beaded curtain at the drinkers and dancers. He always felt like this in bars: isolated, not really there. Which was why he so rarely went into them. "Hey, handsome," said a voice on his left. "Got a light?" "No," he said,

"I'm sorry." The woman wasn't young. She wore earrings that looked like pink walnuts. There was lipstick on her front teeth. "You got a nice mouth," she said. Denis hurried out the swinging curtain and hoped that Brad was too glassy-eyed to witness his departure.

He walked back to school. When he looked in on Mr. Dorn, the new language teacher, he found him snoring in the library. None of the boys were raising hell, however. Most of them were in the common room, glued to "Gunsmoke." Were it Sunday night, only Denis would be down there, rooting silently for Arlene Francis and Dorothy Kilgallen.

He retired to his room, turned off the lights, turned on his stereo. Then he lay down and listened to Sinatra's *Only the Lonely* album. Sinatra had surely gotten laid many times—but where did that lead, except to deeper solitude, and a bed of nails? No wonder he wore a mournful clown face on the album cover instead of a fedora.

Sad songs are all lies, he thought. There is no such thing as a sweet ache.

He played an uptempo album afterwards, which canceled his gloominess.

Shortly before eleven he fell asleep. And he dreamed that an angel, nailed to a cross, was calling to him from the woods. And as he approached the angel, it turned into Cary Tillotson, shivering, in a whirlwind of rain. And as the dripping-wet boy enfolded him in his arms, which were still streaming with feathers, Denis cried out—for the cross, he realized, was nailed to himself, not the boy. And he could not tell if the boy was attempting to wrest him from the cross or was hammering the nails. The whirlwind closed in on them, slashed them with spikes of rain, then tore their bodies apart.

His own startled cry woke him. The pillowcase was sopping with sweat. The next morning Brad asked him why he'd left Sally's so early. *I got sick*, Denis said. *I had too many beers.*

Mr. Stice called him into his office early the next week. The Ruizes had phoned from Venezuela, worried that their sons might not pass English. A peeved Mr. Tillotson had also phoned. He'd paid an additional room-and-board charge to ensure that his son have a room to himself with no distractions; now he feared his son's teacher might be either too tough or too inexperienced. Obviously all three boys had been in recent contact with their parents. Denis could not imagine any of them writing letters, so they must have phoned. And he knew why they were petrified. At the end of the course he couldn't give them a final of his own devising; in order to pass they were required to take the standardized exam. "You're going to have to spend considerably more time with them, Denis," said Mr. Stice. "I suggest you use some of their evening study hall time to work with them individually. We may even need to detain them during the weekends. We can't afford to have these boys flunk." Mr. Stice looked more ashen than usual, as though the school were on its last legs, in desperate need of an infusion of cash, preferably from wealthy foreigners.

Denis was distressed, even hurt by the implication that he wasn't fulfilling his duties. And he was furious with the meddlesome parents for making such unfair assumptions. But his tenseness resulted from fear, not rage. He did not look forward to this project at all.

The individual sessions began, every night, at seven-thirty. He met with Damon and Arnold first, in their room. They were so sluggish and reticent, so stubbornly resistant to nuances of grammar, that by the time he was finished an hour later he wanted to crawl into some foxhole and blank out. Cary provided some relief afterwards, solely because there was only one of him. From eight-thirty to nine-thirty Denis would toil through the same exercises, turning himself into an extension of his Paper Mate, pointing out the conjunctive adverbs, the nouns in apposition, while Cary indicated or mimicked partial comprehension by nodding. In time all three started showing some raggedy improvement. But Denis was always worn out by these sessions, and found himself stinting on his preparations for the next day—which he couldn't afford, given Shoemaker's frequent leaps for the jugular in French class. Sometimes, too, he thought he would suffocate—from breathing in too much of their skin, their smells. At night the rooms were saunas. When he and Damon and Arnold leaned in unison over the grammar exercise book, he felt as though they were bound to each other's waists, like Siamese triplets. He knew the exact colors of their eyes, the length of their eyelashes, the way their nostrils twitched, the number of pimples blossoming on each face. Whenever Cary's arm would brush against his, accidentally, he could at least edge away, discreetly—since there were only the two of them.

Now, after dinner, rather than touch base with Brad before evening study hall, he would hightail it outside where the smokers congregated, lean against the fence that overlooked the lake, and steel himself, stare at the tabula rasa water, empty his head. Students left him alone, mostly because his back was turned to them. And the smokers, like drinkers, preferred to be with their own kind.

One night, though, Cary Tillotson ventured into that quiet space. Denis was not inclined to talk to him, for he would be grilling the boy all too soon, watching him breathe, think, grope, sweat. Still, it was rude to turn away.

"I'm doing better, aren't I?"

"Much better," said Denis. He was casing the sky, not the boy. In several hours the stars would be out, if the night was clear enough. Lyra. Draco. Cassiopeia. The Northern Cross—it would be tipped over now, on its side.

"I'm sorry," said Denis. "I was drifting. What were you saying, Cary?"

"You're lucky, sir."

"Lucky?"

"You didn't get shortchanged."

"I think we're all shortchanged, Cary. None of us is very lucky."

"But you're luckier. Sometimes I think God really messed up with me. Why couldn't he've sprinkled a few more brains my way?"

"If there is a God, Cary, he's not a saltshaker."

"I'm worried about the exam, sir. I'm scared to death."

"I know. But there's plenty of time ahead of us. Now could you just let me be by myself for a little while, Cary?"

We have at least that in common, thought Denis, after the boy had gone. *I have been scared to death too.*

■■　■■　■■

The next Saturday he played three sets of tennis with Shoemaker in the afternoon and won only two out of three. *"Alors! Tu n'es pas invincible!"* Shoemaker yelled after walloping him that one set, 6–1. *"Ne me tutoyez pas!"* Denis shouted back. *"Pourquoi, monsieur?"* "Because we are not intimates." "But, sir, we're intimate adversaries. *Est-ce que vous tutoyez Monsieur Tillotson?"* Denis knew the question had been tossed at him like a gauntlet. Shoemaker had obviously sensed something. *"Mais non, Monsieur Shoemaker,"* said Denis. "He's but another intimate adversary. *Comme toi."* "Bien sûr,"* Shoemaker replied, laughing. "Are you up for doubles with the twins, *les jumeaux terribles?"* asked Denis. The Ruizes were chasing high lobs, so he knew they couldn't hear him. "Impossible," said Shoemaker. "I'm bushed. Truly. See you at dinner, sir." Kenny Osborne had been half working on his serve, half volleying with the twins, so Denis roped in the three of them for a set, he and Osborne each being paired with a Ruiz. By the time they finished, Denis was as wiped out as Shoemaker. He also felt nauseous. The moment he got back to the dorm, he raced to the bathroom and emptied his stomach. Maybe it was summer flu; maybe he'd just overplayed. Whatever, he decided to forgo dinner, and informed Brad. Miss Gload's dinners had to be slept off anyway, so sleeping through one couldn't be that great a crime. He was too preoccupied with his nausea to worry about missing a tutorial with Tillotson. Maybe he could sleep through his dorm duties as well. Brad had already volunteered to drive the boys to the movies. The double feature that night had everyone excited but Denis. *Mothra* and *101 Dalmatians*.

Five hours later, when Denis woke up, he had no idea where he was at first, could not remember falling asleep, did not even know why he was sleeping. He was still in his tennis clothes. The room was pitch black. He felt lightheaded, famished. He groped for a Clark bar in his top dresser drawer. That would have to do for dinner, unless he could scrounge up some ice cream from Miss Gload. When he stepped out into the hallway, he heard what sounded like the keening falsetto of Johnny Mathis. The music, he realized, was coming from Tillotson's room. Still drowsy, he knocked on the door, then opened it.

Tillotson was sprawled on his bed, in a T-shirt and Bermudas, apparently studying. On the floor near his stereo lay a Johnny Mathis album cover. Mathis was wearing a billowy white shirt and white ducks and was strolling through clouds, as though he were performing in heaven instead of Las Vegas. He looked calcimined, unreal—but maybe no sillier than Sinatra in his pink clown getup.

"Aren't we doing noun clauses tonight?" asked Cary.

"No. I mean, yes. I guess. What's that smell?"

"Canoe. My new shaving lotion." Cary shot out of bed, opened the bottle that was on top of his dresser, splashed some of the lime-smelling lotion on his face. "Want some?"

"No thank you."

"It smells great. Tropical, sort of."

All Denis hoped was that it would mask the odor of his tennis clothes.

"Your hair's mussed up, sir. Pretty bad."

Denis ran his right hand through his hair, patting it down in back.

"Better?"

"You look like a cockatoo. Here. Use my brush."

Before Denis could say no, Cary had tossed him his hairbrush. Denis politely gave his hair a few strokes with the brush, not hard enough so that any hair might catch in the bristles; then he placed the brush back on Cary's dresser.

"I didn't know you liked Johnny Mathis," he said.

"What's wrong with him? This is my favorite album."

"I didn't say anything was wrong with him. I'm surprised. That's all."

He did not want to do grammar exercises with Cary tonight. He was hungry, maybe even sick. But the boy had clearly been waiting up for him.

Cary turned down the volume, then set the two desk chairs next to one another at his desk. Denis opened Cary's book to the exercises on noun clauses, then positioned the book at its customary slant so that Cary could point and write more comfortably. Cary was left-handed.

"Ready?" Denis asked, though he knew he himself wasn't.

"I think so."

"OK. First sentence. *We will serve for refreshments whatever goes well with lemonade.* Now, what's the subject of the sentence?"

Cary mulled over this for nearly a minute.

"*We,*" he said.

"Good," said Denis. "And the main verb?"

"*Serve.*"

"What about *will*?"

"That's a verb too."

"What kind?"

"The helping verb."

"Auxiliary. Now, what's the noun clause?"

Cary's fingers roamed across the sentence.

"*We will serve for refreshments.*"

"No," said Denis. "That's the main sentence."

"*Whatever goes well with lemonade.*"

"Good. Now why's that the noun clause?"

"*We will serve.* Serve what? *Whatever goes well.* It's the object of serve."

"What kind of object?"

"I forget."

"Indirect? Direct?"

"Direct object."

"Good."

"If Miss Gload was serving it'd be lemon jelly."

"Focus. Next sentence. *Whoever the senior class picks for president this year will have a most difficult job ahead of him.* Noun clause, Cary."

"*The senior class.*"

"Come on."

"*The senior class picks.*"

"The rule, Cary. What's the clause, the entire clause? All of it."

The boy took hold of Denis's left hand with his one free hand, as though he were clutching a water ski. He had no idea what he'd just done; he simply held on, while his eyes labored over the sentence.

"*Whoever the senior class picks for president this year,*" said Cary. "That's the clause. It's the subject of the sentence."

Denis could not move his hand. He could barely talk.

"Next," he said. "Read."

"*She knows that Ridley's sells the prettiest charm bracelets; what she does not know is how expensive they are.* She knows. *She*'s the subject of the sentence, right? She knows what. That Ridley's sells the bracelets. So that's the noun clause, isn't it? *That Ridley's sells the prettiest charm bracelets.* It's the object of *knows.* The direct object. Now the next sentence. *She's* the subject, she doesn't know. Nope.

Don't tell me. *Is. Is* is the main verb, right? *What she does not know*—that's the subject of the sentence, that's the noun clause. Jesus. Is there another one too? *How expensive they are.* That's gotta be a noun clause, right? That's what she doesn't know. What she does not know is *how.* So if there's an *is* verb, the clause is a predicate object, right? I mean predicate noun."

The hand dug in like a leech. The boy never lifted his eyes from the page. He broke down each sentence, methodically, meticulously. When he found the last noun clause, he let go of Denis's hand. An amazed smile shot across his face.

"I did it, sir. I didn't make any mistakes. Or maybe just a couple. I really did it."

Denis's hand, which had dropped off the edge of the desk, was still tingling, as though it were registering some aftershock from a blown circuit. He could dimly hear Johnny Mathis warbling about a ride on a rainbow, but that kind of ride had nothing to do with what had happened to him, as he'd sat there, in what might as well have been some sort of electric chair.

"Are we through now?" Cary asked.

"Yes," said Denis.

Cary got up and stretched, then turned up the volume of his stereo. Mathis's voice soared to castrato levels. Denis rose, walked to the door.

"Thank you, sir," said Cary. "Sir Denis." The boy laughed. "You know what I mean, sir."

"Yes," said Denis. "Good night."

On his way to his room he did not look back. He still held one of Cary's pencils in his hand, like a grenade. If he even twitched, it would go off. He shut the door behind him, laid the pencil down gently on his desk. He had forgotten his hunger. Then he stood by the window and stared at the night. Somewhere out there, surely, were other dark houses where someone like him might also be peering out a window, wondering if the gaping silence and vacancy and darkness and fear were a forecast of the future, all of it unstoppable. *I have fallen in love with a man. A boy. And I don't know what to do.*

I have spent years hiding from this. Years.

He hadn't once been out with a girl when he was in college. He'd made himself smart, gone out with books instead. Whenever nice-looking girls approached him or seemed to fawn over him at school, he assumed they were mainly interested in themselves, that they were simply using his face as a mirror. He wasn't interested in being handsome. Handsomeness was just a genetic whim.

Now he was not so sure. He saw no reflection of his own face in Cary Tillotson's; he sought none. But that hollow in the boy's chest, the ribs beneath his skin—they pulled at him like some divining rod, a magnet. Whatever these feelings were—longing, love, lust, or something else—they had gathered into a single cord that ran through him like a bell rope.

The summer was not yet half over. He could skip out, but he was too responsible to pack up and run. If he stayed, he would have to dance across land mines like Nijinsky. And if he stayed, he would have to begin preparing now for the end of what had not yet even begun. And did he want it to begin? Or, once begun, could it be stopped? Or had it in fact begun without his even knowing it, the moment the boy had buttonholed him in the library? Was that the worst of the unstoppable things?

God, I need help. I need someone to talk to.

He tiptoed down the hallway. He hated making reverse-the-charge calls but he was short of change. He shut himself in the booth, dialed, and waited until the operator had finished her spiel. Then he heard the hello.

"Dad?"

"Yes, son. How's my boy?"

"Fine, Dad. I—"

"How's the weather up there? Can't be any hotter than it is down here. Except in hell. You lie in bed for more than three minutes, you turn into an omelet."

"It's hot up here too, Dad."

"How're you doing? How's teaching?"

"Fine, I guess."

"I never had a teacher whom I didn't either worship or detest. There's no middle ground. Too many are slugs, believe me."

"Well, I'm not detested. Yet. Can't say I'm worshiped either. Dad? I'm in a—"

What could he say? Was he in trouble? In despair? In a jam? In red chelly jerry? He knew what he was in.

"Denis, I can't hear you, son. Is the connection bad? Can you hear me?"

"Yes, Dad. I can hear you. Can you hear me?"

"Yes, yes."

"I just called to say hello. I'm a little lonely, that's all."

"A little lonely, Denis, is better than a lot lonely. Loneliness is what we find waiting for us the moment we pop out of the womb. No wonder we all howl. Howling's sometimes good for you, though. Maybe you've a touch of the lone wolf in you, like your dad. We wolves are howlers. You need anything? Money?"

"No, Dad. Thanks."

"You'll be coming down to visit us, won't you, before you start teaching in September?"

"Yes, Dad."

"You want me to get your mother? I think she fell asleep after dinner, but I can go wake her."

"No, Dad. Don't bother. Just tell her I called."

"You need to get out more, Denis. See more of the world. Meet somebody. One thing I know will kill loneliness quickly and sweetly—and that's passion. You should—"

"I'll try, Dad. I have to go. Bye, Dad."

No help there. His father was too old, too far away, too out of it. He was also wrong. Passion didn't kill loneliness; it created it.

That night he dreamed the dream again, only the props

changed, the scene was less harsh, softened. There were no crosses, only a pillar of rain and the naked wet angel whose arms beckoned to Denis, circled his body tightly, cunningly, then gently, fingers combing through flesh and feathers while the rain beat on their backs and thighs—and the pillar became a black cleft in the sky through which both of them flew, inseparable, joined at the hip and groin, carnal Siamese twins.

And he knew the next morning what it all meant.

The sheet bore witness.

■ ■   ■ ■   ■ ■

He worked with all three boys together the next week, and the weeks that followed, in one of the downstairs classrooms. That gave him an extra hour at night to prepare for his other classes. That kept him from another hands-on encounter with Cary Tillotson. Yet the more he denied himself those sessions with Cary, the more tormented he was. He did not want the boy to feel in any way rejected, unworthy of special attention. The hunger, the curious compulsion, was in him, not the boy. If he sometimes turned away from the boy's beseeching stare, it was not because the ingenuousness in that face annoyed or threatened him; it was because he did not want the boy to notice the same, though not quite so ingenuous, look in his own eyes. A boy who couldn't read books well could still read faces.

If he learned before dinner on Friday that Cary was planning to stay in the dorm that night and watch television, he would then offer to drive the boys who wanted to go bowling. If most of the boys wanted to see the double feature in town—and he would make certain that one in particular was going—then he would opt for dorm duty and stay behind, watch "Route 66," play records in his room, read Verlaine and Baudelaire.

And this seemed to work smoothly until the Saturday night he heard a knock on his door. He'd been listening to Sinatra's "One for My Baby," and the knock was an unwelcome intrusion, though probably necessary. Even though he identified with the dejected lover spilling his woes to the bartender, he was certain his own private woe was not the sort most bartenders lent an ear to.

Cary was standing in the doorway—naked but for his swimsuit. He clutched a towel in one hand. The cross of hair on his chest looked as soft as cat's fur.

"I'm sneaking out," he said. "I'm going swimming. Nobody's in the dorm except the weenies playing Monopoly, and they won't tell. Come down with me. I'll teach you how to swim."

"In the night? You can't."

"Don't you trust me?"

No, he thought. *Yes. It's I whom I cannot trust. I, predicate nominative.*

"Come on," said Cary. "I'm a good teacher. Really. Let me teach you something. I've missed you, you know. You've been avoiding me. Have I done something wrong? Are you mad at me?"

"Wait in the hall," said Denis. "Let me get undressed." Shyly, he turned his back to Cary. He shed his clothes quickly, then slid into the one pair of shorts he had that looked most like boxer trunks. He had no swimsuit. Then he rolled up a towel and put on his sneakers. Cary was barefoot.

"Don't you need shoes, Cary?"

"My soles are hard as a rock."

"Mine aren't."

"You better take them off, sir. Your shoes. They'll squeak."

The boy was right. He'd probably done this before, and knew the ropes. Denis knotted the shoes together and draped them around his neck, just in case he did need them. They flopped clumsily against his chest.

Then the two of them tiptoed down the stairs. Denis could hear one of the boys in the common room squealing, "I'll buy it! I'll buy it!" Nobody noticed them sneak past. Once they were outside, they raced across the lawn and broke their running pace only when they reached the flight of stairs to the beach. Even the stairs, though, they took at a near gallop. Denis had not looked back once, for fear of seeing a face spying on them from a dorm window.

"We can't make much noise in the water," said Denis. "And I'm really scared. I mean it. Not just about being found out, but about this. The water."

"You're a worrywart," said Cary. "Like my mom. Don't worry so much." He had already slipped into the water and was dog-paddling.

"I can't do this," said Denis.

"Yes you can. It's shallow here. Walk in slowly. You want my hand?"

"No," said Denis. "I'll use the pier to hold on to."

He felt ridiculous, like a grown-up learning how to tie a shoe. When the water reached his waist, he started shaking.

"I'm freezing my ass off."

Cary laughed.

"You don't talk like that in class, sir."

"I'm freezing my balls off too, Tillotson," said Denis. "Now what do I do?"

"All right," said Cary. "Let go of the pier and walk over here, towards me."

"I don't want to let go of the pier."

"Then I'll come over there." He ducked beneath the water and then surfaced, right beside Denis. He looked like the dripping angel in the dream, only darker, colder. "If you get your back and chest wet, sir, you won't shake so much. Dunk yourself, sir."

Denis splashed water on his chest and shoulders, then lowered himself, tentatively.

"I'm shaking even more."

"Keep bobbing, sir. Just keep bobbing. OK. Now, stand in front of me. But turn sideways." Denis's shoulder lodged in the cold groove between the boy's breasts. Suddenly he felt Cary's wet arm gripping his back. Denis tightened his arms. "Relax," said

Cary. "All you have to do is lean back. I've got you. I won't let you go."

"What about my legs?"

"Soon as you lean back I'll get those too. They'll float. Trust me, sir."

"I'm scared."

"Don't you trust me? Are you still mad at me?"

Denis shut his eyes. For a moment it was as though he were safe in his father's arms again, lifted. He smiled. He relinquished himself. Cary's other arm had hooked itself beneath his legs. He was levitating. His crotch rose to the surface, floated beside the boy's waist, below the navel. *I am too wet to ever rise there, too cold.*

"You feel like a large dinner tray, sir."

"I feel like a corpse, Cary."

"Now when I let go, keep your butt up. You won't sink at all, I promise. But you've gotta kick your feet or soon you will sink. There."

The whole of him floated—for the first time ever. He could see stars. The Northern Cross, tipped on its side, just like him. He started kicking, then worried he was drifting too far from the pier.

"Cary?"

"I'm here."

"I couldn't hear you. Don't leave me alone here."

"How can I pass English if I run out on you? You're safe. You're in shallow water. You can stand up, sir. Why don't you hold on to the pier with one hand while you kick? So you won't get lost. Is it OK if I go swimming?"

"Yes. I'm going to rest for a while. As long as I'm still alive."

He wobbled as he walked to the pier. The pebbles were slippery. He saw Cary's arms attacking the water with rhythmic thrusts.

"Don't go too far," he called after him. "You're my responsibility."

But the boy couldn't hear. He had slid under the dark sheet

of water that spread out for miles. Denis climbed onto the pier, then sat there on the edge and waited. He thought he could see the boy's head poking up out there in the distance, hear him splashing. The head would surface in one spot, then another, like some romping dolphin. After a while he heard the paddle-wheel sound of the boy's arms, then the slash of his kick as he swam towards the pier.

Cary hoisted himself up, sat next to Denis, shaking water from his face and shoulders.

"I love swimming," he said. "I love being all alone out there. Just the water and me. And the sounds."

"Here's your towel," said Denis. "You're still pretty wet."

"Did you float some more while I was gone?"

"No. But I'm less scared."

"You're just like me, you know, sir? Sort of like me."

"What do you mean?"

"You can't swim out here. But up there, in English class, I'm the one who's sinking. Hey. Look."

On the moonlit beach human shapes emerged.

"Oh Christ," whispered Denis, "let's get out of here fast."

"No," said Cary. "They're OK, they won't bother us."

The three small children could not have been older than four or five, and were dressed in their undershirts and underpants. The bulky woman was wearing a nightgown or maybe a housedress. Only the man wore anything like a bathing suit, and there was too little of the suit and too much of him. His thighs were massive, his breasts drooped down like a woman's, his bathing suit was nearly buried under his bloat. If any of them had noticed Denis and Cary, they in no way acknowledged it. Slowly they proceeded into the water but went no further than knee-deep. Denis saw the man rubbing his body vigorously with something. Then the moonlight revealed a swatch of creamy foam on his chest. He passed the soap to the woman, who then passed it on to the children. They squatted down and dunked their bodies, then they padded just as quietly out of the water, picked up their towels without even drying themselves, and marched back into the shadows from whence they'd come. They could have been a caveman family. All that was missing were the clubs.

"They're down here every night," said Cary.

"Who are they?"

"I don't know. They live in a Quonset hut in the woods."

"How do you know that?"

"Hey, we know everything that happens around here. You don't think we study every night, do you? We know all about the woman in the bikini too. She doesn't have a boyfriend, in case you're interested. She's even dumber than me."

"Than I am. And you're not dumb. These people—they must not have any running water."

"They probably don't have a toilet either. Did you see how they were sitting in the water?"

"Stop it."

A frothy wake was lapping at the sand. By morning, Denis figured, the suds would be gone.

"We should go back now," he said. "I don't want us to get caught."

"At what? We were just swimming."

He let Cary win the race up the stairs. The boy's legs were longer than his, his feet more nimble. At the top Denis rested for a minute. Cary was still running in place.

"Tell me something," said Denis. "Why did you talk to me that first day of school? In the library."

Cary's feet stopped their dance.

"No reason," he said. "I just did."

"But why? Why single me out?"

"I was curious. You looked so engrossed. With what you were reading. I wondered why. I don't know how to be engrossed. You look at things so closely. I mean, you really like to look at things, study things. You look at me sometimes like that too. You do."

"I'm sorry. I don't mean to."

"That's OK. I don't mind. You're not like my father. He doesn't look at me at all."

"We're talking too loudly," said Denis.

"Mr. Downer, sir. Sometime I'm going to do something so scary to you you won't have time to be frightened, and then you won't be frightened anymore. But I don't know what. I'll figure it out before the summer's over. Maybe I'll drop you in deep water."

Then you would be like my father, thought Denis.

He put on his sneakers before he went inside. Hotels were still being purchased. Apparently no one had landed on Boardwalk yet. He could hear someone yelling at Murchison to shake the dice faster. The Monopoly game would probably last till lights out. With his towel Denis carefully wiped away the damp footprints Cary had left behind.

"Next time I'll teach you how to crawl," said Cary.

"You had better crawl into your room right now and dry off," said Denis. "The other boys will be back from town soon."

"Good night, Denis. I mean, Mr. Downer, sir."

"Good night."

When Brad returned, he told Denis he wished "The $64,000 Question" were still on television. He'd stake out his own special field of expertise: *101 Dalmatians*. He knew it by heart. The two of them raided the refrigerator after the boys settled into bed. Miss Gload didn't hear them. She was sleeping off her half-a-dozen-or-more nightcaps. Denis spooned a little red chelly jerry on his vanilla ice cream. Brad poured bourbon over his. Neither was very talkative. They just ate.

That night, in his dreams, Denis swam—across a green lake slick as marble, his arms pumping steadily like pistons, keeping perfect time with Cary's, until the lake was stopped by a huge black wall taller than any dam. Then the wall opened like the mouth of a whale. He could not remember the next day which of them had been swallowed, which of them had escaped.

What happened during the next two weeks he could not explain, but he feared he was somehow to blame. Cary began to falter badly on his homework exercises; he could no more identify a noun clause than locate Uruguay on a map. The Ruiz brothers, on the other hand, started to click. They carried the discussion in class about the Hemingway short story "A Clean, Well-Lighted Place," maybe because *nada* was a word they at last felt comfortable with. Cary just sat back and listened. On the most rudimentary quizzes he would now make gauche errors. The simplest homonyms tripped him up. *Their* would become the adverb; *too*, the preposition. "You're not focusing," he would tell Cary after class, "you're being careless." "I know, sir, I'll do better, sir." "You must." "Yes, sir," he would mutter. And the next day he would hand in an incoherent, rambling essay peppered with sentence fragments.

On the weekends Cary refused to do extra studying, would disappear from his room. Denis could only hope they'd bump into each other. When he opted now for either dorm duty on the weekends or driving the van into town, he would try to predict Cary's moves in the hopes of spending some time with him, even if that meant they couldn't be alone. But now he was always stymied. Cary had told him yes earlier in the day—yes, he would troop along with the boys who wanted to see the science exhibit Friday night in the town's city hall, an annual booster event sponsored by local businessmen. So Denis had switched his chaperone duty to Friday, only to realize that Cary was not among those piling into the van. He had no choice then but to drive the twelve least interesting boys in school, most of them Murchison's pals, to the exhibit, where he spent nearly two hours herding them through rooms full of percolating beakers and tuberous potatoes and dinosaur models made out of shoe leather. But were he to choose dorm duty on a Saturday night when he knew the boy was exhausted, Cary would then skip out at the last minute and head into town to see *Mr. Hobbs Takes a Vacation* and *101 Dalmatians*.

Cary had closed up. The impish smiles he used to flash regularly in class no longer appeared. When Denis walked past Cary's room late at night during the week, he could sometimes hear the sound of a stereo playing sotto voce, the voice of Johnny Mathis piping like a soprano mouse under the floorboards. Sometimes he thought he heard another voice too—the boy's, talking to himself. Denis did not go in.

The next Saturday night he switched duties with Brad at the very last moment, which pissed Brad off greatly. Brad had no doubt been planning on a quiet night in his room, reading the latest *Playboy*. Denis pleaded stomach cramps and fatigue; he couldn't trust himself behind the wheel of the van. He also knew that Cary had gone into retreat after dinner and hadn't budged from his room.

I've never done anything like this before, thought Denis, an hour later, as he changed into his shorts. He hooked a towel around his neck and left his sneakers under the bed. Then he walked down the hall and knocked on Cary's door. There was no answer. Denis opened the door.

Cary was lying in bed, in his underwear, staring at the ceiling.

"You want to go swimming?" asked Denis. "Maybe teach me the crawl?"

The boy's eyes did not move. "I guess so," he said. He rolled out of bed, and before Denis could even turn away, he had shed his jockey shorts. His lack of self-consciousness befitted a zombie, not a heathen. He put on his swimsuit, then draped a towel over his shoulders like a cape. From waist up he looked almost like a young friar. Denis had glimpsed for only seconds what lay below the waist. But he could not tell whether what he'd glimpsed was power or fragility or both.

Wordlessly they sped across the lawn, then down the stairs to the beach. But before Denis had even set foot on the sand, Cary had raced down the length of the pier, dived in, and was gone. For a while Denis heard the sound of those arms slicing through the water, then nothing but the lapping of a few wavelets against the pier. It was pointless to call him back. His voice could be heard by someone upstairs. Denis sat down at the end of the pier and rubbed his goose-bumpy arms. Even though the night was warm, he was shivering.

He lost track of time. He'd left his watch upstairs. Ten minutes could have expired, maybe twenty. He lay back on the pier, his feet dangling in the water. If the girl in the bikini could acquire her unreal caramel tan here during the day, what might he acquire at night? A lunar glow? A sheen of craziness that left no telltale marks? He had that already. Otherwise he would not be here, nearly naked under the stars, talking to himself. More dark, unmeasurable time passed. Then he was stirred to a sitting position by the sloshing beneath him, by the cold hand grabbing his ankle, by the soaked figure rising before him like some nightmare drowning victim.

"My God," said Denis, "what did you do? Swim across the entire lake and back?"

The boy's eyes were white and fearful. He flung his arms around Denis, dug his face into Denis's shoulder, and shook. "Help me," he said. "Please. Please help me." Denis's arms were pinned. He could barely move his forearms. They lifted, then stalled, like mechanical limbs that had run out of juice. He did not know what was happening. He was too afraid to lay his hands on the boy's back, to calm his shaking, quell the need, whatever need it was. Then the boy broke his grip, leaped away, and sprinted up the stairs.

Denis squeezed his arms—to stop them from trembling.
I have failed. I have failed him terribly.
Cold lozenges of moonlight floated below him, belly up.

■■　■■　■■

The boys were down to the wire during the last week of summer school. Denis had little hope that Cary would get through the course, pass the exam. Damon and Arnold, who'd improved radically and had upped their most recent quiz scores to 75 or better, had begun to slip as well, almost out of sympathy for their classmate. But Denis thought they still stood a good chance of passing. He had said nothing to Cary about that incident weeks ago on the pier; and Cary, in turn, had said nothing. Infrequently, he would laugh, usually over some royal grammar goof either he or the Ruizes had made. But most of the time he appeared remote, unstirrable, vaguely disconsolate. Had they been alone, Denis might have held out his hand to him, his arm. *Take it. Take my blood. Tap me, Cary. Squeeze.* But the time for that had died.

He could do only one thing more for the boy, and it would be risky. He was not even sure it would work. Walking on water was probably easier. But he had no choice.

He waited until well after eleven one night, until after he heard the last toilet flush. Pearson Adams always had to take a leak around then, as a result of having downed eight or more forbidden Cokes during evening study hall. A light was still on in Zalinski's room. He was probably reading *Playboy* under the covers, not Plato. If Brad had been awake, he'd've stormed the room, confiscated the *Playboy*, then tucked it under his own pillow to read late at night. Denis tiptoed past the room, figuring Zalinski would be loath to leave the comfort of his bed.

The main stairs creaked, he knew, nearly every one of them, so he slid down the banister. Now came the first tough hurdle. The front door was locked from the inside; even if he did unlock it, the clangor the door made was immediately recognizable. The window in the coatroom next to the lobby was more manageable. That could be shimmied open quietly. And with the coatroom door shut, any noise would be muffled.

Very meticulously, he jiggled up the window sash, straddled the sill, and then jumped. His bare feet made a louder sound when they hit the grass than he thought they would. Maybe his feet, like Cary's, had toughened. He would need leverage to pry open the bottom half of the unscreened window in Stice's office. And that meant he needed to stand on something. A garbage can wouldn't work. The lid would ripple under the pressure of his feet and make a terrible racket.

So that left only one thing—the sundial. If it was movable. He could perch on it as though it were a birdbath.

The sundial was far heavier than it looked. He didn't want to drag it across the lawn and leave a trail. So he had to keep lifting it up and setting it down.

By the time he'd positioned it beneath the window, he was a mess, his T-shirt drenched with sweat. He mounted the sundial, steadying himself by grasping the clapboards and then the windowsill. As he started to jimmy open the window, a pool of yellow light appeared below him. He pressed himself against the window frame. The light came from upstairs. No doubt the bathroom. Probably some boy who wore glasses and who needed to see the urinal he was pissing in. The pool evaporated. Denis waited a moment, then thrust open the sash and was inside.

If anyone were to hear him now, catch him, his career, he knew, would be ruined, his parents crushed. No one in his family had ever done anything as wrong as what he was about to do.

Mr. Stice looked too beaten a man to lock all the drawers in his office. If the school was taking a nosedive, so was the headmaster. What was there of value in here to steal anyway? Not the swivel-top pen, not the dime-store vase of flowers.

He started with the file cabinets. The ones near the desk contained nothing but personnel files and thick folders of financial statements, budgets, maintenance bills, donations. In the small wooden file cabinet near the door to the secretary's office he found the tests, neatly grouped according to subject. He turned his flashlight on, to the lowest setting, and carefully pored through the English exams, making sure there was only one version of the sophomore test and that there were enough copies. He took one out and shut the drawer. He could afford a smile now; he was halfway home.

On his way out the window he almost stepped on the prong

of the sundial. One yowl, and it would have been all over. He hefted the monster timepiece and staggered back with it; that was the worst part. When he was finished, he looked up at the dorm windows, a row of black eye patches. Maybe someone had seen him, but he did not think so.

He crawled back through the coatroom window, the test rolled up in his hand like a baton. He shut the window quietly. When he stepped out of the coatroom and into the lobby, a hand reached for him. He gagged, his cry of fright emerging as a hiccup.

It was Miss Gload, her gap-toothed face leering at him like some Halloween pumpkin.

"Thought I heard a prowler out here, but it's you. Mr. Sweet Tooth. You're in the wrong room, sugar. Come on out back now. Try something new. You'll like it."

Whatever she meant, he didn't dare go to the kitchen. If Brad was up drinking with her, and saw him sweaty like this and barefoot, saw what was in his hand, he'd be cooked. Behind his back he bent the baton in half, then wadded the clumsy bulk of it into the rear pocket of his shorts. "Maybe you'd like some of the other stuff too," she said. "For a change."

He had no choice. She had grabbed his arm and was dragging him off, like some shoplifter caught in the act. Walking was murderous. The exam kept threatening to spring out of his pocket.

And now Miss Gload was pouring him a jelly glassful of something. It wasn't bourbon; maybe it was scotch. There were just the two of them after all. Denis sipped his drink. It smelled like peat moss, tasted awful.

"I know all about you," said Miss Gload. She was spreading dollops of yellow-grey muck on a batch of Ritz crackers. "I know what you like."

He hoped what she meant by her question was food. He also hoped the crackers were for her, not him. The scotch was bad enough, though he was trying to get used to it.

"That music you listen to? I hear it. Ha. I heard it years ago. I was sweet on him too, believe you me. Mr. Bobby Sox. What a lot of nickels I threw away on him. 'All or Nothing at All.' Boy, I must've played that one on the jukebox till it was coming out of my ears. Now he's not so sweet anymore. Here. Have a cracker. You know something? The song doesn't even make sense. It never did. Tell me. You're the English teacher. Just who in this pissy world winds up with all, huh? Nothing, now that's something else, that's more up my line. How's the marbalade? Pretty good, isn't it. So's the old malt, right? 'Nothing or Nothing at All.' That's what it should've been called, right? You can go on living with nothing. Just barely. Are you listening to me? I know you, sugarboy. You've got secrets. And you better take care of yourself. No more of this creeping-around stuff. I think you know about 'nothing at all,' don't you? Don't you?"

He had drunk all the scotch, not meaning to. Her voice, scratchy and crazy, he'd barely listened to. All he'd heard were the sounds of words repeating themselves, as in a nursery rhyme or a comforting lullaby.

"I'm blotto," he said.

"A big boy like you? On one teeny little drink? Don't believe it."

"I'm off to my room now. My bed is calling me."

"Somebody waiting for you up there? Mr. Frankie? Mr. Nothing?"

Miss Gload laughed. Denis heard her jelly glass knock against her teeth, heard the scotch slosh onto the table.

He propelled himself up the stairs by using the banister and leapfrogging. The stairs squeaked only four times. Halfway down the hall to his room he abandoned stealthiness, since he could no longer walk steadily on tiptoe. He heard stirrings in a few of the rooms. *Only your drunken English teacher,* he wanted to shout. When he was safe inside his room, he unfolded the mashed exam and pressed it flat. *Hide it where no student would dream of looking. Then you can crash*. He reached for the chunky, oversized paperback on his desk. The CEEB Vocabulary Practice Book.

■ ■   ■ ■   ■ ■

"Cary, could I see you for a moment?"

In the past the boy had frequently lagged behind the others on his way out of the class, in order to keep Denis for himself. These days he tended to scurry out before Denis could stop him. Damon and Arnold were the first to leave today, though.

Cary looked irritated, and defeated. He'd been like this ever since that night on the pier. Denis wanted to take him by the arms and shake him, jar some life out of that glazed face. *Is it something I've done? Something I don't know about? Tell me, please tell me. You aren't mad at me, are you?* The boy's eyes were coated with a film of listlessness.

"Tonight, after lights out, I am going to work with you," he said. "I want you to stay up, and be alert. Brad's on duty, so we'll have to be extremely quiet."

"What's the use? I'm going to flunk."

"You're not," said Denis. "I have a copy of the test."

The bell rang for lunch.

"Remember," said Denis. "After lights out. And don't you dare fall asleep or decide to get looped."

"Yes, sir."

"Now scoot. I don't want us to arrive at the lunch table together, like we're conspirators." Or like something else, he thought.

The tennis matches that afternoon were both exciting and distracting. Shoemaker's slick forehand taxed Denis to the limit. For the first time that summer Shoemaker won the first set off him instead of the second or third. Then Denis rallied and took the second set, but only narrowly beat him in the third set, 7–5. The doubles teams had finally started to play tennis instead of volleyball. Even Murchison had learned how to hold his racquet as though it were something other than a fly swatter. Kenny Osborne had done really well by that bucket of dead balls. He'd mastered a wicked first serve; and when he missed, he no longer wasted his second. Denis played one final doubles set against Osborne and Shoemaker, knowing he and Conners would get creamed but not caring any longer. Every time he served he kept counting down: *Five hours left till lights out . . . four and a half hours left.*

He asked Brad before dinner if he could borrow his car for a while after finals were over. He knew Brad was already roped into driving the van. "I need to pick up my dry cleaning," he said. But there was something more important to pick up as well.

That evening the chatter in the room was far more subdued. No stereos twittered. Most of the boys had turned into grinds, reading machines. When the lights finally went out, nobody protested. Fatigue had conquered their anxiety about the next day.

He had become adept at this now—these forays into the night. Once again, Denis lingered behind the barely open door of his room, keeping tabs on the sporadic noises that always followed the announcement of lights out, weighing the pauses between this boy's cough and that boy's dropped shoe, waiting for the trips to the bathroom to cease and the stillness to lengthen measurably before he ventured out. This time he had to be even more cautious and devious. Brad was a carnivore when it came to evening dorm patrol, always eager to pounce on a glimmer of light beneath a doorway—the sign of last-minute cramming under the sheets with a flashlight. Denis didn't dare knock on Cary's door; he simply opened it quickly, then closed it behind him quietly.

Cary had fallen asleep, had not heard the door open or shut. Denis stood beside his bed. He had never really watched anyone sleep before. Or watched like this. Secretly. The boy's forehead was smooth as a washed stone, his breath as steady as the whir of a tiny fan. Whatever he was dreaming, his dream contained him.

On the floor, near the foot of his bed, were his two suitcases and his stereo. He had packed already. Denis could see the empty coat hangers dangling in the closet. It was as though the boy had never been here, never existed.

Denis roused him gently. "What?" muttered Cary. "Shhh," whispered Denis. "Where's your flashlight? Did you pack it?" "It's in the top drawer. Of my desk." Denis tiptoed to the desk, located the flashlight, then pulled down the spare blanket from the shelf in the closet and draped it over him. "You look like a leper, sir." "Thanks." He flicked on the flashlight, sat on the bed next to Cary, and then wrapped the blanket around the two of them. He had no fear. Though barefoot, he was dressed. The boy's arm, though, was flush against his. And their faces were so close he could sometimes feel Cary's breath blowing down his neck.

"I can't stay here long," said Denis. "So just listen. Here is the test you'll be taking tomorrow. I've circled all the right answers—but I've left three blank. It never looks good to have a perfect score. Now I don't care how tired you are. I want you to memorize these answers. Now. Tonight. If I could stay here, I'd drill the answers into you—but I can't. Are you awake?"

"Yes. Sort of."

"Here. Eat one of my Clark bars. Chocolate'll keep you awake."

Cary unwrapped the candy bar slowly, almost as though he were defusing a bomb. It was sweltering under the blanket. But a sheet, Denis knew, wouldn't conceal the flashlight as well.

"I have to sneak back to my room," he said. "I'll leave you another Clark bar, so you'll be sure to stay up. And I don't want you to say to yourself, 'How boring this test is.' Just read it, very carefully. And memorize, memorize, memorize. It won't take more than an hour, Cary. You'll still get a good night's sleep."

The boy bit into the candy. Denis could smell peanut butter and chocolate. The sweetness seemed to emanate from the boy's skin, not his mouth. If he stayed there much longer, he might not be able to resist the urge to press his lips against that flesh, bite into it, devour it. An impossible urge.

"Why've you done this, sir? Why've you done this for me?"

"Because. Because I believe you're valuable. Because if you believed in yourself more, you wouldn't have needed me to do this for you. Because I don't want you or this summer to go to waste. Because—"

He left the sentence incomplete.

"You know what I wish," said Cary.

"What?" said Denis.

"That I could plug into your brain tomorrow. The way I did that night. You remember."

"Go to sleep. Tomorrow it will all be over, all your worries. Cary?"

"Yes, sir?"

"I asked Brad, Mr. Jones, if I could borrow his car tomorrow. I'd like to drive you to the airport myself. I don't think Brad'll mind. Everybody's taking off at staggered hours tomorrow, anyway. At least the ones whose parents are picking them up. It only takes about an hour and a half to drive to Boston, so we could leave here around two or two-thirty, avoid the rush hour. Your plane doesn't take off until after six anyway, right?"

"Yep. That'd be great, sir. I'd love to."

"Now if you choke up on any of the answers tomorrow, don't panic. Remember the rules. Neither *is*, not *are*. Different *from*, not *than*. Pronouns as predicate nominatives always take—"

"The subjective case."

"Right." He could stay under the blanket no longer. The boy's bare foot was touching his. He handed Cary the flashlight and the test and crawled out of the blanket. "Just make sure you don't leave the test behind as evidence. Pack it in your suitcase before you fall asleep."

He slithered out of the room and shut the door. Seconds later, the bathroom door swung open, and Brad emerged, his shaving mug in his hand. Brad shaved every night as well as in the morning. Sometimes he'd catch boys in the stalls at night, he told Denis, wanking off. They were all heavy wankers, even the boy with ringworm.

"Little buggers have packed it all in," said Brad.

"Yep."

"Bet half of mine wipe out tomorrow. Some'll think Jefferson Davis lives at Monticello. Some'll identify Mad Anthony Wayne as Hondo's crazy brother. How's Tillotson? On his way to a third strike-out?"

"I hope not." Brad too had guessed about the two of them, thought Denis. No wonder he'd quit asking him if he wanted to tag along to Waterfront Sally's.

"Miss Gload's throwing a parting bash for her favorites late tonight. Emptying out whatever bourbon and scotch is left, probably not much, into those damn jelly glasses of hers. You joining us? Or are you going to meditate, or whatever it is you do up here?"

Brad already sounded potted. Maybe this was what happened to thirty-year-old men who'd taught in boys' schools for too long, the jocks especially. When they could no longer pass themselves off as overgrown boys, even to themselves, they sought another kind of buddy: like the bottle.

"I'm tired, Brad. One drink would lay me out flat. Say goodbye to Miss Gload for me. It's still OK if I borrow your car tomorrow, isn't it?"

"Sure, kid. Be my guest. Better watch out for splinters. Bare feet can get you in trouble up here. I've never seen you in bare feet."

When Denis lay down in bed his arms were shaking so much he thought the bed would start jumping. He gripped the sides of the mattress. His heart thudded and boomed like a pile driver attacking itself. The noise engulfed him; its loudness banged against the walls. How comfortless, how shabby this room was. How many boys had turned their faces to these walls and muttered curses, wept ugly tears? He'd wanted to read to his classes that poem by John Donne about the lovers waking up together and transforming their bed, their narrow room, into the universe, an "everywhere." Why? Because it had never happened to him. This cot could no more hold two bodies than a saucer two teacups. No one had lain next to him, in his arms, ever. This room was a monk's cell, a Skinner box, a nowhere.

The shrill banging in his head went on for another hour.

Sleep finally crashed in on him like a slammed window sash.

■ ■   ■ ■   ■ ■

The clamor of running showers woke him up. He'd overslept. His alarm clock had failed to go off. The boys were making more of a racket than usual this morning, probably because they knew they'd be free by day's end. Kenny Osborne was adjusting his nylon headpiece when Denis walked into the bathroom. "Breakfast is in eight minutes, sir," he said. "I know," said Denis. He felt weirdly calm. "Sir, I can't find my blue blazer. I was packing my clothes last night, and it's missing. Somebody's stolen it." "I'll tell the headmaster." "And Ricky Dodd's missing his marbles." "Ricky, I think, has been missing his marbles for a long time." "His Chinese checker marbles, sir. They're gone. Not the checkerboard, but the marbles." "I'll talk to Brad."

Denis took a two-minute shower, and shaved in less than one minute. When he arrived at his table, his hair was still wet and slicked back.

"You look like a matinee idol from the thirties, sir," said Shoemaker, after they'd sat down to eat.

"Rudolph Downertino," said Conners. "Take me to the Casbah."

"You mean the twenties," Denis said. "And Marty, you mean Charles Boyer."

"Who's he?"

Miss Gload had gone all out on the last breakfast. The pancakes were colder than usual and looked like cow patties. But for those who preferred jelly to syrup, two petri dishes had been placed on the table, one sporting a gummy deposit of red chelly jerry, the other a gluey mound of the yellow-grey "marbalade."

Tom Brannen was staring glumly at the pancakes. Everybody had dived in except him.

"Tom, I think you should have breakfast."

"I hate pancakes. I'd rather be crucified than eat another of Miss Gload's pancakes."

"I'd rather you stay alive," said Denis. "You need to eat something starchy, especially before exams. Pretend they're tiny pizzas."

"I hate pizza too."

"Then should we send out for nails and a hammer?"

The boys polished off breakfast quickly. They left the jams untouched. They still had to wait, though, for Mr. Stice and his wife to finish before they could be excused. Mrs. Stice was chipping away at her shredded wheat very slowly, and then swallowing each bite as though it were steel wool. No wonder her husband looked as though he were ready to cash in his chips early.

At last they rose from their table, like grey ghosts, and vanished.

"May we be excused now, sir?" asked Conners.

"Wait until Tom has finished his pancakes."

The boys at the end of the table glowered at Brannen. "Chug-a-lug, Tombo," said Shoemaker. "OK OK, Shoelace, but do I get a prize for eating masonry?" The boy stuffed the last wad of pancake into his mouth and swallowed.

"Thomas, are you through?"

He nodded yes. The boys split from the table. On his way to the classroom Denis stopped at the secretary's office to pick up copies of the exams. "For English I and II and French III," he said. "How many do you need for each class?" she asked. "Five for French III. Eight for English I. Three for English II." She rapped on the headmaster's door, then went into his office. Denis could hear the file drawer being opened, then shut. That an exam was missing from the file would never enter her head or Mr. Stice's, he was sure. And the tally of extra exams would always be constantly shifting, what with late enrollees and students dropping out. Besides, if Miss Gload was right, the secretary couldn't add anyway.

She handed him a stack of booklets as though she were passing on top-secret information.

The French exam was tougher than he'd predicted. He was glad he had not skimped on the passé composé. He was also glad he had gone over some difficult poems with them as well as short stories. The major poem on the exam was Baudelaire's "L'Invitation au voyage." When he'd first read that poem in college, one line in the refrain had mesmerized him, and he'd never known why. Now he knew. *Luxe, calme et volupté*. They'd been only exotic abstractions before. Now they had taken on flesh. They were names for what he felt when he'd first seen the vision in the lake.

Shoemaker was the last to finish the exam. Most of them were fuming towards the end. Multiple-choice questions were often the hardest. When the bell rang, nearly all of them groaned—in relief.

"Come on," said Denis. "It was rough, but not impossible."

"What's a *râteau?*" asked Peters.

"A rake."

"Damn it."

They dropped the booklets and their answer sheets on Denis's desk.

"A very foxy test, sir," said Shoemaker. "Too foxy. What in blazes is *hyacinthe?* In that Baudelaire poem. I thought it meant the flower, but I don't think so. *'D'hyacinthe et d'or.'* It was driving me nuts."

"It's a precious stone. A sort of reddish-yellow color. Like a fire opal. Or like the sunset."

"Oh shit, that's so unfair. That's the only line I couldn't translate."

"*Fini!*" shrieked Carson. "*Tout fini. Soyez heureuse, Monsieur Downer!*"

"*Heureux, Monsieur Carson.*"

"*Oui, bien sûr, pardon.*"

Most of the boys in English I, with the exception of Murchison, managed to finish their exams by the time the bell rang. Their pace had picked up. They moved like armadillos now rather than turtles.

When he walked into his English II class, Cary and the others were still leafing through their grammar books.

"OK, guys. You'll have an hour and a half to do this, and there's to be no whispering, no—"

"Can we go to the bathroom?" asked Damon.

"If you can't hold it. Yes."

"Can we use the crib notes on our arms when we go?" asked Arnold. He raised his bare right arm, which had not a mark on it, and pretended to read. "Direct object, prepositional phrase, adverbial phrase."

The other two laughed.

"Now quiet down," said Denis. "Read the directions closely, and don't rush through any of the questions. Take your time, but don't dawdle. If you think you're dawdling, move on to the next question. They're all multiple choice. I'll give you plenty of warning before time runs out."

They started. He could hear only their breathing, and the digging-in of number-two pencils. Once in a while, Cary would look up, and their eyes would appear to connect. Then Denis would turn his neutral gaze towards the others. When the sight of bent-over heads grew too boring, he would shift his eyes to the window. Two girls were playing tennis on one of the distant courts. They didn't belong there. They were probably neighborhood children. Sometimes the pencils were writing in synch to the quiet pock of the tennis ball, sometimes not. When a spell of total silence occurred, he would try to predict which he would hear first, the pencil or the tennis ball. "You have about five minutes left on this particular section."

It all sifts away, doesn't it? Grinding on; sifting away. The exam would come to a stop, and so would his time on this earth spent with this boy. But nothing else would.

The ball pocked; the pencil scribbled; and occasionally Cary looked up; and then the bell rang.

Cary, like Shoemaker, was the last to finish. "It was hard," he said as he turned in his test. "I'm sure you did well," said Denis. "Who knows? You might even have aced it." "I don't know," said Cary, "but I hope so." "I'll come by your room around two," said Denis.

Most of the boys at his lunch table were jubilant, even the generally morose Tom Brannen. "Aren't you glad you ate those pancakes?" Denis asked. "No, sir. I threw them up just before I took my first exam." "Tell us more, why don't you?" said Shoemaker. "Did they emerge in the same shape?" "I know I passed, though," said Brannen. "I don't care if I passed or not," said Peters. "But if somebody doesn't please pass the ketchup soon, my burger will need an IV." "No more Gloadburgers until September. Hooray." "Even the Snack Box burgers are better than these. At least they're hot." "Yeah, and so's the bikini who works there." "That's who you'll really miss, Zalinski." "So will you, Adams. Every time she steams a hot dog she won't be thinking of you, little weenie."

"This isn't great table talk, boys."

"This isn't great food either, Mr. Downer."

Brad was conferring with the headmaster about something. He stopped by Denis's table on the way back to his own. "Stice says we don't have to wait for him and his wife. They want to hibernate over their coffee." "Brad," said Denis, "your car keys." "Oh, sorry. Forgot." He handed Denis the keys, which Denis slipped into his pocket. "All right," said Denis, "are we ready for dessert?" "Dessert sucks, sir. It's pink pie." "Chiffon?" asked

Murchison. "It looks like bubble bath," said Shoemaker. "I witnessed the event this morning." "If it's made out of soap, then Miss Gload didn't make it." "I love chiffon pie." "You'd love to get depantsed, Murchison, and then be dangled from your thumbs out a second-story window." "We'll take a vote on the chiffon pie then, if it's chiffon," said Denis. "Who wants to stay for the pie?" Only Murchison raised his hand. "OK," said Denis, "the rest of you can go." Denis told Brian, the waiter, that there'd be one pie. Brian began clearing the dishes. Denis realized he could not leave Murchison alone at the table, not with the headmaster and his wife still in the room. "You're sure you want this pie, Murchison?" "Yes, sir."

Brian brought in a slice of the pie. Only Miss Gload could have created it. It quivered and gleamed. It was probably aerated red chelly jerry foamed up with milk, then made to levitate. "How is it?" asked Denis, checking his watch. "Yum," said Murchison. The pie was so steep and wobbly it demanded engineering skills to negotiate a polite biteful upon the fork tines. The delay was excruciating. Wedged between Denis and Brad's car was a piece of frothing pink pie.

Finally, Murchison scraped his plate and killed the last pink crumblet. Denis tore out to the faculty parking lot.

About twenty minutes later he was downtown. He picked up his dry cleaning first and deposited it in the car. Then he went to the bookstore.

The book he had special-ordered was a handsome, leather-bound edition of *The Great Gatsby*. "Isn't this beautifully made?" said the woman who managed the store. "Doesn't it smell exactly like a new shoe? Exactly. And the stitching is so elegant."

"You can wrap it here for me, can't you?" asked Denis.

"Oh yes," she said. "And you'll want a card, won't you?" She handed him a tiny cream-colored note with a matching envelope.

What should he do? The book was too beautiful to mar with

some inane inscription. So he'd have to make do with the card, which he knew could either fall out of the book or get tossed out with the wrapping. His Paper Mate dallied in his hand. What should he say? *To a fine student? From your English teacher, Denis Downer? Mr. Downer* wasn't right. Could he simply say *Denis? To Cary—from Denis?* What about *with affection?* Did that sound too stiff, or too embarrassing? He couldn't write the shorter word that meant something different. "Messages are so hard, aren't they?" said the woman. "Just take your time." But he didn't have that much time. Time was taking him.

He left the card and the envelope on the counter. Scott Fitzgerald was dead. How could he possibly mind? He'd been over his head in troubles too. Denis opened the book to the front flyleaf and wrote: *For Cary—who taught me how to float—Love, Denis.*

He picked out a deep blue wrapping paper. The woman wrapped the book expertly, taking special care with the ribbon. Denis hoped the bow would be tied with a little more flair than shoelaces.

"Come back soon now," she said.

"I will," he said.

I won't, he thought afterwards, in the car. *Not ever.* He had plenty of time still. It was only one-thirty. He'd be back on campus before two. He turned on the car radio and hummed along, badly, to dopey songs he'd never heard before. Every now and then he took his eyes off the road, for no more than a few seconds, to check on the book sitting beside him. It hadn't moved.

When he got back to the dorm, he raced up the stairs and knocked on Cary's door.

"I'm back," he said.

He opened the door. No one was there. The bed was made, the sheets turned so tightly they could have passed boot-camp inspection. The suitcases and stereo were gone; so were the shoes under the bed. Only the brisk smell of Canoe lingered in the room.

There's been a mistake. Maybe he's waiting for me in my room. But he wasn't. Denis ran downstairs to the secretary's office. She was squeezing the last drops from her teabag into her mug.

"Yes?" she said.

"I was supposed to drive one of the students to the airport this afternoon. He was going with me. Cary, Cary Tillotson. Have you seen him?"

"Oh, I think he left earlier, in the van. With Mr. Jones and the others. Yes, I remember. Mr. Jones told him it was silly to wait here as long as there was plenty of room in the van. And, you know, the traffic to Boston, it can be so bad. They didn't want to miss their planes, so they left a little early."

Her smile was saying how nice it was when people did favors for other people, lessening the load for others.

"Left? He's left? Left?"

He could not pluck his voice from the groove it was caught in.

■ ■　■ ■　■ ■

The lights in the Snack Box had been extinguished hours ago. The girl in the orange bikini was no doubt totally naked now, dreaming about some muscular coxswain who would wrest her away from her short-order duties and carry her off on his Chris Craft. The homes within sight of the beach, looming over the water like dark crates, had also shut down for the night. From one backyard a dog barked sporadically, then was silenced by some yelping human voice. A barbecue grill still sent up wisps of blue-grey smoke. The frogs were giving the crickets stiff competition. Their croaks ringed the shoreline, then mounted into the woods.

The lake was a deep purple stain. Unblottable. Spreading beyond the bordering trees, into the sky.

He was up to his waist in water, using the pier to hold on to. If Cary were with him, he would force Denis to dip his chest in, all the way to his neck, quickly, again and again—until he shook himself free of the shakes, until he belonged to the water, until it was air that became the alien element, not H_2O, *let it own you, Denis, a cold bed for a cold body, bend to the will of it, bend.* How could the water be so cold, though, when it was August, and the air was sweltering during the day? He had lain in bed all that afternoon, while parents arrived to pick up their offspring. Then Brad had stopped by after returning from the airport; and Denis had lied, said he had a raging fever and wouldn't be down for a parting meal, which he knew would be leftovers anyway, befitting the strays who were still in the dorm. He never wanted to see Brad Jones again in his life. Then he'd fallen into a deep sleep, only to awaken near midnight in a profuse sweat. And after shedding his clothes and putting on his shorts, he had walked downstairs like an invisible man. And the night air had refreshed him, cooled him. But now the water was too cold. And he was not sure he could go through with this at all.

He held on to one of the pilings. He let his shoulders and neck and the back of his head fall back upon the collapsible water beneath him, then thrust up his legs and puffed out his stomach as much as he could, extending his body tautly. For a moment his rear end seemed to weight him down, but then he was on top, floating.

He lay there, his hand still gripping the pier, until his legs would start to sink and pull him below. Then he quickly fluttered his feet, and his legs would lift.

Let go, the frogs were croaking. *Let go,* the trees whispered from across the lake. *Let go,* whispered Cary. *You have to let go of me; otherwise, you will not live. Did you hear, sir, how I made the connection—with a conjunctive adverb? Did you see, sir, how I made it? With a semicolon? Now you have to break the connection, sir. You have to.*

His arms were moving like scissors; his feet were kicking steadily, like a frog's. He was still on his back. He was carving a path straight toward the lake's dead center. The sky flattened above him, like a sheet of glistening tarmac. The stars—they were chips of glass, the leavings of numberless smashed headlamps, windshields. The script from on high was spelled out for him in shredded glass and tar: accident.

He knew he was in deep water. He had known that for some time. If he shifted his head too much to the left or the right, he might swallow water, though shifting his head would be the only way to tell how far he was from land.

His stomach began to growl. *Oh Christ.* Here he was, in the middle of a lake, ready to plummet to the floor like an anchor— and it wasn't his spirit that was protesting, it was his belly. *Why worry about food?* he thought. *You'll soon be food enough for others.*

He did something daring then with his feet. He crossed one leg over the other, shifted his weight onto his hip, and started pedaling, as though he were on a tipped-over bicycle. He was spinning, churning foam like a waterwheel. The spins made him giddy. Gleeful. He almost laughed. Above him now was a dizzying sky, bluer than India ink, littered with pinpoints of dazzle.

He did not want to die.

And now he was panicked. *Keep moving, stay calm,* he whispered. His arms scooped through the water while his legs kicked and he talked to the sky. If he kept on paddling like this, he would have to reach land somewhere, just so long as he steered a straight course and pointed his head like a torpedo.

He choked a little. Some water had splashed down his mouth. He was stroking too fast, stirring up the water too much. He was far too frightened to cry out. He just kept moving, on his back.

Then he glimpsed to his right the steep shelf of rock above which all the dark houses perched, like brooding owls. He was safe, nearly there. He was heading right back to the Snack Box, only he was approaching it from the other side of the pier. He knew he was back in shallow water again at last, and could stand up now.

He curled up his toes before he touched sand. But there was no sand. The water was suddenly over his head. He gagged as he sank, saw bubbles explode out of his mouth. His arms were flailing, his eyes were wide open. The lake had swallowed him, like some large, purple mouth. He thrust himself upwards, broke the surface but his legs pulled him down again. It was as though his body were filled with cement. He could see dim shapes below the water that looked like stakes—stakes that were just out of reach, that he couldn't use as hoists, stakes that he might as well be chained to. He had hit bottom but was still jerking himself upwards, unable to breathe, his mouth either screaming or taking in water or both. His nose was being sucked up through his eyes, his forehead was splitting. And then his head hit something hard, and he somersaulted, and felt his body unwind, soften into flesh jelly, and he knew he was being crushed and taken now, gorging on water that was flushing him free of fear, resistance, loneliness, pain, everything. He was on his way to God, who was dragging him through oily firmaments of water and sky, lifting him by his armpits, heaving, hauling him up to view the heavenly vault, the showcase of slivered diamonds.

He coughed; he gagged again. Water rolled from his eyes. He could see the lights. And he could see God now.

God was an isosceles triangle, a perfect vee of pudgy, sausage-white legs. God was a sack of testicles big as a bull's. God was the hulk from the Quonset hut.

■■   ■■   ■■

He had been in the white room now for a day and a half. He and the room were intimates. Fellow blanks. The life he'd known before had dropped off a cliff. His new life began here, in the white room, or once he walked out of the room, which he knew would be soon, too soon. The words the doctor had uttered he could not translate. They were simple words, clean words. "Viral." "Motor nerve." "Seventh cranial nerve." Even a poem by Mallarmé was less opaque. The words meant nothing; only the consequence mattered. He listened to the doctor carefully explaining the palsy to his mother and sisters. The three of them had been tracked down in New York and had flown to Boston that morning, rented a car and driven here. His father was due in from Florida soon. "It may right itself in six months," said the doctor. "That's often what happens with Bell's. But again, it may not." His mother's lips moved; she was playing with the words, turning them over and over, like a child toying with alphabet blocks. "But what do you think caused it?" asked Dana. "We don't know," said the doctor. "Perhaps the sudden change in temperature when he fell off the pier, or the shock. He may have hit his head on something below the water, a piling maybe. We just can't say. And neither can he."

He could not say, because he was not talking. Because he refused to talk. Because he had decided from that day forward, as the new life began, he would never talk again. He had seen his face already, once—and that was enough. He had tried to smile, but his mouth had neatly split in half. One side tipped up; the other drooped. "You will lose some of your muscle tone on one side of your face," the doctor had said. "You'll be able to eat, though, laugh, do everything you did before. You're a good-looking boy. Hardly anyone will notice."

But he noticed. Something about one of his eyes wasn't right. Even his nose was out of tilt. When he wiggled one nostril, the other just stayed put. His mother kept moaning, "My boy, my beautiful, beautiful boy." He wished she would shut up, or simply leave. Dana tried to calm her, then pestered the nurse with questions he already knew were unanswerable. Roo said nothing. She sat there by his bed, holding his hand in both of hers, stroking it. The one time he started to cry, more out of anger than self-pity, she wiped away his tears.

His father arrived later in the afternoon. Denis could see how distraught he was. The natural quivering of middle-aged flesh could conceal only so much. Denis had not smiled yet, or moved his face at all, in order to spare his father the worst. There would be time; and surely he knew already. No sooner had his father come to his bedside to relieve Roo than his mother shot up out of her chair.

"It's all your fault!" she said, red-eyed and scowling. "You were the one who insisted that he do as he see fit, that he dabble in teaching if that's what pleased him, that he teach at this ridiculous school so far from home. Look at him! Look what your selfish blindness has led to while you go waltzing off. You're never here when tragedy strikes. Where were you? Playing with stamps? Where were you years ago? You think you bear no responsibility for this because you're not here?" Spit flew from her lips. Her face was like some mad bulldog's. Denis was terrified. "You're never here!" she roared at the old man, who had shriveled into the chair beside Denis's bed. "You've never been here! You're still not here!" Then she broke down, sobbing. He watched Dana curl her arm around this suddenly older woman who was their mother, then lead her out of the room without protest. Roo patted his knee and said, "Don't worry. I won't let her behave like this ever again. We'll leave you and Dad together for a while."

The elderly patient who lay in the other bed in Denis's room had not stirred once during this scene. Denis wondered if he was dead.

Like Roo, his father had taken hold of his hand, affectionately. Denis would have liked to squeeze it in return, acknowledging the bond. But his father's hand felt no more remarkable than an ashtray. He was remembering another hand.

"Denis. When the doctor phoned me, when he told me what had happened, I swallowed the words like poison. I didn't want to breathe anymore. My life, my foolish life—I saw it float past me, a ship full of specters, going nowhere. All I wanted, all I wanted to hear, was you, laughing in my arms the way you used to. Remember? I don't know if your mother is right or not. Perhaps she is. I've not been all I should have been. To you. And to others too. Oh, yes. Others too. But I'm here, my boy. I'm here."

Then his father buried his head in the folds of the rumpled blanket. Denis, almost absentmindedly, stroked his father's hair. He did not quite believe either his mother or his father. His father's voice, like hers, often took a turn toward the baroque. He did believe, though, in sudden emptiness. He knew that absence, and not familiar presence, could occupy a seat at a dinner table. He knew that a smile could wilt now in the same way as a tree toppled—for good. He knew that love, any kind of love, could be siphoned away like a swimmer caught in an undertow.

Shadows began to stain the walls. Denis recognized the man with the wet face at his bedside as someone he'd known before, someone from the life he'd put away, someone who did not belong in the white room. It was a wingless, dark angel, bowed down by his own terrible cross.

■■ ■■ ■■

During that fall he stayed at home and gardened. Like his mother, he too was unable to nudge a single rose from the humid earth. But he coaxed up impatiens and even heather. The aloe plants with their bayonetlike leaves needed no tending at all. But he fertilized regularly the fruit trees that grew near the swimming pool that used to be. And he mowed the lawn every other day. His father had had the swimming pool filled in with dirt and transformed into a patio in record time, one day to be exact. By the time Denis had left Boston and flown down to Florida, there was no evidence left that a pool had ever existed, or that an accident had once occurred there.

The weather was beastly hot in September, worse even than those muggy days and evenings up north, in the dorm at Chadbourne. But he tried not to remember. Sometimes, though, when he heard the family next door whacking tennis balls loudly on their private court, he would think of Shoemaker, hear him cackling every time he aced a serve, hear him crowing, *"Tu n'es pas invincible!"* Don't use tu *with me, Shoemaker, that's only for intimates.*

But you're intimate with Monsieur Tillotson, aren't you, sir? He spent most of the day in the front yard, except when he needed to disappear, listen to music. He knew his father was often watching him from his work window upstairs. His mother stayed out of his hair. She was always tense, and could relax only on those few days that preceded her trips to New York.

In November a letter came for him. It had been forwarded from Chadbourne Academy. It was postmarked originally September. He was afraid to open it. He waited until he was out of his father's sight, and in his favorite place. Then he sat down under one of the coconut palms and opened the letter.

It was neatly printed, in pen instead of number-two pencil. Only the salutation was slightly messy. He'd written *Mr* after *Dear* first, then changed his mind. Turning the *M*, though, into a *D* meant crushing the *M*. He read the letter, reread it, read it again— unwilling to consign it to the wind or his dresser, not knowing what to do with it, knowing only that the more he read it, the more he still had to forget.

Dear Denis,

I'm real sorry I didn't get a chance to say goodbye to you. I was in a rush to get home, I guess. Oh well! I suppose you know about the exam. Mr. Stice said I failed. That figures. My father was able to get me into this great school in Arizona, because of connections or something. They'll make me a junior if I do good my first term in English. I bet I will! You were really a great teacher!

I'm married to my girlfriend, Nancy. I bet you didn't know. I'm going to be a father too. The baby's due in March sometime. Maybe you remember how grumpy I was last summer. That's when I found out. But now I'm happy. I hope it's a boy! Still, it's going to be rough going to school and having to be a father too. We can't live in the school dorm, that's for sure! But Mom and Dad are going to pay our rent! That's great, isn't it.

I hope you are learning how to swim now. The crawl is easy. It really is!

I hope you are fine. I learned a lot from you, and I will never forget you.

Very truly yours,
Cary Tillotson

Beneath his signature, a parenthetical phrase had been added: *your friend!*

The exclamation point was enclosed, properly, within the parentheses.

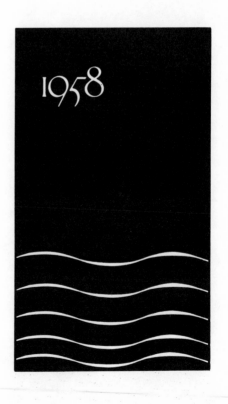

The photographer is grateful there's no fidgety, malcontent dog to deal with too. He has had his tripod and his 4 × 5 Graflex set up on the lawn now for nearly twenty minutes, and the women are still fussing with their hats. None of them seem the least bit concerned about shadows and the shifting angle of the sun, his major worries now. Five chapeaux are five too many chapeaux here, he wants to tell them, but how can he? The mother's hat dominates and leads the others like a lioness patrolling her cubs, and he knows that under no circumstances would she relent and discard it for this shot. She has become her hat, he thinks. It sits on her small head like an immense kidney-shaped swimming pool choked with water lilies. A Gainsborough beauty she isn't. But that's why, he knows, some women who've begun to lose their looks will take so feverishly to wearing brooches big as palmetto bugs and bulky necklaces and hats like portable gardens. Ornament camouflage. She sits on the wicker love seat next to her husband but hardly notices him. Something bigger than the hat, he thinks, has probably kept them together and apart like this for years. Women who love Hedda Hopper hats don't usually like sex.

Unlike the other two, the daughters—who are clearly more warm-blooded and squirmy. Neither of them's up for this hat routine, although the older of the two, the pretty one, the one with the two kids, doesn't look bad in the Givenchy. In fact, the photographer realizes, she resembles Audrey Hepburn a good deal, though an Audrey with breasts. The hat's right and wrong, he wants to tell her. You're not demure enough for it. But he knows she knows. It's the mother who must have dredged up from the attic all these pastel frocks, along with the hats, hoping to resurrect her own Gibson Girl past. The Hepburn daughters are like thin versions of Tweedledum and Tweedledee in drag. Their mother, or the grandmother, had planted skimmers on their heads. But the little girls, no lookers anyway, are wilting in the July heat and melting under their hats. Hepburn's sister is the angry one, and the photographer well understands her anger. The picture hat is all wrong for her. It makes her look like a straitjacketed sunflower or a shooting-range target. She has tried in vain to switch hats with her sister and has taken her hat off at least five times to fiddle with the brim. But the photographer knows where he'd want to jab that hatpin were he one of those women.

The father is oblivious to all this ruckus. So is the teenage boy, who is the real beauty of the bunch, and who is simply waiting politely for his sisters to stop squabbling. No boater on him, thank God, thinks the photographer. The boy's hair is ruffled some by the breeze off the ocean; so is the old man's. But neither of them looks ruffled from within. The father wears a cream-colored suit and an ecru tie with tiny polka dots; the boy's in white ducks and a pale-toffee blazer with a tie like his father's. Even without hats, the two of them belong in Monet's *Terrace at Saint-Adresse*. The others are strictly bad Renoir.

Except for the one who looks like Audrey Hepburn. The photographer remembers a Burne-Jones watercolor he saw once, of a mermaid clasping a drowned man with her long milky arms and torpedo tail. The man was beautiful; his body strong, not at all epicene; his skin was translucent, a pearly white-green; his eyes were closed; his feet were tightly squeezed together as though they'd been nailed, as though he'd just dropped from the crucifix and plummeted into the ocean. The ocean floor writhed like an octopus. The stones that were scattered on the floor gleamed like pieces of eight. And up from the eerie green depths filtered bubbles, strands of bubbles like broken necklaces, bubbles released by the plants or the mermaid or the man before he expired.

The painting deeply disturbed him. It wasn't clear at all whether the mermaid had found the man dead or drowned him herself. Whatever, she had taken him with her to the bottom of the sea and was having her way with him. Her long dusky hair was pulled up and back, like this woman's. And her eyes were riveted on the viewer, the jealous outsider, not the corpse, the shark food, the same way this woman was looking at him now as he hid under the focusing cloth.

What a lovely scary death, the photographer thinks. And what a terrific body on this older daughter, whose hair he wouldn't mind unknotting and drowning in one bit. He must wrap up this photo session fast. He's starting to get hard.

Finally they're ready. The two granddaughters are positioned on their grandmother's right, one of them perching on the arm of the love seat. The older parents are sitting beside each other like good teddy bears. The daughters have momentarily quelled their restlessness. They and the boy stand behind the love seat, the daughters behind the mother, the son behind the father. The hats are casting no awkward shadows.

"Say cheese, everyone," he sings out, knowing none of them will smile, knowing "squeal" or "dreams" would do the same trick, except the words do not apply—since these were the sort of people who had been raised never to squeal, and who, as a result of their good fortune, needed no dreams. If I'd only said "pork," he thinks, perhaps I could have nudged a laugh out of some of them. If they'd said pork, they'd all look like guppies.

He squeezes off one shot after another, loading, unloading. It takes time. The Graflex is slow. The pauses give him time to play out the ritual that always sustains him during group shots. He imagines how each one in the family will bite the dust. The old woman will die of decades-old bottled-up anger and gas, terminal dyspepsia. Squeeze, click. Her husband? In bed with some tartlette young enough to be his granddaughter. Click. The granddaughters are lifeless already and will sweetly dissolve, like sugar cubes, before they reach puberty. Click. The picture hat will be eaten by a horde of wild boars in southern France. Click. Audrey Hepburn will marry a Roumanian vampire, succumb to his mighty incisors, and live on forever. Click. The boy will become a confirmed alcoholic by age eighteen and keel over at twenty-one from too much Johnnie Walker Red and too many women. Click.

As he readies the camera for one more load, the young woman's picture hat breaks loose and swoops off and then double-somersaults over their heads. The mother looks up, apprehensive, and holds on to her hat to make sure it is still anchored. The Tweedledee girls snap out of their listlessness and gawk. The Burne-Jones mermaid and her sister squint as the sun stabs their eyes, then smile suggestively, as a way of rooting for the hat. The men simply watch, neither rueing nor applauding, since they know that runaway hats, like some kites, will always belong to the sky.

They're a blessedly normal family after all, thinks the photographer. A few of them can actually be discombobulated. Would, though, that his camera had been primed at that very moment. He can see how that straw hat with its smoky-white ribbon would hover flutteringly in the corner of the frame, how those startled faces would gape in wonder as though they were about to witness the landing of some flying saucer, and how that quirky disruption would so beautifully jar that too composed, too precious arrangement. He has known this bitter ache again and again and again. It is old hat, but he still fumes. *Shit*. And double shit. He has missed the best shot.

The best shots always miss.

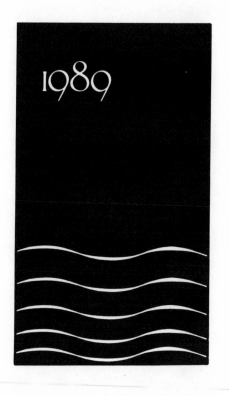

:: ::

::

It was that hour in the afternoon when *le piccole botteghe* in Venice roll down their window-grate armor and close shop, when museums in Florence expel tourists by the droves into the sun-scorched piazzas to suffocate and combust, when churches in Rome refuse to admit either the damned or the truly penitent, insisting they wait outside and burn on the fiercely hot marble stairs as if to prove that patience is no virtue at all, only another sort of hell.

Downstairs, the polo player, Princeton '47, was pouring himself his sixth gin and tonic of the day, having pushed the cocktail hour westward through eight time zones, trying very, very hard to hear—as he rattled the cubes in his highball glass—the final, frantic whinny of the horse that threw him in the last polo match the two of them ever played, that horse which drove its iron hooves through his jodhpurred, handsome left thigh and even more magnificent groin, wrecking him for eager-to-be-saddled debutantes for the rest of his life, and which he then shot through the belly, left eye and mouth his first day out of the hospital. The former aerobics instructor now turned real estate agent struggled to find a way of dressing up her description of an undesirable, first-floor apartment which had but a skimpy patio and provided a glimpse of the Atlantic only if one stood upon a porch chair and looked over the hedge. Accomplished at stretching, she settled for "lanai apt. with surprising ocean view." The sculptor, wearing nothing, not even her Calvins, was sitting in a half-lotus position on a carpet of wood shavings, summoning up a fresh coprophiliac vision, a shape to turn heads, or tails. The man who so desperately adored trains, and who knew that he himself would never go anywhere, oohed as the tiny pink light of the crossing gate flicked on, signaling the approach of the little, the only, engine in life that could. His right hand nudged the transformer very gingerly, as though he were planting a mine.

Nothing moved in that terrific heat but ice cubes in a glass, a Gucci pen scribbling, chips of wood levitating, and a Lionel train.

Eric had removed the Nyasaland King George VI pictorials, the Northern and Southern Rhodesia Queen Elizabeth coronation sets, the Angola birds, the Mozambique fish, the multicolored flowers from the Belgian Congo, and the French Guiana Galibi bowmen from all of their crystal mounts, holding them to the light one by one with his tongs, admiring their brilliant colors, their classic or daring designs. When he turned his gaze from the twenty-shilling elephant with giraffe in rose red and red purple, he saw the man in his bedroom. At first he thought he was hallucinating. The man appeared to be a much older King George VI. He was wearing an elegant, ageless suit, dark blue with a faint pencil stripe; but both he and the suit looked dusty, as though if you blew but gently they both would atomize, disintegrate. Occasionally Denis forgot to lock the doors. But given the publicness of the house and the frequent sorties of his nomadic tenants, there was so little need for locked doors, especially now, in the bald daylight, when the house was hotter than an oven. The French doors in the living room were always left open while Denis tended the lawn, so that the coolness from the sprinklers might snake its way inside. Eric glanced out the window. Denis was nowhere to be seen, vanishing, as he always did, at midafternoon, after the mowing was nearly done.

The man at the bedroom door hadn't moved. Neither had he blown away. Eric thought he might be looking for a place to stay, had heard from someone in town about the sorts of lodgers who sequestered themselves here on indefinite leave from reality.

"I'm out of room at the moment," he said. "Though when my jumping-jack lady sells her first big condo, I imagine she'll move to splashier quarters."

"What's this?" the man asked. He was pointing at the Deco robot Eric had built years ago, that spring in Paris, long before anyone dreamed of the fine-tooled robotic life, that spring in Paris, when he still believed in something.

"A toy," he said. "An indulgence. It never went beyond that. There's only this one."

"How's it work?" the man asked.

"The switch. In the navel."

Eric wondered how the man knew. Knew that it worked.

The man pressed the switch. And the robot waddled forward, jerkily, stopped, twitched to the right, then the left, then continued to slink across the floor. Eric had not seen her move in years. Since that summer of his near-death, when he'd flown it back from Paris as though it were his own coffin (though there was far more life in it than in its creator), the piece had stood against his bedroom wall like a Marisol sculpture, like a mummy case, like a Sleeping Beauty that had given up on princes for good. Now it staggered towards him, a crippled siren risen from the dead. The stained-glass face he'd spent weeks working on reminded him now of Millais's Ophelia or Lorenzetti's Mary Magdalene. Had he deceived himself that thoroughly forty or more years ago? Had only his hands been in touch with the truth, not his head? In Paris the fragile robot had cut graceful arabesques across their parqueted bedroom; it moved without kinks; they had—each of them—even danced with it. How had he not seen through its weird beauty to what lay beneath, both then and now—a debilitating sorrow?

"Cute," said the man.

"No," said Eric. "Anything but."

"I found the Duesie."

Eric recognized the handsome coarseness that even the sag of old age had not completely squashed. He looked out the window again, but Denis was nowhere. The robot had stopped jiggling.

"Not much of a house," said the man. "A big white elephant's what I'd call it. Run-down, just like its owner. You need some new stuff here. Stuff that works. You should call one of those fancy fag decorators. Or should've called."

"Why are you here?" asked Eric, knowing and not knowing.

"I always wondered what she did with the Duesie. She said she was broke in Kentucky, had to sell it after you left her. I believed her. She never lied much. Only when she thought she might get the heave-ho. You weren't so hard to find back then either. Once she came back to me, though, you weren't worth the bother. The car, though. If I'da known she'd left the Duesie here with you, you bet I would have nailed you then. She couldn't've stopped me."

"It still runs. My son drives it around the block occasionally, for exercise."

The man's boutonniere was wilting. He tried to perk it up by repinning it, but the tiny carnation continued hanging its head. Even its color hadn't changed.

"Ever meet her ma?" the man asked. "Of course you didn't. A sweet old lady she was. A real fruitcake. Talked to God a lot, and she didn't use the phone. Poor little Dory. Eight years old, and she's sliding trays of food for her ma through a hole in the bedroom door. Her dad had to keep her locked upstairs she was so batty. Then the aunt comes to live with Dory, another Bible popper, and she goes off her rocker too. Dory's dad—what a shitbum he was. Bet you didn't know him either, did you? He's outa the house by the time she's sixteen, and now she's all alone sliding trays through the door to the two Jesus freaks, the ma and her crazy sister. Boy, they stuck it to Dory. Giving her shit while singing to Jesus. They told her she was the devil. Can you believe that? After Dory and I hooked up, I took care of the fruitcakes for her. Sent them off to the loony bin in Elgin. She wouldn't let me take care of them the other way. They deserved it. They were killers. A razor would've shut 'em up for good. You didn't know any of them, did you?"

"No," said Eric.

"She's gone, you know. I found her in London after you left her again. I took care of her. I always did. All those years before and after. She didn't want to come back to the States. She wanted to 'keep on going south for a while,' she said. South, my ass. London's not south. She wanted to blow you off the face of the earth for what you did to her. I brought her back with me to Reno."

"I never left her."

She was the one she wanted to kill. Not me. I see that now.

"She lied to me again, in the hospital. Just three days ago. I knew what the cancer was doing to her. I knew. I'd been eaten up inside for years, just watching her. All the lights were going out in her like she was some Christmas tree pooping out. And she kept saying, 'It doesn't hurt, Andy, it doesn't hurt so much.' The poor, pathetic liar. So I pulled the plug. And people are looking for me, but so what. Now I'm here."

He could almost see her, those slender wrists of hers, those lips pale as rosewater. If he'd been there instead, could he have done it? Cut her down, watch her expire as though she had never been real, never touched him, scarred him, shot his body through and through with bullets, fire, life?

"You were one unlucky bastard, weren't you?" said the man. "She thought she knew what she wanted, but she didn't, did she? And what did you get? My car. 'Course, all I got is her kids, and grandkids. Plus sciatica, a crummy kidney, and a double bypass. So who cares if I croak? Not me. Not my fuckin' kids. They don't want to clean up the mess. I'll make yours look neat, though. You just got tired of life, that's all, like me. You got a bright family. They'll figure it out. I'm the piece of the puzzle they won't figure. But who cares. So I'm gonna walk quietly downstairs, same way I came in, and sit myself in the backseat of my favorite car, and do what I should've done to Dory's crazy ma. But first there's this."

Eric was half-listening. He'd been fixated on the man's beautiful blue suit, regretting they could not somehow trade clothes as well as places now, wishing he'd at least put on a handsomer bathrobe. Then he remembered the stamps.

"And I won't fuck up this time," said the man.

In those two remaining seconds he had, Eric shoved his stamp albums away from where he knew his bloodied head would fall, watching—with an inexplicable rapture—the fish from Mozambique breakdancing as they flew out the window, the Belgian Congo flowers swirling like corybantic wallpaper roses, the Nyasaland leopards coupling with the Angola birds in a peaceable kingdom of sexual riot, and the slow-waterfall fall of the flame lily from Southern Rhodesia, and the baobab tree, and the prussianblue and deep red-violet Zimbabwe ruins, and the splendid bare torsos of the Galibi bowmen as they tumbled, one by one, to the carpet of green below.

The ocean roared, glowed.

Blue-gold waves broke against one another in an endless shattering.

Denis sat beneath one of the palm trees that lined the beachfront, as he did every day, watching the sand, the water, the sky, everything. No one could see him from the house. He always chose trees that were closer to the private beach next door for his roosting place. But he did not worry much about anyone seeing him, or knowing where he was. The music would play on in the house for hours; it would keep playing, as it had for years now, though he was often not in his room but here instead. Far better, he knew, for his father to be gently deceived than made more uneasy.

Sometimes, like today, when the beach was quite empty, when no trespassers had blundered into view, he would get up and walk down as far as the wet sand, let the cool foam rush over his feet, feel the kelp snake between his toes.

He never went into the water, though. He knew how impossible it would be to float in the ocean. Lying in the trough of a wave would be like waiting for a coffin lid to close down on you. Nor did he expect the ocean to wash up any lucky charms.

But the pain was mostly gone. It had been washed away long ago. And of some things he was no longer afraid.

What he waited for, every day, for more than twenty years, were the visions. Which came, which always came. Predictably, and unpredictably.

Today, as he trod the surf, he was not alone. When he saw the two strangers approach—a boy and a girl—he knew it was time to retreat. The girl was pale and pretty and sandy-haired, barely out of her teens. She wore a wraparound skirt, like a sarong, over her bathing suit. The boy was carrying thick white beach towels and a thermos. Denis should have moved more quickly, but he couldn't. A gold medallion clung to the boy's throat. It glittered sharply. Denis blinked, with one eye.

"Are you cleaning the beach?" the girl asked.

Denis shook his head no. He saw that the girl had noticed. His mouth, his face. The boy smiled at him. He was wearing brightly flowered boxer trunks. His face was like another bright blossom.

"OK, sir, if we catch some rays here?" the boy asked.

He nodded yes. *You've still a handsome smile, Denis, remember that*, his father had said. *It's like a Deco S now. It doesn't droop, it curves. A lovely line. A Deco smile.*

Then he left, without waving good-bye, without needing to. By the time he got to his palm tree the girl had already lathered her body with coconut oil and was horizontal. The boy was up to his waist in the ocean.

Denis stood there in the shade, his back against the tree.

If you could have seen me back then. If you could have held me back then. If you could hold me now.

And he was there. Cary. It was Cary's finger, not his own,

that was tracing a line of sweat across his chest and down his breastbone, as though to bless him.

Cary.

Only the boy's head now could be seen in the ocean. The girl lay still as a log.

Half-smiling, Denis walked back to his abandoned life, the front lawn and mower.

Freshly cut grass shimmered in the sunlight.

Beneath his bare feet birds churred, leopards growled, and naked men thrust spears into the hot, viparious earth.